THE LUCKY SEVEN

THE
LUCKY
SEVEN

One airman's remarkable true wartime story of escape
and evasion from German-occupied Europe,
and the brave résistance fighters
who delivered him to freedom.

NORMAN W. HOLDEN

ISBN 978-1-7362203-3-7 (eBook)
ISBN 978-1-7362203-4-4 (Paperback Edition)
ISBN 978-1-7362203-5-1 (Hardcover Edition)

Library of Congress Control Number: 2023907304

Book cover and interior design by C'est Beau Designs

Printed and bound in the United States of America
First printing 2023

Published by NWH Holdings, LLC
Colorado, USA

www.normanholdenbooks.com

Based on true events

HIS027120 HISTORY / Military / Veterans

First Lieutenant James J. Goebel Jr.

This book is dedicated to the memory of James J. Goebel Jr., his beloved wife, Joan, the Greatest Generation, and, most importantly and with gratitude, the men and women of the Belgium and French Résistance. As a gesture of respect to all those who sacrificed for the safety of others and for those who fought for our freedom, I applaud your bravery and thank you!

It truly has been an honor to bring James's story to life.

With love and admiration,
Norman W. Holden
April 24, 2023

CONTENTS

Introduction   1

Prologue   3

PART ONE: DESTINED TO FLY   5

Chapter 1:   Model Planes   7

Chapter 2:   Reporting for Duty   12

Chapter 3:   Pilot Training   15

Chapter 4:   Combat Team Assignment   27

Chapter 5:   Heavy Bomber Training   32

PART TWO: TRANSGLOBAL JOURNEY   45

Chapter 6:   Port of Embarkation   47

Chapter 7:   Overseas Movement   52

Chapter 8:   From Island to Jungle   54

Chapter 9:   Crossing the Atlantic   62

Chapter 10:   A Sea of Sand   65

Chapter 11:   The Final Leg   68

PART THREE: OVERTURE TO OVERLORD   73

Chapter 12:   Replacements   75

Chapter 13:   Combat Crew Assignment   81

Chapter 14:   Inaugural Mission   89

Chapter 15:   Caterpillar Club   96

PART FOUR: MISSING IN OCCUPIED LAND   109

Chapter 16:   Downed Airmen   111

Chapter 17:   Captured Pavelka   119

Chapter 18:   The Secret Army   132

Chapter 19:   Ultimate Sacrifice   145

Chapter 20:   Command Performance   152

Chapter 21:   Steenweg 79   161

Chapter 22:   Bitching Cold   174

Chapter 23:   Chicken Shit!   177

Chapter 24:   '38 Chevrolet   181

Chapter 25:   La Cathédrale Saint Paul   194

Chapter 26:   The Big Day   230

Chapter 27:   Broken Escape Chain   241

Chapter 28:   Twenty-First Birthday   244

Chapter 29:   An Alternative Plan   247

Chapter 30:   Cruising P-51s   250

Chapter 31:   New Arrivals   252

Chapter 32:   The Lucky Seven   255

PART FIVE: GOING IT ALONE   261

Chapter 33:   A Path of Cards   263

Chapter 34:   The Maquis Bandits   274

Chapter 35:   Scared Stiff   284

Chapter 36:   Train to Belfort   288

Chapter 37:   Lost in the Woods   292

PART SIX: INTERNMENT   297

Chapter 38:   Lots of Indians   299

Chapter 39:   Quarantine Period   307

Chapter 40:   Fresh Duds   312

Chapter 41:   Hotel de Glion   318

Chapter 42:   Repatriation   327

Epilogue: Heading Home   335

Afterword   341

Never Forgotten   343

Acknowledgments   345

Supplemental Information: B-24 Liberator Bomber   350

Supplemental Information: 445th Bomb Group   353

Supplemental Information: Air Forces Escape & Evasion Society (AFEES)   355

Supplemental Information: Fellow Evadee Airmen   358

About the Author   363

References   365

Websites   367

Introduction

THE STORY YOU ARE about to read is grounded on true wartime events. This book is the culmination of several personal firsthand accounts, thousands of hours of research, and hundreds of historical documents. To the best of his ability, the author wove all of these together with the sincerest desire to create an accurate and authentic retelling of history. While this book is based on factual events, people, locations, and dates, the author did take a few liberties in an attempt to connect vital dots and fill in some gaps. The fictional elements were created solely in an effort to share a worthwhile and inspiring story. With the exception of a few attributed quotations in **"bold,"** all dialog within this book was written to add context and color. The men and women in this story are real, so were their sacrifices and efforts to preserve our freedom. It is the author's hope that his retelling of this piece of history honors their legacy.

Prologue

April 24, 1944
Altitude 14,000 ft. above Belgium
0330 Hours

THE FUSELAGE FIRE WAS growing out of control, leaving nothing left for the crew to do but bail out. Second Lieutenant James J. Goebel Jr. stood on the narrow bomb-bay catwalk as he checked his straps one last time. Summoning the courage, he stepped into open space. The overpowering throb of the remaining Pratt & Whitney 1200 horsepower engines were replaced with dead silence. It took less than three seconds for Goebel to reach terminal velocity. With black smoke tracing its final journey, the wounded B-24 continued its plunge toward the earth's surface. The aircraft's descent was punctuated by an orange fireball exploding in an open, grassy pasture.

Nothing prepared Goebel for the experience of falling at nearly 120 miles per hour with no feeling of motion. Recognizing the irony of his situation, Goebel muttered, "Why wasn't this part of my training?" This baptism by fire became his first practice jump. He pulled the rip cord; the force of his chute opening immediately knocked him momentarily unconscious. Floating like a ghost toward the earth's surface under a silken white mantle, he regained consciousness. Trying to shake the fog from his head, he silently observed the quickly approaching foreign countryside, then silently prayed for a safe landing and braced himself for impact. The force of impact drove Goebel's knees hard into his chest, knocking all of the air from his lungs with a loud gasp. Straining for breath, he half-heartedly tugged on his chute, feeling immediate resistance as the barbed wire fence gripped the white silk.

Struggling to break free of the straps that harnessed him, Goebel began to move quickly yet awkwardly. A downed airman in occupied land, he was now a wanted man. In just a few seconds, his fate would rest in the hands of the two men running toward him, leaving him to wonder, **"Were they friend or foe?"**

PART ONE

Destined to Fly

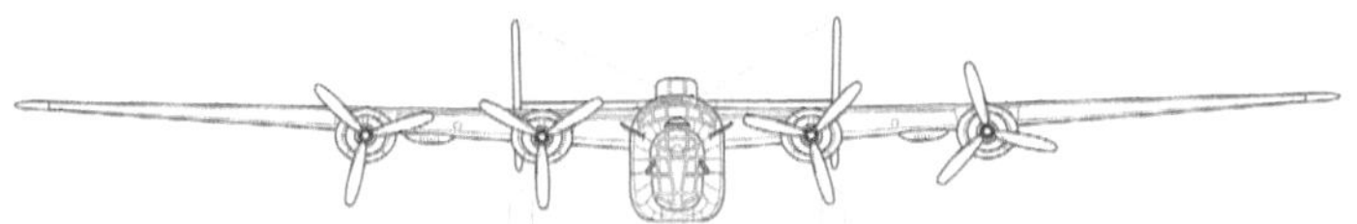

CHAPTER ONE

Model Planes

May 19, 1923
Brooklyn, New York
Midmorning

ON A SPRING SATURDAY, James and Frances Goebel brought their third child, James John Goebel Jr., into the world. A third generation New Yorker, James—or Jimmy as he was affectionately called by his family—was a Brooklynite. Situated between E35th and E37th Streets, the Goebel family home, a two-story brick townhome and their piece of the "Big Apple," sat modestly on 1375 Brooklyn Avenue. A few years earlier, the underground rail had been completed, which connected Brooklyn's outer edge to Manhattan and eventually made the borough a popular spot for thousands of new families to build their homes. Jimmy would know of no other home growing up but Brooklyn.

The Goebel siblings would eventually expand to five children in total. Losing their first child at an early age, Jimmy fell in order behind the now-oldest, Robert, followed Audrey and John. There was nothing special or extraordinary that set this Roman Catholic family apart from the rest of working-class America. The Goebels were the quintessential German immigrant family who settled in their ideal spot, looking to capitalize on the American Dream.

Jimmy's generation came of age during the Great Depression. Tough times were all one really knew; thankfully, though, with youth comes a cheerful and sweet resilience. By the early 1930s, the unemployment rate had soared past twenty percent. Thousands of businesses and banks had failed, with many more to follow suit. A professional cameraman and photographer who worked for Twentieth Century-Fox Film Corporation, Jimmy's father, like other heads of households, struggled to provide for his family. No matter how troublesome things became, the Goebel family always found time to give back to their community. As a young boy, Jimmy fondly looked on as his father volunteered at the local food bank, handing out apples to those less fortunate.

Jimmy and his mates passed the time with games of marbles, kick the can, or street baseball. Countless afternoons were interrupted by men and women returning home from fruitless job hunts, who often found their homes locked, their possessions tossed onto the street, and their families left to wander the streets. The majority were forced to move from town to town, living in makeshift Hoovervilles, also known as shantytowns. Seeing all the gloom surrounding his block, Jimmy would kneel next to his bed each night and pray that his family would be sheltered from the grey storm cloud covering most of the world that he knew.

Listening to the beloved Brooklyn Dodgers playing at Ebbets Field was one of the few things that brought cheers and laughter to the neighborhood. The natural amphitheater of the streets became more animated and colorful on a winning night. On many an evening, the front stoop became the perfect spot for grown-ups to sit and listen to the game and visit with neighbors.

Growing up in the shadow of Floyd Bennet Field, New York's first municipal airport, Jimmy established an early love of aviation and flight. He often looked at the family's photo album with envy; the strapping young pilot standing next to the biplane was his uncle Fred, who served in the Great War. With his trusty pocketknife tightly gripped in his right hand and a scrap of balsa wood in the other, Jimmy would imagine he was taking part in a fierce dogfight while carving his own crude model planes.

At a preadolescent age, Jimmy witnessed Americans elect Franklin D. Roosevelt in 1932 in a landslide vote over Hoover. He saw the New Deal take shape and watched as FDR was elected for a second term. On September 1, 1939, Germany's aggressions toward its neighbor to the east escalated. Germany's invasion of Poland and the beginning of World War II was plainly stated on the morning edition of the *Brooklyn Eagle* daily newspaper: **"QUIT WAR ON POLAND OR FACE GT. BRITAIN, LONDON WARNS REICH."** The *Eagle* informed readers that while Nazi troops raided many cities, FDR vowed to keep America out of this conflict.

During the following summer of 1940, Jimmy, now age seventeen, was sent off for a month of military training. He joined other young men at Plattsburg Barracks in Plattsburg, New York, for a basic course of infantry instruction at the Citizens' Military Training Camp held under the auspices of the war department of the United States. The Yanks involvement in the Second World War seemed to be inevitable, and Jimmy was determined to be prepared. Life in the Brooklyn Borough did not vary much; most everyone scrimped and saved, and unemployment still ran high, with the tide only turning in late 1941.

Entering into his senior year at Erasmus High School, Jim's love of airplanes eventually paid off. He ran for and was elected the President of the Aero Club. The excitement of his achievement was soon overshadowed by the Japanese attack of Pearl Harbor and the reawakening of the American industrial machine. A few of Jimmy's classmates made the choice to leave school early and enlist; the majority of others would enlist post-graduation. Jimmy's older brother, Robert, answered the call, enlisted, and became active duty in the Army.

In the spring of 1942, Jimmy received word that he had won a forestry scholarship to Syracuse University. He decided not to accept the offer and, like many others, enlisted in the Army Air Force just a few weeks after graduation, never to pursue a degree in forestry.

With only eight weeks of time remaining between enlistment and actual reporting for duty, Jimmy put his knowledge and skills to work. As part of the Second New Deal, he had taken advantage of special automotive vocational training offered while in high school. His knack for mechanical repair came in handy, enabling him to take on a number of odd jobs doing light maintenance work on passenger vehicles. Jimmy earned just enough cash so that he could enjoy a movie with a nice neighborhood girl or go with his friends on an afternoon trip to Coney Island for a hot dog while soaking up the seaside entertainment.

The summer nights of 1942 slipped by effortlessly. When early September arrived, Jimmy had let go of his Brooklyn childhood and said his goodbyes to family and friends, then headed off to report for duty.

James (above) at age five, standing on the front steps of his Brooklyn home. James (far left) with two high school classmates working on their latest flying machine (below).

CHAPTER TWO

Reporting for Duty

SEPTEMBER 18, 1942
NEW YORK, NEW YORK
MORNING

AFTER THREE MONTHS OF WORKING as a mechanic's helper, it was time for Goebel to join the military ranks, so on a Friday morning in the fall, Goebel reported for duty. His first stop was the U.S. Army command depot in New York, New York. After checking in, he lined up with hundreds of other enlisted personnel to complete orderly rituals of health examinations, issuance of gear, document signing, and being sworn in. The following morning, like livestock, they were ushered aboard a southbound, coal-burning steam train.

Goebel's mode of transportation came complements of the United States Office of Defense Transportation: an existing steel boxcar converted to a "Troop Sleeper." The Pullman Company had constructed something of a mobile barracks. Each was equipped with thirty bunks stacked three high, which slept twenty-nine service-members plus the Pullman porter. Luck was not on Goebel's side as he was unable to claim one of the few bunks adjacent to a window. The ten window units mounted on each side provided the only source of light and ventilation. After two and a half days in a cramped, musty Pullman, he arrived in the humid fall heat of San Antonio, Texas, where he was hurried though nine weeks of basic training.

At the end of December, Goebel passed the necessary tests to be considered an aviation cadet. He received orders to report to the Army Air Force Classification Center at Randolph Field in San Antonio, Texas. Just northeast of town, he reported to the San Antonio Aviation Cadet Center to begin the next round of training. In Army Air Force Preflight School, Goebel was subjected to a similar series of grueling physical training and coursework. As an aviation cadet, he attended classes in advanced math, Morse code, meteorology, science of flight, course plotting, and all manner of subjects related to plane mechanics and actual flight.

A typical day started pre-dawn with reveille. First, he got dressed in calisthenics garb and then ate a Southern breakfast. Next, Goebel formed up with the rest of the cadets for the ceremonial morning jog and two hours of rigorous exercise. Calisthenics ended with jogging (and unity singing) all the way back to the dormitory for a shower, quick change into uniform, and off to a full day of classes that started promptly at 0900 hours. For most, the only enjoyable relief from their aggressive training was the ten hours of flight instruction in a sixty-five horsepower Piper Cub. This particular aircraft didn't leave the ground; however, the eager cadets were getting closer to actual flight.

Goebel and his fellow cadets endured nine full weeks of training before getting their first leave. Not to stray from tradition, he joined his fellow cadets and headed for the Cadet Club in downtown San Antonio. The thirsty young cadets quickly drank themselves into a drunken celebratory stupor. In the early morning hours, Goebel returned to the base and crawled into his cot with the hopes of sleeping off the evening's events.

Morning reveille was untimely at best. All were present and accounted for, but many jogged as if they were wearing lead gym shoes. Several cadets soiled their white gym shirts with regurgitated breakfast grits and remnants of the prior evening's refreshments. Goebel went on to pass his course and physical exams even with an unyielding headache. Upon successful completion of preflight school, he received orders, gathered his gear, and boarded a train for Sikeston, Missouri.

San Antonio Aviation Cadet Center

CHAPTER THREE

Pilot Training

April 25, 1943
Sikeston, Missouri
Early evening

GOEBEL'S NEXT STOP WAS for primary pilot training. After another day-long dusty and sweaty ride, his train arrived in southeastern Missouri. Aching from his travels, Goebel stepped onto the platform in Poplar Bluff and grabbed his duffle. Making his way to the parking lot, he climbed into the back of an idling truck, which lurched northeast to the nearby base.

The ride was short, and the scenery wasn't much to admire—simply an expanse of vast green pastures budding with new spring crops. Goebel watched as his ride stopped at the checkpoint, then passed through the gate, leaving behind two armed sentries who promptly returned to manning their post. His final destination that evening was the 309th Army Air Force Training Depot, Missouri Institute of Aeronautics in Sikeston.

Goebel's preflight schooling was now going to be put to the test. First thing the following morning, he was introduced to the

Fairchild PT-19 Cornell training aircraft. Known as the "cradle," the PT-19 had over twice the horsepower of the Piper Cub. The PT-19 was an open cockpit, low-wing aircraft, which was pulled through the air by its 175 HP inverted engine. The young cadet went through a brief orientation of the PT-19 aircraft and was soon in the air for his first flight.

The cadet chatter was loud in the evening mess hall as many revisited the day's triumphant milestone. After enjoying another fine Army meal, Goebel went to the post communication office and wired a telegram to his parents at home, notifying them that he'd arrived safely the day prior, provided his new address, then ended on a high note: **"FIRST FLIGHT TODAY AND IT WAS SWELL."**

After two weeks of intensive training and a dozen hours of dual instruction, Goebel flew his first solo flight on May 15, 1943. Shortly after that, on June 23, he completed his final primary pilot training flight. Goebel had successfully completed the required nine-week training course and logged sixty-five hours of flight time, including thirty-four solo hours. He easily went on to pass the strenuous flight test and graduated from primary. The next stop on Goebel's tour would be basic pilot training in Independence, Kansas.

The midsummer heat baked the tarp-covered transport truck as it made its way 380 miles due west from Sikeston. The only view from the open back of the truck was of maturing corn fields and hayed pastures. Goebel bumped along, thinking of home, romantic escapades with girls from last summer, and how appropriate it was that he would spend his first Fourth of July away from home in the sleepy, small town of Independence.

One week after completing his last flight in the Fairchild trainer, Goebel was eager to take to the air again. Jumping from the truck, he eyed the aircraft on the Independence Army Airfield tarmac. Lined in an orderly fashion, the cadets gazed at the Vultee BT-13 Valiants. From a distance, they appeared to be much bigger than the PT-19s. Goebel and his fellow cadets would have to be patient and wait until the next day before being introduced to the Vultee.

Life in Independence wasn't much different than their previous post. On this day, the Army Air Force regimen of physical conditioning, breakfast, and a few hours of briefings were required before their instructor would take the class out to meet their new flying machine. The Vultee BT-13 Valiant—or "Vultee Vibrator" as some would fondly call it—was a big, low-winged aircraft powered by a monster 450 HP Pratt & Whitney engine. It was nicknamed the Vultee Vibrator after a couple curious traits. Simply enough, the aircraft vibrated from the massive stroking of the Pratt & Whitney while at high RPMs. The second and more unusual trait was caused by the action of its tall tail, which normally shook during flight. Some unlucky and inexperienced pilots found out that the tail would twist off during violent acrobatics. Once airborne, the Vultee was steady, making it a very good trainer plane.

Over the next two months, Goebel trained in the Vultee BT-13, 14, and 15 airplanes. It was in the Vultee that he learned the skill of instrument flying. Each cadet logged several hours "under the hood" (a device used to block all reference to the outside). This was also the place that many young cadets who were full of confidence tried their luck in acrobatics and participated in prohibited "dog fights" with other students. Not only did cadets stupidly risk their lives; they also risked the chance of being "washed out" of the training program altogether.

On August 25, 1943, Goebel completed his last basic pilot training flight, ending with a total of eighty-five hours of logged time. Upon successful completion of his exams, Goebel—for the first time in his training process—was given a choice. He was to decide where he would complete flight training based on his ability and interest. The choice was simple: single-engine or twin-engine advanced flight school. Single engine meant fighters; twin engine meant bombers, which Goebel wanted nothing to do with because they were like hulking trucks with wings. He wanted to fly the faster, more agile fighter planes.

After a final review from the camp commanding officer (CO), the decision was made and Goebel received orders to immediately report for Advanced Single-Engine Pilot Training in Eagle Pass, Texas. Excited for the next chapter to unfold, he headed back to the Lone Star State where he'd started basic training almost eleven months earlier.

It was the end of August, and the summer heat and soaking humidity were unyielding. Goebel was not looking forward to another cramped Pullman ride; however, he had very little choice when it came to the Army's selected mode of transportation. He arrived at the 367th Army Air Forces Pilot School located at the Eagle Pass Army Airfield near the Texas-Mexico border.

At Eagle Pass, the advanced training program was made up of four school squadrons, each divided into eight training squadrons. Each school squadron was made up of roughly fifty cadets and had about ten flight instructors. Goebel was assigned to Flight Crew D in Squadron 8 as part of the Class of 43-J, wittingly nicknamed "The Eagles."

While in Eagle Pass, Goebel was taught the art of pursuit and twin formation flying. He logged the majority of his flight time in the North American AT-6 Texan trainer. Most instructors would go on to say that there was never a better aircraft built for training fighter pilots than the Texan. Some in the Eagle Pass cohort would continue on to other fighter/attack warbirds, which included the

Curtiss P-36 Hawk, the Curtiss P-40 Warhawk, and the Bell P-39 Aircobra.

Finally, on November 1, 1943, Goebel made his last training flight as a cadet. During his nine months of flight training, he logged 242 hours of pilot time, including more than 160 hours of solo flight time. As a non-com aviation cadet, Goebel successfully completed the required four nine-week pilot training courses and received an Honorable Discharge from the Army of the United States on November 2, 1943, (S.O. No. 267). Now rated a Pilot, Second Lieutenant. James J. Goebel Jr. became a commissioned officer with 175 other cadets. Regrettably, many would later be shot down, become POWs, or be killed in action during their service in World War II.

Cadet Class 43-J left the following dedication in their annual:

"When the world has been freed from the clutches of the ruthless maniacs with whom we now struggle, history will find among its accounts of glorious deeds, hard work, and sacrifice, an outstanding record. It will tell the story of a particular type of warrior—the Allied pilot.

Unsurpassed by any, these men of the air have set a precedence for those who will follow on that road to victory. Sincerely we pray that we may qualify.

By the way of dedicating ourselves to the job ahead, we of 43-J, dedicate this book to the pilots of the Allied forces all over the world. May we soon see the successful conclusion to this conflict, and an everlasting Peace."[1]

1 (Class 43-J, 1943)

THE LUCKY SEVEN

The life of an Army Air Force Cadet in the time of the early 1940s was a good one. For a young fellow interested in the aviation field and intent upon perfection and the rewards therein, there was satisfaction readily apparent in a job well done. However, the rewards were not without constant risk of failure, injury, or even death. An Army Air Force Cadet went through a battery of mental and physical exams and hundreds of hours of flight training. If a cadet was fortunate not to be washed out or killed in an accident, whatever his assignment, the newly commissioned officer and pilot had achieved something that was truly admirable.

AUGUST 6, 1943
PENTAGON, WASHINGTON, DC

The Adjutant General's Office of the War Department reissued order AG 383.6, "Amended Instructions Concerning Publicity in Connection with Escaped Prisoners of War, to Include Evaders of Capture in Enemy or Enemy-Occupied Territory and Internees in Neutral Countries," which expressly restricted the publication or communication to any unauthorized persons of experiences of escape or evasion from enemy-occupied territory, interment in a neutral country, or release from internment. Effectively, the War Department wanted to protect sensitive information so not to jeopardize future escapes, evasions, or releases. They especially wanted to keep secret and safeguard those persons aiding soldiers and airmen.

Goebel was quick to make friends throughout his training. He became the subject of a fellow cadet's cartoons as illustrated on the following pages. The cartoonist was believed to be Cadet Junior R. Gardner from Delta, Utah.

Cartoon illustrated by Cadet Junior R. Gardner from Delta, Utah.

Cartoon illustrated by Cadet Junior R. Gardner from Delta, Utah.

A cadet during his first solo flight in a Fairchild PT-19 Cornell (top left; the photo taken by The Bach Studio in Sikeston, Missouri, was found in Goebel's personal album; however, it's unknown if the cadet is Goebel). Goebel (top right) taking time out for a quick photo during flight training in the Vultee BT-13 Valiant. Goebel (below) piloting an AT-6 Texan at Eagle Pass, Texas.

Three North American AT-6 Texans flying in twin formation (above).
A final cartoon created in Independence, Kansas, predicted Goebel's future
as an Army Air Force pilot (below).

Photos taken during stages of Goebel's cadet and flight training (above). A studio photo was taken in San Antonio prior to Goebel's commissioning (below).

CHAPTER FOUR

Combat Team Assignment

ON A SUNNY MIDWEEK afternoon in Eagle Pass, Texas, Goebel and his fellow cadets attended the scheduled graduation and commissioning ceremony. Just over a year since his enlistment, Goebel was receiving his silver wings, becoming a Second Lieutenant in the Army Air Force. Those wings represented the greatest achievement and most valuable possession that Goebel had at that moment.

Within a day of his celebrated achievement, Goebel received special orders (S.O. No. 268), assigning him to the Second Air Force and granting him a ten-day leave of absence. Quickly, he packed his duffle, headed to the station, and boarded a train for home in hopes of enjoying a well-earned leave before reporting to his next tactical assignment. After a brief stay in New York, he sadly boarded a train headed west for Salt Lake City, Utah, to Kearns Center. Goebel's anticipation built over the cross-continental trip as he was unsure of what to expect. He had been assigned to the 18th Replacement Wing, and all he really knew was that the unit processed personnel entering the Second Air Force for assignments to other units. Goebel dreaded the prospect of staying in Salt Lake City any longer than he had to, and his impatience grew as he wanted to be back to flying—hopefully, in a coveted fighter.

Goebel stepped onto the platform, covering his eyes to shield them from the bright sun. Once adjusted, he viewed the brilliant blue skies and the snow-capped mountains bordering the small city. At first glimpse, the natural surroundings looked more hospitable than West Texas, yet the base appeared more primitive. Between the swirls of dust and the nonstop movement of men and machines, Goebel's little remaining optimism was quickly dashed when he realized the enormity of the organized chaos that surrounded him.

Located west of Salt Lake City, Kearns Army Air Base was constructed on a 5,450-acre dry farming area, a newly erected shanty town of sorts. In military fashion, the landscape was littered with hundreds of tarpaper-sheathed buildings. In total, the fairgrounds were a temporary home for close to forty thousand troops and another thousand civilians.

After a few moments, Goebel was able to make the necessary arrangements to share a staff car with another second lieutenant. The two piled into the back seat of the olive-green sedan and made the short drive from the station to base command. Upon arrival, Goebel checked into the office of the base CO and received directions to his assigned barracks; luckily, he was going to be housed in one of the few permanent structures on base. Goebel and over four hundred airmen were billeted in a stark, open structure, which was neatly aligned with over two hundred double-stacked bunk beds.

Goebel searched the large open display area for an unoccupied bunk. Finding one, he stowed his gear, sat down, and began a quick conversation with a nearby bunk mate. It didn't take long before he realized the true mission of the 18th Replacement Wing: it took officers fresh from advanced training and formed them into a bomber combat team or reassigned them to fighter pilot training. The newly formed crews or individual pilots would then be assigned to an operational training unit located in other parts of the United States.

Hearing this, Goebel interrupted his new bunk mate in mid-sentence. "I'm going to be reassigned to fighter pilot training!"

Goebel's comment was met with a disagreeable smile and head shake. "Look around. You're surrounded by other pilots, navigators, and bombardiers. Uncle Sam needs bomber crews more than fighter pilots!" Goebel failed to see the humor of the situation, so he quietly ended the conversation by lying back on his bunk.

His flight training prior to his commissioning was all in single-engine aircraft, making Goebel a perfect candidate to become a fighter pilot. After more investigation, he learned that the majority of the airmen stationed at the 18th had been trained in multi-engine aircraft, and Goebel didn't like the taste of that. He had little interest in the four-engine trucks, and the biggest thing he was ready to accept would be the Douglas A-20 Havoc or, with a little pressure, maybe the North American B-25 Mitchell—that is, if he had anything to say about it.

The next day only reconfirmed the reality of his situation. Goebel realized quickly that the tents outside surrounding his barracks were mostly occupied by non-commissioned officers; different sergeant grades trained to be engineers, gunners, and radiomen. He could do nothing but stew, pass the time, and wait for orders. Most entertained themselves by playing cards, watching war-time newsreels and *Casablanca* or *Sunset Serenade* with Roy Rogers. Alcohol provided the only other source of entertainment. But with Salt Lake City being mostly dry, supplies were brought in daily from a liquor store in a neighboring state. The evening's events typically ended humorously when many impaired airmen struggled to find their bunks after returning from the Officers' Club with something of a snootful.

The weekend prior to Thanksgiving, the base put on its version of an air show; an opportunity for a few pilots to show off their abilities and aircraft. Three quarters of the camp turned out to watch the brief show. Things turned tragic when two pilots' signals got crossed, causing their Douglas A-20 attack bombers to collide in midair with both pilots being killed. Luckily, they were not directly over the base and no one else was injured.

While it was not the first of such events, Goebel was still not fully accustomed to losing fellow cadets in training. On average, it amounted to some four percent of the cadet population. This statistic only reinforced the reality of their situation. Sadly, each loss was no easier to swallow than the first. The worst of all was a loss without merit, which was hard to justify in anyone's mind.

Goebel's second week in Salt Lake City dragged on as if time had stood still; the only uplifting news came from the European Front as the British Royal Air Force (RAF) made its first nighttime bombing raids on Berlin. The second major raid was on the night of November 22, causing extensive damage to residential areas west of the town center.

Goebel was not immediately assigned to be a member of a bomber crew, leading him to believe that he would be assigned to tactical fighter pilot training as he had requested. Each day he went out with the others to see what orders had been posted; finally, on Wednesday, November 24, Goebel's name appeared on the transfer list.

He reported to the company clerk and received his special orders (S.O. No. 328) directing him to report to the 302nd Bomb Group in Clovis, New Mexico. Goebel's stomach sank when he read the official document. Turning away from the bulletin board, he approached the clerk who had posted the list and, in an authoritative voice, said, "This has to be a mistake? I'm a fighter pilot!"

Hearing this all too often, the clerk spoke up. "Look, Lieutenant, I don't make the orders. I just type them up! If you have a problem with them, you should go see the CO!" Frustrated, Goebel turned about face and stormed from the clerk's office, slamming the door as he passed through. He went back to his barracks, collected his gear, and arranged for quick transportation to the train station, then hopped on the next available train heading east to Cheyenne. He was not going to spend his Thanksgiving in Salt Lake City.

Goebel elected to take the less direct route to Clovis instead of boarding the Denver and Rio Grande & Western Railroad, a direct line from the base to Pueblo, Colorado, choosing the longer trip though Cheyenne, Denver, and Colorado Springs. Although his travel distance was twice as long, it provided him an opportunity for an unexpected friendship with a pretty young lady that developed along his route through Colorado.

CHAPTER FIVE

Heavy Bomber Training

Late November 1943
Clovis, New Mexico
Afternoon

A WINTER STORM PASSED through Southern Colorado as Goebel headed toward New Mexico; whiteouts were replaced by scattered patches of emerald-blue sky and eventually turned into rain. His mood was as rotten as the weather when he arrived at the Clovis, New Mexico, train station—one day behind the rest of the contingent.

Finding no one at the station platform who resembled the military, Goebel phoned the base motor pool and requested transportation to the Clovis Army Airfield. The better part of an hour passed and, feeling justified, Goebel called the motor pool again, stating, "This is Colonel Gibbons! I'm here at the railroad station. Please send a staff car for me immediately."

About twenty minutes later, a staff car slid up to the platform. When not immediately seeing his intended passenger, the driver jumped from the car and entered the station. Goebel approached him and innocently said, "Can I help you, Corporal?"

"Did you see a Colonel waiting here, Lieutenant?" the driver asked.

Goebel smartly replied, "I did a while back, but he left when someone picked him up. If you're heading back to the airfield, I'd appreciate a lift."

"Well, I might as well. Hop in, Lieutenant, and I'll get you to the base."

Driving away, Goebel smiled while whispering to himself, "Amazing how rank has its privileges."

Passing through the gates of Clovis Army Airfield, Goebel viewed the large sign posted above the guard shack. It depicted a large, pale, irradiated thunderbolt painted below the inscription "302d Bombardment Group." Punctuated on the bottom was the group motto: "Justum Et Tenacem – Just and Resolute." He looked away, trying not to recognize the irony of the words.

When Goebel arrived, he was expecting to have P-47 Thunderbolts in his future. He searched the field for the large four-blade propeller of the single-engine fighters. Instead, he was faced with the presence of B-24s in abundance. He sunk in his seat as things didn't look or feel very promising.

The staff car departed as Goebel entered the company clerk's office. He reported in and received the news that he had been assigned to a B-24 crew as part of the 16th Bombardment Operational Training Wing. Unhappily, he accepted a copy of his orders and quickly spotted his name listed under HB (Heavy Bomber) Crew No. DJ-11. More specifically, he noticed that his name was under another Second Lieutenant named Kendziora, Franklin C.

HB Crew No. DJ-11

Crew Position	Name in Full	Rank	Serial Number
Pilot	Kendziora, Franklin C.	2nd Lt.	0-682879
Copilot	Goebel, James J., Jr.	2nd Lt.	0-697268
Navigator	Czaplewski, Leon	2nd Lt.	0-694342
Bombardier	Tucker, Robert C.	2nd Lt.	0-682743
Eng.-Top Turret Gunner	Irvin, Donald D.	S/Sgt.	18227060
Radio Operator	Westerlund, Charles H.	S/Sgt.	31275855
Waist Gunner	Klinginsmith, Irl J.	Sgt.	17127415
Waist Gunner	Mosher, Norman C.	Sgt.	33459450
Ball Turret Gunner	Weymouth, Charles L.	Sgt.	31316949
Tail Gunner	Chriss, Theodore S.	Sgt.	687034

Like it or not, Goebel was now part of a new family with nine new brothers and the flying Mack Truck called the Consolidated B-24 Liberator, their new aircraft and mode of transportation. Goebel asked where he might find his new barracks and crew, then sharply departed the clerk's office. He realized that he could not buck what had already been predetermined; the United States was at war, and its need for bomber crews was more important than his desire to pilot fighters. While he wasn't happy at all with this assignment, he could accept it.

Walking into his assigned barracks, Goebel saw a group of three officers and six noncoms huddled around looking at the latest issue of *Life* magazine. As he approached, the group turned their attention to him.

Standing opposite, one officer introduced himself. "Hi, I'm Franklin Kendziora!"

Sizing him up, Goebel responded, "I am Jim Goebel!" Hesitating, he continued. "It looks like I am your new copilot!"

"Awe, good. We have been expecting you," Kendziora happily replied as he shook Goebel's hand. Gesturing Jim toward the group, Kendziora began introducing Jim to the rest of the crew.

"This is our bombardier, Robert Tucker. And this is our navigator, Leon Czaplewski!"

Shaking hands, Goebel paused and repeated his name choppily. "Czaplewski?"

Seeing Goebel struggling to pronounce his name, Czaplewski spoke up. "My friends call me Chappie!"

Kendziora smiled and continued. "This is our flight engineer, Donald Irvin!"

Going through the motions, Goebel greeted each member of the crew, who appeared to be good chaps. *Maybe this won't be too bad after all*, he thought. Finding his bunk, Goebel settled—for the moment—into Clovis.

———

In Clovis, Goebel and the rest of Crew DJ-11 were introduced to the Consolidated B-24 Liberator. The B-24 was compared to a 1930s Mack Truck by many of its pilots. Yes, it was fully successful at carrying a heavy load for long distances and at high speeds; yet steering the four-engine beast was difficult and exhausting. With a 110-foot wingspan and weighing in at 56,000 pounds at takeoff, the Liberator lumbered off the ground under considerable strain. Designed to reach nearly 300 miles per hour, the Liberator could carry a 5,000-pound bomb load for more than 1,500 miles before returning home, making it a formidable heavy bomber.

The Liberator was a stripped-down flying machine, a goliath built for one purpose, which had nothing to do with making its inhabitants comfortable. Its shiny silver aluminum skin was so thin it could be cut with a knife, later proving to offer little resistance against enemy flak or bullets. The skeleton within the beast offered endless metallic bards that often provided a sweet kiss to the human skin at every touch—only to burn later as reminder of one's time within its belly. It came equipped without a bathroom, kitchen, or pressurized cabin. Not to mention, it was cramped and cold. It also lacked windshield wipers, making it more than difficult to see during unfavorable weather conditions.

Its interior was cramped, even for the smallest among the group with the only open area located at the rear of the bomb bay near the waist gunners. Every space was efficiently designed for maximum utility. The bomb bay catwalk was the only means to move from front to back as the aircraft was a total of nine inches wide without any form of side railing, rendering it extremely difficult and dangerous to maneuver through the cramped space if needed.

The B-24 was designed for high-altitude flight. At 20,000 feet or higher, wind would rip through the open fuselage, causing the temperatures to drop to forty and fifty degrees below zero. Any exposed skin, especially crewmen's hands, would instantly fuse to metal when contact was made. The airmen's only source of protection was the electrically heated F-2 suit assembly and an oxygen mask. The cumbersome fifteen-piece wardrobe was designed to maintain top body efficiency of the wearer during routine flight training or combat flying; the suit was rated for temperatures of forty degrees below zero.

With a slight lack of synchronization, its four 1200 horse-powered Pratt & Whitney twin wasp engines produced a tremendous roar, vibration, and deafening hum that only subsided when they were intentionally shut off or snuffed out of commission. The lack of noise during flight provided an uncomfortable silence as the Liberator was not known to be much of a glider.

With less than a month to become acquainted, Crew DJ-11 would spend more time in the classroom and/or climbing through the beast than in the air. The specialized heavy bomber training was now officially underway for the Kendziora crew. Over the next four weeks, they were to become familiar with every aspect of the aircraft and with each other's roles, working toward becoming a trusting team. The B-24 was technologically more advanced than the B-17, but that didn't aid the ten-man aircrew or lessen what they were about to undergo.

Goebel and the rest of the Kendziora crew underwent crash courses in the B-24's instruments, controls, pilots, equipment manuals, flight characteristics, and ground crew responsibilities. This coupled with flying, bombing, gunnery, and photographic reconnaissance classes might just make the crew fit for operational readiness.

The B-24 crew setup was designed with built-in redundancy, and their primary and secondary duties were as follows:

Officers

Kendziora: Pilot—Aircraft Commander, Pilot, Navigation Specialist

Goebel: Copilot—Assistant Aircraft Commander, Aircraft Engineering Officer and Assistant Pilot, Fire Officer

Czaplewski:	Navigator—Determine plane position relative to earth, qualified as Nose Turret Gunner, Assistant Bombardier
Tucker:	Bombardier—Deliver payload on target, qualified as Nose Turret Gunner

Enlisted Men

Irvin:	Flight Engineer—Engine Health Monitoring, Top Turret Gunner, qualified as Copilot
Westerlund:	Radio Operator—Communications Handler, Waist Gunner, Assistant Aircraft Engineer
Klinginsmith:	Left Waist Gunner—Enemy Fighter Protection, Assistant Engineer
Mosher:	Right Waist Gunner—Enemy Fighter Protection, Assistant Radio Operator
Weymouth:	Ball Turret Gunner—Enemy Fighter Protection
Chriss:	Tail Gunner—Enemy Fighter Protection (most important defensive position)

December 4, 1943, marked the first and only logged flight that the Kendziora crew flew together in a Consolidated B-24E while in Clovis. On this occasion, the Kendziora crew practiced solo night landings for over three hours. This would be a short duration compared to future flights; typical bombing raids would normally be twice as long, and sometimes as long as ten hours or more.

After their first flight, Kendziora and Goebel's arms felt weak and rubbery from wrestling the two yokes. Like many other pilots, Goebel didn't like the B-24 aircraft as it handled like a boxcar with wings and was big, bulky, and difficult to maneuver. The B-24 wasn't in the same league as his cherished fighters. Goebel desperately and secretly wished he could be back in a prized fighter; the B-24 wasn't a suitable replacement.

After spending less than a month in eastern New Mexico, the Kendziora crew successfully completed the required training expectations of the "302d." Without haste, each crew member received separate orders to report to the 16th Bombardment Training Wing located at Langley Army Air Base. Individually, they gathered their gear and as a group boarded a troop train for the trip to Virginia.

DECEMBER 21, 1943
LANGLEY FIELD IN HAMPTON, VIRGINIA
MORNING

Preparing for their first flight over the Atlantic, the Kendziora crew shivered while commiserating their misfortune of being assigned to the Virginia coast during the coldest months of the year. Starkly different from Clovis, Langley Field sits on the end of a peninsula projecting like a finger into the mouth of Chesapeake Bay. Openly exposed to the Atlantic Ocean, there was no way to avoid the damp humidity and cold of the surrounding waters. Looking forward to a couple of days' leave for the Christmas holiday, the crew turned their focus to the first of many upcoming training flights. Steeped in aeronautical history, Langley Field was currently playing a vital role in the sinking of enemy submarines off the East Coast as well as serving as an operational training center.

Just a few days earlier, and after a full day of rail travel, the Kendziora crew had now settled into their new location. The bitterly cold Langley would be home of their final phase of the specialized heavy bomber training. Exercises at Langley consisted of high-altitude flight, formation work, and nighttime navigation. The crew participated in air-to-ground and air-to-air gunnery sessions. Each crew member got a taste of the waist gunners experience by standing in an open doorway at high altitude and in subzero temperatures, firing fifty-caliber machine gun rounds at a target sleeve being towed by a Martin B-26 Marauder.

Training was progressing reasonably; however, there were several personnel issues to be resolved. It could not be expected that everyone on the Kendziora crew would mesh seamlessly together. Like any other forming team, the Kendziora crew was now storming. Ten individuals with diverse backgrounds and life experiences thrown together in cramped quarters under stressful conditions are bound to produce conflicts.

Unhappy with his own circumstances, Goebel's intolerance of personnel mistakes would become further inflamed when repeated crew issues arose. Goebel especially struggled with Czaplewski, who became the crew clown and goofed off quite a bit. Crew members often turned on each other and fought like cats and dogs over the simplest of matters. The stress of their situation only grew.

During the heart of January, the Kendziora crew participated in day and night navigational training missions, such as sweeping the Atlantic from Virginia northeast to Nantucket, Block Island, and then returning. This was navigated at fifteen thousand feet, and most of it through snow squalls and subzero temperatures. Through the course of ten flights, the crew worked on the specific roles and responsibilities expected of each of them during a typical mission. Like many crews, they suffered with numerous miscalculations, errors, and missteps. Luckily, none of their blunders resulted in a catastrophic event.

While at Langley, Goebel would not let go of his dream. He desperately wanted to get transferred from heavy bombardment, a last-ditch effort to get back to fighter planes. He pleaded his case to anyone who would listen. During his final individual screening, Goebel stated that he didn't like the B-24; he believed his proficiency was good enough for a fighter pilot and his talents were being wasted. Regrettably for Goebel, his appeals would fall on deaf ears as a transfer out of bombardment prior to combat duty was highly unlikely.

January 23, 1944, marked the last training flight for the Kendziora crew while at Langley. A ten-hour and fifty-five-minute flight would be the longest one to date. This flight would mimic the expected duration of a typical bombing run when in theater and would prep an unknowing crew for their upcoming mission. A few days later, the Kendziora crew was given orders to report to the First Air Force Provisional Staging Squadron at Mitchel Field in New York where they would be processed for overseas combat duty.

Mitchel Field was located in the heart of Long Island, just a stone's throw from Goebel's home in Brooklyn. Goebel and the other members of the crew who hailed from the New England region were happy to hear that they would be stationed close to their hometowns. The potential of a few days of leave before getting shipped out further hastened their trip from Virginia to New York.

Mitchel Army Airfield was a flurry of activity when the Kendziora crew arrived in early February. In addition to processing thousands of Army Air Force personnel for overseas combat duty, it was the Air Defense command and control base for the North Atlantic. Goebel and his fellow crew members knew it would not be long before they deployed to an overseas theater of action. But the question was, which one?

FEBRUARY 7, 1944
MITCHEL FIELD—LONG ISLAND, NY
MIDDAY

It was a cloudy Monday when Crew No. DJ-11 received their overseas movement orders. Goebel and the rest of the Kendziora crew were issued a copy of Special Orders No. 31, which directed them to take aircraft No. 42-52733 B-24H (a Ford B-24H-15-F0 Liberator) to Morrison Field in West Palm Beach, Florida, where they would receive further instructions. Their departure date was still restricted information, yet soon they would be joining nineteen other flight crews who together would ferry their aircraft to the East Coast of Florida.

Happy that they were not destined to board a troop ship for a month-long journey, the crew spent the next week calibrating instruments and navigation equipment on their newly assigned aircraft, which included a four-hour flight on February 10. Two days later, and shortly after completing their designated tasks, the Kendziora crew was given a short reprieve of a six-day leave. This would be their last opportunity to visit family or friends before being restricted to base while awaiting final departure orders. As soon as their passes were in hand, Charles Weymouth headed home to Bangor, Maine; Charles Westerlund went to Connecticut; Goebel invited Robert Tucker to Brooklyn; and the remaining members of the crew remained in New York City.

February 15–16, 1944
Berlin, Germany
Night

The Battle of Berlin continued to rage as the British RAF bombing campaign massed its largest raids on the Nazi homeland. Despite cloud cover, the 561 Lancasters, 314 Halifaxes, and 16 Mosquitos (891 aircraft total) hit the Germans most important war industries. Allied bombs struck the large area of Siemensstadt, Germany, with the center and southwestern districts sustaining most of the damage. In all, the RAF lost some ten percent of their aircraft during the one-night raid.

A few days later on Sunday, February 20, 1944, the Allies (a consortium of 8th Air Force and RAF) began its "Big Week" attacks on the Third Reich, a six-day strategic bombing campaign aimed at German plants and airfields. For the first time, over 1,000 bombers were dispatched to three strategic locations with an escort force of 835 fighter aircraft. The winged armada hit its targets with minimal losses, twenty-five aircraft in total.

The following photo and caption appeared in Goebel's local New York newspaper sometime during early December 1943.

"Soldier, Sailor and Marine—*Buddies in service who met at home recently on simultaneous furloughs are, left to right, Marine Staff Sgt. Charles E. Murphy of 558 East 37th St., stationed at Cherry Point, N. C.; Lt. James J. Goebel Jr. of 1375 Brooklyn Ave., pilot in a bomber group at Langley Field, Va., and Pharmacist's Mate 2nd Class William J. MacMahon of 1367 Brooklyn Ave., stationed at Dallas, Texas."*

Transglobal Journey

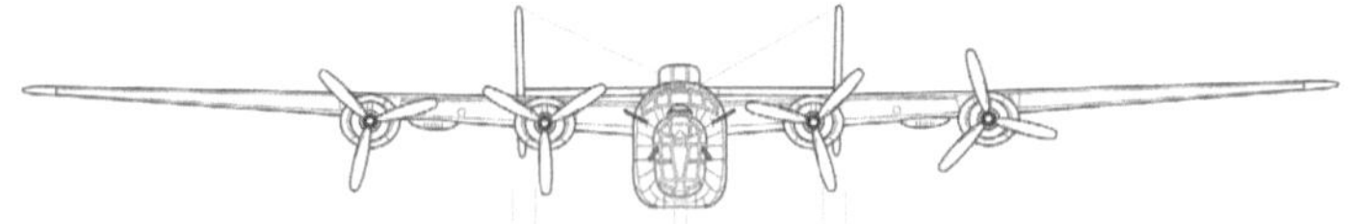

Port of Embarkation

FEBRUARY 21, 1944

MITCHEL FIELD—LONG ISLAND, NEW YORK

MORNING

THE KENDZIORA CREW JOINED with other B-24 crew personnel for a departure briefing. The airmen were given clear directions not to discuss their overseas destination; additionally, they were indoctrinated in matters of security and censorship of all activities. Each airman, no matter their rank, was also prohibited from filing safe arrival telegrams with commercial agencies while enroute or at domestic and overseas destinations. Upon their dismissal, each crew boarded their aircraft, completed preflight, and began the taxi and takeoff parade.

The Kendziora crew (Crew No. DJ-11, now labeled by the USAAF) departed from Mitchel Field with a course set for West Palm Beach. Their predetermined flight plan would take them along the eastern coastline, breaking away from Charleston, South Carolina, in a more direct route to the southern half of Florida.

Approximately two hours into a seemingly flawless flight, they began to experience mechanical difficulties when the number two engine began to falter. Kendziora noticed the issue and yelled to Goebel on the radio while motioning wildly with his hands, "Number two is running rough!" He then called out to Donald Irvin, "What the hell's happening with the number two engine?"

"I'm checking as we speak. Give me a second!" Irvin replied. Moments later, Irvin broke air silence. "Sir, it doesn't look good! We're losing a lot of oil, so you'd better shut it down!"

Unbeknownst to the crew, the number two engine had thrown a rod, rupturing the case, which caused the oil it possessed to spray over the nacelle and the left side of the aircraft. Kendziora ordered Goebel to cut the fuel to the wounded engine. He then triggered his mic and informed the rest of the crew of the situation. With three good engines there was no reason to turn back; they would maintain their planned route to Florida.

Arriving in the darkness of night, the remaining four hours of flight went off without a hitch. A deep sigh of relief passed from one end of the B-24 to the other as the Kendziora crew quietly acknowledged the completion of the first leg of their mission. After rolling to a stop, the crew watched as the ground crews jumped into action and quickly towed the injured B-24 from the tarmac to the repair area. Mechanics promptly tore the engine compartment open and, after a brief inspection, determined the engine failures resulted from the over-dilution of the engine oil by ground maintenance the previous night.

Knowing that at least one engine needed extensive repair, the rest would undergo a round of inspections. The Kendziora crew speculated that they might see another two-day pass in their future. Instead, the crew was informed that they were to transfer their belongings to another new aircraft, preflight the aircraft, and depart immediately. Crew DJ-11 was reassigned a new aircraft No. 41-28742 (Douglas-Tulsa B-24H-10-DT Liberator).

Morrison Field was the United States Army Air Corps "winter" Port of Embarkation. As northern ferrying routes over the north and mid-Atlantic were subject to unhospitable weather, transport missions were shifted south for the winter months. An integral cog in the Allied war machine, the Air Transport Command at Morrison Field was a major departing station for all aircraft heading for southern latitudes and beyond. One thousand men worked around the clock to ensure the readiness of aircraft before returning them to service. It was here that any gripes with the aircraft were corrected. Thankfully, the Kendziora crew had a new ship with a clean bill of health, yet it was still missing something.

The newly minted B-24 was a stark Army green and was missing any form of nose art. Believing that it would bring them good luck, the crew arranged to have a lovely filly—a rather shapely brunette, that is—painted on the left side of their plane.

The Kendziora crew had no problems agreeing to the portrait image; however, the name was another subject. Goebel spoke up first. "We have to name her."

Mosher replied, "Let's name her Jiggles!" The group became silent in response. Seeing his cue, Mosher continued. "Come on! You guys know? Kind of like the way a woman walks." He mocked the swaying motion for the crew. "Different parts of her go in different directions at different times. Somewhat like how a B-24 flies!"

Hearing his description, the crew unanimously agreed with Mosher's idea. "Jiggles" was scripted beneath their newly adorned goddess. Together, they pooled their funds, chipping in eight dollars each to pay the groundman. When completed, the newly decorated B-24 was something that they looked at with pride. The new paint and the warm weather were a boost to the crew's morale.

The crew's stay at Morrison Field was as abbreviated as possible to expedite their continuation toward a designated theater of operation, which, at departure, was completely unknown when they left New York. Later the day prior, Crew DJ-11 received final movement orders (O.O. No. 573) to proceed to its initial destination of the British Crown Colony of Trinidad and on to a still classified front.

JUNE 20, 1944
MALMO, SWEDEN
MORNING

The Kendziora crews originally assigned B-24H (42-52733) aircraft eventually made it overseas to the European Theater. It was transferred to the 446th Bomber Group, 704th Bomb Squadron, where it was eventually assigned to Second Lt. Harry E. Grafton and his crew. The B-24H Liberator, coincidently named "Jiggs," flew its final mission on June 20, 1944. After bombing a synthetic oil plant in Politz, Germany, its crew was forced to land at an airfield outside of Malmo, Sweden, as a result of intense and accurate flak. The aircraft was immediately stripped of valuable parts and scrapped. The Mississippi native and his entire crew landed safely; however, they were placed in an internment camp for the remainder of the war.

CHAPTER SEVEN

Overseas Movement

February 24, 1944
Morrison Field—West Palm Beach, Florida
Morning

AFTER SPENDING THE LAST couple of days stocking up with the needed essentials, the Kendziora crew was ready for departure. Loaded up and in line with nine other aircraft, each B-24 pointed east. Taking turns, one by one they took off over the sandy Florida coastline. Crew DJ-11 departed in their newly painted B-24 (41-28742) from Morrison Field and the Continental United States on its leg to Waller Army Airfield in Trinidad and Tobago. For all of the members of Crew DJ-11, this was understandably the first time any of them had traveled outside the borders of their home country.

As ordered, one hour out of Morrison and over the Atlantic, Kendziora was allowed to open the sealed envelope marked only with his name and the word "Classified" in bold red letters. Crew DJ-11's operational orders outlined a very specific route, the anticipated timeline for each leg, and their designated final destination: "FX 200 DJ."

Although his orders didn't specifically state it, Kendziora knew his crew's new home was to be in England as part of the European Theater of Operations (ETO). Kendziora broke radio silence and announced the news to his crew: "We're headed to Germany, boys!" A loud cheer erupted in response.

Their designated route and lower altitude allowed the crew to enjoy the sights of the tropical teal-green waters of the Caribbean Sea. The nine hour and thirty-five-minute flight took them directly over the Bahama Islands and the Greater and Lesser Antilles. Due to the capacity of the B-24, the Kendziora crew and their fellow heavy bombers were able to fly longer routes, thus skipping intermediate fueling stops.

Crew DJ-11 landed safely in the northern half of Trinidad Island at Waller Field. Located within the ten-square-mile confines of Fort Read, Waller and Read combined created an immensely busy United States Army Base. Fort Read was one of the largest bases in the Caribbean. In total, the United States had at any point 130,000 troops deployed or passing through the tiny country; understandably, this created immense social challenges for a country with a population of only 450,000 citizens.

The Kendziora crew was able to eat a hot meal, wash off the day's grime, and find a fresh rack for a few hours of sleep. Early the next morning, the crew checked on Jiggles to ensure that the ground crew had corrected all minor maintenance issues and topped off the thirsty 3,000-gallon fuel tank. Once all preflight checks were made, the crew loaded up and joined the queue for the only two usable runways.

CHAPTER EIGHT

From Island to Jungle

DEPARTING FROM WALLER FIELD, Crew DJ-11's third trans-global leg would take them southeast across the equator along the coast of South America and the Northeast Region of Brazil. Their intended destination was Val de Cans Airfield near the jungle port of Belém, Brazil, located along the banks of Rio de Pará. A former Naval Air Facility and home to the Pan American and Brazilian Airlines, the airfield at Belém and its two 5,000-foot paved runways had recently been converted for military use. A more primitive yet efficient facility, Belém was simply a refueling stop before heading farther south down the Brazilin coastline to a larger air base in Fortaleza.

On the way to Belém, Jiggles was flown at an altitude of five hundred to a thousand feet over the jungle, allowing the crew to observe the mouths of the Amazon River in great detail. The natural beauty of the lush landscape was comparably as picturesque as the Caribbean to the north.

The flight to Belém, although scenic, was damp and very warm. The rising heat from the thick green jungle combined with the warm waters of the South Atlantic made for an extremely rough trip. Crew DJ-11 successfully completed the eight hour and forty-minute flight with the crew landing in Belém on the afternoon of February 25, 1944.

FEBRUARY 26, 1944
VAL DE CANS AIRFIELD—BELÉM, BRAZIL
0800 HOURS

Goebel taxied Jiggles and the Kendziora crew to runway one for an 0815-hour departure from Val de Cans Airfield. Crew DJ-11 was soon wheels-up, and Belém quickly faded into the jungle as they headed along their designated course. Their fourth leg flight to Fortaleza, Brazil, took slightly more than five hours, and they were back on the ground by 1330 hours.

Located roughly one hour flight time northwest of Natal, Fortaleza was home to Adjacento Field. The Fortaleza Air Force Base was the smaller companion to the Parnamirim Field in Natal, Brazil. When fully constructed, Parnamirim Field became the largest United States Air Force Base outside its own American territory. Combined with one other nearby facility, during the first half of 1944 they were they busiest air bases in the world and impressive symbols of American fortitude.

The United States and its Allies recognized (in the early 1940s) the strategic importance of winning Brazil over to the Allied side. Brazil's eastern peninsula was the closest point in the Americas to Africa. Natal and Fortaleza would become the **"The Springboard for Victory"** as coined by President Roosevelt.

Prior to their Atlantic crossing, the heavy equipment was stationed at Fortaleza while the smaller twin-engine equipment was held at Natal. While the clear weather existed, the twins were scheduled toward Africa, and when the weather worsened or traffic allowed, the heavies were released. U.S. aircraft regularly departed for Africa like angry wasps leaving a disturbed nest.

February 27, 1944
Adjacento Field—Fortaleza, Brazil
Morning

The Kendziora crew was scheduled to remain at Fortaleza for two additional days while the ground crews conducted the required fifty-hour inspection and maintenance on Jiggles. The air base was at peak capacity when they arrived; with all of the barracks full, the Kendziora crew was billeted in standard Army-issued tents. Each tent was simply equipped with four cots and mosquito netting. The tent canvas and its contents smelled musty and wet as if it was intentionally staged. While malaria was a concern, it seemed that the digs provided little reinforcement against a continuous onslaught from the local inhabitants. Unimpressed, Fortaleza was an obvious step down from their previous accommodations.

The airmen were not allowed to hang around; all were assigned duties either working on aircraft maintenance or other base-related duties. Goebel was assigned to an eight-man aircraft recovery team. He was happy to have a break from the unforgiving aircraft; however, he deeply hoped that there would be no need for his services, as good things never come from crashing planes.

The following night during a heavy downpour, Goebel's fears would come knocking as tragedy struck at 0055 hours on February 28, 1944. There was a report of a major fire southwest of the field. Too strong to be a normal house fire, a crew and plane were ordered to scout the area. When a local Brazilian reported that a plane had crashed, a ground team was sent out to investigate before the air crew could report back their findings.

Upon arriving at the site of the fire, Major Ernest E. Dryer found that it was an accident involving a B-24 model airplane, and the tail number 42-52645 was still intact. Members of the local police and fire department of the city of Fortaleza were already on the scene and were working to keep the fire under control. Major Dryer sent a messenger back to base to inform the medical officer to bring ambulances and military police. The aircrew recovery team was immediately alerted and assembled.

Goebel and the rest of his team were ordered to gather their gear, litters, lanterns, additional volunteers, and jeeps. Following the lead vehicles, Goebel and another Second Lieutenant closely trailed the group off the base and down a well-used path toward the direction of the accident scene. Luckily, the path led the recovery team within a few hundred yards of the site, removing the need for fighting the entangled forest. The light from burning wreckage allowed the recovery team to find the remains of the aircraft. Unfortunately, scavenging marauders were also able to find the wreckage. They had made quick work and slipped into the darkness of night before help had appeared.

The recovery team solemnly arrived at the crash site only to find airplane parts, broken bodies, and personal belongings scattered in a 1,000-square-foot area. In fairly dense brush and palmettos, the wing sections had broken off and were burning; the main plane fuselage was partially intact and didn't burn, yet it had left a trial of disintegrating parts along its pathway. The body of one crew member was lifelessly hanging from a rain-soaked tree limb. Immediately, the team searched the wreckage for survivors, but there were none; all ten crew members had perished in the crash.

All ten bodies were recovered, but not before someone had removed everything of value from them, pocket contents pulled free and laying about. Goebel was stunned by the carnage and the immediate acknowledgment that this could have easily been his crew only a few days prior. The pit in his stomach dropped beyond any point imaginable. He stood quietly, looking into the destruction. His stare was suddenly broken by a passing litter. The faint recognition of a motionless face caught his attention.

"Stop!" Goebel yelled as he maneuvered toward the lifeless body, realizing that the deceased copilot being pulled from the wreckage looked familiar. Upon closer inspection, Goebel murmured, "Wear." He then spoke loud enough for the two bearers to hear. "This was an old classmate of mine from Advanced Pilot Training, Class 43-J, Eagle Pass." Goebel sadly identified Second Lieutenant Robert D. Wear from New Orleans, Louisiana, who had perished alongside his fellow crewmembers.

Goebel could not bear to look any longer. He turned and went to work helping to free the other crewmen. Trying not to dwell on the loss, the team hurriedly completed their duties before 0300 hours. With the rain subsiding and observing no one else returning to the scene, they began their ride back to the air base.

Upon returning to camp, the two lieutenants met with Major Dryer to report their findings. They handed over the deceased crew's lasting belongings as the rest of the team members transferred the crew's remains to the base morgue.

From the tail number, it was later determined that this was the last departing B-24 for the evening on its ferrying mission to Dakar, Africa. Having experienced engine failure, it turned back. Unable to make it to the base, the troubled aircraft crashed approximately five minutes after takeoff. The doomed flight had been commanded by Second Lieutenant William M. Brock Jr. from Oklahoma. He and his entire ten-man crew were lost. Their bodies were buried in Fortaleza and were later transferred to the United States in 1947.

FEBRUARY 28, 1944
ADJACENTO FIELD—FORTALEZA, BRAZIL
EARLY MORNING

After finishing with their reports, the group left the Majors compound to finally gather near a cluster of tents. Sitting on wooden benches under the flicker of a nearby hanging lantern, the men started to converse while appreciating a smoke. Exhausted, soaking wet, and covered from head to toe in sticky reddish-brown Brazilian mud, the group calmly but sadly recited the night's events.

From the shadows of their lantern, a small, furry creature scurried across the center of the sitting men. Suddenly, a little black spider monkey about a foot long, not including its tail, leapt into Goebel's lap. Stunned, he sat motionless to see what the small pot-bellied primate would do. It became apparent that the creature had been raised and cared for by different residents of the base because it acted tame and somewhat curious.

Feeling no fear, the monkey quickly opened Goebel's shirt pocket and pulled the cigarette pack free. The small beast began shredding each cigarette, one by one. Out of cigarettes and seeing the lit one in Goebel's hand, the little rascal snatched it and placed it between its legs, then began to urinate all over the cigarette and Goebel's muddy flight suit. A burst of laughter erupted from the watching aviators. For a split-second Goebel wasn't sure if he should laugh, be embarrassed, or strangle the little creature, but he chose to laugh as that was what he needed most of all. In response, the monkey let out a screech and jumped to an adjacent empty bench.

Not to be outdone, Goebel saw the humor of the moment and was quickly convinced that he had to keep the monkey as a pet. He thought of all the fun and games that little monster would provide him during his remaining stay at Fortaleza. Little did he realize the trouble it would cause!

Religiously, Crew DJ-11 prepared each day for the next flight by preflighting their plane, draining all the sumps, running up the engines for a brief period, and checking all systems to the extent possible. One morning, Goebel failed to keep the monkey out of the plane, and when they discovered its absence, it took the entire crew the better part of an hour to locate it in the plane and another hour to clean up its leavings and check the position of all switches. Kendziora was pissed at Goebel and let him know. This only happened once, and Goebel's primate obsession quickly waned.

As a result of the plane crash and the continued storms, the air base ground activities and scheduled departure flights were backed up, creating an extended stay. An unhappy Kendziora crew spent those few days in Fortaleza flightless, only venturing out once for a solo flight lasting only an hour and forty-five-minutes to ensure that all systems checked out for the impending Atlantic crossing.

After the crew completed their morning ritual with Jiggles, they were granted an afternoon pass allowing them to go into town. A short walk brought the airmen to the nearby village. Unfortunately, it turned out to be a small and dusty town with narrow dirt streets. The four lieutenants found their way to the outdoor market where Goebel purchased a small trinket for his mother from the local vendors. They then discovered a cantina where they would try the local cuisine: horse meat. Luckily, no one suffered negatively!

Later that afternoon when returning back to the base, the airmen passed the civilian airline offices. They watched as a Pan Am crew came into view and entered the saloon next door with their starched shirts, pants, and neat ties. The watching airmen looked at each other and realized that their oil-stained flight jumpsuits looked rather tired. Suddenly aware, the commissioned Kendziora crew all felt like a bunch of slobs. Returning to their tents and rut sacks, they all put on some decent attire, including ties, in spite of the heat. The change of clothing provided the crew with a much-needed morale and self-esteem boost, which had been slipping away with the conditions they were being exposed to.

The following morning, Crew DJ-11 was informed that their stay at Fortaleza would finally come to an end. Their long-awaited departure was scheduled, allowing Jiggles to take off for the Atlantic crossing, ending their stay in the Brazilian jungle.

CHAPTER NINE

Crossing the Atlantic

MARCH 3, 1944

ADJACENTO FIELD—FORTALEZA, BRAZIL

EARLY EVENING

POISED IN THEIR FLIGHT POSITIONS and sweating from inactivity for more than four hours, Crew DJ-11 waited in frustration for their turn to take off. It was approaching 1800 hours, their scheduled departure time. Finally, the radio cracked to life and the call came in, signaling them to start their engines and begin the slow move from the hardstand.

Kendziora radioed to his crew "Okay, boys! It's our turn! Let's get going."

As the crew came alive, Goebel leaned toward Kendziora, expressing little confidence when he stated, "Chappie better have his act together tonight, or we'll be swimming!"

Angered, Kendziora replied, "Shut up, Jim. Worry about your own damn job and let me worry about Czaplewski."

Hearing the remark, Goebel looked past his pilot as the first of four 1200 horsepowered engines shuttered to life. Once the fourth Pratt & Whitney matched the pulse of the rest, Goebel taxied Jiggles into position behind six other waiting aircraft. A few minutes later, Kendziora adjusted the controls, bringing Jiggles to a full roar. Releasing the brakes, she progressed onto the concrete strip. Assuming their place in line, they joined the winged procession and rolled off the paved runway toward the oncoming open water. Taking flight, Crew DJ-11 left the Brazilian coastline and the South American continent behind them. Aimed for West Africa, the ten-man crew and their ship had over two thousand miles of open water to traverse. Leg five of their journey was now underway. Their destination was now Mallard Field in Dakar, Senegal—French West Africa.

The crew could not have asked for better weather. The forecast called for clear traveling, tropical yet mild temperatures, and, thankfully, very little turbulence. Within thirty minutes, the sun crept slowly below the shrinking black outline of the coast. As the Brazilian landmass disappeared behind them, the immensity of the Atlantic and the darkness of night swallowed them whole. Besides the accompanying heavies at the wing tips, endless water, white-tipped waves, and an occasional reflection of an aircraft silhouette was all one could see.

At first, the sky and ocean appeared to be as one until a waxing crescent moon painted a silver sheen on the tops of the waves, creating a mesmerizing seascape. When duties allowed, each crew member stared at the open water; the calming effect evoked pleasant thoughts of those left at home, washing away any homesickness.

Close to midnight, Jiggles neared and then crossed the equator for the second time. Moonlit cumulus nimbus clouds stood like sentinels, defining the margin between north and south latitudes. Kendziora and Goebel took turns at the controls, allowing the other to rest their eyes and sore arms.

In the early morning hours of March 4, 1944, Crew DJ-11 approached the West African bridgehead. Their prescribed destination was the city of Dakar, located on the Cape Verde Peninsula. To the Allies, Dakar was an important strategic naval port, land base, and air link. To the airmen making the nighttime overseas journey, it was a welcome sight. The trans-Atlantic crossing took just over ten hours to complete, and Crew DJ-11 landed safely on the western tip of French West Africa.

Dakar was to be an abbreviated one-day layover, allowing time only for refueling, restocking of supplies, minor plane repairs, a little sleep, and—if they were fortunate—a trip into town, which surprisingly enough was okay with the weary aviators. It was evident from the time they landed that the atmosphere at Mallard Field was as different as night and day from Fortaleza. Dakar had many of the same characteristics as Brazil; the place was hot, humid, and a little rancid. However, it was abundantly clear to the airmen that the honeymoon was over. A great deal of Allied blood had been lost over the Dakar acquisition a few years earlier. Strict military authority and a no-nonsense approach was the minimum expectation for a trooper while on base.

CHAPTER TEN

A Sea of Sand

March 5, 1944
Mallard Field—Dakar, Senegal
Early morning

TAKEOFF TIME WAS SCHEDULED for 0730 hours. As with the previous five legs, crews were briefed two hours before takeoff. While the pilots, navigators, and radio operators attended the morning briefing, the rest of Crew DJ-11 completed its required tasks, loaded-up, and prepped for departure. After wheels up, Jiggles and her crew turned northeast, paralleling the inland coast of Africa and the western edge of the immense Sahara.

The entire trip was flown at a dangerously low altitude, almost skimming across the Sahara sand. Kendziora reevaluated his selected altitude when Westerlund radioed, informing him that they had just lost the trailing antenna anchor weight on an unsuspecting sand dune, which was reeled out to 125 feet. At a modified elevation, the cascading sun exposed the shadows of desert dunes, making them look eerily familiar to the black waters of the Atlantic. It was an endless sea of sand.

Their day-long trip passed over the fertile Senegal River valley and an unending expanse of sand dunes. Every so often they spotted a distant Bedouin camp—or so they thought. It was possible they were only seeing a mirage skipping across the many shades of brown. In the late afternoon sun, the crew navigated the Atlas Mountain range and landed at Menara Airfield in Marrakech, French Morocco, without incident. Crossing the African continent took just under nine hours.

After two days of hard flying and little restful sleep, the Kendziora crew was happy to be on the ground. Grabbing their gear, they went straight to their assigned barracks for some much-needed shut-eye. Waking for evening chow, the Kendziora crew got cleaned-up, changed into a cleaner flight suit, and scarfed down the local Army fare. After dinner, Kendziora and Goebel went to check on their departure schedule while the rest of the crew followed-up on Jiggles and the repair to her antenna wire. Catching up to the crew, Kendziora informed them that they were scheduled to remain in Marrakech the following day. Though they would be part of the first wave out, departing at 0400 hours on Tuesday morning.

MARCH 4 AND MARCH 6, 1944
WESTERN EUROPE
DAYTIME

While Jiggles was crossing the Atlantic Ocean, the 8th Air Force was preparing to conduct the first of many raids on Berlin. On March 4, 1944, the Americans sent 300 bombers across the channel in an attempt to bomb Berlin. Two days later on Black Monday, the 8th Air

Force began its assault in earnest when it launched a massive sortie of over 700 bombers and 900 fighters for Berlin during a daytime raid. The heavy bomber caravan made up of B-17 Flying Fortresses and B-24 Liberators stretched out over 93 miles (150 kilometers).

The train of bombers left an imposing wake of contrails across the skies of Western Europe, providing a beacon for the defensive forces. The Allied Air Force would meet with strong resistance by anti-aircraft artillery and fighters, losing nearly ten percent of its aircraft. Between heavy losses and sporadic bombing accuracy, the day's results were less than desirable for the Americans, yet it was hopefully the beginning of the end for the German Luftwaffe.

CHAPTER ELEVEN

The Final Leg

March 7, 1944
Menara Airfield—Marrakech, French Morocco
Early morning

PREPARATIONS FOR THE FINAL LEG began early on Tuesday morning. Rising at 0230 hours, Kendziora and Goebel assembled themselves for the morning debrief. The remaining crew gathered their gear and then stopped by the mess hall to fill their thermoses and grab an egg sandwich on the way to board and preflight Jiggles. Anxious to be at the front of the pack this morning, the crew hurried through their final checks and prepared their aircraft for a quick taxi out. Once in the air, Kendziora made a sweeping turn northwest out over the Atlantic. Crew DJ-11's flight path would take them due north, paralleling the neutral Portugal-Spain shoreline. The seventh and final leg of their transglobal journey was proceeding as planned.

As they progressed north, the air temperature steadily dipped; once out over the open waters of the Atlantic, they dropped even more. The angrier the seas appeared, the colder the air became. Kendziora radioed the crew, instructing them to change, one by one, into their heated flying suits, which consisted of long under-wear, woolen shirt and regulation trousers, a jacket, gloves, and felt shoes. He further instructed Weymouth and Mosher to move their gear out of the sling in the bomb bay. As ordered, Weymouth and Mosher went to work collecting each crew member's cold weather gear from the stowed duffels.

The crew, now properly suited up, was comfortable—except for Goebel. Regrettably, his electric jacket and trouser inserts were missing. Frustrated, Goebel had to be content wearing his lamb-skins, a less-than-desirable alternative as he was freezing his butt off. In addition to the unwanted chill, Goebel was losing his agility because of the bulky clothing. Eventually, his missing gear was later discovered in his barracks bag. A hard lesson learned for Goebel.

Maintaining an altitude of 500 feet, the crew watched as the seas were being whipped by the progressing weather front. The white caps on the black-slate sea indicated a stronger than twenty knot surface wind from the northwest. As they neared the British Isles, the weather worsened in an ominous way, seeming to foretell what their immediate fortune might be on the approaching besieged island. The weather was **"British Miserable"** with the scud around the heights and a drizzling ceiling at 2,000 feet.

Kendziora called out to Chappie and Westerlund, "Keep us clear of Ireland! We can't afford any mistakes, especially in this soup!"

During their preflight debriefing in Marrakech, the Kendziora crew was forewarned to stay clear of Ireland. Ireland's neutrality during World War II kept the island off-limits from Allied flights. With the exception of a narrow strip of British airspace at the top of the island, the only permissible route open over the "Emerald Isle" was the Donegal Corridor linking Northern Ireland with the international waters of the North Atlantic Ocean. This was not part of their designated journey; therefore flying over this neutral land-mass was prohibited.

On a cloudy midafternoon, Land's End broke into view as a dark escarpment being battered by a nasty sea. The crew worked their way northeast, following the St. Georges Channel along the western shoreline of Wales.

North Wales, a small, flat island on the eastern shore of the Irish Sea, was Crew DJ-11's final destination and port of entry. The USAAF ferry terminal (Army Airfield No. 568—Air Transport Command) was based at the Valley airfield in the Isle of Anglesey. Crew DJ-11 arrived cold, tired, and unharmed, completing the last and longest leg of their transglobal trip, lasting eleven hours as a result of the worsened and unwelcoming weather.

Upon arrival, the Kendziora crew was directed to a designated hardstand and was told to unload all of its gear. No sooner was this done when two nondescript troopers hooked up and promptly towed Jiggles from their area. The Kendziora crew had unknowingly given up their B-24 Liberator, unaware it was a replacement aircraft needed elsewhere. Jiggles, their transglobal partner, was taken away to the modification center where armor plate was attached to both sides of the cockpit area, shielding the proudly adorned nose art and given name. Finally broken in, Jiggles would not transport the Kendziora crew on any future missions. The replacement B-24H (41-28742) aircraft, painted and nicknamed Jiggles by the Kendziora crew, was assigned to 392nd Bomb Group, 579th Bomber Squadron.

March 18, 1944
Skies over Southern Germany
Midmorning

The reassigned Kendziora B-24H (41-28742) was in flight conducting its first sortie for the 392nd. It had been assigned to First Lt. Dallas O. Brooks and his crew. The Brooks crew promptly nicknamed the new plane "Old Glory" just before takeoff. They had flown together on seven previous missions. Sadly, Old Glory was shot down by fighters about 130 kilometers northwest of Friedrichshafen, Germany, on the return route. Failing to return home, all but one crew member was killed in the crash.

The B-24H (41-28742), originally nicknamed Jiggles and then Old Glory, was never officially named. To be able to officially name an aircraft, a crew must first complete several successful missions. Upon completion of this milestone or "rite of passage," an aircraft is permanently assigned to the crew and an official aircraft name is recorded.

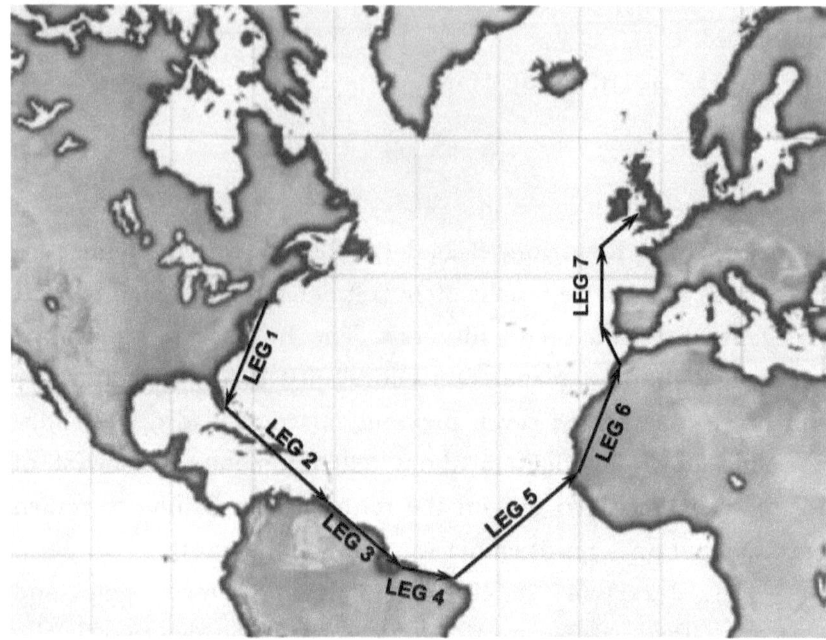

The map above outlines the 16-day, 9,400-statute-miles (15,130 kilometers) transglobal route taken by the Kendziora crew (Crew DJ-11) while transporting a replacement B-24 Liberator aircraft from Mitchel Field in Long Island, New York, to the Isle of Anglesey. During the winter months, the South Atlantic air route to Europe quickly developed and became the most often used method of getting aircraft to the African Theater and European Theaters of war.

PART THREE

Overture to Overlord

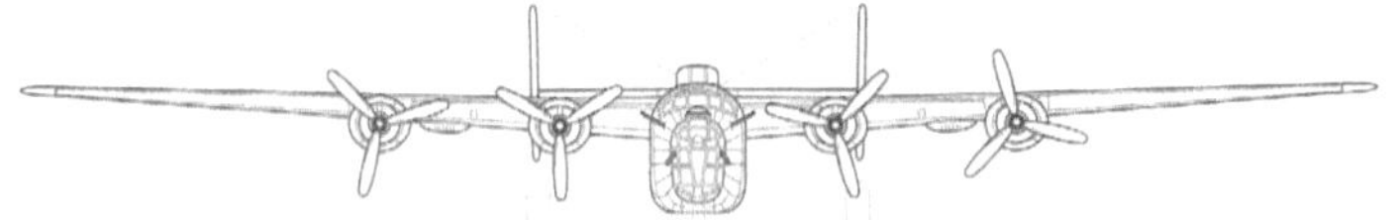

CHAPTER TWELVE

Replacements

MARCH 7, 1944
WEST MIDLANDS, ENGLAND
EVENING

"In our new planes, with our new crews, we bombed,
the ranges by the desert or the shore,
fired at towed targets, waited for our scores,
and turned into replacements and woke up
one morning, over England, operational."

—RANDELL JARRELL[2]

GRABBING THEIR GEAR, THE ten-man crew walked through a steady drizzle to the base commander's office. Kendziora and Goebel went inside while the rest of the crew waited under a dry overhang. The two lieutenants approached the first office, which

2 (Gardiner, 1992)

was occupied by a clean-cut major manning his desk. Both pilots saluted, stood at attention, and waited for the officer to acknowledge them.

Not looking up, the major curtly spoke; "At ease! Let me see your orders!"

Kendziora handed over the operational order marked "FX 200 DJ." Reaching toward the major, he asked, "Permission to speak, Sir?"

Looking up and taking the form from Kendziora's hand, the major smartly replied, "Granted!"

With approval, Kendziora added, "Sir, what are they doing to my aircraft? You see—"

Cutting him off, the major jumped in. "Well, Lieutenant, that aircraft doesn't belong to you; it belongs to me and the Eighth Air Force! As a matter of fact, you and your crew belong to the Mighty Eighth! Now, go two doors down and my corporal will arrange for your transportation."

Saluting again, the two aviators sharply turned and left the room.

After consulting with the assigned corporal, the Kendziora crew loaded into the back of a waiting soft-skinned transport truck and promptly left for the train station with the other airmen. Their escort, a freckle-faced private, was ordered to guide the aviators to a replacement depot located in the "Six Towns" area of Staffordshire County.

The airmen, along with their escort, traveled by train through Chester and Crewe and terminated at the Strafford station where they loaded into waiting troop trucks bound north for Yarnfield. Now deep in a foreign land, it was all very confusing to the tired airmen. Still raining and now darker, they were said to be somewhere in the British Midlands. The only thing for certain was the fact that they were now part of The Mighty Eighth and the European Theater of Operations. The major had made that point abundantly clear.

The airmen were soon deposited in a nondescript installation, and with a passing declaration their young escort abruptly disappeared. Crew DJ-11's new home was a troop processing camp (a non-airfield), a replacement control depot just south of Stoke-on-Trent. The camp was overflowing with troops and supplies; it was truly a sprawling military metropolis. The offices were billeted to an old hotel converted into barracks, dining hall, and offices, while the noncoms of the Kendziora crew were housed in huts. Upon reporting in, the airmen were informed that they would remain at their current post for at least ten days before being shipped out for low-level flight training. Additionally, they would all be assigned—including the officers—to work details, ground defense positions, maintenance crews, mess-hall duties (KP), and mail censors.

The hotel itself became the hub of all social activities in the area, with the multitude of troops from various services and countries attending the nightly dances and social hours. Things certainly became a little risqué, especially at the end of the evening when drunken troopers fought for the attention of the few available women. Like many other airmen and soldiers, when not on duty, Goebel enjoyed the company of the young, local British ladies. Trying his luck, Goebel did his best to charm them with tokens of silk stockings or the equally sought after milled toilet soap.

Like most other United States military personnel, Goebel was not as pleased with the native food or accommodations. The abundance of mutton, greasy potatoes, and weak tea (always with milk) did nothing for their appetites except make them long for the comforts of home. The Brit plumbing, electrical service, heating systems, and lack of modern appliances all dated back to the turn of the century. It was obvious that the British were under the duress of wartime conditions and rationing. The British weather wasn't much better, with the month of March producing twenty inches of rain and the winds at an average mean wind speed of fourteen knots. It was easy for a young trooper to become more than a little gloomy and homesick.

The prescribed ten days passed without further direction, and the military idiom of "hurry up and wait" was fully implanted. After little more than three weeks had passed, no flying and too much idle time had the crew on edge. On April 1, the Kendziora crew received orders that it would be moving out. Already pre-warned by other airmen, the crew knew they were headed for more training. Any training at the moment sounded exciting. First, they would participate in additional low-level flight and formation training. Once completed, they would be assigned to a bomber squadron. Frustrated with their situation and surroundings, the airmen could do nothing but follow orders and advance to their next objective: Cluntoe Airfield in Northern Ireland.

April 2, 1944
Cluntoe, Northern Ireland
Afternoon

The trip from Yarnfield to Cluntoe was relatively uneventful. The Kendziora crew lined up with hundreds of other airmen and boarded the array of military transports. The train took them northwest to Liverpool where they boarded a ferry that shuttled them across the Irish Sea. Once on land in Northern Ireland, they boarded troop trucks that transported them in a caravan to a remote part of the

English-occupied territory. The small village of Ardboe in County Tyrone, located on the western side of Lough Neagh, is a rural but homely farming community where the airfield was situated.

Originally built in 1941, the RAF station was later transferred to the USAAF 8th Air Force in November 1943, becoming the No. 4 Combat Crew Replacement Center. Training at the airfield immediately began with B-17 crews only to later evolve to include B-24 crews in February 1944. The site became No. 2 Combat Crew Replacement Center in March 1944 just weeks prior to the Kendziora crew's arrival. The following months, May through to August, would be the busiest for the airfield and the surrounding tiny town.

The primitive village of Ardboe was independent from electricity; its sole population consisted of farmers and herders, who still depended on horses and carts. Thatched and whitewashed stone cottages bookended the town's few shops, which housed a farmers' market, a shoemaker, a pub, and two blacksmiths.

Arriving to Station No. 238, the Kendziora crew was assigned to a twenty-foot by forty-foot quonset hut. The half-round tin and pressed-wood structures were lined neatly in rows. Each hut was equipped with twenty-four cots and one centrally placed potbellied stove, with its black tin chimney passing up through the thinly insulated roof. The main source of heat in the hut burned coal, which left a generous coating of black dust on all interior surfaces.

Over the next week, the Kendziora crew would attend training and briefings conducted by experienced pilots leaving the European Theatre. These war-hardened airmen would meet with new recruits to pass on the benefits of their experience. In early April 1944, Crew DJ-11 participated in two low-level training flights. The Kendziora crew honed its formation skills, flying at haystack height across the open countryside and the nearby Irish Sea.

APRIL 10, 1944
CLUNTOE, NORTHERN IRELAND
MORNING

On Monday morning, Crew DJ-11 received special orders (S.O. No. 93) assigning them to the 445th Bomber Group. These new orders confirmed what they had been anticipating: their assignment as combat crew personnel. As part of the 445th, they would transfer to Army Air Force Station 124, Tibenham Airfield, located in Norfolk County, England.

On that same day, the RAF dropped a record 3,600 tons of bombs in a single raid on Germany, Belgium, and France. While many Allied servicemen were unaware, the preparations for Operation Overlord were well underway.

CHAPTER THIRTEEN

Combat Crew Assignment

April 12, 1944
Cluntoe, Northern Ireland
Early morning

DEPARTING CLUNTOE EARLY IN the morning, the Kendziora crew would retrace their previous travels. Loading into the back of a soft-skinned GMC truck, Goebel and his fellow airmen headed back to the eastern port. They crossed back over the Irish Sea and boarded a train in Liverpool headed for the southeast coast of England. Their travels took them through dozens of little towns that all looked the same. The soggy English countryside rolled together as they sat viewing the scenery from their steam carriage. It consumed the better part of the day to trek across mainland England, only to arrive late in the evening.

Tibenham Airfield first opened in November 1942; its first occupants were Martin B-26 Marauders, the 2nd Bomb Wing, and the 320th Bombardment Group en route to North Africa. One year later, the airfield was transferred to 445th Bombardment Group with its B-24 Liberators. Combined, the 700th, 701st, 702nd, and 703rd Bomb Squadrons would fly 282 combat missions during their stay, ending in May 1945. Tibenham also boasted to be the home of actor Jimmy Stewart who, at the rank of captain, was the 703rd BS Commander until his promotion and transfer to the 453rd Bombardment Group in March 1944, just one month before Goebel and Crew DJ-11 arrived.

The grounds at Tibenham consisted of the standard concrete A-shaped runway, a three-story concrete control tower and watch office with operations, observation deck, and crew briefing rooms. Surrounding the airfield, the flat farmland allowed for plenty of aircraft storage, flight crew billeting, and support operations.

On arrival to the base, the four officers were assigned and given brief directions to a smaller dank nissan hut, a smaller version of a quonset. They were given a fair warning they were going to be billeted near an active dairy farm. In an effort to overcome the stench, cigarettes hung from each of their mouths as the four aviators searched for their hut. Paranoid, the men stared at the ground hoping not to step in the brown bovine landmines. They arrived without incident only to find that their designated hut was occupied with another crew's gear. Placing their duffels on the ground, the airmen proceeded to take another smoke break while debating their next step.

Just as the last Camel was lit, a jeep with a young buck private pulled to a stop near the four lieutenants. Jumping from the jeep, the private walked toward them and saluted, then went to the door of the hut.

Kendziora spoke up first. "There's no one in there!"

"Yes, sir! I'm just here to collect the Pavelka crew's effects," the private retorted.

The private went on to explain that the previous occupants, the Pavelka crew, had been shot down and listed as MIA from an early morning bombing raid. "We dispatched B-24s this morning; they were on a mission to bomb some German industrial targets when things were scrubbed because of cloud cover."

"Their ship didn't return?" Goebel quietly inquired.

Looking at the ground the private hesitated a moment, then answered. "Nope, They're MIA! I heard they were last seen over Belgium."

Saddened by the news, the four aviators stood silently as the private went about his business. Waiting respectfully outside, the men stared at their feet, not wanting to address the news. After a few moments, Kendziora, Goebel, Chappie, and Tucker were granted access. Stepping inside the small hut, they began unpacking their gear. Kendziora noticed that the mood in the hut was still somber and needed to be changed.

Addressing his peers, Kendziora spoke up. "Not to worry, boys! That won't be us! Besides, it's not like we knew the chaps. It's important that we clear our minds of this and get prepared for the task ahead."

The following morning started with Crew DJ-11 receiving special orders (S.O. No. 96), officially assigning them to the 702nd Bomber Squadron. After twenty months and traveling halfway around the world, the Kendziora crew was finally getting closer to actually performing the role that they had been trained for.

Over the next four days, Crew DJ-11 would participate in short local training flights consisting of one or two hours at most. While absorbing all the information made available to them, time was not on their side. Too many idle hours were spent waiting to be engaged in a war that was raging in front of them.

While watching as their comrades depart for Germany as part of 626 bomber and 871 fighter armada, the loudspeaker cracked and squealed in an attempt to make an announcement: "Your attention, please! I have a message from Supreme Headquarters Allied Expeditionary Force as of 0000 hours this morning. General of the Army Dwight D. Eisenhower formally assumed authority over air operations for the European Theater. It looks like Ike's calling the shots from now on!"

Unfortunately, with good news came more frustrating news. The airmen were informed that before Kendziora could lead his own crew, he must first complete five missions as a copilot. Hearing the news, the rest of the crew felt deflated. Kendziora was soon assigned and participated in the next two strategic operations. Bombing Mission (306) dispatched on Tuesday, April 18, 1944, and Bombing Mission (308) dispatched on Thursday, April 19, 1944.

Upon returning each afternoon, Kendziora would brief his crew on what he saw and experienced. As best as he could, Kendziora tried to prepare them for what the future held: "The German 88mm flak is the worst part. Black plumes of exploding, bone-rattling flak all around. We were greeted by German antiaircraft artillery as soon as we hit the European coast!"

The remaining members of Crew DJ-11 patiently waited for Kendziora to complete his obligations. Goebel and his other crew members had been in Europe now for more than six weeks. Irritated with not being provided the opportunity to prove themselves was becoming more than a little frustrating. Each day of waiting compounded more nervous energy onto the next. In their anticipation, it was difficult not to think about all the dreadful things that could go wrong: flak, mechanical failures, or being shot down by enemy fighters.

A break in the monotony for Goebel and the others came on Friday, April 20,1944, when Crew DJ-11 was assigned to perform a channel sweep. Taking off as a small contingent of B-24s dispatched to Mission 309, Crew DJ-11 flew their B-24H out over the English Channel, completing their last formation practice flight. In their travels, the airmen would look down upon the movement on the ground and along the shoreline. Unaware they were witnessing only a fraction of the area's events; Allied forces rehearsed their roles in preparation for the impending Allied invasion of the European continent. In the early months of 1944, more than four million Allied servicemen would travel through England's bases and ports in preparations for Operation Overlord.

On Saturday, April 22, 1944, Kendziora was dispatched again as a copilot on Bombing Mission 311. Returning safely and successfully participating in three missions, the 702nd BS Commander relaxed the five-flight requirement as the squadron required more active crews. Kendziora was now deemed experienced enough to lead Crew DJ-11 and as a result his crew was reclassified as "combat-ready."

Crew DJ-11 would be part of the next strategic bombing operation. On Sunday afternoon, Kendziora and Goebel went to the message board outside the commander's office. Boldly listed was their crew's name. Drawing his finger across the notice, Kendziora saw that he was assigned aircraft No. 42-110060 B-24J (Consolidated B-24J-130-CO Liberator) with the call sign of T-Tare. Being new and on their first mission, Crew DJ-11 was simply relegated to one of the available working aircraft, and that was all Kendziora could expect. Leaving the dispatch office, Kendziora and Goebel strolled out onto the hardstand in search of their new B-24.

Crew DJ-11 and their newly assigned aircraft previously named "Ruthless Ruth" were dispatched on Bombing Mission 315, scheduled for the next day, Monday, April 24, 1944.

APRIL 13, 1944
SUPREME ALLIED COMMAND HEADQUARTERS—LONDON, ENGLAND
MORNING

When General Eisenhower assumed official control of the Allied Air Forces on April 13, 1944, he was immediately faced with the decision of how best to support the invasion of Europe and capitalize on his newly acquired forces. Ike was presented with two major proposals.

As the Commander of U.S. Strategic Air Forces in Europe, General Carl A. Spaatz wanted to focus on German industry. The "Oil Plan" objective was focused on the destruction of German oil refineries and major manufacturing by heavy bombers to immobilize the German Armed Forces. Opponents of the Oil Plan argued that the desired results would not happen soon enough to affect the Normandy invasion.

Alternatively, Eisenhower's Deputy Supreme Commander, British Air Chief Marshal Sir Arthur Tedder, proposed the "Transportation Plan," which focused on the destruction of German/French rail marshaling yards and other transportation targets to isolate German armies in the invasion area. Opponents of the Transportation Plan argued that it did not make effective use of the heavy bombers and, worse, would kill or wound many French civilians.

Wanting the French perspective first before making his final decision, Ike consulted French General Marie-Pierre-Joseph Koenig, the leading commander of Free French Forces and an American military representative.

Eisenhower ordered implementation of the Transportation Plan, but in order to minimize civilian casualties, he banned attacks on moving trains and restricted their initial efforts to marshaling yards and bridges. In conjunction, Eisenhower also ordered strategic attacks on German industry.

★ ★ ★ ★ ★ ★ ★

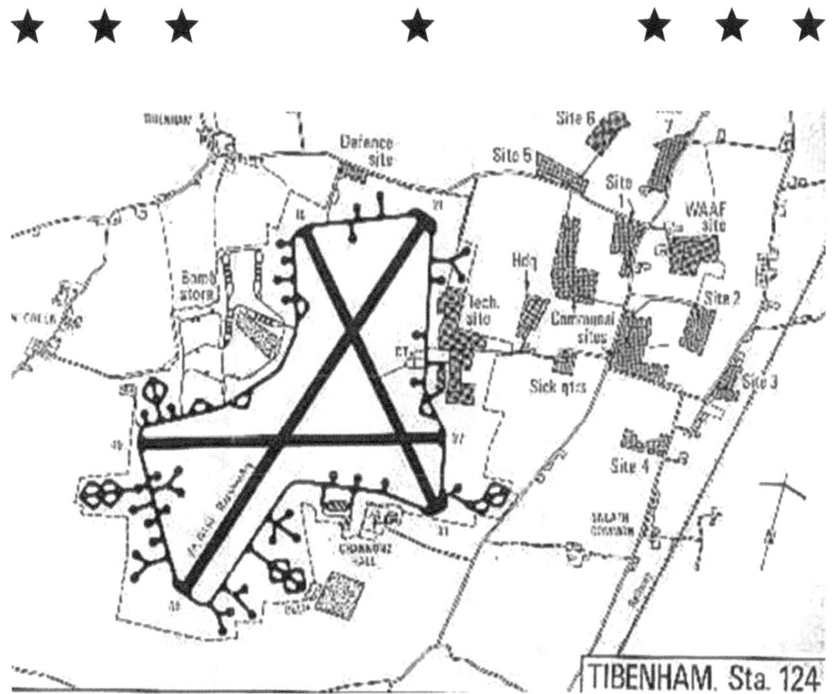

Plan view of Tibenham Airfield, USAAF Station 124 (above), utilized the typical triangular A-shaped pattern used by the Allied forces during World War II. Photo © 2004 445th BG website.

(C) 2004
445th BG
Website

Awaiting the return of the group

*The actual air control tower as seen by Goebel at Tibenham (above)
and the 702nd orderly building (below).*

(C) 2004
445th BG
Website

702nd Bomb Squadron
Orderly Room Staff

CHAPTER FOURTEEN

Inaugural Mission

APRIL 24, 1944
TIBENHAM, ENGLAND
EARLY MORNING

"April 24, 1944[3]

AT 0315 AN ORDERLY rushed into our hut and called out the four officers' names of our crew: Kendziora—pilot, Goebel—copilot, Czaplewski—navigator, Tucker—bombardier. This was our first mission with the entire crew participating. It was to be a big day for us, and we hurried into our clothes with a vigor. I washed my hands, leaving my face unwashed to prevent chapping.

Kendziora and I grabbed our various flying gear and meandered to Mess Hall No. 5. After heaving down a fresh egg breakfast, we headed for the briefing room to see what gives! We were early and had plenty of time to grab a smoke before business got underway. The crew

3 The following excerpts are Goebel's own words taken from his personal diary written in September 1944.

collected together and throughout the room there was a lot of fast chatter and sparse laughter. "At ease" was called and the "briefing" began. The screen was lifted from the European map and our target was clearly marked; it was München. A chill shot up my spine, and I laughingly said to Ken, "Well, they're really starting us off with a bang!" Hell, if all our missions were to be this caliber, we'd be lucky to finish ten, let alone "thirty." I had figured on a "milk-run" to start our career, but Operations didn't think the way I did. The briefing didn't take long; our specific target was to be an airdrome northwest of München, which was not only an air base but a large supply depot as well. Bombing technique was discussed, pictures shown, and then the weather was covered. Light cirrus was about the only cloud formation over the target. Stratiform over England proper; Altocumulus over the French Coast diminishing to a clear sky over the interior. Fighter cover was to be provided; that in itself took three quarters of the load off our shoulders. Briefing finished with special information for the Radioman and Navigator. Our bomb load was fifty-two, one-hundred-pound incendiary bombs. Every detail seemed to be covered completely and to a green crew it looked as if it would be a "lark."

Leaving the briefing room, we went to the ready room to pick up our heated suits and parachutes. I had a brand-new backpack parachute, and I handled it with care; hell, I might have to use it, who knows? After putting on our suits and chutes, I turned and asked Ken, "Taking your G.I. shoes?" "Hell, no," was the reply! Our crew was a very confident one, to say the least. I agree, anyone would. It'd be just too ironic to get slapped down on your first hop! Haw!

Takeoffs were to be at thirty-second intervals, starting at 0900 hours; our takeoff time was 0920. Our position was No. 2 man in the #4 element of the high right squadron. As planned, it was a damn good position for a green crew from any attack by fighters. Too damn bad we didn't hold it! Takeoff went off easily, and after forming at

20,000 ft. we started on our way. We passed over the southeast English coast at 1128 hours; it had taken us almost two and half hours to get into the air and form.

Weather was as predicted, and following a Fortress wing in, we would circumnavigate the flak areas as they plowed through them. About five minutes in over France, we started to meet aborters heading home, some with one or two engines cut out. North of Paris we saw a Fort spiraling down aflame but still under control. P-47 cover was all over the sky, and we had no fighter worries. Farther in, the 47s left us and 51s picked us up. The sky was crystal clear, and we all felt good. Irvin, our engineer, reported that he felt sick. I asked him if he wanted to be replaced by Charlie Weymouth, ball-gunner, but he refused, saying he'd stick it out. All other ships had their top turrets slowly rotating. Ours was not and I made a mental note to speak to Irvin on that account. Approaching the Wing I.P. we could see the snow-covered Alps on our right and B-17 Fortresses crossing them to the south-east. They were in terrific flak concentrations, and I counted twelve torches proving the accuracy of the flak throwers. I can't say the flak was accurate on second thought because the whole sky was covered with Forts, and it was just like a duck shoot. By this time, all fuel was in the main tanks. Our element leader was Miller; he was the poorest pilot I've seen in quite a while. Occasionally, we'd have to drop flaps and pull our turbos in order to stay with him. Such radical changes in settings are not necessary. "Peters" flying left wing in our element became disquieted and hooked onto another element. We hadn't the experience to follow suit. Our Wing I.P. was Dillingen, Germany. Here the wing broke into groups. Approaching Group I.P. our leader had placed us entrail of number 3 element, a complete shift to the right! Some formation flying!

This position rubbed us into #3 element where bombs were released and put our ass over the fire as far as fighters were concerned.

We broke this entrail position just prior to bomb release and resumed it again after leaving the target area. Charlie Westerlund, radio operator, had opened the bomb bay doors and had checked all bombs clear. After flak had popped in front of his face a few times he hastily closed the doors without much ado. It would be modest to say a strained expression on our faces. Flak was so heavy it was like running through a field of black cotton. Over the target, my hands were practically idle, and I sat in my seat as if I expected a 105mm shell to come up and splash me around. A poor copilot has a hell of a position in times like these. We could tell just when we came to the edge of the flak zone, and we breathed mighty easy once out of that hell! We checked over the ship for battle damage and no one had anything to report. One piece of flak had caught us just fore the instrument panel, but I doubt if it penetrated.

Well, the rough part of the mission was over with; we had only to return safely, and we could chalk one up. Everything had seemed easy, looking back at it. Ahead lay flak concentrations, but with a little luck these could be completely avoided. We were a tail-end wing at the end of a huge procession. I studied the peaceful landscape that Germany presented from the air and wondered how a country such as that could possibly protect itself. All that was visible were cultivated fields, wooded areas, and scattered communities. We passed south of Stuttgart and noted that fierce fires were ragging in the dock area, evidently oil fires. Our cover over the target had consisted of P38s and 51s, and they were mighty beautiful to see. Just past Stuttgart I noticed we had the P-51 cover briefing said we would have. Everything was running smoothly. The Navigator rang out over interphone that at 1531 we'd pass over the Belgian-German Frontier; at this point P-47 cover would be provided. We could see the Mustangs picking up vapor trails as they left us just prior to the coming of the Thunderbolts.

There was perhaps a five-minute interval that we had no fighter cover. We were fast approaching the Frontier when things really happened. All men were at their positions, but still we had no warning whatsoever in the cockpit. I was just about to inquire where the hell the K ration was at. Charlie Westerlund was on his hands and knees selecting the proper frequency to receive weather conditions at our base. Ken was smoking; his face was flushed and definitely acted sluggishly. We were in pairs instead of briefed formation; the formation reminded me of a herd of cows going out to pasture.

I heard a bunch of muffled reports, then green-white flashes burst all about the nose of the ship. Some of them burst twenty feet ahead of us. They were exploding 20mm shells. There were at least twenty bursts at one time and the bursts just kept repeating themselves. After the fire ceased, I heard the tail turret open up, then the top-turret and one waist gun.

Instantly, we poured the soup to all engines, but it was no use, we were too far out! At 3 o'clock, about a thousand feet below us, I caught sight of a green-and-yellow-patched ME109 F or G doing a wing over. Shortly after that we saw 20mm exploding about ten yards short of the only silver Lib in the wing, which was flying alongside and to the left of us. Luckily, Jerry had miscalculated and failed to score any strikes.

Number 2 started to run away but slowly. The pilot called my attention to this, and first I played with the toggles, they were useless and so were the feathering buttons; the only thing left was to retard throttle to approximately 15 inches. At least she was pulling her own weight. Charlie started shouting "Fire!" and after looking into the bomb-bay, I told him to try and put it out. No. 2 being out, the ship had lost formation in an instant of confusion. The pilot was on the right rudder, but he was banking to the left! Showing his ability to think clearly was shot to hell through lack of oxygen over a period of time. Altitude was at that time about 22,000 ft.

Meanwhile, I was trying to help fly the ship and give the fire my attention also. The engineer slid out of the top turret. Charlie helped him slip on his chute, and the next time I looked around, Charlie alone was standing on the catwalk. Leaving the controls, I jumped on the catwalk and grabbed the CO2 extinguisher. Leaning against the first brace, I reached toward the base of the fire and pressed the trigger. To my astonishment and dismay, all that came out was two small chips of dry ice! A swell scene for a comedy!

The only thing left to do was to open the bomb bay doors and try to blow it out, not only that the draft kept the fire away from us. Oxygen and all electrical equipment were out of commission. We couldn't make contact, nor see, the rear section of our ship. Staying with the ship 15 to 20 minutes after we were hit, the fire had steadily grown worse. We had the windshield open but still were coughing our lungs out. Finally, I suggested to Ken that it was a lost cause. He agreed and I gave Charlie the "okay" to bail out. This he did with great speed, and I saw his silk blossom out before I lost sight of him out of the bomb bay.

I stood in the catwalk and checked all my buckles, then yelled to Ken I was leaving. Then I just stepped out into a void that had no depth. To insure my not pulling my ripcord, I kept my arms free and used them to control my position. The ship quickly left me, and I was all alone to experience the unique sensation of seeming to be supported by air alone. I was in a supine position with my legs spread and angled slightly higher than my body.

I put my right arm out and turned over. Facing the ground, the air whipped at my face and my eyes watered so quickly that I could scarcely see. I again put out my right hand and turned over on my back. I couldn't judge my height, but when I noticed some green coloring of the landscape growing over my shoulder, I grabbed my rip cord and pulled it about two inches.

A flock of white passed my head, and the next instant a terrific force jerked the living hell out of me. For a fraction of a second, I lost consciousness. When I came to, my arms were at my side and I still had the rip cord. I was wearing a two-piece electric suit, so I tied the rip cord to the extension wire, for what reason I do not know. I judged my altitude at opening my chute to be close to 14,000 ft. I saw the plane in a dive, then I saw the pilot tumbling out. I can't swear whether his chute opened or not. I believe it did. It may have been the Navigator or Bombardier. I saw Charlie below me, a mere white speck in the sky that contrasted the earth below. I was quickly nearing the ground so prepared for a good landing.

I worked the shroud lines all the way down and by looking past the toes of my heated boots I could gage my drift. There was a small village to the north, and I could see people running out of town. I could see bicycles very plainly. I passed over two men in the center of a large field at a height of approximately 250 ft. I waved to them and then prepared to land. I was facing in the direction I was drifting and had my feet together and ready to take the shock. I should have made a good landing.

The last 200 feet rush by you, and with a swish you've got a half acre shoved in your face. My legs jacked-knifed into my chest, and I went down with every bit of air knocked out of me. My chute dropped over a barb-wire fence; I had landed in the very corner of the field."

CHAPTER FIFTEEN

Caterpillar Club

April 24, 1944
Skies over Eastern Europe
Early afternoon

HEADING WEST, THE KENDZIORA crew crossed the Belgium border at 1135 hours. With good fighter coverage and fairly good formation, the flight was uncomfortably peaceful. Looking down at the countryside, it was hard to believe there was a war going on. That soon changed once they reached their initial point (IP), Gablingen Airfield. Their target was reached at 1355 hours. The skies immediately erupted in heavy black and red flak as soon as the first of the formation arrived. The crew watched in disbelief as three B-17s exploded one by one in front of them. No parachutes were witnessed. Just an explosion of flame and debris, then the planes were gone. The sight of the vaporized aircraft rocked them to immediate reality that their chore for that day was extremely real and unforgiving.

Suddenly, the sky turned into an exploding field of black cotton. Several abrupt course changes were made until the release point was reached. The crews of the heavies only had one purpose: place their bombs on their intended target. Releasing their bombs was only part of the mission. Making it back home to Tibenham intact was the true end goal. The sudden release of their payload caused Ruth to lurch upward, the crew maintained control and banked to return home. Set on a straight-line course from Augsburg to their home airfield, and 5,200 pounds lighter, Ruthless Ruth was now able to inch closer to her maximum elevation of 28,000 feet and an airspeed of 290 miles per hour. Grouped with other aircraft positioned at the end of the procession, the Kendziora crew was ready, alert, and nervous, to say the least.

Heading northeast, the Kendziora crew passed over Stuttgart. The German manufacturing hub was in flames. This fact would not impede the enemy though. Ahead, the German antiaircraft remained in the flak fields. The hulking giants would have to negotiate through exploding 57-pound shells that were able to easily reach a ceiling of 37,000 feet, well above their cruising altitude. A striking shell could easily incinerate the drab-green aircraft and its unlucky crew.

Crossing the burning German city without incident, the crew of Ruthless Ruth soon saw the Rhine River. Seeing this, they knew the Belgium border was still more than an hour away. With this knowledge, Kendziora continued to push his B-24, almost willing it home to safety. Crossing the Belgium/German border at 1521 hours and with a heading toward the city of Liège, they passed the halfway mark. For the moment, things appeared to be going smoothly for the Kendziora crew.

Irl Klinginsmith, Norman Mosher, Charles Weymouth, and Theodore Chriss

Stocking his lumbering prey, the Luftwaffe pilot hung back, watching as the Allied P-51 Mustang escort fighters dropped away to return to their base in need of fuel. Knowing that he would be unchallenged, the pilot pushed his fighter toward the trailing B-24s. Seeing the enemy Messerschmitt on its approaching attack, Chriss, Weymouth, and Klinginsmith opened fire. The ME109 found its target and replied, revengefully watching as his rounds pierced the upper left side of the beast. The Luftwaffe pilot was experienced as he knew where to direct his kill shots. The Messerschmitt 20mm rounds sliced through the paper-thin skin and struck the interior of Ruthless Ruth. Their path was unobstructed, only to be replaced by a stream of exterior light that entered the dark fuselage interior. The rounds exploded when hitting solid objects within, ultimately taking out the hydraulics, communication, and wounding Klinginsmith in the left arm and right eye.

Klinginsmith yelled out over the wind noise of his open waist door: "Damn it! I've been hit!"

Mosher heard his partner's call for help and stepped toward Klinginsmith, noticing the smoke from the exploding round. Mosher turned from Klinginsmith and instantly assumed Weymouth's position.

Shouting, Mosher informed Weymouth of the impending hazard: "Charlie, Irl's been shot and we're on fire! Go grab Chriss and find the source of the smoke, and I will help Irl!" Unable to do much for Klinginsmith's wounds, Mosher assured him that his chute was in good condition and properly secured.

Weymouth and Chriss were instantly engulfed in smoke. Sensing that Ruthless Ruth was losing elevation and unable to extinguish the blaze or contact the front of the plane, the four airmen came to the decision that it was time to get out. Chriss made haste, opening the main floor hatch in the aft cabin. Standing around the exposed hole, the four airmen checked their chutes and gestured the order of departure. Before stepping through, each man looked at one another and said, "Good luck!" then quietly disappeared.

Weymouth helped Klinginsmith into position, double-checked that he had his chute handle securely in his hand, gave him the okay signal, and watched as Klinginsmith jumped free. He was followed closely by Mosher. After double-checking the buckles on his chute, Weymouth jumped next. Finally, Chriss looked around the smoked-filled cabin one last time, crossed his arms on his chest, and leaped forward into the opening. Unbeknownst to them, the four rear occupants were the first group out of Ruthless Ruth. They landed in a three-kilometer spread near the towns of Stavelot and Stoumont, Belgium, respectively.

Robert Tucker and Leon Czaplewski

Except for the time it took to facilitate his bombardier duties, Tucker had spent most of the trip to and from Augsburg in the hydraulically driven nose turret. The first signal for Tucker that something was terribly wrong was when tracers flew dangerously close beneath him, streaming forward from the rear. Then the corner of Tucker's right eye caught the image of the German ME109 at the one o'clock position, flying level with the hulking B-24. The swirling black-and-white checkerboard nacelle was only twenty-five yards away. Tucker was able to clearly see the enemy pilot's head turn to look at him as if to survey for possible damage.

Tucker's face squinted with surprise and dogged determination as he turned the turret guns to the right in an effort to offer his deadly response. He then bared down on the ME109, unleashing his twin .50 caliber machine guns. Sensing impending danger, his counterpart maneuvered his aircraft, rolling down and away. Tucker's bullets missed their mark. In pursuit, Tucker forced the controls but to little avail. The turret had lost complete mobility and the hydraulics were out. Tucker continued to fight the controls in an effort to center the turret and align the rear hatch. Trapped and unable to move, fight back, or get out, Tucker was a sitting duck!

Realizing Tucker's predicament, Czaplewski jumped from his position and began to manually crank the turret back. Once properly aligned with the navigator/bombardier compartment, Czaplewski snatched the metal hatch doors open, freeing Tucker. Climbing free, Tucker thumped Czaplewski on the back of the shoulder and said, "Thanks, Chappie! I owe you one! Have you heard anything from Irvin on what happened to the hydraulics?"

Humbly shrugging off his friend's gratitude, Czaplewski replied, "No, nothing. The radios are dead too!"

Czaplewski and Tucker listened for the bailout bell, unable to contact the flight deck by radio. Smoke was beginning to fill the cramped quarters, and they concluded that it was time to abandon Ruthless Ruth. Unable to wear the bulky chest pack in the turret, Tucker immediately reached for his chute that was still hanging on the compartment wall. After clipping it securely and giving it one final check, they gave each other the thumbs-up signal.

The two men moved to the nose gear compartment, and Czaplewski pulled down the emergency release handles that opened the nose wheel doors. The doors slid open, exposing open sky and the earth's surface below. Czaplewski motioned to Tucker to go first. With the plane flying straight and level, Tucker climbed out. His body flashed instantly out of sight, almost as if the wind had sucked him clean from the wounded fuselage. Czaplewski climbed into position and leapt from the wounded aircraft. Simultaneously, the B-24 dropped violently, twisting to the left and causing Czaplewski's head to strike the bottom of the hatch opening, knocking him unconscious.

Czaplewski's hand, already gripping his rip cord, reflexively deployed when the force of the wind struck his falling body; thus saving his life. Now floating under his deployed canopy, Tucker looked up to check on Czaplewski's progress and saw that his chute was open. Thankfully, Czaplewski appeared to be descending as gracefully as possible; however, they were traveling farther apart by the second. That moment was the last time Tucker would see Czaplewski for the remainder of the war.

Tucker descended quietly, landing unharmed in the small Belgium town of Huy, northwest of Stavelot. Czaplewski would suffer a much worse fate. A sharp, stabling pain woke him from his unconscious state. Feeling the burn and warm liquid run down the inside of his pant leg, he realized he had been shot. As the blurriness cleared from his vision, Czaplewski was able to make out the silhouette of the hostile figure running in his direction below. Impatiently waiving the muzzle of his Schmeisser submachine gun, the German Wehrmacht soldier barked to his approaching comrades and the unsuspecting injured airman. Czaplewski, bleeding from his head and leg, was eagerly greeted by his unwelcome captor, who proudly handed him over to a Gestapo agent for interrogation.

———————————

Donald Irvin, Charles Westerlund, James Goebel, and Franklin Kendziora

With the fire burning out of control and no way to extinguish it, there was little left to do but get out before the plane exploded. Knowing that they had limited time remaining, Kendziora and Goebel fought to steer their burning aircraft away from unsuspecting civilians on the ground. Ruthless Ruth's last maneuvers were intentional. With flames clearly seen from the ground, and at a low speed, the pilots pulled Ruth in a hard one-hundred-eighty-degree turn to the right to avoid the town of Andenne. Ruthless Ruth shunted again as it made its final correction, a second ninety-degree right turn to avoid the village of Couthuin.

The only means of egress for the remaining members of the Kendziora crew was through the smoke- and fire-infested bomb bay doors. One by one, they each left their stations and abandoned the mortally wounded aircraft. Irvin led the way, followed by Westerlund, then Goebel, and lastly, Kendziora. Each man walked onto the catwalk and jumped into the smoke, only to punch through into the clear-blue sky.

The unmanned B-24 quietly glided toward the earth, only to be swallowed up by a fireball on impact. Ruthless Ruth struck the forested ground just east of Namur, Belgium. The final wave of fleeing airmen landed in an area stretching five kilometers, covering an arching strip that reached from Nonceveux to Andenne, Belgium. All four airmen landed safely, yet were dispersed randomly along the foreign Belgium countryside, far from the security of England or their homeland.

Scattered across the Belgium countryside like dandelion seeds in a brisk wind, the members of the Kendziora crew were now considered missing in action (MIA). After being hit, Ruthless

Ruth would travel for more than sixty kilometers in a northeasterly direction before banking a hard left and slamming into the ground approximately two kilometers south of Couthuin, Belgium (twenty kilometers east northeast of Numar, Belgium).

APRIL 24, 1944
SKIES OVER BELGIUM
AFTERNOON

That afternoon, while jumping to safety from their B-24, Goebel and the other members of the Kendziora crew unknowingly all became eligible for membership into one of the world's most exclusive organizations, the **"Caterpillar Club,"** which is an informal association. It has no meetings, officers, or formal organization, but the requirements for membership are rigid; members <u>must</u> have saved their lives by jumping from a disabled aircraft with a parachute. To date, there are less than 100,000 estimated members of the Caterpillar Club, with the majority of members qualifying during World War II.

THE LUCKY SEVEN

April 24, 1944

European Theater of Operations Combat Chronology[4]

Strategic Operations (8th Air Force): Mission 315: 754 bombers and 867 fighters are dispatched to bomb airfields, aircraft production industries and targets of opportunity in Germany. The bombers claimed an estimated 20 KIA, 1WIA, and 36 MIA Luftwaffe aircraft and the fighters claimed an estimated 124 KIA, 6 WIA, and 58 MIA Luftwaffe fighters; Allied aircraft lost 40 bombers and 17 fighters.

The details are as follows:

1. *Of 281 B-17s dispatched, 109 hit Erding Air Depot, 84 hit aviation industry targets at Oberpfaffenhofen, 57 hit Lansberg Airfield and 18 hit targets of opportunity; 27 B-17s are lost and 112 damaged; casualties are 4 KIA, 22 WIA and 260 MIA.*

2. *243 B-17s are dispatched to bomb aviation industry targets at Friedrichshafen/Lowenthal (98 bomb) and Friedrichshafen/Manzell (58 bomb), industrial areas at Friedrichshafen/Manzell (58 bomb) and Neckarsulm (15 bomb); 3 also hit targets of opportunity; 9 B-17s are lost and 119 damaged; casualties are 7 KIA, 4 WIA and 71 MIA.*

3. *230 B-24s are dispatched to bomb airfields; 120 hit Gablingen Airfield, 98 hit Liepheim Airfield, and 1 hit a target of opportunity;* **4 B-24s are lost and 26 damaged; casualties are 1 WIA and 40 MIA.**

4 As documented by the Eighth Air Force Historical Society and the 445th Bomb Group.

4. *Escort is provided by the 8th and 9th Air Force. 131 P-38s, 490 P-47s and 246 P-51s. P-38s claim 4-1-0 Luftwaffe aircraft, 1 P-38 is damaged beyond repair and 7 damaged; P-47s claim 2-1-0 aircraft in the air and 36-0-16 on the ground, 5 P-47s are lost and 15 damaged, 5 pilots are MIA; P-51s claim 64-4-2 aircraft in the air and 21-0-20 on the ground, 12 P-51s are lost and 8 damaged; 12 pilots are MIA.*

Mission 316: 5 of 5 B-17s drop 1.12 million leaflets on Amsterdam, Rotterdam, The Hague and Utrecht, The Netherlands, Lillie, Reams, and France at 23:22-23:44 hours without loss.

*8 B-24s are dispatched on **CARPETBAGGER** operations*

From the perspective of the Eighth Air Force and the combined crews of the more than 714 B-17 and B-24 aircraft, Bombing Mission No. 315 was a complete success. Reaching their assigned target, the majority of B-24s, including Ruthless Ruth, rained their deadly cargo on the Gablingen Airfield located near the town of Augsburg in southern Germany, just fifty-seven kilometers northwest of Munich (München). The Gablingen airdrome was the home of three Luftwaffe flying schools and two sets of runways. In a single strike, the American raid delivered more than 1.7 million pounds of ordnance, destroying most of the facilities, including the Leipheim headquarters, hangers, barracks, officers' quarters, aircraft shelters, and runway.

THE LUCKY SEVEN

After failing to return back to USAAF Station 124, Crew DJ-11 was officially reported missing. The base Intelligence Officer (IO) on duty completed in triplicate a Missing Air Crew Report. MACR No. 4293 was filed, listing all ten members of the Kendziora crew as missing in action (MIA). The IO also collected any ascertainable information that other flight crews may have seen at the time that aircraft No. 42-110060 B-24J was shot down.

In early 1944 "Operation Carpetbagger" was a general term used for the aerial resupply of arms, equipment, and agents ("Joes" to occupy Europe), in support of the résistance fighters in France, Belgium, and Italy by the U.S. Army Air Forces (USAAF). Two squadrons were placed under the 801st Bomb Group (Provisional) at the beginning of 1944, and the first missions were carried under the command of a World War I Medal of Honor recipient, General William J. ("Wild Bill") Donovan and the Office of Strategic Services (OSS).

In April 1944, the group moved to RAF Harrington airfield (USAAF Station 179), a more secluded and thus more secure airbase located in Northampton County, England. In May 1944, in advance of the expected invasion of Europe, the group was expanded to four squadrons to increase its capabilities. In total, the "Carpetbaggers" conducted twenty-one night missions.

German Fighter Messerschmitt BF 109G

PART FOUR

Missing in Occupied Land

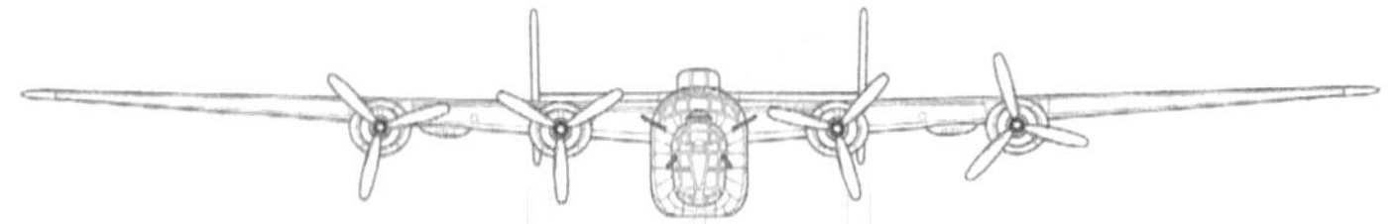

CHAPTER SIXTEEN

Downed Airmen

APRIL 24, 1944
SOUTHWEST BELGIUM
1530 HOURS

AS THE TAIL END of the heavy bomber procession traveled northeast overhead, the crew of Ruthless Ruth could only hope that their brothers above would see their descent to the ground below. Later, back at AAF Station 124 in Tibenham, a company clerk would compile in triplicate a Missing Air Crew Report (MACR) documenting that the crew of ten and their aircraft was officially reported missing.

Klinginsmith

Bailed at 21,000 feet
Landed near Stavelot, Belgium
Status: prisoner of war (POW)

Klinginsmith landed in a field near the edge of some trees. He was seriously wounded by flying shrapnel from a 20mm exploding round.

Klinginsmith was losing blood and in need of immediate medical attention. Upon examining him, the locals turned Klinginsmith over to the Germans as they were unable to provide medical aid or medicine. His right eye was later cut out by a German doctor before being hospitalized, interrogated, and shipped off to a POW camp named Stalag Luft IV, located in Gross Tychow, Pomerania. Klinginsmith would remain in Luft IV for the majority of the war until being shipped to Stalag Luft I to avoid the Russian Army. Klinginsmith would later be liberated by the Russians as they made their way across Germany.

Mosher

Bailed at 21,000 feet
Landed near Stavelot, Belgium
Status: missing in action (MIA)

Mosher was also hit with shrapnel above his left eye, yet his wounds would not prevent him from being assisted by the locals on the ground. Mosher witnessed three other open chutes as he floated down and landed safely alone.

Weymouth

Bailed at 20,000 feet
Landed near Stoumont, Belgium
Status: missing in action (MIA)

Weymouth landed safely and without incident on Belgium soil and was quickly picked up by the locals and kept away from the Germans.

Chriss

Bailed at 19,500 feet
Landed near Stoumont, Belgium
Status: missing in action (MIA)

The last of the group to leave the back of plane, Chriss floated safely to the ground. Separated from the others, he was quickly greeted by the locals, who wasted no time in stripping him free of his chute and harness. Chriss was whisked away before the German patrols arrived.

Tucker

Bailed at 16,500 feet
Landed in Huy, Belgium
Status: missing in action (MIA)

Tucker landed hard in a plowed field between a nearby high-tension line and a barbed wire fence. Momentarily stunned from the impact, he rolled over once and started to unhook his harness. Before he could get the second buckle unlatched, the local people had surrounded him. In a singular, well-orchestrated movement, one man cut off Tucker's chute; another took off his harness; and a third removed his flight jacket. Tucker was helped into a pair of overalls and, as he pushed his arm through the sleeve, was handed a napkin with bread by a young woman.

As the adrenaline from the fall wore off, Tucker felt a twinge in his left knee. He reached down and confirmed his fear. His knee was swollen and quickly expanding like a balloon as he struggled across the field. Making their way to the nearby road, women and girls approached, crying. They kissed and hugged Tucker as he confirmed he was an American. Now in significant pain, Tucker could barely walk. Recognizing Tucker's limitations, the group put him on the back of a young man's bicycle. Gripping the rider's chest tightly while grimacing, the two rode off only to be passed by German patrols looking for the downed airman.

Czaplewski

Bailed at 17,000 feet
Landed near Andenne, Belgium
Status: prisoner of war (POW)

Grounded yet hurt, Czaplewski's chute was caught on top of a telegraph pole like a large, white flag and could easily be spotted by his enemy's search party. Due to his head and leg injuries, Czaplewski was immediately picked up by the Germans. Wounded, Czaplewski was hospitalized in a Wehrmacht hospital in the area of Saint-Gilles, Belgium, before being taken to Dulag Luft. Dulag was a transit camp for interrogation before being transferred to a permanent POW camp. Czaplewski would eventually be detained at Stalag Luft III, located in Sagen, Lower Silesia, Nazis Germany, 160 kilometers southeast of Berlin. Stalag Luft III was a Luftwaffe run prison that held captured Western Allied Air Force personnel.

Irvin

Bailed at 17,000 feet
Landed Southwest of Nonceveux, Belgium
Status: missing in action (MIA)

The first of the flight deck crew to depart, Irvin safely escaped Ruthless Ruth. He landed without incident and was quickly surrounded by the locals on the ground. Irvin would be successfully hidden away from the Germans.

Westerlund

Bailed at 16,500 feet
Landed near Heron, Belgium
Status: missing in action (MIA)

Third from last to jump, Westerlund safely made it away from Ruthless Ruth. Waiting until about 5,000 feet, he pulled the red handle and deployed his chute. Floating silently to the ground, he witnessed Goebel and Kendziora as their chutes opened. He watched as Ruthless Ruth banked hard, then careened into the earth in an exploding cartwheel of fire and debris. Landing without incident, Westerlund was met by several locals on the ground and was kept away from the Germans.

Goebel

Bailed at 14,000 feet
Landed in Couthuin, Belgium
Status: missing in action (MIA)

Waking from his momentary blackout, Goebel was relieved to see that he was afloat under his silk canopy. Knocked unconscious from his opening chute, he tasted the metallic flavor of blood that ran from his nose into his mouth. Attempting to wipe it clean, he watched as the ground rapidly approached. The last two-hundred feet seemed as if he were falling like a rock. Preparing for impact Goebel, tried to brace himself.

"With all the wind knocked out of me, I couldn't straighten out and I laid there in a semi-paralyzed condition for perhaps thirty seconds. A couple men rushed up, turned me over, and unfastened the chute harness. I'll swear that I heard someone ask me if I was hurt as they lifted me to my feet, but when I gained my senses everyone spoke French. By this time, a small crowd had gathered, and everyone was jabbering. I just nodded and smiled at anyone that addressed me. My face was covered with blood because I had minor cuts on my face, and my nose had taken a beating when the chute opened. The men were all anxious to help me, and the women stood about, crying over me, pleading with their son and husband to stay out of danger.

A young fellow came up to me and motioned me to follow him; with that, he took off like a deer into a wooded section. I followed as fast as I could and managed to keep up with him. As I ran, I glanced back and saw a stout woman running across the field with my chute bunched up in her arms. We ran for two to three minutes and stopped while I changed into some old clothes that an elderly man had brought to me. After that, we left and again started to run farther into the woods. Five minutes later we sat on a towering hill and surveyed the scene of the crash less than a mile away. Germans had already arrived at the ship, and we spotted three or four motorcycles scouting the surrounding roads and fields. I pulled out half a pack of

Lucky Strikes, which I had managed to salvage along with my dog tags, watch, and pencil. I asked the boy what part of Belgium we were in, and he replied, "Couthuin." I had no idea where Couthuin was; there were so many small towns and villages not shown on the aerial maps. All I knew was that I had landed in Belgium. We sat there approximately fifteen minutes and did a lot of gesturing and subdued laughing. There wasn't a damn thing to laugh about, but I was in a very good humor that day and it didn't take much to start me laughing. The Belgian I learned was a farmer, twenty-three years old, and he showed me a picture of his blond wife who was quite pretty.

Our rest period over, we started walking toward the small town; I was given a small birch tree to carry. We walked about a mile and then he told me to lie in some bushes and wait for him; he indicated that he'd return in one hour at 1640. I laid down and then I realized my back ached like hell and my kidneys felt as if they had been jerked loose. As I lay there in the thick carpet of leaves, I began to think of what a lucky bum I was."[5]

Kendziora

Bailed at 13,000 feet
Landed near Andenne, Belgium
Status: missing in action (MIA)

5 The preceding excerpts are Jim's own words taken from his personal diary written in September 1944.

Kendziora didn't see another crew member after reaching the ground. The locals efficiently hid his parachute, and he didn't see any Germans near where he landed.

CHAPTER SEVENTEEN

Captured Pavelka

April 24, 1944—Day One
Couthuin, Belgium
1540 Hours

GOEBEL WAS EXTREMELY FORTUNATE. He had made it safely to the ground and found himself greeted by friendly civilians who were willing to risk their lives to protect a downed airman. Many others suffered a much different fate by landing in more densely populated areas or territories occupied by Nazi sympathizers. Often, these airmen were greeted by hostile soldiers, farmers, or villagers. It was not uncommon for a fleeing airman to be shot on site or for the more fortunate be imprisoned for the remainder of the war. Goebel had no way of knowing who could be trusted.

Finding what he believed to be a secure area, the young farmer instructed Goebel to conceal himself. Struggling to communicate, the farmer conveyed that he would return for Goebel as soon as the Germans had given up their search. Standing alone on foreign land, Goebel watched as the farmer's outline faded into the landscape. Still unsure of the young man's intent, Goebel moved about a hundred yards away, found an undisturbed area, then sat down on the ground. He rested quietly and surveyed his surroundings. The Belgium farm country was green and soggy from the spring rains, and there was still a chill in the air, especially in the shade. Through the budding oak trees and firs, Goebel could see the edge of an empty open pasture. He remained silent as the forest returned to its natural form, and a light breeze stirred the trees around him. The swaying branches lulled him into a calmer state of mind as he reflected on the day's events. After a moment of collecting his thoughts, Goebel went to work creating an adequate hiding spot. Finding a decaying fallen tree, he piled brush and leaves together, all the while trying not to disturb the natural landscape.

After about an hour, Goebel heard approaching footsteps. Motionless, he watched as three individuals tromped around in the leaves and scattered dead branches. He immediately recognized the young farmer. However, the two other men were new, which made Goebel suspicious. Unable to find what they had come for, they began to thrash about the leaves, looking frantically for him. Goebel continued to watch the young men.

With his flight suit covered by the clothes that the old man gave him, Goebel was now technically out of uniform. He would be seen as a spy instead of a downed airmen and a potential POW. Knowing that he could be shot on the grounds of treason, Goebel had to be sure. Once convinced they were acting in reverence and were truly worried about the missing airman and were not there to harm him, Goebel stood up and walked to them. The faces on the young men sprung wide with relief when they saw him appear. Enthusiastically, they all individually offered their arms to Goebel in a sincere embrace.

Standing there in the early evening light, the adrenaline of the day's actions had fully vacated, and the effects of Goebel's less-than-graceful landing was starting to befall his tired body. His right ankle was stiff and sore, and his back and kidney area were very tender and throbbed, but at least the bleeding from his nose and face had stopped. Drained, hungry, and thirsty, Goebel wanted to get the hell out of the woods. However, more pressingly, he wanted to know where he was and if his trusted new friends had seen any of the other members of his crew. Unfortunately, language barriers prevented a thorough exchange of information. Nervous and frustrated, the young men pulled at Goebel and in broken English repeated, "We go! We go!"

Remaining in the forested areas for cover, the four men ran through the trees until reaching an open pasture. On the opposite edge of the field, Goebel could see the grey shadow outline of what looked to be a farmhouse, barn, and several smaller out-buildings. Gesturing this was their intended destination, the men continued on, skirting the pasture until reaching the wooden structures. The three men with Goebel slipped inside the darkness of a large shed. Completing his first evasion effort, Goebel and his escorts had traveled little more than a kilometer to the neighboring village of Heron.

Once inside, the young farmer pointed at his watch and spoke in a combination of French and broken English, explaining to Goebel that he would have to remain there for several hours. One of the two new men lit a lantern while the other disappeared into the shadows of the structure, only to return a few moments later with another man trailing behind him. As the new figure got closer, Goebel could make out that it was Westerlund, the crew's radio operator.

In disbelief, Goebel stepped toward Westerlund and said, "Charlie, is that you?"

"Oh, buddy, am I happy to see you!" Westerlund replied, giving Goebel a bruising brotherly embrace.

The farmer and his two other liberators broke up the impromptu celebration by hushing the two airmen. Westerlund and Goebel were instructed through hand gestures to remain in the shed and be quiet. Extinguishing the lantern, the three exited the shed, latching the door behind them. Westerlund walked Goebel over to his previous hiding spot, which was clear of sight and the entrance. The two men sat down and in a low whisper shared their experiences thus far.

Starting off, Goebel asked, "Have you seen any of the other crew?"

"No, you're the first," Westerlund replied.

"How long have you been here?" Goebel questioned.

"Almost two hours. I was ushered away immediately after hitting the ground. We ran for about thirty minutes before arriving here. Everyone so far has been really friendly. I believe these guys must be part of the Secret Army[6] that they briefed us about. Do you know where the hell we are?" Westerlund asked.

"Not really. The farmer told me that we were in Couthuin!" Goebel shifted his weight, trying to find a comfortable spot. "That was one hell of a landing. I got beat up pretty good. You?"

"I'm okay. I sure hope everyone one got out!" Westerlund acknowledged.

Goebel inaudibly sighed. "Me too!"

---

6 The Secret Army (aka Armée Blanche or the "White Army" or "Helpers") was a faction within the Belgian Résistance and was active during the German occupation of Belgium during World War II. Founded in August 1940 as the Belgian Legion, the Secret Army changed its name on a number of occasions during its existence. It was the largest résistance group active in the country.

Closing his eyes, Goebel drifted off only to be woken by Westerlund whispering in a low tone. "Jim, Jim! Someone's coming!"

The two sat still and soundless, waiting to see who or what appeared at the shed door. The sound of the door latch and hinges notified the two airmen that they were no longer alone. They heard the door close and saw a faint light glowing in the opposite corner. Goebel and Westerlund waited to move until the farmer's face peered around the edge of the stall opening.

It was 2100 hours, and Goebel and Westerlund were now enjoying a drink of water and some freshly baked bread while being introduced to yet another new figure. Speaking better English, the gentleman introduced himself as Edmond Wanzoul, a member of the "résistance."[7] Wanzoul appeared to be in his mid-forties, and even with a smile he still looked hardened. He assured Goebel and Westerlund that they were in trusted hands and that he would be moving them to a new hiding spot: an abandoned and partially destroyed farmhouse near another small village called Oteppe.

After a heartfelt thanks, the two airmen and their new guide left the shed and the young farmer behind. Having lived in the area most of his life, Wanzoul was very familiar with the best routes to Oteppe. On foot, they traveled seven kilometers along fence lines, dirt roads, and dairy pastures. Just over ninety minutes later, the three men arrived at the small village, making their way around the community outskirts. Leading them past a stately stone chateau,

---

7 For their own safety, most résistance members did not share their full or true identity when handling downed airmen. It is believed that Goebel provided his full name and home address and requested that the underground member write to him after the war, and most did. Starting as early as May 3, 1945, Goebel received multiple letters from his Belgium and French helpers.

Wanzoul escorted the two airmen to a standalone tool shed. From the outside, it appeared completely dark. Opening the door, the light from within leaked into the blackness of the night sky. Quickly climbing in, Goebel and Westerlund were confronted with three strange faces sitting on makeshift benches. The light from one dimly lit kerosene lamp showed no signs of friendliness on any of their features. No one spoke as Wanzoul disappeared as quickly as he had arrived.

Left standing there with Westerlund at his side, Goebel stared at the three men, sizing up the opposition. The first guy appeared to be a few years older than Goebel, possibly a Westerner with a stockier build than Goebel's, black hair, and mustache. The second fellow sitting nearer to the first chap also looked like a yank but with a slighter build and thinner sandy-colored hair. The third, who sat alone, looked larger in stature and angrier. This guy definitely wasn't a Westerner; he had a weathered, Slavic look. All were wearing similar tattered clothing not much different than Goebel's.

Finding a spot on the dirt floor opposite the two Westerners, Goebel and Westerlund sat with their backs against the outside wall. Goebel's first impression was that they seemed harmless, except for the larger one, who chose to remain isolated. After a few moments of noiseless staring, Goebel decided to ask a few questions. Looking at the guy with the mustache first, he asked, "Hey, bud, what's your name?" Goebel's inquiry was met with no reaction. He repeated his question.

This time the black-haired fellow spoke. "Pavelka. Who wants to know?"

"Hey, Mack, this isn't an interrogation. I just wanted to know who I was sharing this lovely shack with!" Goebel snapped.

It was obvious that these three were sticking to the most basic of military rules when in a hostile situation: Don't speak unless spoken to. If questioned, only provide your name, rank, and serial number. Hearing an American accent and feeling more comfortable, Goebel continued. "I'm Jim Goebel, and this is Charles Westerlund."

Pavelka softened a bit, pointed to his left, and said, "This is Philip Solomon, and I'm Joseph Pavelka."

Goebel nodded in acceptance and appreciation. Looking at the lone man, then back at Pavelka, he added, "What's his story?"

Pavelka paused and then explained. "I don't know his name, and he doesn't speak any English. The résistance chap that delivered you here brought this guy in yesterday. He told us that "Mr. Happy" over there is a Russian soldier who recently escaped from a German work camp."

More at ease, Goebel continued his inquiry. "Are you two air jockeys?"

Hesitating, Pavelka answered, "Yes, we belong to a heavy crew. I'm the pilot, and this is my navigator."

"So are we. Well, I am. Westerlund here is a radio operator. We were forced to bail out this afternoon. What's your story?" Goebel said.

"We've been on the ground a lot longer," Pavelka explained. "We were shot down twelve days ago, then landed in Malmedy. I hit hard, like a bag of rocks. My legs got pretty banged up and are still sore."

"Wow, sorry to hear. What were you flying? A Fortress or Lib?"

"Liberator, you?"

Spitting as he spoke, Goebel exhibited his dislike for the B-24. "Yeah, we were in one of those damn Mack trucks also. What group?"

Loosening up, Pavelka went on to tell Goebel that he and Solomon were assigned to the 8th AAF; 445th Bomb Group, and 702nd Bomb Squadron.

Shaking his head in disbelief, Goebel busted out, "You have to be kidding me! What are the odds? We're assigned to the 702nd also!"

Joining into the conversation, Solomon fired his first question. "What barracks and what bed?"

"The No. 4 Nissan hut," Goebel answered. "On the top of the hill! And I was bunked in the second bed on the right as you enter."

Solomon jumped to his feet like he was ready to fight. "Son of a bitch! He's got my bed!" Both Goebel and Westerlund jumped to their feet to meet Solomon. Pavelka stepped forward in an effort to separate Solomon and Goebel when the door opened and Wanzoul entered.

Wanzoul was aggravated by the ruckus the airmen were raising, and rightfully so. He was terrified that they would wake the neighboring homes. There were no guarantees that they wouldn't be turned in by a Nazi sympathizer or discovered by patrolling Wehrmacht soldiers. Either scenario was a death sentence for him and a certain one-way ticket to a POW camp if the airmen were lucky. Bringing calm and silence to the small shelter, Wanzoul gritted his teeth and scolded the young men in a low hiss for their lapse of judgment.

Quietly, Wanzoul informed the group that it was time to move to a new location. At around 2300 hours, the escort and five men arrived at a new house. Before entering, Wanzoul informed them that they would only be there for a brief time while he gathered another airman. After making their way in, Wanzoul led them to a back room where they came face-to-face with a familiar figure. Westerlund recognized him first and blurted out, "It's Tucker!"

Tucker sat at a small table with his left leg resting on an adjacent chair. Recognizing his crew mates, Tucker extended a greeting, yet remained sitting. He shared with Goebel and Westerlund his accounting of the afternoon events, including his injury and escape from the Germans.

Collecting everyone's attention, Wanzoul informed the group that they were going to leave. They moved one by one, following their guide. Struggling to walk on his own, Tucker was aided by his fellow crewmates. After a brief jaunt, they made their way to a new house inhabited by a widow named Mademoiselle Feron Lannoy and her baby. After a very brief introduction, Wanzoul escorted the group to a little straw-filled shed attached to the back of the house. Once inside, the six men slumped into a spot around the available space. Assured that everyone was settled, Wanzoul reached into his jacket and pulled out a bottle of locally brewed wine. He informed the young men that he would return later tomorrow and they should remain inside and silent. Handing the bottle to Tucker, Wanzoul slipped through the door and was promptly gone.

Settling into their individual spots in the now-cramped space, the six men passed the bottle of wine around, allowing each man to have two celebratory swigs. The grape elixir had an instant calming effect on the stressed group. Pavelka, the ranking officer, stayed awake for the first two-hour watch and assigned the order for the remaining to follow. The members of the Kendziora crew were all in desperate need of sleep; even the thought of getting a few hours of light sleep was welcome. The tension of being in an unknown land coupled with their destiny being in the hands of others was nerve-racking.

After most had drifted off, Goebel began to search the contents of his new clothes. Reaching into his trouser pockets, he found a worn but blank scrap of paper, evidently left by the previous owner. Looking the paper over, he pulled a salvaged pencil from his flight suit pocket. Starting to write, Goebel hadn't evaluated the risk of what he was about to do. He began to record a chain of words, a coded diary of sorts, definitely a map for the Nazis if found. Goebel's first entry was as follows:

**"4-24 – Fire – Couthuin – Chateau –
Hut – Heron – Captured Pavelka"**[8]

APRIL 12, 1944
MALMEDY, BELGIUM
MIDAFTERNOON

As a part of Mission 300 to bomb Zwickau Airfield and a Messerschmitt 109 assembly plant in Zwickau, Germany, the Pavelka crew were one of five B-24s lost as part of operations for the day. Under attack by enemy fighters, the Pavelka crew was shot down over the very same stretch of Belgian countryside as the Kendziora crew. Ironically, these were the very same airmen that the Kendziora crew replaced.

Raised in Cleveland, Ohio, First Lt. Joseph Pavelka was a tall, dark-haired Christian man. Like most pilots, Pavelka was the last man to bail out of his burning ship. In the process, he severely sprained one leg, bruised the other leg, and injured his lower back

8 While helpful in retracing Goebel's steps and establishing historical events, maintaining a written record of his interactions was misguided as it created a significant risk for Goebel and his handlers. If caught, Goebel most likely would have been interrogated and executed as an enemy spy.

on impact. Hobbled, Pavelka was unable to help himself. Angered by his situation he lay in the open field, struggling to free the white canopy that betrayed his position. The sun was still high in the sky and daylight was his enemy. Looking at his watch, Pavelka reconfirmed that it was still only 1330 hours.

Luckily, Pavelka's navigator, Second Lt. Philip Solomon, had landed within a kilometer of his pilot. Banged up but able to move, Solomon began walking in the direction of where he last saw Pavelka. A local villager named Roger Catoul would reach the downed pilot first. Vulnerable and lying on his back Pavelka watched as the stranger approached. Speaking in French to the pilot, the stranger worked to remove Pavelka's chute. Injured and separated from his crew, Pavelka could do little other than trust the man offering aid.

Catoul spoke no English. French and German were his only tongues. Unfortunately for both men, Pavelka spoke neither. Pavelka let out a scream of agony as the man pulled him to his feet. Not far away and hearing Pavelka's voice, Solomon ran the remaining distance to his comrade's side. Arriving on the scene, Solomon found Catoul struggling to help Pavelka. Knowing that Solomon spoke French, he asked his navigator to tell the man to stop because he obviously couldn't walk.

In a language that the man could understand, Solomon explained that his pilot would need to be carried. Instinctively, Solomon went to work trying to lift half of Pavelka's body mass, but Solomon's own condition lessoned his ability to muster the needed strength and endurance to help. Seeing the shape that both men were in, Catoul realized that without help, he would be unable to move Pavelka fast enough to stay ahead of the Germans.

Together, Catoul and Solomon dragged Pavelka to the nearest tree so that he could at least sit upright. Catoul explained to Solomon that he would go for help and could not return until after dark for fear that he would be caught. Translating the message for his pilot, both airmen clearly understood Catoul's concern. Thanking him, the two airmen watched as Catoul marched away.

Returning after dark as promised, Catoul was accompanied by a ruggedly built farmer. Together the two of them were able to form a seat for Pavelka by putting their arms together. Solomon would take the lead and act as the group's lookout. It was a devilish trek even over open field! The roads were to be avoided as truckloads of unpredictable German troops often passed by on their nightly patrols in search for downed Allied airmen, bandits, or Secret Army guerrillas. To further complicate matters, the Wehrmacht soldiers intermediately stopped to investigate the surrounding woods with dogs and lamps.

Guarded German aerial spotlights, radar stations, and anti-aircraft artillery were situated all over the countryside, slowing the process down even more as Solomon and Catoul would have to scout ahead to find the safest path. The four men lurked in the shadows, which stood under constant surveillance of the Germans. When ditches were absent, they were obliged to slink half bent over when they were close to enemy areas. Just prior to the morning's predawn light and after much suffering and anxiety, the four men reached the farmer's home. Pavelka and Solomon were forced to hide within the confines of an underground root cellar hidden beneath the main house until they had fully recuperated from their injuries.

Little more than a week later, their hosts could no longer risk being caught. Now well enough to travel, the two downed airmen would be escorted north toward Liège. Over the next several days, members of the local résistance would smuggle Pavelka and

Solomon some sixty-five kilometers to Oteppe where they would be left in the entrusted hands of Edmond Wanzoul and the Comète Line.[9]

9 Starting in January 1943, the Comète Line rapidly organized itself and concentrated its existence on the saving of airmen who had been shot down. Thanks to the multitude of helpers in the form of farmers, mountain dwellers, printers, and false stamp manufacturers, the obstacles of smuggling Allied airmen through German occupied territory became a possibility.

CHAPTER EIGHTEEN

The Secret Army

MAY 10, 1940
ANTWERP, BELGIUM
0445 HOURS

"To all whose love and defense of Country helped bring back freedom."

—YVONNE DE RIDDER FILES[10]

THINKING FRANCE AND BRITAIN would not come to the aid of the Polish state, Hitler invaded Poland on September 1, 1939, igniting World War II. Two days later, France responded to the German onslaught of Poland by declaring war. Over the next eight months, Belgium's neutral monarchy remained steadfast as tensions grew on its north and west borders.

On the morning of May 10, 1940, Hitler's armies struck westward across Europe. A historically convenient battlefield in

10 (Files, 1991)

wars between France and Germany; the smaller, densely populated country was prepared more than others for World War II. Repeating its World War I footsteps, the German army began its march to Paris through the small, neutral country of Belgium. The Western Europe landscape was enveloped in a fierce battle until Belgium's controversial capitulation on May 28, 1940. Blitzing German panzer divisions forced Belgium's surrender, splitting the British and French armies and leaving 300,000 Allied troops stranded and Belgium's government divided.

The Secret Army grew out of the ranks of the Belgian Army who, under German oppression, did not consider surrendering at any point during the war. Soldiers, ex-officers, and civilians of different races and religions collaboratively joined in arms to create the Secret Army. By mid-April 1944, with support from the Allied Commanders in England, the Belgian Legion and Secret Army matured to almost 50,000 strong.

Occupying Germans Wehrmacht soldiers viewed the Secret Army members as "Bandits," "Outlaws," and "Guerillas," and for the unlucky résistance member who was caught, a "Nacht und Nebel"[11] person. If captured while harboring an Allied service or bearing arms, a Nacht und Nebel person would be imprisoned, tortured, or killed on the spot.

Always evolving, the Secret Army was a complex network of groups or lines working independently. Each line was commanded by ex-soldiers who were experts in tactical fighting. Pockets of

---

11 The "Nacht und Nebel" ("Night and Fog") decree was a secret order issued by Adolf Hitler on December 7, 1941. It allowed German authorities to abduct, arrest, and either shoot or spirit away under cover of "night and fog" (meaning clandestinely) to concentration camps any "persons endangering German security" in the German-occupied territories of Western Europe.

résistance maintained contact with England and the OSS through dropped "Joes" (French and Belgian agents). Lines were often shut down when members were arrested, killed, or when penetrated by Gestapo "De Zitter"[12] agents. Surviving members went underground, hiding for weeks until German searches stopped, only to recreate a new branch.

Four years of shared hardships, constant blackouts, curfews, rationing, harassment, and oppression by their occupier only hardened the Belgium and French people. Their hatred for the unwelcome inhabitants of their homelands was solidified as time crept on. Thankfully, by the spring of 1944, the Germans were feeling the strength of the Allied bombing of their Vaterland. These events emboldened the Secret Army; regrettably, so did the German reprisal against them. Over the course of the war, no one line was more successful than others; all fought without a uniform in complete anonymity. Members of the Belgium and French undergrounds armed with a common goal selflessly risked their lives to aid Allied airmen so that they may return to fight another day.

APRIL 25, 1944—DAY TWO
LENS-SAINT-REMY, BELGIUM
EARLY MORNING

Knowing the airmen would eventually be found, Wanzoul wasted little time before setting out to contact the next member of the line.

12 Prosper De Zitter was a Belgian traitor who, under German control, operated a fake escape organization for Allied servicemen in Brussels.

Heading north on his bicycle, he pedaled the nine kilometers to the village town of Lens-Saint-Remy. Going to the designated café, Wanzoul met fellow résistance member Jean Cambron. Cambron was an eager eighteen-year-old son of a local farmer. He was a student and proclaimed royalist who vowed his loyalty to his nation and countrymen. As a young member of the Comète Line, he fought proudly for his king. Jean was willing to take risks and, if required, spill his blood in order to protect his beliefs and country from the occupying Germans.

Sitting in the corner of a busy café sipping coffee, Wanzoul cautiously explained to Cambron there were five airmen hidden locally who desperately needed to be moved. Although he did not betray his thoughts, Cambron was surprised that Wanzoul had accrued such a large number of airmen. Expressing little concern to Wanzoul, Cambron told Wanzoul to return to his home and he would meet later that evening in Oteppe.

Left alone at the café, Cambron finished his coffee as he mulled over his options. His few safe houses were already full of escaped Russian soldiers from the German prison camps. Knowing that he could not take in so many men at one time, he had to seek out additional help. His cousin René Londoz would know what to do.

Borrowing a car, Cambron drove north to his cousin's home in Gingelom near the province line of Limburg and Liège. Londoz, also eighteen, was a student graduate civil engineer and could speak fluent English. He was an idealist in support of his country's struggling democracy and passionately fought against the Hitler dictatorship.

Upon hearing the news, Londoz instructed Cambron to assemble a few men he could trust and move the airmen to the Gingelom safe house. Londoz agreed to meet Cambron at 0030 hours to interrogate the airmen and verify their legitimacy. As part of the

Comète Line, it was Cambron's job to question the downed airmen. Only after confirming they were true Allied fliers and not spies sent by the enemy to discover their escape line would they be passed on to fellow patriots.

Cambron returned to his hometown and collected Fernand Masset (nicknamed "Petit-Louis") and his brother, Jean Masset, who were both trusted résistance comrades. As planned, in order to avoid German patrols, later that evening the armed trio would drive in an easterly route to Oteppe. On schedule, they would arrive at Wanzoul's home at 2000 hours where they would wait until the late evening before moving their human cargo.

April 25, 1944
Oteppe, Belgium
0630 Hours

Tucker woke first and struggled to get to and use the makeshift privy, a metal bucket in the corner of the room. Hurting more, his knee would barely move. Returning back to his spot, Tucker tried to ignore the pain, silently hoping that it would not get worse, and closed his eyes.

Goebel woke in a cramped position. His body was now stiff from the prior day's fall. He looked at his watch and saw it was 1030 hours. Happy for the result, Goebel managed to sleep two more hours after his turn on watch. He looked around the room and saw that the Russian and Tucker still had their eyes closed. Pavelka, Solomon, and Westerlund were gathered together playing cards. Getting up from the floor, Goebel stretched, commenting to himself, "I need to brush my teeth." Turning, Goebel slowly gimped to Westerlund's side and said to the group, "Where did you guys get those cards?"

"They're mine!" Solomon replied without looking up at Goebel. "I suppose you want them, too, since you already got my bunk!"

Ignoring Solomon's dig, Goebel looked over Westerlund's shoulder and said, "How about dealing me in on the next hand?"

"Sure, no problem," Pavelka replied. "Pull up some straw."

Anxious about their unknown future, the group passed the day by silently playing cards mixed with periodic conversation conducted in low whispers. After reawakening and collecting his thoughts, Tucker joined the card game. Sharing his thoughts with Westerlund and Goebel, Tucker described his pre-departure experiences from Ruth.

"Chappie saved my butt," Tucker said with a thankful smile. He went on to tell his two crew members that he had landed near the town of Huy, and farmers quickly scooped him up. Tucker repeatedly expressed his concern about the others. "I only counted four other chutes!" Listening intently, neither Goebel nor Westerlund could relieve Tucker's worries.

It wasn't until 1300 hours before the airmen would see Wanzoul. Entering from the back shed, he carried two wooden buckets; one contained water, bread, and cheese rations for the six men, and the other was to replace the existing waste container. He did not stay long, but paused momentarily before leaving and said, in broken English, "I have made plans, and you will leave tonight!"

With the door now closed, Tucker threw his cards down and blurted sarcastically, "That's it? That's the only news we get?"

With no details to go on, their imaginations ran amuck with all sorts of scenarios, mostly negative and much of which was not shared with the other members of the group.

Wanzoul would return again after dark; this time accompanied by three armed men. Goebel and the others weren't sure what to expect from the new strangers. Until this point, no one had pointed a weapon at them, yet these strangers made sure to display their sidearms. The apparent leader of the three spoke in a language that none of the airmen could understand. Even Solomon, who spoke French, couldn't make out the conversation.

Speaking in Flemish, Jean Cambron wanted to know why there were six men and not five as Wanzoul had earlier told him. Wanzoul informed Cambron that the Russian was not going with him, and he had made other arrangements for him to leave the following day. Satisfied with Wanzoul's plan, Cambron turned and left the cramped space with his two trusted comrades Petit-Louis (Fernand Masset) and Jean Masset in tow. Wanzoul paused before following only to inform the airmen that they would be leaving in a few hours.

Later in the evening at around 2330 hours, under the slight visibility of a crescent moon, the five airmen were ushered by gunpoint to the back of a 1938 Ford sedan. Cambron, Petit-Louis, and Jean Masset armed with two sidearms each piled into the front seat. Weighted down and with extinguished headlamps, the Ford rolled away.

Stacked like cord wood and with their mouths clamped shut, the airmen left their hiding spot with no idea of where they were headed. In accordance with their previously discussed plan, Jean Masset drove north on the westerly route to Gingelom. The thirty-kilometer trek in complete darkness would take almost an hour if all things went well. Previous scouting reports indicated that there had been light German activity on their intended route with only intermittent patrols. The fact that traveling during curfew without a pass was a significant offense on its own did not deter Jean Masset or his comrades. The reality of the curfew offense was inconsequential compared to the possession of a firearm or the fact that they were harboring and aiding five downed Allied airmen. This crime was punishable by execution.

With a third of the trip behind them, they approached the southern side of the village Moxhe. Their luck soon ran out though. From a distance, Jean Masset could see the lights and outline of a parked open-top Opel Blitz troop truck. Its Wehrmacht squad was scattered out in the ditches on both sides of the road; they were obviously looking for something or someone. A few troops milled around the rear of the truck with readied weapons.

Jean Masset brought the Ford to a stop. Staring at the Germans, he began to converse in Flemish with his two partners. Crouched in the back seat, the airmen listened in an effort to understand what was being discussed. The three résistance members were clearly trying to choose what course to take. Finally deciding, Jean Masset turned on the Ford's lights, lifted his foot from the break, and applied pressure to the gas. The sedan leaped forward and began to speed toward the parked truck. Goebel and the other airmen began yelling at the driver to stop. Ignoring all of the men, Jean Masset rolled closer to the Wehrmacht patrol.

Noticing the lights from the oncoming car, the troops at the rear of the truck moved to the center of the road and began to wave, signaling the car to a stop. Jean Masset slowed, got within five yards of the truck, and came to a complete stop. Three Wehrmacht troops began to move in to check on the contents of the vehicle. Pausing, Jean Masset watched as the soldiers walked within a few feet of his front bumper. Slamming his foot on the accelerator, Jean and Petit-Louis brandished their revolvers and began to unload them onto the approaching Germans. The Ford swerved as it ran through the remaining enemy troops. Returning fire peppered the trunk and rear window of the escaping sedan.

Once out of German site, the airmen sat up to survey themselves. Luckily, during the exchange of gunfire, no one within the car was injured. Leaving his lights on, Jean Masset raced the remaining distance to the Gingelom safe house, arriving at 0020 hours. Shutting off the lights, Jean pulled the sedan into a barn; on cue, Petit-Louis jumped out and quickly swung the barn door closed.

Like nothing had happened, Cambron exited the barn, leaving Petit-Louis and his brother to guard the five airmen. Entering the back of the house, Jean Masset was greeted by René Londoz and Arthur "Zoro" Deroye. Deroye was a battle-hardened commander who was tasked with the Secret Army Judiciary and dispensing justice. In the event that any (or all) of the airmen was determined to be a spy, it was his job to deal with the false airmen in what he called the **"right manner."**

At fifteen-minute increments, each airman was escorted from the barn to the house at gun point. Once inside and surrounded by Londoz, Deroye, and Cambron the legitimacy process began. After a line of specific questioning, the airmen had to be found genuine. To do so, each man had to correctly answer seven specific questions and provide verifiable personal information. The questions were provided to the résistance via OSS "Joes," and as part of their mission briefing the airmen were instructed to memorize the answers.

Once satisfied with their legitimacy, Londoz formally introduced the others and himself. Additionally, he assured the airmen that members of their Secret Army Line would do everything possible to see that they were safely liberated. Moved to yet another room, each airman was asked to complete an intelligence service questionnaire. When completed, the airman would provide the résistance group a record of his name, rank, serial number, crew role, aircraft type flown, unit information, and home address. The formal process was concluded by Londoz taking their photos for false Belgian identification cards, which they would receive at a later date.

Upon completion of their technical efforts, the résistance group provided the airmen with clothing in exchange for what they were wearing. Although warmer, their blue flight suits, military gear, and leather boots were a dead giveaway for the Germans. Each man received misfitted pants, a coat, and shoes. In the process, Goebel cut the embroidered wing patch from his flight suit and kept the bronze lieutenant bar as a keepsake and hopeful proof of his status. By donning civilian clothing, however, Goebel and the others lost their Geneva Convention rights and ran the risk of being shot as spies if captured.

Almost two hours after the interrogation process started, the five airmen were finally together again. Smoking cigarettes and passing around a jug of water, Goebel and the others shared their thoughts about the evening's events.

"That was a pretty hairy ride over here. I thought those resistance fellows were going to get us all killed," Tucker commented.

Their exchange was soon interrupted by an overheated discussion in the opposite room. This time, most of the conversation was in French; therefore Solomon was able to eavesdrop. Realizing that Solomon knew what was being said, Pavelka asked, "What are they talking about, Phil?"

Solomon paused to listen, then translated. "I'm only picking up bits and pieces, but it sounds like that René Londoz chap isn't too happy about our run-in with the German patrol. Also, something about unsettled family matters."

While Cambron continued to prattle on about the trip to Gingelom, Londoz quickly decided that these five should be moved. Cambron dismissed Londoz's concerns, insisting that the Germans had no idea who rammed through the earlier blockade. Londoz was obviously unsettled by the group's tales and was determined to find the airmen a new home, so he instructed Cambron and the others to immediately head home and find safe hiding spots until things settled. Londoz had a secure place for the airmen, and he would take care of getting them there. After a quick embrace, the Secret Army patriots went their separate ways.

Londoz gathered the five airmen and led them four kilometers by foot to the neighboring village of Landen. There, he deposited them at the home of a family, who graciously accepted the young men. Londoz instructed Goebel and the others to remain out of sight. He would return later that day once their false identity cards were complete. Secured in the barn, their accommodation for the night would be a spacious hayloft. Finding a comfortable spot, Goebel pulled out his dairy and added the next entry.

**"4-25 – Hay Bed – Widow – Kid –
Cards – Ford – Pistols – Landen"**

1/ How do you call a leave-form?

2/ How do you call your identity-cart?

3/ What is a 6.6.4.B?

4/ what is "George"?

5/ What is "Mickey Mouse"?

6/ What is a"Sister"?

7/ How do you call a life-buoy for the sea?

    -:-:-:-:-:-:-:-:-

1/ 2.9.5 (Two nine five)

2/ 12.5 (Twelf,fifth)

3/ The exchanging cart for clothing

4/ The automatic pilot

5/ The bomb   distributor

6/ The enemy Cartridge

7/ A"May West"

    -:-:-:-:-:-:-

*Interrogation questions given to Londoz by the OSS (above left),
and answers (above right) were provided to the airmen for memorization and
verification. A Belgium false identity card (below) for a younger
René Londoz, similar to what René would make for the airmen.*

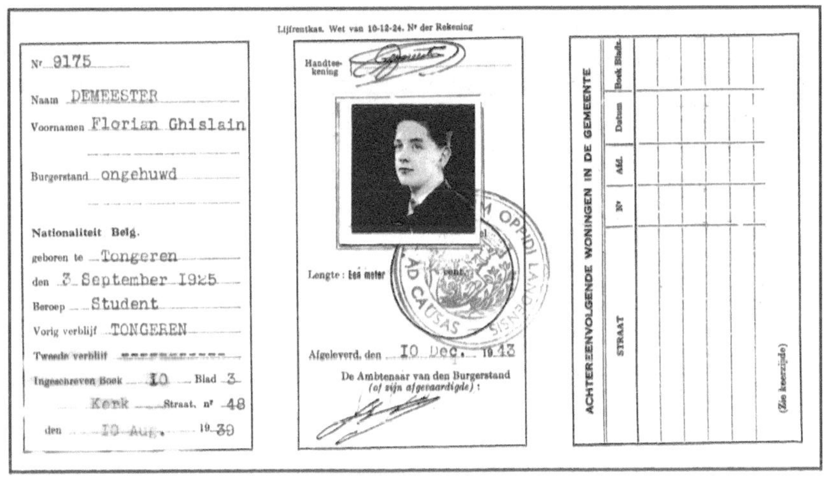

Post-war photo of Lieutenant René Londoz in his Belgium Legion uniform.[13]

13 During the war, René Londoz remained an active member of the Comète Line. He also aided airmen through his efforts in many other secret organizations, namely "Athos" (Belgian Military Intelligence Service), group "CONE," "Marc," "Luc-Marc," "Bayard," and "Relief to the Allied Broken Wings."

CHAPTER NINETEEN

Ultimate Sacrifice

APRIL 26, 1944—DAY THREE
LANDEN, BELGIUM
0230 HOURS

AFTER TWENTY MINUTES OF intense discussions, Cambron, Petit-Louis, and Jean Masset left for home as Londoz had directed. Now driving, Cambron coasted slowly out of town with all the lights extinguished so he would navigate the less-conspicuous route home. Exhausted and worried about another run-in, the trio drove home without a word spoken between them. Arriving safely back in Lens-Saint-Remy, Cambron purposely stopped in an area close to, but far enough away from, Jean Masset's home. If they were being followed or watched, Cambron wanted to exercise some caution. Without any acknowledgement, Petit-Louis and his brother climbed from the Ford sedan. Retreating to separate homes, both found refuge and a place to sleep.

At a low idle, Cambron continued through the village court-yard to his mother's farmhouse. He decided to hide the borrowed and damaged car in a barn at his mother's home. He would wait until the Wehrmacht search had cooled before returning the sedan. More importantly, he needed to complete a few obvious repairs before the Ford could be road-worthy in daylight hours. Arriving safely, he crept the Ford quietly into what he believed was a secure spot. Closing the barn doors, he turned toward the dark house and went inside only to collapse onto his bed. Now fast asleep, Cambron was unaware that the Gestapo had been tipped off by a German sympathizer and was quickly moving in on him.

Less than two hours later, the Gestapo encircled the small village of Lens-Saint-Remy. Their efforts would first focus on the arrest of Petit-Louis. Following their strongest lead, Wehrmacht soldiers controlled by Gestapo officers arrived at the Masset haven in force. The black-booted Jerries[14] skulked around the property, searching all of the out-buildings and secured the perimeter. A quick inspection produced nothing of interest. Without haste, they turned their search toward the peaceful and unassuming home.

The house was awoken by the sound of loud commands from unwanted visitors and a rifle butt being used to break in the front door. Prepared as usual with his loaded six-shooter under his pillow, Petit-Louis rolled from bed and flipped the dresser onto the mattress, creating the best shelter possible. Waiting for the German raid to reach his room, Petit-Louis reflected on the fact that being caught by the Gestapo now meant most certain death.

Already wanted by the Germans, Petit-Louis had refused to go to work for them, and as a precaution he had been in hiding for the past several weeks. He also knew that the unmerciful Gestapo would interrogate and torture him if he did not give up his comrades and the downed Americans. If they were successful in breaking him, he would at best be shipped off to an undisclosed location

14 "Jerries" was a British slang for a German soldier.

or concentration camp where death would be prescribed faithfully from the application of a firing squad. Petit-Louis knew that he had no choice. He must defend his fellow patriots and, if possible, save his skin, right down to the last bullet.

Hearing the invaders storm through his house, he knew it would not be long before they reached his location. He was at least satisfied with the fact that the Germans would only find him as the rest of his family was safely hidden in another town. Petit-Louis braced himself, poised below the edge of his stacked barricade. The door to his room was propelled open by a swift heel of a leather boot. The first Wehrmacht soldier entered the room only to receive a bullet to the chest. Without a pause, a second trooper stormed in. Petit-Louis aimed and fired the next slug right through the head of the charging Kraut, dropping the lifeless German in his place. The third invader was already standing in the doorway, covered in blood and brain matter, and he turned to retreat. While backpedaling out of the room, Petit-Louis put a round into the fleeing soldier's back.

Realizing their current tactic wasn't working, a remaining angered Wehrmacht trooper lobbed a grenade into the room. The explosion slammed the dresser and Petit-Louis against the wall, causing the metal shrapnel and pieces of wood to rip through his body. Slumping to the floor, Petit-Louis was knocked unconscious. His battered and bleeding body lay amongst the shattered debris. Once the smoke cleared and no signs of movement were noticed, the Gestapo moved in to capture the Secret Army bandit.

Petit-Louis awoke while being towed by his arms to the adjoining room. Now placed and bound to a wooden straight-backed chair, Petit-Louis regained consciousness. As the fog cleared in his head, he realized his station. A Gestapo officer gave Petit-Louis an eerie grin as he approached. In German, he openly observed to his captive: "I see the grenade blast did not mortally wound you. We will see what we can do about that."

With one Nacht und Nebel person already in custody and actively being interrogated, a second German patrol departed the Masset home in search for fellow collaborators. Unaware, Jean Cambron's own interrogation was about to commence. The Gestapo found their way to Cambron's home and the hidden Ford. Their search of the sedan produced an American watch, cigarettes, empty shell casings, false identity cards, and the two revolvers belonging to Jean Masset.

The documents given to Jean Cambron by René Londoz earlier that evening were reserved for Russian prisoners who had escaped a German held Belgium coal mine. With evidence in hand, attention quickly turned toward the Cambron farmhouse, knowing that the bandit they were hunting was most likely inside.

The Wehrmacht troopers stormed the dark farmhouse and a struggle soon erupted. Without any shots fired, Cambron was dragged from his bed and taken outside to the front courtyard. Screaming at the top of her lungs, Cambron's mother was pulled by her hair to her son's side. Upon refusal to cooperate, he was beaten to the ground before his mother's eyes by the direction of a young Gestapo officer. They would not immediately kill him, not yet. They desperately wanted information from him first.

With his body now held against the house exterior brick wall, the Wehrmacht soldiers continued Cambron's beating. They started by bashing him about the face and chest with the butt of a rifle. As they delivered one crushing blow after another, they barked at Cambron in German, asking him for the names of his fellow résistance members. Cambron never uttered a word; he would never speak of his relations. They continued to strike him but couldn't get a word from him. His mother could do nothing but watch as her son was beaten to death by the insufferable barbarians. The possessed troopers struck him harder and harder, matching their increasing levels of frustration as they were desperate to know the names of his patriots and the airmen. With gritted teeth, they continually hissed the same question: "Where are they hidden and who arranged for their refuge?"

The intense beating rendered Cambron unrecognizable. While spitting out blood and teeth, his mother began to speak to him in a soft, motherly tone, repeating the same phrase in a Flemish dialect that the Gestapo would not understand. "Don't tell them anything, my son. It will soon be over. Don't tell them anything." Jean Cambron acknowledged his mother by nodding his head and maintaining his silence.

A Mercedes staff car pulled up and stopped in front of the Cambron home. Two Gestapo officers climbed out of the vehicle and demanded that the Nacht und Nebel prisoner be brought to the back of the car. As ordered, the Wehrmacht soldiers halted their beating only to drag his battered and bloody body to the back of the Mercedes. As Cambron and his escorts approached the back of the staff car, the driver opened the trunk. Standing while assisted by his captors, he stared into the open trunk. Even with blood blurring his vision, he instinctively knew that the crumpled body belonged to his comrade, Petit-Louis, who had been shot execution-style—one bullet to the head.

One of the two Gestapo officers grabbed the back of Cambron's neck and proceeded to shove his head closer to Petit-Louis's lifeless face. Like an angry dog, the Gestapo office barked at Cambron. He demanded to know the names of other members of their line and asserted that the body belonged to a fellow traitor. Cambron shook his head and grunted a response of defiance.

Seeing that Cambron was not cooperating, the Gestapo officers ordered that Cambron's mother also view the lifeless body. She was led to the rear of the car where she was subjected to the same questions. She briefly looked at the badly beaten corpse and turned her head away. Physically forcing her to face Petit-Louis, she closed her eyes and stated that she could not identify the dead man.

Cambron's mother was thrown to the ground as he was loaded into the back of a waiting truck. Wedged between his captors, he was driven away from his home never to be seen again. In the forthcoming days, Cambron's family would only be told that he had been taken to a concentration camp in Germany. Jean Cambron disappeared that morning, never to return or be seen again.

After killing Petit-Louis and hauling Cambron away, the Gestapo wanted to send a clear message to the other résistance members. Both Petit-Louis's and Jean Cambron's family farms were set ablaze and burned to the ground, destroying all of the structures and killing most of the livestock. They continued through the village in a reign of terror, picking ten other local men for questioning. The Gestapo continued to surround the village, holding all residences hostage until 1000 hours.

The only member of the Belgium Secret Army not picked up in the Lens-Saint-Remy raid was Jean Masset. He managed to escape the small town one hour after the Gestapo released its grip. Jean Masset and his ten-year-old son peddled their bicycles back to Gingelom to notify René Londoz about the death of his brother and the capture and beating of Jean Cambron.

Jean Cambron

CHAPTER TWENTY

Command Performance

April 26, 1944
Landen, Belgium
Midday

IT WAS MIDDAY WHEN René Londoz received the news of what had happened to his cousin and comrade. Alarmed with this report, Londoz immediately returned home from the café to share the disturbing news with his father, Jean Londoz, who immediately began to question his son about his personal safety and the family's security and safety. Londoz responded that he had no way of knowing if his cousin Jean Cambron had been broken by the Gestapo. A nervous shiver traveled through Londoz as his thoughts reaffirmed his concerns for his family's safety and his own. They were all now in grave danger.

Londoz set out to contact fellow members of the résistance line and immediately gave orders to change the hiding places of the American airmen. Londoz was very active in the Secret Army and in the Comète Line; he knew that it would not be long before the Gestapo traced things back to him. For his own safety, he needed to distance himself and go into hiding. Londoz arranged for a young runner to shuttle an envelope filled with identification cards to a known résistance hiding spot in town. While Londoz felt obligated to oversee the movement of the airmen to new and safer shelter, it was equally important that the airmen were relocated without him knowing their actual final destinations or the circumstances behind their hasty relocation.

Goebel and the other airmen could sense that something was severely wrong when Londoz did not return at the appointed time. Unexpectedly, a few hours later, three different résistance members entered the barn. Stressed and startled by the untimely meeting and the absence of Londoz, the airmen jumped to their feet. As the senior officer of the group, Pavelka approached the three résistance members and asked, "What's wrong? Where is René?" One man stepped forward and offered little explanation, yet made it clear that they all needed to leave.

In broken English, the résistance leader shared news. "Our line has been invaded by the Germans, and we must find you all new hiding spots."

As the rest of the airman gathered around, Westerlund asked, "We're going now? In the light of day?"

"Yes, we have identity papers for you all, and we will be leaving in smaller, separate groups. Now that is all I can tell you. You must trust me!" the résistance leader replied.

Brief, first-name introductions were made. Tonny Heslenfeld, the résistance leader, handed over to each airman their newly made Belgian identity cards. "Pavelka and Solomon, you will go with Eugène Demal and Roland Prinsen. Goebel, Tucker, and Westerlund, you will come with me," Heslenfeld stated. "We have to go now!" Somewhat dazed, each airman glanced at their identity card, examining the photo and their new European name. Throughout the exchange, there was no mention of Londoz or the fates of Jean Cambron or Petit-Louis.

Motioning the duo toward the door, Solomon and Pavelka were separated from the group first. After wishing each of the other men "the best of luck," Solomon and Pavelka were quickly escorted by Demal and Prinsen from the barn. On bicycles, the four men rode in an easterly direction out of town only to arrive a few minutes later at a sugar mill located on the western side of Gingelom. For the time being, Pavelka and Solomon would be secured in the mill's pump house until things had cooled and a new plan could be formulated.

Goebel, Tucker, and Westerlund would temporarily remain in the village of Landen. Heslenfeld led them on foot to a nearby farm where they would all remain until dark. Heslenfeld was a young Dutch man, about twenty years of age and a proud member of the Secret Army. He enjoyed boasting about his accomplishments and victories over the rotten Germans. That afternoon, while passing time, Heslenfeld told the three airmen tales about underground activities. "Our army is amazingly successful with its guerrilla tactics and covert operations," he boldly stated. "I have personally helped to make off with supplies of dairy products, meat, produce, and even some train loads of coal, which is no easy task!"

Twice during that afternoon, Heslenfeld's stories were interrupted by the abrupt sounds of antiaircraft batteries. The German guns relentlessly pounded the sky, threatening the lives of fellow American airmen. It was a surreal experience for the airmen. After living through the black balls of flak firsthand while flying, they were now listening to it as it was being dispensed. They could hear the drone of hundreds of bombers returning in waves, no doubt headed back to bases in England. Each time the airmen sat silently, anxiously awaiting and dreading the exploding report of a downed Allied aircraft.

Heslenfeld looked at his watch and decided it was time to move. He got up from his spot and went outside to look around for a moment. Feeling comfortable with his surroundings, he led the three airmen from their sanctuary. It was 2030 hours, and the sun was beginning to set. The group had to move and be in place before curfew at 2100 hours, which was sunset. Westerlund, Goebel, and Tucker blindly followed Heslenfeld as he pushed his bicycle through the village center. With the locals looking on from their dwellings and neighboring businesses, Heslenfeld guided them through town in a single-file line.

"We stick out like a sore thumb!" Goebel whispered over his shoulder to Tucker.

"Yeah, hopefully no one will snitch to the Germans," Tucker replied.

Once past the last home, Heslenfeld stepped off the street and began trekking across open country.

After fifteen minutes of hiking, they crossed a wire fence and road to another open field. As they headed across a pasture in the same formation, they spotted a German Messerschmitt 110 approaching their direction and flying very low while firing its guns. The group dove to the ground as the rounds thudded nearby. With the plane roaring overhead, Goebel and his companions looked up in time to notice the radar night-fighting equipment on the nose of the plane. While pulling themselves up, they wiped moist chucks of the manure and mud from their clothing. They were pleasantly surprised to find themselves alive and unharmed. The bullets were not intended for them; the 110 was actually attacking a firing range. Not wanting to stick around for another pass, the airmen hustled to the edge of the field and dropped back into the thick cover of the bordering brush and trees.

After traveling little more than three kilometers, the group arrived at the adjoining village of Overwinden. They moved quietly through the empty streets, working diligently to avoid the town's occupiers. Heslenfeld led the airmen directly to the local parish house where they would be deposited for the time being. Entering the parsonage, Heslenfeld introduced the three airmen to a friendly elderly priest. He then informed the group that different members of the Underground would be by on Friday evening at 2100 hours to fetch them. Before departing, Heslenfeld offered each man a hug and wished them all the best. Leaving, he climbed on his bicycle and rode off in the opposite direction from where they had come.

Later that evening for only a few brief hours, the three airmen were joined by two escaped Russian soldiers. They were put in a separate room from the airmen and would leave later that night. Goebel and his fellow airmen were given the chance to wash their hands and face, have a hot cup of black coffee, and enjoy their first opportunity to listen to the radio. Unfortunately, the local radio stations were continually interrupted by German propaganda. As they sat and listened to French melodies, Goebel made his third entry into his simple diary. It was 2300 hours when they finally turned in. The three crew members would settle into a pleasant room and, for a change, sleep off the ground.

"4-26 – Overwinden – Priest – Russians – Tony – 110"

April 27, 1944—Day Four
Overwinden, Belgium
Late morning

Up at 1000 hours, the airmen had a simple breakfast consisting of coffee and bread before a brief listen to the radio. Throughout the next thirty-six hours, the airmen enjoyed a rather peaceful stay at the parish house. During the day, Goebel and his fellow airmen were sequestered in a cellar room out of sight from possible visitors. Playing cards, the men sat quietly below, listening, while life above went about its normal activities. As people moved about, dirt and dust from the floorboards sprinkled down, filling the air of the small damp room.

Besides the priest, the only other souls who met the airmen was a woman caretaker and a young Dutch boy around the age of seventeen. The priest had the older lady come by during the day to help with the housekeeping and meals. The Dutch boy, who spoke fairly good English, brought the airmen an electric razor so they could clean up. While in the care of the local parish, the small group received three solid home-cooked meals, which they greatly appreciated and devoured.

Only at night were the men allowed to exercise outside in the garden or return to the small room where they listened to the radio and slept. That evening, when the last visitors left the parish, the airmen gathered closely around the radio. Westerlund worked the knob until they heard what they had been missing. **"You're listening to the Armed Forces Radio Network,"** cracked a voice from the speaker. Goebel, Tucker, and Westerlund marveled as they listened to "Command Performance,"[15] featuring songs from Frank Sinatra, Bob Hope, and Judy Garland.

APRIL 27, 1944
OVERWINDEN, BELGIUM
2110 HOURS

As expected, two new Secret Army friends arrived at the parish on Friday evening. The three airmen thankfully greeted Paul Lindekens and Edgard Thierie, members of the local résistance from Landen. While quickly gathering their coats, each man expressed in their own way their gratitude to the cheerful priest. Within fifteen minutes of arrival, the three airmen were exiting the rear of the parish house, trailing their new guides on their way back to Gingelom.

Lindekens and Thierie were more conservative in their approach of leading the three evades. They would leave nothing to chance, sticking strictly to pastures and wooded groves as they traveled. The waxing moon would provide the only light during their seven-kilometer, two-and-a-half-hour night march as Lindekens and Thierie refused to use the hand torches they were carrying. Even after repeated run-ins with dense thickets, producing more than a few scratches on each man's face, they ignored the airmen's requests.

15   A "Command Performance" was a radio program which originally aired between 1942 and 1949. The program, consisting of 293 episodes, was broadcast on the Armed Forces Radio Network and transmitted by shortwave to the troops overseas and not domestically.

Their refusal, though inconvenient, was prudent as the group was walking uncomfortably closer to the largest German Luftwaffe airfield in Belgium. The Sint-Truiden Air Base was located in Brustem, Belgium, less than ten kilometers northeast of their current location. With the air base came a division of Wehrmacht soldiers who were tasked with manning antiaircraft batteries, providing airfield security, and keeping the Belgium population at bay.

During a short rest, Thierie educated the airmen on why they weren't going to use the torches and further enlighten them on local German activities. The résistance patriot went on to tell the airmen about the Jerries' activities in the surrounding area. In broad detail, he told them about the airdromes, special function groups, night fighters, radar installations, arsenals, and supply sources. To this point, Goebel and his fellow airmen had not been informed that great amounts of German troops were massed in and around the nearby Castle of Gingelom.

Aggravated with being kept in the dark, Goebel spoke up. "That's just great! All this time we have been traipsing around in a Kraut hotbed. Why the hell didn't someone say something sooner?"

Sarcastically, Tucker chimed in. "That Tonny chap, with all of his grand tales. He certainly failed to mention this part in his stories!"

"It all makes sense now! The Messerschmitt target practice, the antiaircraft batteries, and the damn shoot-out with the Kraut patrol," Westerlund added.

Nothing more was said about the Germans or their predicament. On cue, each man stood up and continued with the task at hand, following their escorts like criminals slinking in the darkness of night.

As they got closer to town, the German patrols were noticeably more frequent. With a renewed and heightened awareness, the three airmen would follow in lock step with their Secret Army guides. Arriving unnoticed at the designated résistance safe house, Goebel sat down and looked at his watch; it was 2200 hours.

JUNE 6, 1944
LANDEN, BELGIUM
LATE AFTERNOON

Later during D-Day, Tonny Heslenfeld would help to hide two other downed American airmen, Walter W. Swartz and Ernest B. Fitzpatrick. Heslenfeld was himself liberated in Belgium on September 7, 1944. By mid-October 1944, Heslenfeld was walking around in an American uniform attached to a cavalry division.

CHAPTER TWENTY-ONE

Steenweg 79

April 27, 1944
Gingelom, Belgium
2200 Hours

UPON THEIR ARRIVAL TO the résistance safe house, Goebel, Westerlund, and Tucker found themselves once again face-to-face with Arthur "Zoro" Deroye, the Secret Army commander. He informed the airmen that their planned original departure by truck to Brussels had been scrubbed. He refused to tell them about the events that led to the canceled trip. Additionally, he remained tight-lipped about any details regarding their impending departure. "It's in your best interest not to know," Deroye firmly remarked. "The only thing I can tell you is that I have radioed your names back to England. Your people know you're safe and in good hands."

"However, that won't prevent our families from getting the standard Adjutant General missing in action telegram," Goebel noted to his two crew members.

"You will now need new identity papers," the commander stated, ignoring Goebel's comments. He then turned to his aide-de-camp. "Take pictures of each of these airmen, then escort them to the pump house." The young bandit snapped to attention and escorted the airmen from the room. Goebel, Tucker, and Westerlund were soon being ushered to the sugar mill pump house where they would temporarily hide until new plans could be made.

The aide unlocked the door to the ten-by-fifteen-foot masonry structure. Goebel, followed by Westerlund and Tucker, stepped into the noisy equipment room. The door closed behind them with the lock quickly clamping shut. Goebel went to work, surveying the cramped space with the kerosene lamp the aide provided. As he stepped around an obstacle, he found two quiet masses huddled near the back of the pump structure. Stepping closer, he noticed that the two faces looked familiar. Goebel knelt down in front of the two and smiled as he held the light closer. "Pavelka! Solomon! It's good to see you!" he said cheerfully.

Pavelka and Solomon were startled by Goebel's appearance. The two sleeping airmen had not heard the three arrivals as their ears were packed with scraps of cloth. Goebel watched as they plucked the bits of cotton fiber free. "I'm sorry. I didn't mean to sneak up on you. How long have you been here?" Goebel asked.

Pavelka rose and shook Goebel's hand, then replied. "For two days, since we left you. We received a reprieve last night and this afternoon for a few hours when we met with that Arthur chap and had a meal. We were out long enough to warm up. But not long enough for the damn ringing to stop in our heads." It was noticeable to Goebel and his two crew members that things had not gone as well for Pavelka and Solomon as it had for them.

Recognizing that it was going to be extremely difficult to continue any safe level of conversation, Goebel, Tucker, and Westerlund took up places around the pump house. They sat on the cold concrete floor with their jackets pulled up over their heads in an effort to insulate themselves from the room's mechanical noise. Once stationary, they soon felt the effects of the cool night air on their stone shelter. Combined with the dampness of the pump house, all shivered silently, waiting for their guardians to return.

They sat crouched on their haunches for what felt like an eternity. Without warning, the pump house door opened and three men stepped inside. An older man named Eugène Demal and two younger White Army guerillas stood calmly in front of the five shivering and temporarily deaf airmen. As assigned, Demal would take Pavelka, Solomon, and Goebel. Westerlund and Tucker would follow the two bucks to their next safe house site. Once again on foot and separated from Solomon and Pavelka, the small band hurried along the factory perimeter. With Goebel in the number-three position, followed by Tucker and Westerlund, the five-man group crept through the woods toward the edge of town.

Now within the more densely populated area, they ran in quick bursts from one shed, barn, or building to the next. Their young Secret Army escorts covered their route along the way, each time going ahead to ensure that all was clear. Signaling between them, the group snaked their way through town, utilizing the glowing amber of lit cigarettes and hand gestures. Their prearranged final destination was "Steenweg 79."

A white, unassuming two-story building occupied the Gingelom address. The masonry structure with its clay tile roof sat starkly on the street corner. Its exposed main façade was neatly lined by a wide brick walkway, which was adjoined by the primary roadway through town. A cobbler's shoe shop, café, and residences above were the buildings main occupants.

The front entrance was a flurry of activity with patrons coming and going from the active café. Others milled around on the front walk only to be disturbed by the passing patrols of Wehrmacht elite. As anticipated, the renegade team would only have periodic clear access to enter from the rear of the building. Arriving as scheduled, one young sentinel went inside to confirm things were still safe. After a few moments, he returned to lead the group the remaining distance. The five men stealthily approached and then entered the rear door. Stepping into a dimly lit hallway, they made their way up the staircase without raising any suspicion.

It was 2330 hours when they arrived at the second-story home of the Loyaerts family. Once inside, the airmen were quietly introduced to their new caretakers: Arthur Loyaerts, his wife, their son, Eduard, and his parents. Together in the front room, the Dutch family, along with Goebel, Westerlund, and Tucker, stood cautiously facing each other. Goebel internally took notice: *This family has agreed to risk everything for three young American men.* Then aloud, and on behalf of his two brothers, he openly thanked each member of the Loyaerts family for welcoming them into their home. Acknowledging Goebel's gratitude, Arthur Loyaerts escorted the airmen to a resting place within their modest dwelling. The juxtaposition of the evening and their presence in this family's home brought the airmen comfort and peace; yet at the same time their existence in this foreign environment was extremely unsettling. Especially with the knowledge that their mere being at this location had lethal consequences for this good family.

Eugène Demal was no stranger to sacrifice. A veteran of the First World War, he volunteered to escort the two airmen to his home and their new accommodation. Solomon and Pavelka left the pump house, following quietly behind Demal. Demal's home was located on the opposite side of town, and in an effort to limit their exposure, he decided to take a less direct route through the open country. Their walk, lasting little more than an hour, ended cleanly. When the three men arrived at the Demal house, it was very dark inside and out. Taking no chances, Demal instructed the two airmen to wait in the shadows of the house while he stepped inside.

Demal turned and quietly made his way back to the front of the house. For safety's sake, the occupant had locked and bolted the door. Unable to get in, Demal softly knocked on the thick wooden door. Receiving no initial response and having no other choice, he knocked again, but louder. Rattled awake by the pounding, the home's sole occupant made her way to the door in a muffled uproar. Initially frightened that the untimely visitor may be Wehrmacht soldiers, the woman refused to open the door. After some convincing, the nervous woman partially opened the door to confirm the intruder's identity. Seeing that it was only her brother, she stepped aside to allow him to pass. Demal paused, then waved to the hiding men that things were okay. Seeing Demal's signal, Pavelka and Solomon were quick to move. Now on Demal's heels, all three simultaneously pushed their way inside the house. Demal's sister let out a yell of shock as the two strangers stood nearby. Immediately, she pleaded with her brother in Flemish.

"Eugène, you have to go to another place with these men. It is not safe for us with them here. Please, Eugène, I beg you to take them away. They may be Duitsers!"[16]

It was public knowledge that the Germans were actively searching for the local Secret Army line and escape trails. Furthermore, in an effort to trap members of the résistance, the Gestapo regularly dropped Wehrmacht troops in the region wearing American clothing. Demal's sister knew he was at risk. Again, she asserted that she would not allow her brother to remain in their home with these two strangers. Reluctantly, Demal obliged his sister's request. Without telling her where he was going, he left his family's home with Solomon and Pavelka in tow.

Demal spent the next hour guiding Solomon and Pavelka back to town. Lost for ideas and with no place else to turn, he led the young airmen to his comrade's home located at Steenweg 79. When they appeared at the stairwell entrance, it was evident that the Loyaerts had already settled in for the night. It was close to 0130 hours on an early Saturday morning when Eugène delivered the unexpected knock on the door.

Loyaerts paused momentarily and raised a finger to his mouth, signaling to his wife. He wasn't expecting anyone. The unwelcome knock most likely meant an unwanted enemy visitor. Pushing the curtain aside, he peeked through the front window. Relieved, he released a deep breath when he saw no additional troops outside.

Startled by the knock, Goebel moved to his feet, first looking at the entrance door and then to Loyaerts, who entered the front room followed by his wife. He signaled to his wife and the airmen to hide in the adjoining bedroom. She moved the three airmen back to the master bedroom and closed the door behind them. Once the

16 *Duitsers* is Dutch for "Germans."

166

area was clear, Loyaerts went to the door and sternly asked, "Who's there?" A familiar voice answered, "It's me, Eugène!" Loyaerts opened the door and there in the hallway stood a very embarrassed Eugène Demal, shadowed by Solomon and Pavelka.

Loyaerts let the three men into his home, and Solomon and Pavelka joined Goebel and the others. Demal explained his situation and asked if the two Americans could stay with him for the rest of the night while he looked for another suitable hiding spot. Loyaerts was not happy with this proposal. However, he knew too well there were no other alternatives as the résistance members were out of hiding places. Reluctantly, he agreed. Demal vowed to return for the two Allied airmen and then left the Loyaerts's home, expressing his thanks.

Arthur Loyaerts was obviously unsettled. His family and the airmen were at much greater risk now that they were all grouped together. Cramped, there was barely enough room for his extended family. Never mind five additional grown men.

By 0200 hours things had finally settled again. As they made themselves as comfortable as possible on the wooden floor, the airmen began reciting their stories of the evening's events. Solomon and Pavelka talked about their run-in with the angry sister. Goebel, Westerlund, and Tucker described how the café below was full of drunken Kraut soldiers, who sang a sobering rendition of "Eins, Zwei, Drei, Saufen" while they sat in silence, afraid of being detected. Through all of the regaling, Goebel lay quietly, making the following entry.

"4-28 – Sat Nite – Shoe Shop – Good Food – Five Fredrick"

THE LUCKY SEVEN

About an hour later, Demal crept through town, quietly avoiding all inhabitants. He made his return back to the Loyaerts's home after finding a suitable new shelter for his two evaders. Without delay, Solomon and Pavelka were once again led away by Eugène Demal. Goebel, Westerlund, and Tucker would remain in place, spending the balance of the early morning hours and the next day above the café.

Shortly after the trio's departure, and noticing that their guests felt out of place, Loyaerts and his wife made every effort to better a very strange and uncomfortable situation. While limited, a meal was the easiest means to ease the awkward silence imposed on the airmen. The young airmen settled around the kitchen table where each man received a small but equal portion of food from Loyaerts's family's stores. A noticeable strain on their resources, he insisted they eat. He saw his family's sacrifice as their duty to support the honorable Allied cause. After the brief meal, the airmen thanked their hosts and returned to their designated resting spot where they quickly fell asleep.

Like most families, the Loyaerts worked to be self-sufficient. They raised a few chickens, baked their own bread, and grew vegetables in a small, shared plot of land behind their home. What they didn't have, they either did without or, periodically, were able to purchase needed supplies from other family farms in the village. That is to say what was left that the Germans had not confiscated.

Upon their initial occupation, Wehrmacht soldiers measured each farmer's land. It was then dictated what crops would be produced and if any of those crops the farmer was allowed to keep for his own consumption. They counted all chickens and again dictated how many eggs were to be supplied to the Third Reich. As one can imagine, there were often shortfalls from the German estimation and actual returns. In these circumstances, one would be forced to make up the difference from the "Black Market." That in itself was a dangerous thing to do. Many families would resort to hiding small livestock so that they could meet their own needs. The Loyaerts family was no different.

Like other Belgium locals, the Loyaerts were forced to pay exorbitant prices. However, if it was made known that the rations were meant to help fugitive persons, like the airmen or other escaped Allied soldiers, there was no cost. If for some reason a farmer refused to provide the needed supplies, the Secret Army would simply liberate crops from the unsuspecting farmer during the darkness of night.

A late morning meal of fresh eggs, bread, and coffee was appreciated by all. The airmen politely sat at the kitchen table, listening to Arthur Loyaerts's stories of his town and the impact of the German occupation. Sitting next to Goebel was Arthur Loyaerts's young son, Eduard. He curiously stared at the strange men at his family table.

Noticing, Loyaerts remarked in Flemish to the young boy about his rude behavior: "It's not polite to stare at our guests!"

"I know, Papa. I'm sorry. I just wanted to learn about their airplane," the boy explained.

Arthur apologized for his son and translated to the airmen his request. Goebel was happy to oblige. For the next hour, the group sat and talked amongst themselves as Goebel drew crude sketches. With hand gestures, he did his best to explain to the boy how their plane had been attacked, each of their positions in the plane, and their escape from Ruthless Ruth. When completed, Goebel folded up the piece of scrap paper and handed it to the boy, who immediately stowed it away for safe keeping. Seeing this, Loyaerts recognized the hazard of his young son having such a drawing. He asked to see it, and after a quick glance, he tucked the drawing in his front pocket. The boy protested, yet he reluctantly obeyed as his father explained why he could not keep it.

The next task would be just as challenging, if not more. In turns, each of the airmen was allowed to visit the outhouse located in the garden behind the main building. The garden and rear court-yard was lined by a waist-high brick wall that provided some cover. It was important that the men moved quickly but not conspicuously, as this facility was also used by the patrons of the café. Once inside the little shack, one was greeted by the usual stench of ammonia, a rough-sawn wooden shelf, and a few scraps of old newspaper. Spaced so not to raise suspicion, a successful trip ended with only a black-stained buttock.

Upon returning from their backyard visit, the airmen were treated to a shave and a cold-water wash. Arthur's Loyaerts's father was also a veteran of the First World War and was well experienced in using the very dangerous straight razor. While he was shaving the men, it seemed strange to the young boy that these men didn't speak a word the entire time. Eduard asked his grandfather, "Bompa, why do these people not speak while you are shaving them?"

"Don't be worried. These boys are deaf-mutes," Bompa replied with a smile.

Their strange silence was a mixture of nervousness and the adherence of orders. They had been warned, and their instructions were absolutely clear: "Limit conversations with the locals, and most of all, do not to speak in public." Few could be trusted as each village had its share of citizens who were sympathetic to the

German cause and would be happy to snitch to the Gestapo. Even though this family had come to their aid, they still weren't going to take any chances.

In the midafternoon hours, while the café was closed to the public, the airmen were allowed to move downstairs in a back room where they listened to the radio. While catching up on the local news, a visiting member of the Comète Line stopped in to check on the fallen Allied troops. Without hesitation, he purposely informed the airmen of the week's tragic events. "Do you remember the fellows from the other night? The ones who helped you few with the car ride from Oteppe?"

Goebel spoke for the group. "Of course we do. How could we forget? Those three almost got us killed."

"I thought you should know that two of them were picked up by the Jerries in their hometown." The résistance member went on to share more. "My close friend, Petit-Louis, was executed after a gun battle with the Krauts. Also, the driver, Jean Cambron, was severely beaten and hauled away and hasn't been seen since."

Hearing the news, Goebel and the others were openly stunned. Lowering his head and staring at the floor, Goebel slowly shook his head in disbelief. A sickening tightness in his throat quickly sunk to his stomach. He struggled to come to terms with the fact that someone whom he met by sheer chance had lost his life in the efforts of saving theirs. Goebel wanted to ask more questions but couldn't bring himself to speak. Before this point, the gravity of their circumstances hadn't truly registered. It was now painfully obvious to Goebel and his comrades that the Germans considered his guardians "Bandits," and the gravest of consequences were to be expected if caught. This thought terrified Goebel.

*"Steenweg 79" (above picture) which occupied the shoe shop (far right door),
and the café (main entrance and lower windows on the left).
The second level above the café was the Loyaerts's residence.
Goebel's sketched pictures (below), drawn April 28, 1944, were returned to
the Goebel family May 2006.*

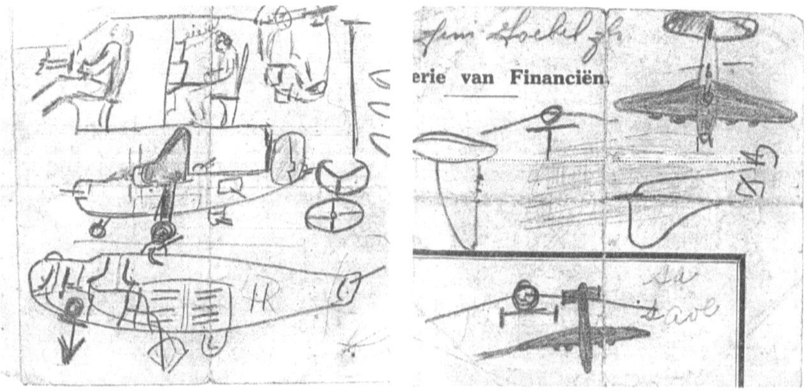

Farewell and thank-you letter from Second Lt. Philip Solomon (above left). Photo (above right) of First Lt. Joseph Pavelka (left) and résistance member Gilbert Mazy (right) was taken in the Landen/Gingelom area during their stay in April 1944.

CHAPTER TWENTY-TWO

Bitching Cold

April 28, 1944
Gingelom, Belgium
Nearing midnight

AS THE CLOCK APPROACHED midnight, the airmen could sense something was unsettled. Arthur Loyaerts broke the news that they would be forced to leave the comfort of the Loyaerts's home. While conveying this message, Arthur was interrupted by an unexpected knock at the door. Cautiously, he approached the door and verified that the visitor was friendly and then he partially opened the door. A murmuring voice could be heard by the rest of the inhabitants, who stood waiting in silence. Arthur said nothing but was given urgent directions. Once delivered, the visitor quietly turned, descended the stairs, and exited into the darkness of the night.

He closed the wooded door, paused momentarily, and turned to the group. The ashen look on his face presented an undeniable air of fear, as if he had just seen a ghost. Repeating the message, he tried not to overly alarm his wife and young guests. The visitor had delivered news that Wehrmacht soldiers had arrived in force and were engaged in an active search of the neighborhood.

Digesting the news, the group sprang into action. The airmen gathered their few belongings, helped to straighten up, and worked to remove any sign of their presence while their host family hurried around gathering what little rations they could spare. The ingredients for a few dry-cured bacon sandwiches and the remainder of a quart of crème de menthe was stored away in the airmen's pockets. In a hurried fashion, the airmen thanked each family member for their kindness and generosity and gathered into position at the door.

Arthur escorted the three men out the back entrance where they were met by a waiting Secret Army member. The German disturbance could now be easily heard throughout the small village above the noise of the rain. Silently, they each expressed their gratitude to Arthur and then quickly marched single file into the foggy blackness. Closely following their escort, Goebel, Westerlund, and Tucker safely made their way out of town.

Nearing 0020 hours, they met up again with Pavelka and Solomon and walked together in the cold night rain for about ten kilometers. None of the airmen had anything more than the shirt on their backs and a thinning, tattered wool coat that someone had generously donated. None had shoes that fit properly, and they were certainly not equipped for the rain and mud, making the long hike even more unpleasant. Their journey ended on the outskirts of another quiet village at an unassuming small stone-and-wood shed. Once inside and with the door securely closed, their guide lit a hanging kerosene lantern. The new light source revealed what appeared to be narrow gauge railroad rails and other assorted construction equipment.

It was made known to the airmen that for their own safety they would be locked in the shed for at least the remainder of the day. Their guide motioned to the door and suggested that if anyone had to relieve himself, he'd better do it outside while able. One by one, each man in the group took advantage of the invitation. Once back inside, they were instructed to use the lantern sparingly and keep quiet. Their guide soon departed, closing and locking the heavy shed door. Its sounds were punctuated by the final twist of a key and the mechanical device locking them inside.

The five airmen were now confined to a maintenance shed, measuring roughly twenty-by-thirty feet. Most of the space and the dirt floor was consumed with materials and equipment and only spared a small fraction of the cleared area to rest unencumbered. With little room to move around, the men settled where they could find a less-than-awkward spot. The earthen floor only radiated a chill and provided little comfort. Soaked through and cold and exhausted from their hike, the airmen all sat quietly, staring at the floor. Sleep was not an option at the moment. Unfortunately, nerves and uncontrollable shivering made this simple task unattainable.

Their sole source of heat for the night was six bottles of wine given to Pavelka and Solomon earlier by Eugène Demal. The combination of wine, fatigue, and the cramped space led to a confrontation between Goebel and Tucker. Goebel was trying to impose his authority once again. Between the wine and his still-sore knee, Tucker didn't want to hear it. The bickering was quickly shut down by Pavelka, who outranked the members of the Kendziora crew. Once settled, they all quietly waited for dawn.

"4-29 – Barn – Dirt Floor – Piss in Corner – Bitching Cold"

CHAPTER TWENTY-THREE

Chicken Shit!

April 29, 1944—Day Six
Unknown Location, Belgium
0430 Hours

THE DAWN'S LIGHT PIERCED the cracks of the upper wooded facade. The stone shed allowed little light to penetrate, yet a few rays managed their way into the cramped space, which spotlighted the resting inhabitants. While the rain had stopped, the morning air was still thick with moisture, and the stone structure trapped a chill within its confines. Life within the shed had not improved for the airmen.

One by one, the men awoke from a rigid slumber. Remaining perched on whatever partially level spot they could find, each man sat somewhat paralyzed. The hours of nonstop shivering had stiffened their bodies and made it difficult to move. With no room to stretch within the frigid, cramped space, they had little choice but remain in a sitting position at their chosen post. When nature called, it seemed as if it took them the better part of an hour to be able to stand erect. Unable to go outside, the men were forced to urinate in the confines of the locked quarters. A designated spot was identified in an accessible corner.

The airmen napped and took turns pacing in a small circle. There wasn't room for more than one at a time. Their food supplies consisted of little more than a few raw bacon-fat sandwiches, leftover wine, and crème de menthe and was rationed equally. The spring day and early evening hours seemed to drag on forever. Discussions on "what to do" if their guides didn't return were rehashed over and over, only to be interrupted by the sounds of solitary planes passing in the distant sky.

Later that evening as planned, armed résistance members returned, arriving just before midnight at 2330 hours. Pavelka and Solomon departed separately again. Goebel, Westerlund, and Tucker were escorted to a nearby home. Even in the darkness as they approached, the structure appeared to be a more than a modest home. Following their guides, they traveled to the back of the property where they met the family in a well-manicured garden. After introductions, the airmen received small gifts of cigarettes, food, and water. Allowed to rest for only a short period, the men were on the move again. They continued walking for about another eight kilometers while sounds of British Lancaster bombers filled the night sky.

Walking single file in silence, the three airmen followed their guides across the countryside. Unlike the previous evening, the night sky exhibited a full show of stars. Pausing for a moment on a hillside, the group looked down on the shadows of the neighboring farmhouses and work structures. As ordered by their occupiers, all homes and businesses were blacked out at night. Seeing that they had arrived, the résistance leader halted the group while he went ahead to confirm that the designated safehouse was still secure. Upon his arrival, the résistance fighter was startled to find that there was no one to meet him at their intended stop for the night.

Returning a few moments later, the leader conveyed the news to his companions. Unsure of what happened to their comrades, they made the decision to take the three airmen to an alternate hiding spot. On their way to the secondary hiding location, they passed by the burnt remains of a farmhouse and a partially destroyed barn. Goebel could still see the glow of embers as he passed by the blackened structures, but the inhabitants were long gone. Near the barn's remains was a small, well-used abandoned game keeping hut.

Unhappy with their guide's choice of accommodations, the three airmen reluctantly climbed inside. The résistance members gathered some additional straw from the remains of a nearby barn. Directed to remain in place, the two guides departed. Left alone again and sealed in the stench of animal waste, smoke-stained straw, and a dirt floor, the three men had little to do but try to get as comfortable as possible in the space allowed. Their guides returned a little more than an hour later bringing provisions of drinking water, a blanket, and replenished their supply of bacon-fat sandwiches. Despite their location fatigue and a lack of sleep, exhaustion finally caught up to the three young men. Huddled together sharing their coats as blankets, they finally managed to get some sleep.

Goebel awoke a few hours later as the morning light beamed into the dark hut. He watched as it slowly moved across his still body and landed on the whitewashed wall next to him. He got up, went to the exterior wall, and peeked through a small knothole where the light had entered the confined space. The brightness temporarily blinded him until his eyes were able to adjust. Looking again, Goebel viewed a beautiful pastoral scene. The dark-green trees in the distance fenced in a dew-covered meadow. He peered as guernsey cows fed on the lush spring grasses. The whole scene was alive with color illuminated by the low sun angle.

It was Sunday morning. As Goebel stood gazing, he thought about his family back home in Brooklyn. He reminisced about past family gatherings. Five full days had passed, and he hoped they had received news that he was alive and well. As he admired the morning coming to life, he was abruptly reminded of his current situation and the ammonia smell wafting from his clothes. Chicken shit!

The two other hut occupants were later awoken by the ominous thunder of a large formation of American bombers passing overhead on their way to dispense their deadly cargo on an unsuspecting factory, airfield, and/or city. Also unexpected were the reporting sounds from the business end of the ordnance being delivered. A position close enough to them so that the bombardment could be clearly heard.

Goebel's knothole became the only source of entertainment and means to pass the time. The airmen took turns watching as people passed on the road or were busily working nearby. Throughout the day and early evening, each took turns trying to nap. Unfortunately, sleep did not come easily as the well-traveled road right outside their hut saw little idleness. This combined with the interrupted sounds of air raid sirens coming from a distant neighboring town preparing to be assaulted made sleep just out of reach. The three airmen could do little but wait to be liberated from the stench.

"4-30 – Pump House – Chicken Shit Straw – Cold – Hungry"

CHAPTER TWENTY-FOUR

'38 Chevrolet

April 30, 1944—Day Seven
Unknown location, Belgium
2300 Hours

LATER THAT EVENING, THE résistance army boys returned, closely accompanied again by Pavelka and Solomon. After a brief greeting and little discussion, it was time to move. Not knowing where they were being taken, the five airmen obediently but blindly followed their guides. At the edge of a tree line just outside another small village, the group came to an abrupt stop. Only able to see the shadow of a few blacked-out structures, the airmen paused to catch their breath. The leader of the group spoke in a low voice in broken English. "We wait here!"

A few minutes later, a lone figure cautiously approached the group from the darkness of the woods. He stopped at a safe distance and lit a cigarette. Goebel's guides acknowledged the gesture in kind. This benign gesture signaled to the approaching man that they were friendly. As he neared, his mannerisms revealed that he was not a young man. Greeting the guides, the stranger turned and then turned to Goebel. Examining his facial features, Goebel estimated that he was of similar age to his own father. Jean Londoz introduced himself as "Shorty." As part of his greeting, he declared to the airmen, "I am René's father."

Shorty informed the group that he would escort Goebel, Westerlund, and Tucker, and Pavelka and Solomon would once again be taken a different direction by the other two guides. Hearing the news, the airmen began to separate into their corresponding groups. Each time neither group of men knew if they would see the other again. Recognizing this reality, each man wished the other good luck and sealed the departure with hardy handshake. Now separated with their respective guides, each group headed off in different directions.

Shorty with Goebel, Westerlund, and Tucker in procession marched without incident about three kilometers to their new shelter. Arriving safely and before entering the rear of the two-story structure, Shorty announced to his guests that this was his family home. Once inside the home, the airmen were treated to a hot drink and the opportunity for a cold-water wash. While they took turns cleaning up their face and hands, Shorty informed them that his son René was still underground hiding from the Gestapo. While René was safe, he would never be seen again by the airmen.

Now in the confines of the Londoz family kitchen, the three airmen could not shake the events of the last twenty-four hours. No matter how much they wanted, they couldn't get away from the smell embedded in their clothes. Shorty smiled and shrugged when he realized what was bothering the young men. He offered all that he had, but unfortunately there was nothing more he could do for them at the moment.

Shorty motioned to the young men, signaling to them to be quiet and to follow him. He stepped away from the kitchen with the airmen in tow and brought them to a modest room with a single bed and nightstand. Standing in the doorway, Shorty informed them that it was René's bedroom. Before departing the room and closing the door, he told the men that they would stay with him until tomorrow evening when they would be taken to Brussels.

Left alone, the three airmen climbed on top of the soft bed. Tucker and Goebel claimed the outside edges, and Westerlund took the middle. Rank had its privileges, even in these circumstances. They were finally able to sleep in a bed again. It was cramped, but off the ground. Just as soon as they drifted asleep, they were rattled awake once by the RAF. The windows shook as the low-flying planes rumbled past overhead. The British Lancaster crews were hard at work that evening bombing the nearby town of Liège.

MAY 1, 1944—DAY EIGHT
GINGELOM, BELGIUM
0800 HOURS

Even in a cramped setting, the three airmen had the best night of sleep in several days. It was amazing what a warm, dry bed did for their soul and demeanor. Waking to the smell of freshly cooked eggs and potatoes, the airmen made their way back to the kitchen where they were greeted by Shorty and his wife, who was visibly younger and very pretty. She smiled softly and shook each of their hands. Standing in a small circle, she noticed the animal aroma still wafting from her three guests. Without speaking, she gestured to the men to follow her. She set up a wash bowl and razor, then took their overcoats and hung them outside in the fresh air. Following the unspoken cues, each man took turns. One by one, they cleaned up and shaved with the straight, dull razor. Managing to escape serious injury, the three men returned to the kitchen, once presentable.

During their meal together, Shorty explained to the young men that the German occupiers had forced him to work for them. As he pointed in an upwardly motion, he stated that he was a finance officer for the Germans. "Hah!" He laughed indignantly at the idea of helping the Germans. Shorty went on to tell the airmen how proud he was of his son, and the efforts being made by members of the Underground. Seeing distress within her facial expressions, the airmen recognized that Shorty's wife was uneasy with the discussion of her son's exploits.

Goebel saw this as an opportunity to change the subject by asking questions about their current whereabouts. Shorty explained that their family home was located on the edge of Gingelom. The airmen quickly realized that they had been moving in circles all this time and hadn't progressed greatly beyond their original starting point. In a week's time, they had traveled roughly thirty-five kilometers north from their respective landing points. This conclusion triggered a quick debate among the airmen, each voicing similar concerns that their caretakers, while extremely hospitable, may not have a fully baked plan. Sensing that the airmen now needed a distraction, Shorty got up from the table and went to another room for a moment and came back with a deck of playing cards. Placing them in the middle of the table, he attempted to assure the young men that everything was going to be okay. With Shorty's words of hope, the young men happily accepted the deck of cards, and his wife kindly looked at the airmen and quickly started a game of rummy.

Just after 1400 hours, a black two-door sedan stopped in front of the Londoz home. Without haste, two young men quickly jumped out and went to the front door. Expecting the visitors, Shorty got up and went to greet the two men. After exchanging brief pleasantries, he brought them to the kitchen where the three airmen were still playing cards. Shorty entered the kitchen with the visitors following closely behind. Goebel, who was facing the door, saw the strangers and quickly stood. Westerlund and Tucker reacted in suit, turning to face Shorty and the two men flanking him.

Introducing them only by their first names, Shorty said, "This is Roger and Fernand, and they will be taking care of you."

Roger Jamblin and his partner, Fernand, were about the same age as the airmen they were now in custody of, yet they were much more experienced in the art of war than the Americans. Hardened by four years of German occupation, Jamblin, the leader of the group, was well-acquainted with Gestapo tactics. Jamblin had joined the Mouvement National Belge (M.N.B.)[17] soon after the Germans moved into Belgium. Alongside of other M.N.B. members, Jamblin had participated in ongoing sabotage, intelligence gathering, distribution of propaganda leaflets, recovery of caches of explosives dropped into Belgium, harboring Jewish neighbors, and smuggling airmen through Belgium and France. Sadly, by May 1944, assisting a few airmen was becoming commonplace for the young Belgian helper.

Goebel paused and looked inquisitively at Shorty and asked, "It's the middle of the day. Are we going now?" Not waiting for a response, Goebel added, "I thought we weren't leaving until tonight."

Unfazed, Jamblin stepped forward and responded forcefully in his broken English. "We go now. You are not safe here!"

17 The Mouvement National Belge (M.N.B.) was a major résistance group established in German-occupied Belgium during World War II and was founded in December 1940 in Brussels by Aimé Danboy.

Accepting this instruction, the airmen showed their appreciation to Shorty and his wife and followed Jamblin and Fernand from the house to the car outside. As directed, the three airmen paused so that their hands could be secured behind their backs before being wedged into the backseat of 1938 Chevrolet sedan. Once the three parcels were secure, the four-passenger car marked similar to the local police sped away from the Londoz home. Armed with forged police papers, Jamblin was prepared for his German occupiers. If the car was stopped, his ruse was simple. Jamblin and his partner would present themselves as real police bringing in arrested felons.

After a few moments of silence, Goebel inquired about their intended destination and expressed his concern that they would be captured while traveling during the day. Jamblin, sitting in the passenger seat, turned to face the three airmen sitting behind him. He bluntly responded in broken English before restating in French for Tucker. "I cannot tell you where we are going. However, we are very familiar with this area, and we know where the Germans are. In fact, we are running on gas stolen from the Germans." This was the only exchange between the two groups for the remainder of the trip. Fernand did not speak at all during their journey, yet he drove the group with a heavy foot along back roads, through pastures, and zig-zagged across the countryside all in an effort to avoid the German occupiers.

Unbeknownst to the three passengers, they were taken to the résistance headquarters in Liège about forty kilometers southwest of Gingelom in the center of Nazi occupation. Arriving around 1630 hours, Goebel, Westerlund, and Tucker were taken to House No. 15 located within the cloisters of The Holy Cross Church near the center of town. The home of Lambert Hosdin was marked by worn blue and white numbers like the other houses in town. Now the nerve center for the local résistance and the assembly point for downed airmen, the cloister cells had once been occupied in previous centuries by monks but were now inhabited by seemingly ordinary families. The access to the four small dwellings, including House No. 15, was directly through a corridor along one side of the church. Conveniently for the helpers it could also be reached through an independent entry a short distance down the street near the rear of the church.

Once inside, Roger Jamblin introduced the three to a Belgian woman, Madame Hosdin, who spoke surprisingly good English. She explained that her husband was an American and was also the head of the local résistance group; therefore for those reasons, they would not meet him or know her true identity. She went on to inform them that the intended plan to transport them to Switzerland was no longer an option since the Germans had broken up the larger résistance outfit. She took their names and promised that they would be radioed back to England. She also informed them that for the time being, they would remain guests in her home.

Later that evening, Goebel, Westerlund, and Tucker were invited to have dinner with the lady of the house; her two daughters, Malou (age eight) and Betty (age ten); and local friends. Even with this news of their ruined getaway, the three airmen were able to have fun playing cards with a group of young guests, friends of the résistance. They were able to talk openly, without worries of being caught, and laughed for the first time since their journey had begun. That evening, Goebel and Westerlund would share a bed, and Tucker would enjoy the couch to himself.

**"5-1 – Slept 3 In Single Bed at Belge House –
Potatoes – Picked Up by Roger in Chevrolet –
Went to Liège Driven by Fernand"**

MAY 2, 1944—DAY NINE
LIÈGE, BELGIUM
1000 HOURS

The next morning, Roger Jamblin returned with his brother Josse, who stopped by to gather up the three airmen for some sorely needed personal hygiene. Together, the three airmen were taken to a nearby public bath house and then treated to a shave and haircut. This was their first opportunity to really get clean. They were dirty; in fact, quite crusty. After the much-needed cleansing, Jamblin took them to an unknown woman's house for a couple of drinks, then back to House No. 15. Once settled within the tiny home, Goebel, Westerlund, and Tucker were outfitted with newer clothes, wool suits, and slightly small shoes. A familiar hazard for the American airmen with bigger feet.

Near 1500 hours, Jamblin told the three airmen that it was time to move to their next hiding spot, which was a short walk across town. While their final destination was not shared, it was clear that they were moving into the heart of the medieval city and in the center of German occupied territory. This was an uncomfortable transition for the three young airmen, yet it did not seem to bother Jamblin. He was calm and collected as he went about his chaperoning with brazen defiance of the Germans. In the midst of passing numerous Germans in the streets, the airmen would naturally tense up, and Jamblin would whistle, **"It's a Long Way to**

Tipperary."[18] The experience was unsettling yet exhilarating. The trio thought Jamblin was crazy; however, they did not betray their leader's confidence.

The Jamblin brothers were rebellious and lucky. Moments of indiscretion frequently occurred with surprisingly little consequences. On one occasion, Josse Jamblin went to the public swimming pool with an Allied pilot named Overkamp. Overkamp jumped into the water of the pool, which was being used by fifty German soldiers. Without thinking, Overkamp had forgotten to take off his dog tags. Luckily, nobody was the wiser, and Josse was able to correct the oversight without calling attention to his Allied companion.

JUNE 1944
HOUSE NO. 15—LIÈGE, BELGIUM

In early June, the Gestapo was closing in on the cloister. Three downed carpetbaggers, Ernest B. Fitzpatrick, Jr. (pilot); Walter W. Swartz (engineer); and William E. Schack (gunner) from the 406th Bomb Squadron, had recently been shot down and were in hiding in the fabled home. During the evenings of May 29 and 30, 1944, as part of Operation Osric 14, the Fitzpatrick crew was forced to bail out over Belgium. While at No. 15, a fourth evader arrived,

18 "It's a Long Way to Tipperary" is an Irish hall song written by Jack Judge and Harry Williams in 1912, which was later made famous when it was recorded by John McCormack in 1914. It became a popular marching song for soldiers in the First World War as it evoked memories of home.

yet something didn't seem right to the three Americans. Sensing that something was wrong, the airmen addressed their concern with their Belgium Helper, Lucien Theelen. Theelen confirmed their suspicions.

It was quickly decided that the new arrival would be evacuated by three guides. Roger Jamblin was one of the three selected for the mission. The traitor was handcuffed and placed in the back of the car with an armed guard at his side. Prior to picking up their parcel, the three résistance members had drawn lots to determine who would terminate the newest arrival.

The three guides escorted the suspicious man out of the valley toward Oreye. After twenty minutes of silence, the car pulled to a stop in a remote location. All four made their way to the rear of the car, and under the cover of night the guide who drew the short straw shot the undercover Gestapo man in the back of the head.

Later that evening back in Liège, Theelen was preparing for the worst. He had the three airmen transferred to a nearby firehouse and then helped scour House No. 15, removing any evidence of the recent Allied inhabitants. The next morning, the Gestapo stormed the cloister residence and arrested Madame Hosdin. She resisted their hard questioning for several days and was eventually transferred to a German concentration camp where she would remain until June 1945. Not only did the Gestapo fall short in their infiltration scheme; they had also missed the Jews hiding in the cloister next door.

While it is impossible to say with certainty, after the war it was determined that well over one hundred Allied airmen had passed through the cloister. By the end of the war, countless American, English, and Canadian airmen had crossed through the hallowed cloister grounds, most likely without fervent recognition of their whereabouts. Only to remain for a brief time in a modest home flanked by a small garden, the adjacent alley, and an enemy only too happy to know their whereabouts. Their time was spent awaiting a false identity and working cards, new clothes, and nourishment until the opportunity for the final trip to France and Switzerland was coordinated. By May 1944, the bombing of Germany had intensified in preparation for D-Day. Steadily, more and more Allied aircraft were shot down. It is safe to say that the tower of the Holy Cross Church (and other cathédrales) attracted airmen similar to a crippled ship in search for the first glimpse of a friendly harbor.

AUGUST 1944
GINGELOM, BELGIUM

Four months later, the Gestapo did visit the Londoz home. A warrant for René's Londoz's head had been issued with a 100 Belgian franc reward. In a time when workers only earned roughly 50 francs ($1.14 U.S.)/day, many would turn on a résistance member, even family members. René Londoz had not come back to his home for some time. He was deep in hiding for good reasons. He had been snitched on by an agent of the Geheime Field Polizei who penetrated the line. Like the rest of the résistance members in his line, he was forced to hide for weeks and months underground while the survivors recreated a new line. Only when he could be assured the lives of his family's members were out of harm's reach would he revisit. When he did not surrender, the Germans came to take René as a prisoner.

Wehrmacht soldiers stormed the Londoz family home in search of René Londoz or learn the whereabouts of his hiding spot.

After a good ransacking of their home, René's father, Jean Londoz (Shorty), was instead arrested and threatened a worse fate if René didn't turn himself in soon. All of the pleading and tears from Jean's wife did not sway the stone-faced and determined Gestapo. Jean was dragged from his home at gunpoint and placed in the back of a tarp-covered truck. Only after days of brutal interrogation was the Gestapo convinced that Jean did not know the location of René. Jean was later liberated from a local POW camp and returned home without further incident. René Londoz was never seen again by the airmen but would later return safely to his family and home.

Post VE Day
Liège, Belgium

With all his exploits during the war, Roger Jamblin was thankfully never arrested by the Germans. After the war, Roger finished school and went to work for the Americans in a quartermaster company as an accountant. Both Roger and Josse volunteered for the Belgium Army; however, Roger was sent home due to being sick and having to wear eyeglasses. In 1948, Roger was awarded the Medal of Freedom, which was presented by Admiral Goodrich Kirk, the acting United States Ambassador to Belgium. Roger was also honored by the Belgian Government for his participation in Groupe Marcel, an affiliate of Mouvement National Belge (MNB).

Jean (Shorty) Londoz's home in Gingelom

CHAPTER TWENTY-FIVE

La Cathédrale Saint Paul

May 2, 1944
Liège, Belgium
1530 Hours

AS THE GROUP MARCHED closer, the gothic cathédrale grew larger. Just west and near the banks of the Meuse River, the airmen were led to their next hiding spot, located in the heart of Liège. Originally founded in the tenth century, the Liège Cathédrale was now shrouded in vertically ornate dark-grey stone. It was an impressive structure and not very conspicuous, Goebel noted to himself. However, there was value to hiding in plain sight. Goebel had been told that if he was ever separated and in an unknown land, he should make his way to the nearest Catholic church as the priests were sympathetic and knew who could be trusting in the surrounding area. This was comforting to the young Catholic pilot.

Arriving to the rear of the complex, the airmen were escorted to the residence of the church caretakers. A couple in their fifties, Desiré and Maria Demelenne, fifty-eight and fifty-four years old respectively, would be become the trio's new guardians. After initial introductions were made, Roger Jamblin informed the airmen to expect to remain at this location for at least a week. Jamblin turned to Desiré and Maria, spoke briefly in French, and exited back onto the street, vanishing into the cool afternoon haze.

Leaving the airmen with their new hosts, Desiré and Maria were quick to move the young men upstairs to an improvised living room. Here, there was a couch and a mattress on the floor. Desiré disappeared momentarily and returned with a small radio. Gesturing to the younger men, he placed the radio on a small end table adjacent to the couch. Their initial exchanges were awkward as the couple didn't speak anything other than French. Thankfully, Tucker took French in school and could get by with some rudimentary dialogue.

The couple left the airmen and later returned with a loaf of bread, a pitcher of water, and three glasses. Short on supplies, their caretakers brought what rations they had available. The airmen gratefully accepted and wasted no time devouring the meal. Once complete, they were taken on a quick tour of the Demelenne dwelling. The semi-clumsy procession deposited the airmen back to the upstairs room. After a quiet evening of listing to the radio, the men adjourned. Tucker took the couch and Goebel and Westerlund split the mattress. Before dozing off, Goebel scribbled in his diary the following footnote:

"5-2 – Moved to St Paul's Cathédrale,
Maria + Desiré, Bread Water + Hungry as Hell"

THE LUCKY SEVEN

The date for D-Day was delayed from 31 May. The Allied planners determined that two periods in the following month were identified as suitable target dates based on the amount of moonlight and the tides: 5-7 June and 18-20 June.

MAY 3, 1944—DAY TEN
LIÈGE, BELGIUM
0900 HOURS

The follow morning, Goebel, Tucker, and Westerlund woke from a peaceful slumber and were greeted by Maria, who escorted the young men to the kitchen where she served a modest meal of coffee without milk, but offered ersatz sugar, jam, and a loaf of brown bread. After breakfast, Desiré took the trio on a tour of the cathédrale grounds, then showed them the interior cloister and courtyard. Desiré, through Tucker, explained that these areas were accessible during the day and night if no one else was present. He took them to the outer boundary of the cathédrale but not in, then made it clear that this area of the sanctuary and the chapel were off-limits.

The Liège Cathédrale was shelter for more than the three Allied airmen. Unbeknownst to them and their caretakers, at the opposite end of the cathédrale the bishop of Liège was hiding

Jewish refugees. The Gestapo led by a German named Lück was on constant lookout for downed airmen and other escapees, as well as members of the underground and soul who choose to provide aid. The utmost secrecy between the underground members and other friendly locals had to be maintained for survival's sake.

The remainder of their first day at the cathédrale was limited to their assigned living quarters. The airmen passed the time, playing cards, listening to the radio, and relaxing. No one complained as the rest was needed, not only for their nerves but for their bodies. It had been almost ten days since being shot out of the sky. On the mend, Tucker's leg was still healing. While not one hundred percent, he could almost bend down. In the moment, the solitude that this sanctuary provided them was essential.

MAY 4, 1944—DAY ELEVEN
LIÈGE, BELGIUM
0900 HOURS

On the first Thursday of May, Goebel and company spent their first full day in Liège. They woke and had a modest breakfast, followed by card playing and listening to the radio. They had some new company, a fellow airman named Bill. After a brief exchange, Bill and Tucker realized that they had both been through the same B-29 training unit based in Denver, Colorado. While they didn't know each other from the past, Tucker and Bill shared stories about their time at Lowry Field. After some reminiscing, Bill's tone changed; anger surfaced regarding being held in Liège since March 4, 1944. He expressed his disappointment that there was rumored to be over two hundred English and American airmen all waiting to leave. In a sullen tone, Bill said, **"You boys will be lucky if you leave Liège within two months."** His words quickly sucked the air from the room and lowered everyone's morale.

Thankfully, Bill's chaperone revived their spirits. Bill had been accompanied by a very cute flaxen-haired girl by the name of Juliette. At twenty years old, the local beauty was slender with soft features. Juliette did not speak English, so she stood quietly as the airmen talked, yet her smile warmed the room. After a few moments, she spoke to Bill in French, which led to a prompt round of best wishes and the two departing the sanctuary.

The three airmen spent the rest of the day alone, making the most of the time, remaining out of sight, waiting to explore their safe haven after dark.

MAY 5, 1944—DAY TWELVE
LIÈGE, BELGIUM
0900 HOURS

The following morning arrived with a similar ritual. They spent the morning hours lying around and listening to the radio. Their guests had scrounged up some new reading material. While the content may have seemed corny to the young airmen, at least the books were in English.

It was evident that their hosts lived a modest existence and didn't have much to offer. Goebel and his fellow crew members missed the creature comforts of home, yet they were grateful for their newly adopted parents. Maria and Desiré scrimped, and knowing visitors donated what they could. Under the circumstances, the airmen were fed fairly well. Food was tightly rationed. They received one porkchop for the three to split as their daily meat allocation; however, they had plenty of bread, oleo (margarine), jam, and oat coffee in the morning and an ample number of potatoes in the afternoons. It was more than enough to appease the hunger of the young Americans.

Around midafternoon, Roger Jamblin returned to check on their well-being. After verifying that everything was okay, Jamblin reminded the airmen of all the things they shouldn't do. In his broken English, Jamblin said, **"You doesn't must do . . ."** and proceeded to list numerous don'ts. The airmen tried not to laugh at Jamblin's use of the English language. He obviously meant well, yet his delivery brought amusement to their day.

After reciting his rules, Jamblin gathered the three airmen around a small table in the center of the room, pulled out a map, and began to show the three how easily it could be arranged to fly the three back to safety. **"If only the English would cooperate . . ."** Jamblin lamented in French to Tucker. He went on to describe as best he could the résistance organization around Liège. They were well-equipped and ready to oppose their occupiers with plenty of guns and ammunition. While the English may have not been helpful in flying Allied airmen back to England, the English were good at parachuting supplies in under the cover of darkness. Jamblin remained with the airmen for about an hour and left without much exhibition.

Later that evening, the airmen joined Maria and Desiré in the kitchen. Goebel and Westerlund didn't speak anything but English; thankfully, Tucker knew a little French. Between a French dictionary and what he had learned in school, Tucker could translate for the other two. Goebel and Westerlund sat quietly while Tucker conversed with their hosts. They talked about life before the war, travel, and Tucker told them about life in the United States. They sat and chatted until almost midnight before the group retired for the evening.

MAY 6, 1944—DAY THIRTEEN
LIÈGE, BELGIUM
1000 HOURS

The next day little changed. Entering the fourth full day at the cathédrale, the monotony of their existence was beginning to rule. After breakfast, Goebel, Westerlund, and Tucker remained in their room listening to the radio. With boredom and frustration settling in, the group debated the merits of the local radio programming. It seemed that the Germans put out better content as the English BBC kept with only classical music. Supposedly, the BBC felt the Allied troops would rather listen to the elegance and balance of classical rather than the catchy American "swing jazz." Little did they know that back home, Bing Crosby was topping the *Billboard* singles chart with "I Love You."

Their boredom was interrupted in the afternoon by another set of visitors. Two young White Army boys who were sent by Jamblin stopped by to check in on the airmen. Surprisingly, both were under the age of sixteen. The local résistance maintained very youthful ranks for a good reason. Most war age Belgium men were either taken as prisoners of war or were sent off to work in German factories. The remaining older men were under the watchful eye of their occupiers. Therefore young boys were often enlisted to support the cause. These two scouts were a welcome relief as they spoke broken English learned from exchanges with other downed airmen.

The five found seats and played a thorough round of question and answers, only to be broken up by the distinct sound of a very low-flying German Focke-Wulf Fw 190. The roar of the single-engine fighter erupted as it passed over the top of the gothic chapel. The immense noise caused the windows to rattle as bits of dust sprinkled down from the ceiling. Pausing, the group waited to see if there was going to be an ordinance report. With an all-clear sigh of relief, the group wrapped up their discussions, and the two young résistance members departed down the stairs, needing to complete their afternoon assignments.

The remaining afternoon and evening were quiet. Tucker stepped away from Goebel and Westerlund as they played cards and went to visit with Maria and Desiré down in the kitchen. Tired of speaking French, Tucker knew the time with his two hosts would only improve his usage of the language.

MAY 7, 1944—DAY FOURTEEN
LIÈGE, BELGIUM
0800 HOURS

Sunday morning arrived with little fanfare. Goebel and Tucker pondered the idea of attending Mass downstairs, yet ultimately decided that it was too dangerous. They knew it would be for the best as they didn't want to give themselves away or expose their hosts. Remaining in their assigned quarters, the airmen passed the time. Tucker's leg was almost healed. He could walk on it fairly well and without any sign of a limp.

The afternoon brought a new group of visitors. This time it was friends of Maria and Desiré, Maurice Lemal[19] and his wife. Lemal came into the caretaker's home with a suitcase full of black-market items. Setting the case down, he unlatched it and popped it open only to reveal a host of pantyhose, ties, shirts, scarves, perfume, cigarettes, and a few forbidden food items. Lemal turned to the others in the room, waving his hand in a low sweeping motion, and presented his wares. Chatting in French, Maria walked closer and took a look at his inventory.

The airmen stood by awkwardly as the group conversed in French. Lemal's wife, a contemporary of Maria, took interest in Goebel. The ruggedly built brunette wore a flower-style dress and smelled as if she had bathed in French perfume. The overpowering fragrance wafted throughout the space and mixed with the smoke circling the room. Looking at Goebel and between puffs of her cigarette, she began to repeat the same phrase in a smoke-induced raspy voice: **"Je vous aime beaucoup! Je vous aime beaucoup!"** Goebel acknowledged her with a polite smile and nodded.

Not comprehending what was being said, Goebel turned to Tucker for help. "Tucker!" Goebel whispered. "What is she saying?"

Again, she echoed, **"Je vous aime beaucoup!"**

"Tucker, what is she saying?" Goebel barked again under his breath.

"She is saying, 'I love you very much,'" Tucker mused.

---

19 Maurice Lemal was arrested by the Gestapo on July 24, 1944, for illegal trading and was sent to a German concentration camp, never to be seen again.

Goebel's was now blushing, unsure of what to make of her gesture. Sensing his uneasiness, Tucker smiled and replied in French to the madam by acknowledging Goebel's reciprocation.

Goebel quickly questioned Tucker: "What did you tell her?"

Pausing momentarily as a sarcastic grin emerged, Tucker replied, "I told her that you appreciated her well wishes, but you were just shy." Not surprised with Tucker's response, Goebel's face remained red.

The three airmen enjoyed a very decadent afternoon tea. Combined, they were treated to three different kinds of cake and two variations of pie. While provisions were scarce, the delicacies were made from supplies stolen back from the Jerries by local partisans. After tea, the group split up into what appeared to be family units and went out for an afternoon walk. The town was alive with activity while their occupiers remained vigilant. Goebel saw plenty of Nazis, which was an uncomfortable reality. The evidence of their existence was overt. Swastikas, banners, and other German paraphernalia draped from buildings. Pill boxes and barbed wire fencing stood as sentinels against the local population.

Maria, Desiré, Lemal, and his wife were well aware of the risk, yet they took great joy in openly pulling something over on the Jerries. The afternoon stroll allowed their hosts to show the young airmen their town. Their pride was exhibited in a little extra zip as they stepped about the cobblestone walkways. Upon safely returning to the cathédrale, the group entered from the rear into the caretaker's quarters. Between the constant concern of being discovered, the fresh air, and the afternoon walk, the airmen decided to retire to their upstairs sanctuary.

THE LUCKY SEVEN

While Goebel and his hosts were out enjoying a Sunday afternoon walk with his hosts, the Mighty Eighth (the U.S. Eighth Air Force) conducted a massive 1,500 bomber raid attacking Berlin, Hamburg, Dresden, and other surrounding cities.

The local air raid sirens began to wail during the midmorning hours, but no planes came overhead. Maria had always been deathly afraid whenever she heard a plane, the result of the German Stukas of 1940. Each time she heard a plane, she went into hysterics, cried, screamed, and ran down into the church cellar.

At 1400 hours, the sirens pierced the afternoon with their shrill warning. This time the American B-24s were on their way. The intended target was a railway station a half mile from the church. One of the flying forts fell victim to German ground fire, which took out the number three engine and quickly engulfed the plane in flames. Some of the crew was able to bail out. Three parachutes were immediately spotted; two drifted into town and were captured, and the third got away. The plane crashed just outside of town. News arrived later informing the group that two other airmen had also jumped, but their chutes had not opened.

In between air raids, the airmen were allowed to walk around the interior gardens. Protected by the cloister, the airmen enjoyed the small open-air sanctuary. The grass was greener by the day and the flowers were blooming in an array of colors. The weather was also beginning to be noticeably warmer. The oasis confined within the holy walls was in contrast to the chaos and the existence of war on the outside.

When unknown visitors were in play, Goebel would explore the out-of-sight portions of the church grounds. From the tower, he would access the wood framing that supported the roof just above the vaulted cathédrale ceiling. Goebel would then climb through the open void, trying not to disturb the inches of centuries-old dust. Other times, he would go into the three different burial levels beneath the cathédrale. This was more entertaining as he could study the dates and the construction of the shelved coffins, many of which dated from 800 AD to 1300 AD—the years the cathédrale was under construction.

Later that evening, with the light of a full moon piercing through the window, the boys spent the remaining hours listening to Axis Sally wax poetically, warning the Allied fighters that **"There is danger ahead!"** The American broadcaster and traitor dished out Axis propaganda while trying to stir Allied troops with sentimental talk and good-old memory tunes. The radio and Axis Sally was finally silenced at 2300 hours.

THE LUCKY SEVEN

"General Eisenhower fixes 5 June as D-day, the date for the invasion of Normandy."[20] This will be signaled to the commanders on May 23, 1944.

MAY 8, 1944
BROOKLYN, NEW YORK
1300 HOURS

The doorbell pierced the air on a muggy Monday afternoon. Going about her daily routine, Mrs. Frances Goebel was interrupted by a visitor at the door. Standing on the front stoop of 1375 Brooklyn Avenue was a young messenger holding an envelope. His bicycle was left draped against the stone steps behind him. Frances slowly opened the door and greeted the young man. In response, the teenage boy removed his cap, extended his hand forward, and said, "You have a telegram, Ma'am." Not expecting the brown Western Union envelope, she thanked the young man, closed the door, and remained motionless in the foyer. Paralyzed, she was too scared to open it because she had two sons overseas. The young boy had unknowingly delivered a heavy burden, and she was not prepared to receive the bad news.

20 (Buell, 2002)

Regaining her wits, Frances opened the envelope and removed the contents. As tears ran down her cheeks, quivering, she read the following:

"THE SECT OF WAR DESIRES ME TO EXPRESS HIS DEEP REGRET THAT YOUR SON SECOND LT. JAMES J GOEBEL JR. HAS BEEN REPORTED MISSING IN ACTION SINCE 24 APRIL OVER GERMANY."

This was the first and only information regarding James Goebel's condition that the Goebel family had received. It had been more than two weeks since he was last seen. Shocked, slightly relieved, and prayerful, Francis was hopeful that her son was alive.

MAY 9, 1944—DAY SIXTEEN
LIÈGE, BELGIUM
0900 HOURS

Another beautiful spring day shone over Liège. After breakfast, the three airmen went out into the atrium garden and walked or jogged laps around the outer perimeter of the confined space. They went fifty times in one direction, then reversed course and walked another fifty laps. All wanted to remain in shape for the trip that they hoped would soon be ahead of them. In between exercise sessions, the three hung around playing cards and reading.

Later that evening, Desiré took Goebel and Westerlund for a walk. Unknowingly, Goebel's six-foot (183 cm) stature put him and the others at risk. Taller than his fellow crew mates and Desiré and towering over Maria, Goebel did not look like the native Belgium and German occupants of Liège. Recognizing this and the fact that Goebel and Westerlund were unable to speak French, Desiré steered his two young companions to less visible areas near the cathédrale.

Maria and Tucker went separately in a different direction, walking south toward the railyard. Along the route they passed a German hotel across the street from the station. Nazi officers were sitting just inside, drinking beer, smoking, and partaking in a moment of revelry. Maria was on edge. The mere site of a German would give her nervous fits. Each time she saw one, she would grab for Tucker's arm. This was not a good habit as it could trigger an eager Jerry.

Together they continued along their route. Eventually, they made it to the southern edge of town where the valley floor butted up against the western slope of the river Meuse. Soon they began to walk up a very steep hill. Unsure of Maria's end destination, Tucker faithfully followed. At the top, they stopped at the Inter-Allied Memorial. Inaugurated only seven years earlier, the monument was dedicated to the allies of WWI and to the heroic resistance of Liège and Belgium. This was a source of pride for Maria and the citizens of Liège.

From this vantage point, they could better survey the bomb damage. The Allied bombers had done a good job. *They had really messed up the railroad yards*, Tucker thought. He was witnessing the business end of his profession. He could see the devastating effects on innocent people who had been bombed out of their homes and were now picking through the rubble, looking for any sense of belonging. Ambulances rushed about their business, like bees harvesting nectar and pollen. The scene below made Tucker pause. After a short visit, the two departed from Cointe Hill and made their way back to the cathédrale without incident and well before the 2100-hour curfew.

Later that evening when the three were rejoined in their up-stairs haven, they shared stories of their ventures. Comparing notes, they noticed that the Jerries here were either very young or very old. For the most part, their morale seemed pretty low. Their uniforms were awful; hardly any of them matched. All together, they sure didn't look like supermen.

May 10, 1944—Day Seventeen
Liège, Belgium
1200 Hours

Like most days now, the three were sequestered to the confines of the cathédrale property. Kept mostly out of sight of the public, they found themselves marking time for the majority of the day. They were getting used to one good meal for the day with bread and jam for the other two meals. Besides reading and playing cards, Tucker tried teaching the other two French. His French was becoming more fluent where Westerlund knew a little, and Goebel was lost as he could not speak or understand any of it.

In the afternoon, the respective groups (Desiré, Goebel, and Westerlund, and Maria with Tucker) went out for afternoon walks. Today, Maria ventured a little farther than normal. Knowing that Tucker could get by with his French, she was more confident about taking him to other parts of town. Together they boarded a small one-lung passenger steamer that transported them across the river. Once on the eastern shore, they stepped onto a streetcar to continue their journey. On both modes of transportation, Maria and Tucker were not alone. Along with other civilians, there were

German soldiers moving within the crowds. Some were in uniform, and others were more cleverly disguised. The Gestapo often wore civilian clothes in an attempt to blend in with their occupied population. Tucker was getting used to seeing them, and Maria's anxiety had waned slightly, but he couldn't help imagining what these Nazis would give to know he was an American.

Maria stopped at a millinery shop where she had a simple brown wool fedora made for Tucker. Knowing the shop owners were sympathetic to the résistance cause, Maria felt comfortable calling herself Tucker's "Belgium mother." While they waited, Maria and the milliner's wife talked about the recent bombings. Speaking in French, Tucker was able to follow along as the two women exchanged the news for the day. Tucker sat quietly, trying to go unnoticed. He silently hoped that the two women would not engage him in their gossip session, and he prayed the shop keeper's little girl would not start babbling at him. Once completed, Maria and Tucker departed the shop and retraced their steps back to the other side of the river.

The remaining evening was quiet. There were no bombing raids or visitors, just a peaceful evening of Axis Sally pedaling her poisonous wares.

MAY 11, 1944—DAY EIGHTEEN
LIÈGE, BELGIUM
1215 HOURS

A little after noon, Roger Jamblin stopped in again to check the airmen. However, this time he was not alone. With him was a downed RAF Flight Sargent named Donald Brinkhurst. A member of the 101 Squadron, Brinkhurst was a Mid-Upper Gunner on a Lancaster bomber and had been shot down the night of March 30/31, 1944, over Germany as part of the Nuremberg raid. One of only three members of his eight-man crew to survive, Brinkhurst had escaped Germany on his own, still wearing his RAF uniform and flight boots as he journeyed to Belgium.

Brinkhurst was a friendly but tough British chap. From the western port town of Bristol, Brinkhurst had volunteered for his aircraft duties. As a gunner on his crew, he was seated in the mid upper turret, which was an unheated section of the fuselage. As a downed airman and evadee, Brinkhurst was bold and determined.

During his brief stay at the church, while teaching Tucker and Goebel some British card games, Brinkhurst shared his evadee exploits. He went on to tell his story about walking alone at night in Germany for four days. Apart from two raw potatoes that he scrounged on the last day, he'd had nothing to eat. Resting in the daytime, on the first day Brinkhurst had lain in a rut of a ploughed field with Germans working in the next field. The subsequent days he found refuge in an empty house, an old barn, and in the forest on the edge of a German town.

Continuing, Brinkhurst shared with his Allied companions his early experiences with the underground movement in Belgium. He had stayed in a village for three weeks before being found out. Members of the résistance had been bringing him food each evening to a little schoolroom where he was hiding. The Germans caught word from a local collaborator that an airman was in the area and an ensuing raid was coordinated. The raid resulted in the capture and execution of ten local residents believed to be offering aid. Hearing this news, Brinkhurst fled to Holland. After a short stay, he made his way to Liège where he had spent the last couple of weeks under the supervision of the local White Army boys.

Dominating the conversation, Brinkhurst proceeded to describe a more recent German encounter. Like the others, Brinkhurst took trips into the Liège town center. While on these trips, Brinkhurst kept the company of a young married woman named Madame Jennie Smet.[21] In addition to being Brinkhurst's resident guardian, Jennie's sole responsibility when in town with Brinkhurst was to make sure he stayed out of trouble and out of the hands of the Germans. On one such occasion, Brinkhurst and Jennie were crossing a small wooden bridge. When they were halfway across, there came four German Luftwaffe officers approaching from the opposite direction. Realizing there was no way out and a quick about-face would have been an obvious alert to the Germans, Brinkhurst stood cool and took Jennie in his arms and kissed her for an extended time. The German officers passed, staring at the kissing couple, offering their congratulations to Brinkhurst for his good choice and taste.

Later that afternoon after Jamblin and Brinkhurst had departed, the two White Army boys also made another stop in. Their reason for dropping by was less tactical and more hubris. They went on to openly share with the airmen an outline, diagram, and plans to hold up an armored car containing 15,000 Belgium francs ($341 U.S.). Hopefully, there would be no grave consequences from their impending escapade.

That night, the two groups went out again for their separate walks. Maria and Tucker went out to the central square in town. Maria was tired, so they found an empty bench to rest. The two sat and talked. Tucker tried to improve his French by pointing at objects and calling them out for Maria. A few early evening stars

21 While this passive résistance member existed, the surname "Smelt" cannot be confirmed from piecing together different resources.

were shining, so Tucker began to point up at the different ones and identified in French what he was seeing. Without noticing, two German officers stopped alongside the couple to see what Tucker was pointing at. Pausing, Tucker froze in mid-sentence. Maria nervously explained that they were looking at the stars, and the two officers went on their way. Both Maria and Tucker took a deep breath of relief, rose to their feet, and quickly departed the square. Tucker never said anything to Maria, yet he thought that her nerves were going to give them away.

MAY 11, 1944
NORMANDY, FRANCE
2300 HOURS

U.S. and British forces raided airfields and coastal installations in Normandy, hitting Calais particularly hard as part of the deception plan to make the Germans think the impending invasion and landings would be made there. As well, four B-24s were dispatched on CARPETBAGGER[22] missions.

22 Operation Carpetbagger provided aerial support of weapons and other material to résistance fighters in France that began January 4, 1944.

THE LUCKY SEVEN

Around 0200 hours, the night air was interrupted by the RAF that passed overhead to destinations unknown. Unfortunately, the sounds of aircraft set off Maria's hysteria—the result of the German Stuka dive-bombers that came with the German invasion four years earlier. Intended to damage enemy morale and cause physiological damage, the sound of the propeller-driven siren fitted on the bottom of the German aircraft permanently terrorized Maria.

Later that morning around 1000 hours, the USAAF offered an even more terrifying encore for Maria and the residents of Liège. With the air raid sirens wailing, North American A-36 Mustangs began a ground attack of the rail station. In addition to dive-bombing, they strafed the German ack-ack batteries. Maria was losing her mind.

Later that afternoon at 1300 hours, two more A-36 attacks occurred. This time the Germans threw up everything they had to combat the American dive-bombers. Fifty-caliber rounds, light ack-ack, and one-pound pom-poms. Thankfully, they didn't hit any Allied flyers.

During the exchange, Goebel and Tucker moved to the open window to observe the action. Watching, they could clearly see the Mustangs peel off into their dives. Their wings were spitting sheets of orange flame and lead. A piece of ack-ack shrapnel broke a pane of window glass two inches behind Tucker's rear. Simultaneously, fragments began to shower onto the cathédrale's roof, with most landing in the garden below. Soon, the bombs erupted, setting off compression waves low and overpowering. The cacophony of war had overtaken their sanctuary, driving them back into their room. The only sound that interrupted the melee was the hysterical screaming from Maria as she made her way to the basement.

Again, at 1900 hours another attack came. The third of the day. This time it was P-47 Thunderbolts. Equipped with eight .50-caliber machine guns, the Allied fighters strafed the German gun crews. Yet again, the three airmen found themselves in a precarious spot. Watching from their window, they witnessed German tracers arching toward their direction in an effort to hit their prey. Rounds bounced off of the surrounding buildings. Bits of stone and lead fragments ricocheted about, close enough to cause the three airmen to seek refuge under and behind furniture within the room.

The evening's events brought unexpected guests to Desiré and Maria's home. Friends of the Demelenne's had been bombed out of their home, bringing them to the church doorstep. Parents with a teenage daughter, who was also audibly distraught, entered the foyer. Between the cries and commotion, Tucker could make out part of the conversation below. Straining to make sense of the words, Tucker repeated in a low whisper an English translation for Goebel and Westerlund. It seemed the daughter had been in the house at the time the bomb struck. Physically unharmed, the young woman had been rattled to her core. The family had no other place to go, so they sought shelter here for the evening.

Once settled, Desiré made his way upstairs and confirmed with Tucker what he had previously overheard. The new houseguests unknowingly brought with them an added level of complexity and risk to the cathédrale. Goebel and his crew members were now forced to hide in their room. They could not be seen by the new houseguests. The concern was real. Even though they were casual friends of the caretakers, their loyalties were still somewhat unknown. Therefore the family could not be fully trusted. One mention of the hidden guests to the wrong people would surely result in the Americans' capture and their caretakers' most certain death.

As the chaos of the evening subsided, and even with the added risk within the walls of their sanctuary, the airmen could only think of one thing. When was the Allied invasion coming?

MAY 13, 1944—DAY TWENTY
LIÈGE, BELGIUM
1100 HOURS

The airmen had remained secluded within their upstairs room since the previous evening. The new houseguests had not left; therefore the three were confined to little movement, interaction, or noise. Unknowing of the new visitors, Brinkhurst arrived at 1100 hours. Without being seen or heard, Brinkhurst made his way upstairs where he found the three lying about the room, reading. Goebel quietly greeted Brinkhurst and explained the situation. Hearing the news, Brinkhurst offered to take Tucker out for the afternoon as he was the most fluent French speaker of the group. Without telling Maria, the two left for a walk.

Now out on the streets, Tucker followed Brinkhurst as they made efforts to evade local German patrols. The Germans were actively stopping civilians and checking identity cards. While Tucker had a forged ID, an alias of Fernand Louis Mass, and he could speak some French, he had no desire to intentionally interact with the enemy.

After a twenty-minute walk, Brinkhurst had led Tucker to his shelter. The home of Madame Jennie Smet and her two daughters, Julye (age eighteen) and Hilda (age fourteen). Jennie was Belgian and spoke English. Her husband was an American but was currently in a German prison camp near Paris. He had been picked up soon after the United States entered the war against Germany.

While playing cards in the kitchen, an unexpected knock arrived at Jennie's front door. Brinkhurst motioned Tucker to hide, then did the same himself as Jennie made her way to the door. Before opening, Jennie cautiously pulled the curtain back to see who was at the door. Seeing familiar faces, she opened the door and greeted her unexpected guests. The family informed Jennie that they had also been bombed out of their home on the previous day and had nowhere else to go. Forced to seek new shelter, they had in hand all that they could carry. After getting them settled, Jennie went to her neighbors to secure a few additional rations to supplement dinner for the group.

After dinner, Brinkhurst, Tucker, Jennie, and her girls left the family to rest and went out for a walk. Brinkhurst and Tucker wanted very much to go over to the rail station to survey the damage. Fearing for their safety, the girls would only let the group get within two blocks. Their concerns were valid as the Germans were out rounding up young people to go work in Germany. Afraid that her daughters might fall into the same fate as their father, Jennie would not allow the group to advance any closer.

Even from a distance, the carnage was evident. The station was severely battered; no windows remained, and the building was visibly pockmarked by bullets, shrapnel, and other flying debris. The chaos of recovery was in full bloom. Ambulances of every make and model were being employed. Casualties with blood-soaked bandages walked aimlessly through the rubble, looking for anything or anyone recognizable that made sense.

Seeing enough, the group turned toward a safer part of town, quickly creating distance from the spectacle they had just witnessed. Jennie wanted to head back home, and Brinkhurst knew it would be best for Tucker to return to the cathédrale. Splitting apart, the two groups traveled to their agreed destination.

Arriving just after 1900 hours, Brinkhurst and Tucker were greeted by a side of Maria that they had not seen before. Fuming mad, Maria barked at Brinkhurst, demanding that he leave immediately. Turning to Tucker, crying, she insisted that he must go now as well. Doing as he was directed, Tucker went upstairs and collected his few belongings. Returning a few moments later, he found Maria still in tears. But now when she looked at Tucker with his kit in hand, she changed her mind, only to tell him to return upstairs.

Later in the evening, once Maria had quieted down, Tucker made his way downstairs to speak with his Belgium mother. Maria told Tucker that she had been extremely worried about him. Thinking that he had been picked up by the Germans, or a fate much worse. Apologizing for his misstep, Tucker and Maria made amends. Maria divulged that Tucker, Goebel, and Westerlund were the first Americans they had helped, and they felt a higher level of duty and responsibility to protect the young airmen. Thankfully, by evening's end life in the cathédrale had returned to normal. No visitors, no Allied planes, and no hysteria—just quiet.

LA CATHÉDRALE SAINT PAUL

The church bells beckoning its congregation to Sunday's Mass rang out, breaking the morning silence. By midmorning, Jamblin stopped by to check in on the boys and to inform them that they would be leaving early Tuesday morning. Jamblin went on to tell the airmen that the hardest and riskiest part of the remaining journey would be crossing the Swiss border as the Nazis patrolled with dogs in search of escaped prisoners, fleeing Jews, and downed airmen.

A few hours later, Jennie came by to visit Maria. Aware of the previous day's incident, Jennie asked Maria if it would be okay for Tucker to attend dinner at her home again that afternoon. Agreeing, Jennie escorted Tucker to her home where Brinkhurst waited.

Upon arriving, Brinkhurst and Tucker quickly started up a new round of cards only to be interrupted by another visitor to Jennie's door. This time it was a Jewish fellow who was a member of the White Army. Hidden away in the next room, Tucker and Brinkhurst listened as the visitor ranted about his situation. Specifically, he was ranting and raving against the Americans. Unfortunately, he had been bombed out of his home, was temporarily angered, and was sounding like an enemy combatant. Enraged at the fact that he was homeless, the visitor admonished the Americans as "young kids, unmarried, who got drunk before going on missions." After about an hour, the visitor left without incident and dinner went on as planned.

Later that evening, in separate groups, Jennie, Brinkhurst, and Tucker went to the local movie house. Roger Jamblin and Goebel were also in attendance. The movie was in French, yet that didn't matter to the airmen. Just the opportunity to get out and live life somewhat normally, even under the watchful eyes of the German occupiers, was a blessing upon itself. The venue had the Belgian Jimmy Dorsey and his orchestra to support the stage show. It sounded funny to the airmen to hear "Rancho Grande" and other tunes in French, but the entertainment was well worth it.

Sitting separately, Goebel and Jamblin were located in a booth adorned with wicker furniture. Enjoying himself, Goebel was engrossed in the feature on the screen. He didn't have to know the language to understand the plot. It was a typical love triangle between two men fighting over one woman.

Focused on the show, Goebel failed to recognize the scene unfolding in real time. A colonel in the Luftwaffe came into the booth next to Goebel's, bringing a very attractive girl with him. Her perfume was tantalizing, and Goebel glanced in the direction of its origin. Momentarily, and without noticing the obvious threat, he internally applauded the man's taste in companionship, then turned his attention back to the screen.

Goebel and the man were separated by a three-foot-high divider. Wide enough, both men were comfortably able to use the partition as an arm rest. Glancing again at the couple, Goebel realized the man was in uniform; he was a colonel. Freezing momentarily, he examined the proximity of the colonel, then looked at his own wrist, resting mere inches away from the German. His stomach sank as he saw that his military-issued Bulova wristwatch was fully exposed. Goebel carefully eased his arm off of the ledge and pulled his wrist back into his sleeve while not taking his eyes off the screen.

Almost in full panic mode, Goebel realized that Jamblin was no longer seated beside him. Looking to his right, he saw Jamblin standing in the shadows against the back wall, motioning to him with frantic hands, urging him to get out post haste. Making the move, and without bringing attention to himself, Goebel got up and left the booth. Now noticeably shaken, Goebel's face was white as if he had seen a ghost. Without a word spoken, he quietly followed Jamblin out of the theater. Staying off the main streets, the pair skirted around many Germans on their way back to House No. 15.

Later that evening while recapping the night's events with Tucker and Westerlund, Goebel noted that good fortune, not intelligence or caution, was with them that evening, and he was thankful to have gone unnoticed.

MAY 14, 1944
BROOKLYN, NEW YORK
1100 HOURS

Shortly after attending morning Mass, Mr. and Mrs. James Goebel headed to the local meeting hall to attend a solemn Mother's Day ceremony. Still reeling from the recent telegram and the uncertainty of her son's whereabouts, Frances Goebel not only attended as a grieving mother; she also helped to support members of her local community. Despite her own worries, Frances stepped forward to lead. As the current president of the Kings County Chapter for the American War Mothers organization, Frances fought back tears as she oversaw the morning's events.

THE LUCKY SEVEN

The next morning, Brinkhurst was back at the cathédrale and under Maria's watchful eye. The group remained in the kitchen and played cards. After a couple of hours and with Maria's permission, the card game broke up with the intent for the group to go for a walk. The five broke into two groups, one trailing the other by a couple of blocks. Tucker, Goebel, and Maria were followed by Brinkhurst and Westerlund.

Around 1400 hours and about two kilometers from the cathédrale, the air raid siren went off. A group of B-17s flew overhead with a delivery for the Germans. Their target was the Liège railroad station and rail line. It appeared as if the bombs had been unloaded right over their heads. The racket made would scare the devil out of any bystander. Taking cover, the swoosh of bombs being expelled, followed by a few moments of silence and then a deafening delivery response rattled the life out of all exposed.

Feeling a safe distance away, the airmen watched the action as it unfolded. Goebel and Tucker looked on as the silver fortresses traveled overhead. The German ground to air artillery was still accurate. They got a direct hit on one B-17, hitting the right wing and taking it clean off at the fuselage. The wounded metal bird immediately burst into flames. It shifted with the nose down, spinning toward the earth like a top. Only three parachutes were seen, with one landing half a block from the onlookers. Thankfully, the Germans were too busy to capture the downed airman, and the Belgian police were able to help him to escape.

During the excitement, Tucker and Goebel failed to notice that Maria had disappeared. After updating Brinkhurst and Westerlund, the four airmen split up again in search of their missing Belgium mother. After several concerning moments, she was discovered a few houses away, hiding in the cellar. Together again, the group headed back to the relative safety of the cathédrale.

Later that evening, Roger Jamblin came by to see the airmen. In addition to scolding Goebel again for his careless mistake, he shared a similar story with the trio regarding a less-than-fortunate downed airman, who failed to see the issue with carrying his toothbrush in his front coat pocket. With oral hygiene not being at the forefront for many in Europe during the war, a simple toothbrush was a flag to the enemy. It screamed, "I am an American!" Fortunately, luck was on Goebel's side. Thankfully, they could also reflect and laugh about his blunder.

Jamblin also informed them that the plan to move them the next morning had been canceled. Apparently, there was something wrong with the transport truck. Now the plan would be to wait until Wednesday morning to leave Liège. Jamblin went on to describe the upcoming journey. Ordinarily, the trip to the Swiss border took six days.

The airmen retired to their room, excited about the news and the prospect that they may be in Switzerland within a week. The idea of being free from the Germans and the ability to contact home was uplifting for the young men.

THE LUCKY SEVEN

The final D-Day briefing for Allied senior officers took place at St Paul's School, London. It was attended by King George VI and Prime Minister Winston Churchill.

MAY 16, 1944—DAY TWENTY-THREE
LIÈGE, BELGIUM
1300 HOURS

After a quiet morning, Tucker and Maria went for one final walk together. Headed north, Maria chose to escort her adopted American son to Fort de Pontisse. Located seven kilometers northeast of the center of Liège, the unreinforced concrete fortress was one of twelve forts built as part of the fortifications of Liège in the late nineteenth century. As a swastika flew above the formidable-looking structure, it now was occupied by the very invaders it was originally designed to repel.

Staying at a safe distance, Maria explained the history of this defensive structure. She then went on to tell Tucker that it now housed Belgian prisoners. Sadly, she shared stories of her fellow countrymen who were executed by the Germans. They had been lined up against the exterior concrete walls, shot, and left for all to see. The act was a grim reminder of the penalty for betraying Germen authority and rule of law. Both Maria and Tucker were at risk for just being in the vicinity, yet doing so was Maria's silent protest and display of disdain toward the Nazi occupiers.

Returning back to the cathédrale, Tucker met with Goebel and Westerlund, who had spent most of the day at House No. 15 with Roger Jamblin. Goebel confirmed the plans for their departure. They would all meet back at House No. 15 in the morning.

The remaining evening was quiet. A somber mood fell over the elder couple, especially Maria. She wanted very much for the young men to remain hiding at the cathédrale until the end of the war because she was worried that something bad would happen to them. Agreeing that they would be careful and remain safe, she finally relinquished. Both Desiré and Maria requested that each send photos of themselves in their uniforms once they were able.

One by one, each man said their farewells in their own way, expressing their gratitude and well wishes. The next day all men would experience a bittersweet departure from their surrogate parents. While they were excited to leave, they recognized that the Demelenne's provided much-needed grounding in a chaotic world. Collectively, the elder couple would be fondly remembered by the airmen as "Pappy and Mammy."

Excited and anxious for the next day, the young men gathered their few belongings and provisions for the trip and retired early. At long last they would be moving on.

THE LUCKY SEVEN

The liberation of Liège finally arrived in late summer when the U.S. First Army, commanded by General Courtney Hodges, captured the Belgian city from Nazi Germany. The liberation occurred during a swift six-day advance across the country from France to the German border.

Between mid-May and their Liberation, the Demelenne's continued their defiance of the Germans. As staunch résistance members, Desiré and Maria went on to hide additional Allied evaders. Goebel, Westerlund, and Tucker were the first American airmen who sought refuge within their home in Liège. Prior to the American trio, on separate occasions, twelve Frenchmen had been hidden with the caretakers. After the three original American airmen departed, Desiré and Maria hosted at different times English, Canadians, and more American serviceman. The last in hiding was an English serviceman who left on September 11, 1944, after Liège's liberation from the Germans. It is rumored that this Englishman would later return and stay on at the cathédrale for four more months.

La Cathédrale Saint Paul bore harder times after Goebel's departure. The cathédrale was exposed to three months of air bombing, which drove its occupants to sleep in the cellar. Nothing struck the holy structure directly; however, one evening a bomb fell near enough to blow out its stained-glass windows and front doors. In the Demelenne's apartment, their furniture, clothes, the room where Goebel had slept, and other places of refuge were severely damaged by the explosion.

A copy of the telegram received by Goebel's mother on May 8, 1944 (above).
Desiré and Maria Demelenne in 1945 (below).

A group photo of the three airmen taken with their Belgium Pappy and Mammy just outside La Cathédrale Saint Paul (from left to right) Tucker, Desiré, Maria, Goebel, and Westerlund.[23]

23 Believed to be taken on Sunday, May 14, 1944, by Roger Jamblin.

*1944 postcard photo of La Cathédrale Saint Paul – Liège, Belgium,
Goebel's home for fifteen days in May 1944.[24, 25]*

24 Goebel's extended stay in Liège was primarily the result of the anticipated Allied invasion (D-Day), which was postponed on numerous occasions in May due to unsuitable weather conditions.

25 Throughout his travel to freedom, Goebel spent a considerable amount
of time hiding in churches and monasteries, yet he and the others never
had the opportunity to attend an actual Mass. However, they all did their
share of praying.

CHAPTER TWENTY-SIX

The Big Day

MAY 17, 1944—DAY TWENTY-FOUR
LIÈGE, BELGIUM
0500 HOURS

PREDAWN ARRIVED LIKE CHRISTMAS morning. Still dark, the three airmen were wide awake and almost giddy with excitement. They were apprehensive about the unknown, yet excited and ready to go. After waiting about an hour, Goebel, Westerlund, and Tucker collected their belongings, headed downstairs, and said their final goodbyes. The only shortcoming on that Wednesday morning was their provisions. Instructed to each have enough food to last three days, Maria was only able to produce two hard-boiled eggs and one sandwich. It was barely enough for one man; however, they would have to make do.

As directed, they made their way to House No. 15 where Roger Jamblin and other members of the résistance were preparing. The ten-minute walk went without incident, and the three airmen reached Holy Cross and House No. 15 before the appointed time of 0630 hours. Arriving first, Goebel, Westerlund, and Tucker were greeted by Jamblin, who asked them to remain inside and out of sight until the remaining travelers arrived. In the meantime, Jamblin would rejoin his team in a nearby firehouse and return to his preparations. Before heading out the door, Jamblin informed Goebel to expect three other Americans and five British airmen. He also confirmed the code for verification. "You doesn't open the door," Jamblin explained in his broken English, reinforcing the expected protocol to the group.

Within a few moments, a familiar knock pattern on the door pierced the silence. It was the first of several to take place over the next thirty minutes. A pattern of three consecutive taps, then a two-second pause followed by two more taps was expected and was successfully received. Goebel opened the door to find two Brits standing in the courtyard. Ushering them inside, the three strangers stood quietly until Goebel spoke and conducted introductions.

"I'm Jim Goebel, and this is Tucker and Westerlund."

The shorter of the three stuck his hand out. "Hi, mate, I'm Reggie Weeden!" His companion, James Lewis, was more cautious and simply acknowledged Goebel with a nod.

Soon, Donald Brinkhurst would arrive, followed by the last two expected Brits, George Flather and Kevin Doyle. Both had been on the same Halifax bomber that had been shot down several weeks earlier on April 28. Lastly, they were joined by three other American airmen, Joseph Pavelka, Philip Solomon, and Charles Weymouth (the ball turret gunner from the Kendziora crew). Goebel, Tucker, and Westerlund were happy to be reunited with their fellow crew member.

Weymouth provided his fellow crew members with a recap of what occurred in the rear of Ruthless Ruth as she went down. He recalled that only Klinginsmith was severely wounded, believing that he had received three slugs in the arm. Weymouth went on to describe the news that had been conveyed to him by his helpers.

Apparently, a horrible event happened to Klinginsmith when he hit the ground. His eye was torn out by a barbed wired fence upon impact, and he was captured by the Germans as the locals could not provide the necessary medical attention. As far as Weymouth knew, everyone else had gotten away safely.

The group of men congregated in the modest home, anxiously awaiting the next move. It was a huge liability having twelve Allied airmen sitting in one location. Anxiety continued to build as things seemed to be taking longer than planned. Roger Jamblin returned and verified that all eleven of the men were in place. He provided a brief update and left No. 15 as quickly as he arrived. At 0800 hours, Jamblin returned to House No. 15 with a fellow helper named Franz Caubergh and what looked to be an ambulance.

A young Flemish man of their same age, Caubergh was tasked to aid them in the next leg of their journey. Like Jamblin, Caubergh had been hardened by the German occupation. A year earlier, when the Germans were losing ground and many men, the Third Reich decreed that all young men within occupied countries about the age of twenty were obliged to join the steel industry in Germany. At the moment, Caubergh had been conscripted as an interpreter for a German commander as he was able to speak English. Before long, his overlord decided that Caubergh would be of more use to them in Germany.

As part of the Nazi forced labor policy, Caubergh soon received orders and a railway ticket for Brandenburg near Berlin. Along the way, he snuck off the train and became a "refractory," or work refuser. In this moment, Caubergh started his life on the run, constantly hiding and running, seeking forged papers and assistance from sympathetic compatriots. Eventually, Caubergh would become a member of the résistance with the hopes of seeking liberty for himself, his family, and his fellow countrymen.

As part of the résistance, Caubergh would aid the local "Group Firquet" by securing hiding places and lodging, obtaining ration coupons, money, and supplies where they could be found. On this day, Caubergh was to accompany the large group of airmen to France and the Swiss border in an effort to gain repatriation. Armed with three other underground members, some French false identity papers, and genuine money needed for the trip, Caubergh was up for the adventure.

It was a crisp spring morning, and it would become a day of enormous chances and a day in which a single fault could have disastrous consequences. After each member of the traveling congregation was issued their new papers, each man was also handed a Red Cross brassard to wear on his arm. Gathering together outside, the priest from Holy Cross offered a blessing over the truck and its soon-to-be contents. As part of the impromptu ceremony, the priest sprinkled holy water on the truck and its occupants and wished them a safe voyage.

Just prior to their departure, it was decided that a group photograph should be taken. Similar to a family gathering, twenty souls posed together to memorialize the occasion. Not only were the hiding airmen in the picture, so were their aids and those who were present at House No. 15 that morning. What a terrific treasure for an unsuspecting German soldier or Gestapo agent had it been found.

At 0830 hours, the group piled into a small, cramped truck with a newly painted Red Cross banner on the front hood and roof. It was a small vehicle, not at all equipped for the transportation of sixteen full-grown men, eleven airmen, four Belgian escorts, and one driver. Earlier that morning within the nearby firehouse, Jamblin and his team spent the predawn hours assembling the interior benches with the hopes of creating enough seating for what was going to be a long journey. Packed like sardines, the young men were cramped but apprehensive, and they were ready for the mission.

The truck pulled away from the back alley and House No. 15, following closely behind a single motorcycle riding advance guard. The caravan passed many German soldiers walking along the road—the very same Germans the Allied forces would later meet when the invasion took place. Only the Belgian escort and the truck driver were to know the exact route through the Ardennes. Unaware to the rear occupants, the truck was to travel through Dinant and Philipville with the goal of crossing into France at Flarenne.

Only providing escort for part of the journey, the motorcycle and the truck separated. Unbeknownst to the others riding in the cab, the truck driver, now unsure of his way, mistakenly took a wrong turn and inadvertently crossed into a German airfield and encampment. The occupants in the rear of the truck had no idea of the impending danger, except Caubergh, who was able to watch the entire spectacle through a small hole in the front of the truck's tarpaulin. Not revealing this disastrous turn of events to his fellow passengers, Caubergh steadily watched and grimaced at the potentially deadly folly that unfolded in front of him.

Caubergh watched as the truck passed by camouflaged German planes, most likely Messerschmitts that were parked alongside of the roadway. The truck's occupants soon heard the distinctive roar of aircraft engines from nearby planes that were readying themselves for takeoff on the very same roadway that their little truck had just made the wrong turn onto. The sound of the idling German aircraft piqued the interest of the men under the tarp. Almost in unison, the airmen blurted out, "What the hell?" Caubergh quickly gestured for them to remain quiet.

Now realizing his mistake, the truck driver scanned for an immediate escape route. Seeing a widening gap and enough room, he made an abrupt U-turn in an effort to make a speedy getaway. As expected, the large airbase was guarded by numerous German guards, and now many were alert to the out-of-place truck, and they watched curiously as the lone ambulance passed by. The driver suddenly saw a means of exit. Trying not to be overly conspicuous, the driver fell in line and started following a departing sedan. The German sentry at the gate motioned the little car to a stop and then signaled the truck driver to halt as well.

The truck driver hesitated but ultimately did not heed this direction and drove straight through an opening adjacent to the gate and the parked sedan. As the truck passed, a German soldier raised his rifle, readied to fire, but did not. Caubergh, watching the German, wondered why he didn't fire his weapon. Did the man just change his mind? Did the Red Cross emblem persuade him otherwise? Or was it simply because the truck's occupants just happened to be lucky that day? For if he had fired, he could have easily taken out several enemy fighters, or at least made a fine capture, which no doubt would have secured him the German Cross of Merit.

Thankfully, the remaining voyage continued without incident, with the truck arriving near Bois de Brûly, Belgium, near the French boarder at 1200 hours. The occupants were aligned in pairs. They removed their brassards, unloaded, and vanished into the nearby woods. As quick as the men were free from the truck's confines, the driver wasted no time in heading back to Liège.

The group started off in a long column of fifteen men, then worked themselves far enough off of the roadside and into woods where they could safely stop to eat lunch and hide out for some time. Approximately two hours later, after a small meal and a rest, the group continued down the road in a semi-inconspicuous pattern, paired off at 300-yard intervals, with Caubergh and his companion, Charles Westerlund, situated in the middle of the group.

After a couple hours of combined walking and hiding in the woods, the group arrived at a small village near the town of Brûly, Belgium. A few days earlier, the underground had contacted the Brûly customs officer, informing him about the impending arrival of the airmen. Arrangements were needed to secure a proper hiding location. Unbeknownst to the airmen, their guides had made their own arrangements. For once they arrived, these accommodations would be preferable and much more comfortable, yet off limits for the Allied evaders.

Progressing faster than anticipated, the group arrived at the village earlier than the appointed time. Without the needed local escort being present, the group was now at a standstill. After a quick assessment, one of the résistance guides went forward to verify that all was safe and nothing had changed. Now somewhat in the open and seeing the need for cover, Caubergh moved the group in pairs to a less-conspicuous location. A sympathetic tavern owner located on the edge of town welcomed the men inside for a quick beer. After adequate time passed, the group left the tavern, found the rail line, and then proceeded down the railroad tracks until two Belgian policemen stopped their guides.

The airmen in the group became nervous when the two patrolmen looked directly at them while questioning their guides. Feeling exposed, the airmen felt relieved when they learned that these policemen sided with the Allies and would opt to lead the group away from danger. Without haste, they were guided through the woods around the nearby small town occupied by Germans. Their walk continued for approximately twelve kilometers, arriving at 1730 hours at a farmhouse near Brûly, Belgium, adjacent to the French border.

After dark, the airmen were lodged upstairs in a room above a café near the main road through town. After safely depositing his human cargo, Caubergh was taken by his local guides to a nearby chateau. The modest home was occupied by a fine family from Oostende, who at the time were hiding several Jewish children. His Belgian companions were to split up; some stayed at the café with the airmen, and one was boarded at the customs officer's house.

Later in the evening, after Caubergh's supper, the lady of the chateau, Franz's hostess, decided that she would like to say hello to the Allied boys. Together with some other members of her family, they made their way down to the center of the village. When Caubergh and his guests got near the café entrance, they suddenly heard the sounds of voices and cries, and upon opening the upstairs door, the visitors saw what appeared to be a pitched battle going on between bunch of men who were obviously drunk, including one hysterical woman, who was not in the least kicking furiously at the lot.

Caubergh tried to intervene by calming them down and attempted to draw attention to their responsibility and the danger they were about to bring down on all of them. Caubergh was angrily ordered to shut up; they were the perceived bosses. In their eyes, he was still a green-horn and new on the job. The noise went on for quite a while and could clearly be heard from outside. This was a huge transgression as the main road was right outside, and German convoys were passing by regularly. Caubergh was frustrated with the irresponsibility of his counterparts, especially from those who were supposedly charged with his and the airmen's lives. In Caubergh's eyes, their arrogance, carelessness, and indiscretion explained why so many underground members died at the hands of the Germans.

Prior to Caubergh's arrival, the airmen were awakened by the sound of the drunken brawl. Unsure if they should also intervene, they quietly waited in their separate room. Finally, once the feuding men were completely drunk and had fallen asleep, Caubergh, with the aid of people from the chateau, gathered the airmen and told them that they would be leaving the café and moving back to a nearby safehouse.

Now close to 2300 hours, the group quietly departed the café and headed back along the railroad tracks from which they arrived. Thankfully, without any further incident, they made it safely back to the Oostende family chateau. In an impromptu manner, each man received a blanket and was then escorted to their final resting place for the evening.

Fortunately, near the chateau there was a separate farmhouse with an accompanying barn with a large, comfortable hayloft. After receiving final instructions from Caubergh, the airmen climbed up the wooden access ladder and piled into the hay. After settling in, each man took off their shoes to nurse the many blisters earned during the long hike earlier that day. Now quietly resting, the group silently burrowed deep inside the hay for the remaining night's sleep. Goebel got out his journal and reported on his latest news:

"5-17 – Liège To Brûly To Barn – More Hay. At Cul De Sarte."

Group photograph taken prior to leaving Liège, Belgium – Franz Caubergh (1), Donald Brinkhurst (2), Charles Westerlund (3), James Goebel (4), Robert Tucker (5), Joseph Pavelka (6), Philip Solomon (7), Reginald Weeden (8), George Flather (9), Charles Weymouth (10). There is one British airman, James Lewis, and one Canadian airman, Kevin Doyle, known to be in the photo but remain unidentifiable. As well, there appears to be seven résistance members and one young girl within the group. It is unknown if Lambert Hosdin (and/or his daughter) is one of the unidentified individuals.

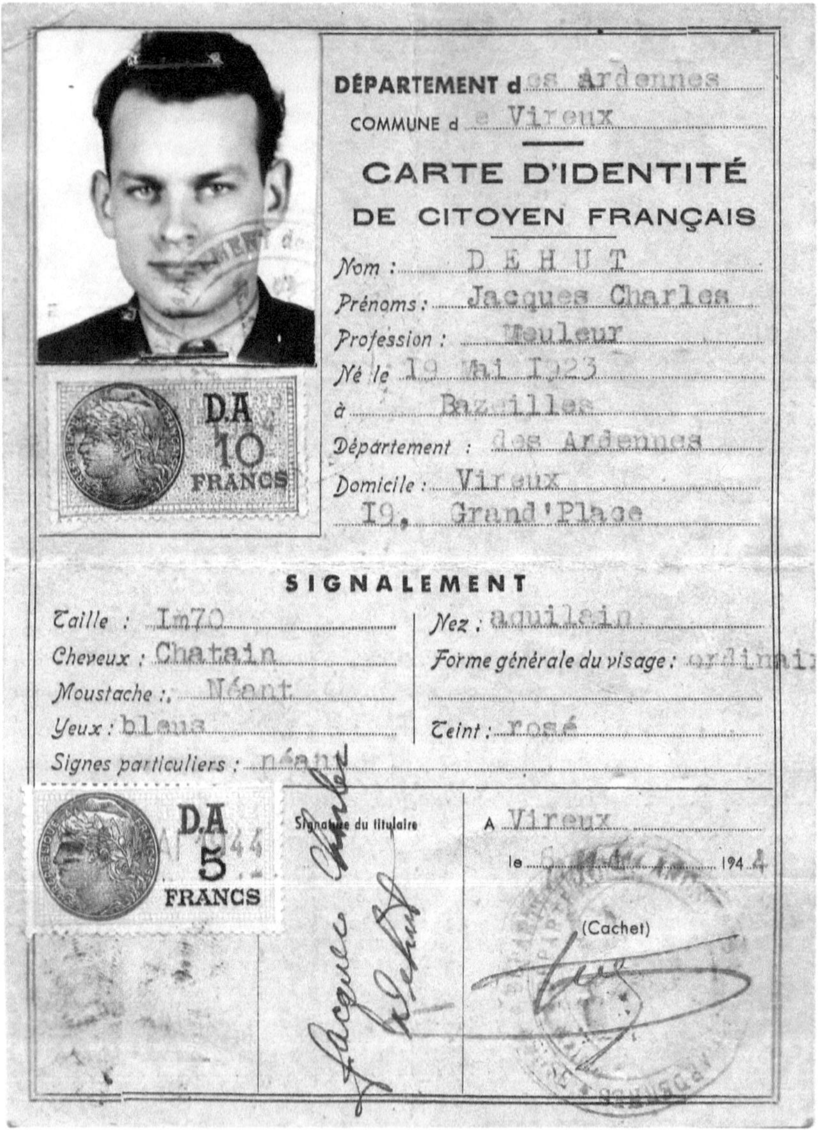

DÉPARTEMENT des Ardennes
COMMUNE de Vireux

CARTE D'IDENTITÉ
DE CITOYEN FRANÇAIS

Nom : DEHUT
Prénoms : Jacques Charles
Profession : Meuleur
Né le 19 Mai 1923
à Bazeilles
Département : des Ardennes
Domicile : Vireux
19, Grand'Place

D.A 10 FRANCS

SIGNALEMENT

Taille : 1m70
Cheveux : Chatain
Moustache : Néant
Yeux : bleus
Signes particuliers : néant
Nez : aquilein
Forme générale du visage : ordinaire
Teint : rosé

D.A 5 FRANCS

Signature du titulaire

A Vireux
le ... 194.
(Cachet)

Goebel's French false identity papers, believed to be provided to him by Roger Jamblin and Franz Caubergh before leaving Liège, Belgium. Goebel's alias was Jacques Charles Dehut, who resided in Vireux, France, a small town on the Belgium/France border.

CHAPTER TWENTY-SEVEN

Broken Escape Chain

May 18, 1944—Day Twenty-Five
Brûly, Belgium
0600 Hours

EARLY THE NEXT MORNING, Caubergh confronted the two very hungover and now ashamed men. Faced with the reality that the eleven airmen, whom they were responsible for, had been kidnapped right from under their noses, they stood red-faced. In the midst of the younger résistance member chastising and admonishing his older compatriots, a local informant arrived and notified the group that their planned departure was delayed due to the railroads being bombed out between Brûly and Charleville, France. The long-established escape chain and part of the Comète Line had been broken.

Upon hearing this news, the four guides unanimously decided that going forward now with the Allied airmen would be futile and dangerous. It was agreed that they would separate. The two eldest guides would go ahead to determine when the entire group could continue on safely while the other two would remain with the airmen. Agreeing to a path forward, Caubergh and his one assigned companion returned back to the farmhouse to inform the airmen.

Hearing the bad news from their guides, the airmen's posture visibly sank for a moment. Now listening closely, Caubergh informed the airmen that they would be remaining in the barn until safe passage could be arranged. Realizing that their fate was unknown and that there was little for them to do at the moment, the airmen turned to the pastime that easily occupied their attention: playing cards.

Held up within the confines of the barn, the airmen exchanged stories and played several rounds. Pavelka told the group that he had gotten up during the night to relieve himself and on the way to the ladder struggled to see where to walk. Between the darkness of the loft and the fact that everyone was thoroughly buried in the hay, he fully expected to step on his fellow fliers.

Around midday, their guests and a couple of townspeople arrived at the barn with lunch for the eleven hungry evaders. The locals were absolutely friendly and giving, bringing treats of sandwiches, red cabbage, meat, and beer. The airmen enjoyed the small feast of food and companionship, almost forgetting their circumstances for a moment.

The afternoon would become even more entertaining when the group pitched in to buy a bottle. One of their visitors agreed and made the trip to the nearby tavern. Returning with two bottles of locally distilled gin, the airmen circled up and passed the beverage amongst themselves. In the midst of their midday celebration, a local Belgian border guard stopped by the barn to check on the young men. The unexpected guest was welcomed with the invitation of a couple snorts.

The party broke up abruptly when two German soldiers on motorcycles were heard heading their direction. All but Brinkhurst and Tucker scampered into the loft and buried themselves under the hay. The Germans parked their bikes, lit cigarettes, and stood under the shade of a tree. Brinkhurst and Tucker quietly stood guard within the interior shadows of the barn, peering through the cracks of the siding and watching the soldiers' every move. Remaining motionless, the two airmen kept an eye on the Germans, who positioned themselves in front of the farmhouse. After more than two hours, the Germans got back on their bikes and ultimately rode off. Once out of sight, Brinkhurst and Tucker signaled all-clear. The other nine men emerged from the hay and returned to the barn floor. With the Germans safely gone, the party continued.

Later that evening, another good meal was brought to the barn. Dinner was complemented by drinks, which were sent over by local townspeople from the nearby tavern. The party lasted until 2300 hours and, after enjoying a small feast of food, libations, and companionship, the group piled deep inside the hay for another warm night's sleep.

CHAPTER TWENTY-EIGHT

Twenty-First Birthday

May 19, 1944—Day Twenty-Six
Brûly, Belgium
0100 Hours

ANY HOPE OF SLEEPING off the side effects of the previous day's celebrations was cut short when their slumber was interrupted by Caubergh and his fellow résistance guide. Growing concerns over the amount of local attention surrounding the presence of the Allied aviators had reached its peak. Caubergh decided it would be best for the group to move, and move fast.

Now fully awake and gathered together, Caubergh informed the airmen that they would be leaving the barn for a new hiding spot. Concerned that a Belgian collaborator would soon tip off the Germans, Caubergh did not want to risk spending another night here. All thirteen men slipped out of the barn and into the chill of the predawn darkness, made their way to the rail line, and ran down the tracks to a nearby chateau.

Waiting for them as arranged by Caubergh was a small truck large enough to accommodate five comfortably. All eleven piled in with the driver, leaving Caubergh and his fellow guide behind. The small truck plodded about seven kilometers without the lights on to a monastery located in Petite-Chapelle, Belgium. Upon arrival, the airmen were received by a young, bearded monk. The driver and the monk exchanged pleasantries, then the truck quietly rolled off in the direction that it had arrived from.

The young Capuchin monk greeted the group of eleven men cautiously. Speaking broken English, he led the way and escorted the airmen inside the modest stone structure. The airmen were divided into two groups. Goebel, Brinkhurst, Westerlund, Tucker, Pavelka and Solomon went in one room; Weymouth, Weeden, Flather, Lewis, and Doyle were assigned to the adjacent room. Each shared room was sparsely outfitted with only six spring bed frames. The men claimed their spot and lay on a thin straw mattress. Happily off the ground and out of the hay, the men had the comfort of being sheltered.

Later that morning, they were awakened at 0900 hours for breakfast and were led to a dining room where coffee, bread, and jelly were on the table. Wanting to better understand who their hosts were, the airmen, through Tucker and Solomon speaking French, peppered the young monk with a barrage of questions. The airmen soon learned that the only inhabitants of the monastery at the moment of their arrival were the monk and his older sister. The monastery was located in a very small town only two hundred meters from the French-Belgium border. The town's only other structures were a church, four houses, and a tavern.

Later that morning, Caubergh and his partner arrived on borrowed bicycles. Caubergh had befriended the monk and his sister as they were also of Flemish descent. Thankfully, for the sake of the Allied airmen, Caubergh was able to make quick and easy contact with the couple. With the monk insisting, Caubergh and his résistance partner would remain with the airmen at the monastery from that point forward.

Caubergh rounded up the airmen in the dormitory and informed them of the latest report. The two eldest guides, who had previously left the group in Brûly, returned with bad news that the railroad was impassable. Separately, the four guides agreed that the following day the same two eldest guides would return to Liège. They would meet with résistance leaders and fetch the truck for a planned return trip back to Liège. Now sullen, the airmen stewed on the news.

The group broke up, with some heading outside to get fresh air. The bucolic estate was picturesque with rolling hills and an open meadow. The only distraction was a single German soldier who passed by on patrol riding a motorbike. The main road was far enough away that the airmen could easily hide themselves behind the stone structure.

That evening, Goebel and his cadre of friends would celebrate his twenty-first birthday with a delicious meal comprised of pork chops and trappist beer, followed by an evening of cards. All would retire by 2200 hours.

**"5-19 – 0100 Petite Chapelle –
Capuchin Monk and Sister – Meat – Um"**

CHAPTER TWENTY-NINE

An Alternative Plan

May 20, 1944—Day Twenty-Seven
Petite-Chapelle, Belgium
0800 Hours

AFTER A FOURTH NIGHT of sleeping in their clothes, the airmen were in dire need of a spruce-up. With little more than a basin of hot water and a bar of soap, each man took turns using the only safety razor available to the group. Missing their electric razor and fearing the need for a facial graph from the irregular grader-like effect, the men took care not to scar themselves.

Once done, the men made their way to the commissary for another fulfilling meal. If there was one thing the airmen could not complain about, it was the fact that they certainly received enough to eat. The monk's sister did an excellent job preparing meals for the group.

A rainy chill enveloped the monastery and the surrounding countryside. The sour weather, their unknown future, and the waiting were beginning to grate on the airmen. The Englishmen, specifically Reggie, did not appreciate the Americans' ribbing and friendly arguments about the RAF versus the USAAF. The men sat in small circles and played cards while trying not to freeze.

Later that afternoon, Caubergh and his companion discussed the possibilities of the entire group returning to Liège for the duration of the war with the intent to fight with the White Army. Hearing this plan, Brinkhurst, Tucker, and Goebel began discussing an alternative plan. Together, the three departed from their dorm room only to corner the monk alone in his abbacy. After sharing their plan, the monk pulled a map of France from a drawer and soon the group was huddled around a small table. Advising the group of what he thought would be the best route, the young airmen concluded that they would go it alone if the news from Liège was unacceptable.

The trio thanked the monk for his guidance and the map. They departed only to adjourn back to a secluded spot within the dormitory. With the most experience evading the Germans, Brinkhurst headed up the planning session. The three contemplated their options and roughed out a plan to Switzerland. They were determined not to return to Liège.

May 20, 1944
Brooklyn, New York
Afternoon

The following telegram was sent by Goebel's older brother, Robert J. Goebel, to his parents upon hearing of his brother James's fate. Robert was a First Lieutenant serving within the U.S. Seventh Army. As an officer in the U.S. Army Signal Corps, Robert operated in the

European Theatre of Operations (ETO) as a trained photographer and cameramen. It is believed that Robert was stationed on the Italian front at the time of this communication.

"SENT SANSORIGINE[26] ON 20 MAY 1944

MR JAMES GOEBEL
1375 BROOKLYN AVE BROOKLYN NY
JUST RECEIVED YOUR LETTERS ABOUT JIM
MISSING PERIOD WIRE ME WHEN YOU RECEIVE
MORE NEWS BOB GOEBEL"

★ ★ ★ ★ ★ ★ ★

First Lieutenant Robert J. Goebel

26 *Sansorigine* is French for "without origin," meaning his origin is being kept secret.

CHAPTER THIRTY

Cruising P-51s

May 21, 1944 – Day Twenty-Eight
Petite-Chapelle, Belgium
1400 Hours

THE AFTERNOON WAS CLEAR and sunny, much improved from the day prior, but still a little cool. The airmen had migrated outside to get some much-needed exercise. Each man was growing weak and lazy from little physical activity and all the idle card playing.

Caubergh departed earlier on his daily trip to the surrounding villages and farms to collect needed food supplies. Armed with his basket and cash, he cycled around seeking meats, vegetables, breads, and cheeses that were still available at the time. Luckily, their location in the small villages and peasant country had better provisions than the larger towns as they were closer to the actual food source. With the money he had been previously given, Caubergh was able to obtain provisions enough for the fifteen inhabitants of the monastery.

The monk's sister did all the cooking for the group, and each individual could honestly admit that their stay at the monastery was not disagreeable at all. The monastery was clean and tidy with a large dormitory that easily accommodated the visiting group. The beds were comfortable, and the airmen were disposed to play on a large exercise ground. Unfortunately, on more than one occasion, Caubergh was forced to speak to the young men about being less conspicuous as the main road was not far from the monastery compound, making it easy for the few local residents to spy on the new visitors in town.

The excitement for the day came when two P-51 Mustangs cruised overhead. The American airmen gawked as the fighters flew past, waving and taking to the pilots as if they could be heard over the roaring 1500 horsepower engines. At a minimum, it gave the airmen a sorely needed morale boost. This chance experience also further cemented their plan to hit the road to Switzerland if the news from Liège was unacceptable.

By late afternoon, Westerlund, Pavelka, and Solomon had agreed to join the three original musketeers. Now there were six, with Charles Weymouth still on the fence. The initial plan created by Brinkhurst, Tucker, and Goebel (based on the monk's recommendations) was to move forward without the assistance of the Comète Line and head for Besancon, France. They would leave the monastery, cross the border, and pass-through Maquis country, hoping to make contact with the rural guerrilla bands of French résistance fighters.

Day three came to an end with no news from Liège. By now, all of the occupants of the monastery were becoming a bit frazzled. For the airmen, the earlier morale boost was waning, and the thought of playing cards was only made better by the possible sentence of utter boredom.

CHAPTER THIRTY-ONE

New Arrivals

May 22, 1944—Day Twenty-Nine
Petite-Chapelle, Belgium
0900 Hours

AFTER BREAKFAST, THE GROUP made their way outside to soak up the morning sun. A similar performance to the prior day, the days were getting longer and warmer. Now fully aligned in tribes, the team of six versus the others continued planning for their alternative escape route. Gathered together, they challenged as many of the details as possible. Ultimately acknowledging that there would be great risk going forward alone. It would be especially rough if they were unable to secure help along the way.

While the airmen were outside, the monk approached Caubergh with the news that the group had to leave the monastery as soon as possible because the next day he was expecting a group of clergymen who were coming for a religious retreat. The monk could not run the risk of the two groups meeting as he was unsure of his visitors' political opinions. It was well-known that some of the clergy, at least in Belgium, had manifested some sympathy for the social democratic regime of Germany, both before and during the war. Hearing this announcement, Caubergh was very unhappy with the monk, to say the least. Unfortunately, there was nothing else to do but look for a new shelter. Acknowledging this request and the monk's obvious fear for his and his sister's lives, Caubergh immediately shifted his focus. Without a word to the airmen, he left the monastery, got on his bicycle, and began the search.

Making matters worse, earlier that morning Caubergh's companion guide became frustrated with the two eldest guides and their delay in returning. He decided to take it upon himself to head back to Liège and find out what the holdup was, subsequently leaving Caubergh as the sole guardian to eleven airmen.

Unaware of what was brewing, the airmen passed the time outside training on their makeshift exercise course. That afternoon, while Brinkhurst was climbing up a rope, Tucker began swinging him when the rope unexpectedly gave way. Brinkhurst cascaded to the ground, making a three-point landing on a stone pathway. Tumbling onto his head, he was dazed but thankfully not unconscious.

Within a few hours, Caubergh had returned with good news for the monk. Luckily, he had found an old, deserted house not far away. Once a parochial patronage where the youth met and performed theatre, it was now partly destroyed and full of rubbish, but it would have to do. Sharing his plan with the monk, Caubergh intended to move the airmen over after their evening meal. Hearing the news, the monk still exhibited some trepidation. Caubergh now only had to break the news to the airmen.

Just before sitting down in the commissary, a new arrival appeared on the front steps of the stone sanctuary. The monk greeted the two men while everyone else stayed out of sight. After a brief conservation, the monk returned inside with his newest guest. A new young face joined the group in hiding, an American P-38 pilot named First Lieutenant Jack W. Holton. Holton's P-38 suffered mechanical failure over Belgium earlier that month while on a sortie escorting B-17 bombers to Germany. Holton was delivered by his benefactor, a local farmer who had been caring for him but needed assistance connecting Holton with the White Army boys. Wanting to get to Switzerland, Holton easily joined his winged fraternity, increasing Cauberg's total headcount to twelve.

Soon after their meal was complete and once the skies had fully darkened, Franz escorted the airmen across the open ground to their new palace. One by one, the airmen slipped from their stone sanctuary into the darkness of night. A new moon and a clear sky made it difficult to navigate, yet each trip for Caubergh became a little easier. With only the clothes on their backs and some rations of food, the airmen made the short ten-minute journey.

The nighttime air was cold, and the entire group (except Brinkhurst) would pass the night shivering. The shrewd one, Brinkhurst, had quickly found some old theater cloth to wrap himself in. Later that evening around 2200 hours, the monk came over, openly scared, expressing his concern that the townspeople knew the airmen were there. This was grave as these people were treated badly by the Germans and in an effort to gain favor, a local might give them away. The monk, wanting them to leave in the morning, offered them 10,000 French francs ($200 U.S.). However, the group insisted on waiting one more day for the guides to return from Liège. Frustrated, the monk returned to the monastery while the thirteen men settled in for a frigid night's rest on the worn stage floor only sparsely covered with a few sprigs of straw.

CHAPTER THIRTY-TWO

The Lucky Seven

May 23, 1944—Day Thirty
Petite-Chapelle, Belgium
0730 Hours

THE CRIES OF CURIOUS children peeping through the broken windows startled the slumbering men awake. In an instant, they ran off before anyone could rise to their feet. Stiff, drowsy, and cold, the team of thirteen began milling around their new surroundings. In addition to looking for a private spot to relieve themselves, they also scouted for what treasures they could find. The structure had been abandoned for many years, and it was stingy when it came to relinquishing items of value.

The group wanted to start a fire, but doing so would give their position away to the Germans. That is, assuming the townspeople or the children had not done so already. By now, it had to be known widely to the inhabitants of this private village that a bunch of strange men had moved in.

No different than any previous morning, playing cards were pulled from pockets, and the pairs of airmen went to work passing time. Some continued to scrounge for any items of interest. Tucker found a single dart after rummaging for about an hour. This find quickly led to a new pastime. Taking turns, the group played darts for a few hours.

Soon after the morning alarm from the local children, Caubergh realized that they were no longer safe, and he had to move the men. Telling the group his plan, he set out to look for new shelter. From his earlier rounds of collecting food supplies, Caubergh knew he had little options. Pedaling, he made his way back to the chateau in Brûly. Returning to the farmhouse, he once again summoned the help of the truck owner. Together, they formulated a plan to relocate the twelve airmen.

Before returning to the abandoned theatre in Petite-Chapelle, Caubergh rode his bike to the local tavern where, to his surprise, he stumbled upon the two eldest guides and his recently departed companion. Now angry, Caubergh wanted nothing more to do with these men of consumption, yet he knew that twelve souls were still depending on him.

Between sips of their beer, the two eldest informed Caubergh that the White Army leaders back in Liège had given up on the original plan of guiding the airmen to Switzerland. He was also told that the Allied invasion was rumored to take place any day now, and they were instructed to bring the airmen back to Liège. The group had orders to get their organizations in order and prepare for an impending invasion. Caubergh knew they could not simply pack up the entire group in the middle of the day and risk being caught by the Germans. He also knew that the men were sitting ducks at their current location. The risk was high, yet Caubergh had to stick with his original plan. Making final arrangements with the White Army trio, he departed the tavern and cycled back to the airmen.

Returning midday, Caubergh found the group entertaining themselves with a single dart. Anxious, they quickly gathered around him to hear what the next steps would be. Caubergh advised the group that they would be leaving momentarily; however, he did not mention a word about returning to Liège. They were to leave from the back side of the abandoned playhouse and enter the woods. Out of sight of any roads or other structures, the men still darted in a synchronized formation from their shelter to the adjacent forest. Once together, the group marched through the neighboring woods for little more than an hour. The four-kilometer walk was quiet; not a word was spoken. Caubergh led the group while he pushed and sometimes carried his borrowed bicycle.

Arriving near the prearranged meeting location, the group halted and rested on the ground. The late afternoon sun cascaded streams of light onto the forest floor. Each man adjusted themselves, finding a comfortable spot to catch the available rays of warmth. After eating their only meal for the day, consisting of dry jellied bread with no water, Caubergh confirmed the time and got up to leave. He quietly pointed to three of the men and signaled for them to follow.

Caubergh led the smaller group to the edge of the road where the farm truck was parked. Even though he and the truck driver had picked a secluded location between Petite-Chapelle and Brûly to meet, the group remained vigilant. Visual cues directed the airmen to their positions. Two men lay in the bed of the truck with a tarp pulled over them, while the third man crouched on the floorboard next to the driver. The driver safely deposited his cargo at an isolated farmhouse located six kilometers away. The thirty-minute round trip returned the truck back to its pickup location where Caubergh and the next three airmen awaited.

It was nearing dusk when the last load, including Caubergh, disembarked at the farmhouse. After an acknowledgement of their safe arrival, Caubergh hugged the driver, gave him a handful of francs for his efforts, and watched him drive away for good. He turned and walked to the barn where the airmen were directed to congregate. Now safely united, Caubergh broke the news about his orders and their impending return to Liège.

Donald Brinkhurst was outraged and would not hear of backtracking to Liège. Brinkhurst had a goal, and it was to get to Switzerland. He challenged the other airmen on their decision to go back or continue on. Brinkhurst was successful in his efforts as six others agreed to join him. To the Americans' surprise, Charles Weymouth decided to return to Liège along with the four remaining British airmen. It was decided. Brinkhurst, Tucker, Westerlund, Holton, Goebel, Solomon, and Pavelka would go it alone. The rest (Weeden, Lewis, Doyle, Flather, and Weymouth) would return to Liège with the White Army boys.

For some, the reality of their decision began to take root. For Goebel, it brought a wave of exhilaration and trepidation all at once. Recognizing the significance of their next moves and the impending risk, Goebel sat quietly and reflected. After a few moments, he collected a dozen small pieces of paper and a pencil. One by one, Goebel and the other eleven airmen recorded their name or next of kin and home address. While there was some risk carrying this information, the group agreed to notify each other's family once they were liberated.

Later that evening, the group was treated to dinner at the farmhouse. After a filling meal, their host brought out an old radio. One of the Americans quickly found a radio station that broadcasted Allied Air, which played their favorite songs. Hearing the big band and swing music, the group provided their Belgium hosts and their faithful guide with an exhibition of how the boogie-woogie could be danced. This quick musical interlude allowed the group to dance and forget their precarious situation, if for only a moment. The evening was rounded out with a toast to their future endeavors. Raising his glass of wine, Jack Holton toasted his six fellow airmen and coined a name for the group choosing to head for Switzerland. Cheers to **"The Lucky Seven."**

Franz Caubergh (1944)

PART FIVE

Going It Alone

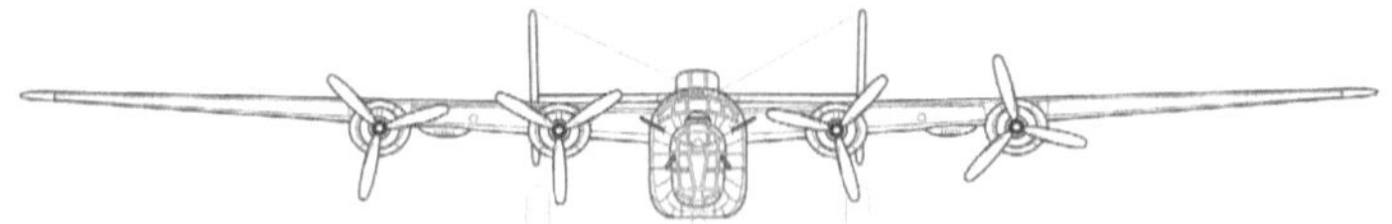

CHAPTER THIRTY-THREE

A Path of Cards

May 24, 1944—Day Thirty-One
Near Petite-Chapelle, Belgium
0430 Hours

THE AIRMEN ROSE AT the appointed time in preparation for their planned departure. Still dark, the men crawled from their burrows nestled within the large, comfortable hayloft. Making their way from the accompanying barn, they crossed the courtyard to the farmhouse. Still in the low fifties, the cool air helped to cleanse any residue of sleep from their bodies. Pausing to relieve himself near a large tree, Goebel looked up at the early morning sky, deducing that it would not be light for another sixty to seventy minutes. Apprehensive about the coming day, he shook the cobwebs from his mind and walked the rest of the distance to the rear of the farmhouse.

Once inside, the madame of the home had prepared a bucket of hot water for the young men to wash up before sitting down for breakfast. The farmhouse kitchen wasn't large enough for all twelve of the airmen to sit at one table, so the men dispersed themselves accordingly. While waiting for Caubergh, the airmen made small talk and confirmed the group promise that the first to get through would make the proper family notifications.

After the previous evening's festivities had wrapped up, Caubergh had made his way back to Brûly to join up with his three underground companions. Armed with a list of items needed for the travelers to Switzerland, he scavenged for any items that he could find in the early morning hours. The four résistance members climbed into the makeshift ambulance and headed to the farmhouse where the airmen were awaiting their arrival.

At 0600 hours, the White Army boys pulled into the yard and parked the small truck behind the barn and out of sight of any German patrols. Before departing, Caubergh issued the Swiss travelers each a few hundred francs and offered a handful of provisions to split between them. While doing so, he apologized to the group, wishing it could have been more. Accepting the parting gifts, each man was truly grateful for all that Caubergh had done for them over the past seven days. Caubergh and his group of airmen felt more connected than at any point in the past week; however, soon their roads would diverge.

The two eldest guides were in a hurry and quickly loaded the group into the back of the small truck. They headed a few kilometers back to Petite-Chapelle, stopping short of the edge of town, yet near enough to the French border. Before exiting the truck, Brinkhurst, Tucker, Westerlund, Holton, Goebel, Solomon, and Pavelka said their goodbyes and offered the others good luck wishes. Two guides then escorted the group of seven to a path that led to the border crossing. Signaling the way, the two turned, walked back to the truck, got in, and drove away, leaving only a cloud of dust as evidence. With less than 4000 French francs ($80 U.S.) amongst them, false identity papers (some without pictures), and over five hundred kilometers to travel, the determined group of seven airmen embarked on their journey to find freedom.

May 24, 1944—Day Thirty-One
Belgium-France Border
0615 Hours

Before crossing, the airmen divided themselves into three smaller units to reduce the risk of the entire group being captured. Tucker and Brinkhurst were the first group, then came Westerlund, Holton, and Goebel, followed by Solomon and Pavelka. Each unit left in five-minute intervals with the goal to cross the French border and regroup safely on the other side. The first group made it across with only a disconcerting glance from the border guard. The second group was stopped by the guard. Recognizing that these three were not regular commuters, the guard started questioning the young men. As none of the three spoke French, Holton unwisely offered up that they were Americans. Hearing this, the guard paused, then in broken English asked them if they had enough food. Affirmatively nodding their heads, the trio moved forward without delay. Luckily for them, the guard was unsympathetic to the German cause. The last group passed with only a wink and a smile as they slipped over the border five minutes later.

Now strung along a half-kilometer line, the seven airmen walked the six kilometers from the Belgian frontier through the French Ardennes to the edge of the ancient fortress town of Rocroi, France. Along the way, they witnessed many signs of war as they passed the remains of abandoned and destroyed French defensive pillboxes and concrete fortifications.

At a brisk pace, they were able to reach the town just after 0700 hours. Brinkhurst and Tucker arrived at the bus station first, only to realize that they were an hour early for the next scheduled bus headed south. Soon, the other two parties arrived. Now gathered together, they quickly realized their group looked suspicious loitering around town while they waited. Not wanting to stand out any more to the locals, the airmen quickly dispersed around town. A few cafes, the network of narrow streets, and the great bastions surrounding the small town provided adequate cover and hiding holes for the men.

Agreeing to return ten minutes before the hour, the airmen made their way back to the station only to witness the morning ritual of townspeople leaving in trucks on their way to do war work for the Nazis. The bus arrived and the seven airmen tried to board without bringing attention to themselves. As scheduled, the 0800-bus departed for Charleville-Mézières, France.

The thirty-kilometer bus ride took more than an hour, making several stops along the way. The bus passed through Nazi-infested territory where they would have had no hope of traveling on foot past so many well-armed soldiers. From their seats, they watched as the French people struggled in a German-occupied life.

Their bus arrived in Charleville-Mézières, just in time for the daytime bombing by the Americans. In an effort to avoid the bombing, the driver stopped the bus on the northwest edge of town. The driver's chosen location could not have been more unsettling for the airmen. Now parked in front of what looked to be a German prison camp, the airmen sunk in their seats. The stout structure was decorated with barbed wire, fortifications, and numerous red, black, and white swastika flags. The bus sat idle as the German ack-ack batteries hammered the sky and German soldiers ran around their parked bus. Motionless, the bus remained in place for a half hour while bombers completed their mission and relative silence once again dominated the landscape.

A larger town of roughly 21,000 French residents, Charleville-Mézières was being softened in preparation of an impending invasion. The rail marshaling yard and the German manufacturing infrastructure were the primary targets for the Allies. Ironically, two weeks earlier Jack Holton had helped to escort B-26 Marauders on a bombing raid of the town's central train station. Holton shared this revelation with Goebel as their bus meandered its way through town. Moving once more, the bus continued its route into town, but it did not stop at main bus terminal, confusing the airmen. Instead, they were ultimately dropped off in what appeared to be a Third Reich den.

MAY 24, 1944—DAY THIRTY-ONE
CHARLEVILLE-MÉZIÈRES, FRANCE
1000 HOURS

The airmen disembarked from the bus and headed down the first street they came upon without Germans. Unfortunately, after a few hundred meters, it dead-ended into the Meuse River. Now feeling cornered, the group realized they had to spread out. Again, the seven men broke into their three smaller groups. With Brinkhurst and Tucker assuming the lead, they looked for a viable way across the river. The other two groups also dispersed with the goal of meeting on the eastern bank of the Meuse.

First, Brinkhurst and Tucker attempted to cross a railroad bridge but were stopped by the sight of a German sentry box and machine gun posted across the river on a hill. They immediately backtracked and tried walking along the railroad yard. As they progressed through the bombed-out but very active yard, the pair passed three separate German guards in elevated towers manning machine guns. Finding it difficult to avoid their line of sight, it became obvious to the pair that these sentries were positioned to guard against thieves trying to steal coal from the German-occupied freight yard. The men realized that in lieu of trying to sneak through the yard, it was safer to walk as if they belonged there.

Goebel, Westerlund, and Holton, followed by Solomon and Pavelka, backtracked up the street towards the bus stop. While looking for an auto bridge to cross, the group quickly realized that something was off. The streets were empty. The townspeople were clearly expecting something more as they were all still in shelters from the earlier bombing raid. Unencumbered, the airmen progressed across town, traveling separately through the railroad yard and quiet streets.

The lead group finally found an avenue that seemed like a safe place to cross, but in the process had managed to get separated from the other five airmen. Tucker and Brinkhurst waited for a short period and then backtracked to find the others. Making their way through town, they found the group in an alley near a small town square only a few blocks from the railroad yard. Unfortunately, it seemed like every sizable building near the park appeared to be part of German headquarters.

As if on cue, the all-clear siren rang. People started moving back out onto the streets. This gave the airmen the break that they needed, allowing them to move safely away from the park. As they walked with the flow of people, the men became concerned with how they would cross the bridge and exit the town as there was a Wehrmacht officer on their tail. The German began to speed up as he wanted to intercept the airmen. Unexpectedly, the air raid siren went off again, signaling another impending bombing raid. Thankfully, this gave the group the opportunity to run across the nearest bridge and away from town in a mix of scared townspeople. Now on the east side of the Meuse, the airmen broke into smaller groups, hustled to the outskirts of the populated area, and inconspicuously slipped into the woods.

Now in a full run through the trees, the airmen pushed themselves for about twenty minutes in an effort to gain distance from town. Upon reaching an isolated area, each group slowed and then began hobbling around in small concentric loops until all had made it safely. Desperate to regain their wind from the run, they stopped, caught their breath, and surveyed for a comfortable spot to rest. One by one they fell to the ground. Each was overwhelmed by the extreme pain throbbing within their feet resulting from the ill-fitting shoes. All seven pulled their shoes off and examined their feet for damage. In unanimous agreement, they took an hour-long break and ate the small lunch provided by Caubergh.

Before resuming, the group discussed methods of marking the trail. They needed a way to ensure that they didn't get separated from each other again. Looking at their available resources, they decided to employ the use of their playing cards. As agreed, the lead group would start dropping playing cards at one-hundred-meter increments as they moved along, thus marking the trail for the next two groups. The middle group would reposition the cards as needed to ensure visibility, and the trailing group would gather them up so no one else could follow. With fifty-two cards in a deck, that would extend out to five kilometers, at which point they would regroup, take a break, and start over.

Now aligned on their planned direction, the groups started out again in five-minute intervals. Heading southeast across country, they traveled through fields, forests, and farms. As much as possible, they tried to stay off of the roads. In their travels, they came upon a .50 caliber waist window gun from a Liberator lying in a field. This was a sobering discovery for the airmen.

Later, during one of their breaks, Brinkhurst and Tucker had an unexpected exchange with two German sentries. While sitting alongside a road resting under a tree, two Germans came along on motorbikes. The lead rider stopped adjacent to the resting pair. Without dismounting, the soldier began questioning the young men in German about their papers. Brinkhurst and Tucker stood but did not move toward the soldier. At the same time, the second rider pulled up, motioned to his partner, and sped off. The first German disengaged from the airmen, put his bike in gear, and sped off. Another lucky break for the men that day.

Progressing south, the airmen walked about fourteen kilometers in total, with very little to nothing to drink all day. They desperately wanted to stop, but ultimately, they pushed on. Luckily, on the outskirts of one small town, they were able to find a clean source of water flowing from a spring that fed into a horse trough. The men dropped to their knees and with cupped hands gulped as much of the cool fluid as they could.

At approximately 1700 hours and overcome by lassitude, the airmen staggered to a stop in a grove of trees. In the distance, no more than a hundred meters away, the airmen could clearly see a farmhouse with several children playing and a woman who was scrubbing clothes in the yard. Quickly spotted by the young eyes, the airmen became a topic of interest, receiving funny looks from the children. Fatigued by little food and water, the group sat with little care and some complacency while they each tended to their swollen and blistered feet. While not moving from their resting place, a small boy approached and, without prompting, offered his name and asked if they would like to rest at his house. Weary and somewhat skeptical, the airmen gratefully accepted the young boy's offer with very little internal debate and began to follow him.

As they neared, the madame of the farm paused from her chores and listened to her youngest son's explanation. Looking up at the seven young men, she motioned them closer. The venerable woman stood calmly as the men approached. In relatively good English, Madame Marcelle Hourrier introduced herself and her youngest son, Serge. The airmen reciprocated by sharing their names and nationalities and conveyed that they were on their way to Switzerland.

After brief introductions, Madame Marcelle explained that she was the head of the house with twelve children of her own, Serge being the youngest. There were two other children and five other individuals on the property who she was supporting, totaling twenty souls. And now she was looking at seven more mouths to feed, thanks to her son's impromptu invitation. She could not offer them much, but they were welcome to stay. Hearing this, the men gracefully declined the boy's offer, yet Madame Marcelle would not hear of it.

She went on to explain that not all in her keeping were her own kin. She had recently taken in another family that had been living in Charleville-Mézières but had been bombed out by American bombers two weeks ago. This revelation made the airmen feel a little uncomfortable as their efforts were leading to hardship for good people.

Undaunted by the extra mouths to feed, Madame Marcelle insisted that the airmen stay with her, if only to ensure that the airmen would receive the help necessary to escape to Switzerland.

After a brief tour of the farm, Madame Marcelle invited the young men into her busy home. As if a human whirlwind, she swiftly presented the airmen sardines, bread, and wine. She even butchered and prepared a rabbit for dinner.

Feeling sorry for the young men, she filled a small tub with water after dinner so that each man could soak his exceptionally dirty and pained feet. Lastly, each was guided to an upstairs bedroom where they were given straw and a blanket to sleep on. They concluded their long day at 2300 hours with relatively full bellies, sore feet, and still in their dirty, unchanged clothes.

> **"5-24 – Depart Alone – Rocroi – Bus – Suspicious –
> Charleville – Bombing – Running – Cards – Water –
> Flub Dub – Overcoat – Walking – Lousy Shoes –
> Met Horroia Family – Boar – Rabbit – 12 Kids –
> Germans – Ju 88 Off Deck"** [27]

MAY 24, 1944
LIÈGE, BELGIUM
1600 HOURS

Soon after departing from the airmen in Petite-Chapelle, Caubergh separated from his White Army counterparts and began the trip back home alone to Liège. He made his way to the local depot and boarded the next available train headed north. The four-hour

27 Goebel's journal entry appears to be a combination of two days, May 24 and May 25.

journey stopped short of entering the town of Louvain as Allied bombers had recently worked over the region. Regrettably, in addition to the train station, their payloads had also hit the local hospital, creating more chaos than normal. Unable to progress any farther by rail, Caubergh looked for an alternative means of transportation.

With roughly eighty kilometers to go, he made his way to a nearby road where he hitched a ride on the back of a large delivery truck on its return route to a local brewery. Now positioned on an empty beer cask, Caubergh braced himself for the bumpy two-hour ride to Sint-Truiden. Thankfully, the last leg of his trip home was by tram. Arriving late afternoon, he was finally able to return home after an almost two-week absence.

The other Allied airmen who chose to return to Liège would ultimately end up in camps established by the Comète Line, hidden in locations within the Ardennes. It is believed that Reginald Weeden, George Flather, Kevin Doyle, James Lewis, and Charles Weymouth would end up in camps located in Beffe and Porcheresse, Belgium. These camps were part of Operation Marathon.

Eventually, some of the Allied airmen would return to Liège and were lodged at La Cathédrale Saint Paul. The cathédrale's caretakers and their adopted guardians (Pappy and Mammy) would accept the young men with open arms. Caubergh would visit from time to time, only to find happy, spoiled sons of the kind, adoptive parents. The young men did not stray as they enjoyed themselves, all patiently awaiting liberation by their comrades, who were nearer than they imagined.

CHAPTER THIRTY-FOUR

The Maquis Bandits

MAY 25, 1944—DAY THIRTY-TWO
NEAR BUTZ, FRANCE
0900 HOURS

LED BY YOUNG SERGE, the airmen were awoken by the horde of Hourrier children. Making their way down to the kitchen, the airmen entered the epicenter of chaos. Still unsure of the names of each child, chaos quickly converted to confusion. Each time they blinked or would turn around, there seemed to be a different child standing before them. The airmen were ushered to the kitchen table and served bread and Nescafé blended with milk. This was a generous offering from a family with so many mouths to feed.

Conspicuously missing from the gathering was Madame Marcelle. Upon inquiring, the airmen were informed that she had left several hours earlier to travel to Charleville-Mézières. Unbeknownst to her new house guests, Madame Marcelle had traveled the fourteen kilometers north to see if she could contact the Maquis,[28] the local French Résistance.

After breakfast, the crew headed outside to enjoy the morning spring air. The days were becoming warmer, paired with sunny skies and green foliage. Finding a comfortable spot, playing cards were shuffled and delt as the airmen passed the time. Between hands, pairs of airmen would wander off into the nearby woods for a short walk.

A little after noon, Madame Marcelle returned home from her fact-finding mission. No less composed, she stated rather frankly that she'd had no luck. Apparently, the Jerries had recently broken up the rural résistance guerrilla band. A betrayal that was still somewhat fresh, the head of Maquis was believed to be hiding somewhere in the woods outside of Charleville-Mézières.

Not long after Madame Marcelle resumed her daily chores, they were interrupted by a neighboring family who unexpectedly called on the Marcelle farmhouse. Addressing Madame Marcelle, they gestured to the airmen loitering in the yard. Unable to make out the conversation, the airmen instinctively knew they were the topic of discussion. To all appearances, the family seemed harmless. Their observations were soon supported by the display of cakes and other baked goods that were held up for the airmen to see.

Once welcomed into the yard, the airmen gathered around the visitors. Curious, the airmen inquired how the family knew of their existence. The visitors informed Madame Marcelle, who then translated for the airmen. Seemingly, on the previous day, a member

28 Emerging at the end of 1941, the Maquis were one of many rural French Résistance fighters that fought against the German Occupation and the Vichy regime during the war.

of the family had spotted Brinkhurst and Tucker drinking at the horse trough. Now receiving the baked gifts, the airmen were thankful and amazed by the generosity of the locals but also unsure of how they could afford to spare such treats.

After a quick visit, life at the farmhouse returned to normal. The airmen resumed their rounds of cards and walks. On one turn, Goebel elected to head off by himself. Wanting to stretch his legs, he wandered into the nearby woods, out of sight but not too far from the farmhouse. Walking in silence, Goebel was startled by a rustle in the brush about three meters away. Pausing, he stood quietly and squinted harder to make out the origin of the disturbance. Taking a step closer to the source of the noise, the ruckus became more aggravated until a small, dark figure leaped toward Goebel. Squealing as it ran past, Goebel jumped from his skin as he tried to avoid a collision with the wild boar. Upon gathering his wits, he quickly headed back in the direction of the farmhouse.

As Goebel moved toward the edge of the woods just opposite the farmhouse, he heard the whine of approaching aircraft. Standing still, Goebel watched as a Focke-Wulf Fw190 German fighter screamed across the treetops, and a few moments later a twin-engine Ju88 lumbered behind. After pausing to make sure the skies were now clear, Goebel crossed the field back to the Marcelle sanctuary without haste.

Arriving back to the farmhouse, he was greeted by yet another Marcelle family member. Madame Marcelle's oldest child had arrived at the homestead while Goebel was dodging the local wildlife. About eighteen years of age, Gilbert was on the run from the Germans. A member of Maquis, Gilbert had been forced into hiding. Making his way through the woods, Gilbert traveled on foot from Charleville-Mézières to the family farm just outside of Butz. Living life on the run was nothing new to Gilbert. Having recently escaped from the Germans while being transported to a work camp, he was becoming skilled at evading the enemy.

Aways suspicious, Gilbert conducted an impromptu interview of each airman. After examining their papers and interrogating each man with the same specific questions, Gilbert was confident that their stories were true and these were not German infiltrators. Moreover, their walk, accents, and prominent facial features also corroborated that these were foreign fighters. Once complete, Gilbert gathered the seven together and informed them that their current identification papers were insufficient to travel any farther. They were missing French work cards, which would allow the men to travel more freely. Gilbert then went on to convey that he had the ability to get them the proper papers; however, it would take a couple of days.

Once relaxed, knowing that his family was safe, Gilbert joined the airmen in a few hands of cards and shared evasion stories as they became better acquainted. Gilbert went on to share that while he had not seen him for quite some time, his father was also a member of Maquis. Père "worked on" the railroads at night. As a result of their German occupiers, sabotage had become a family pastime.

After dinner, Gilbert departed his family farmhouse with the mission to secure papers for the airmen. It seemed the entire Marcelle family would make considerable sacrifices for the young airmen. The family slept in one room in three beds while the airmen slept in the children's room. Unbeknownst to the airmen, Madame Marcelle also used the children's food ration cards to obtain the needed supplies to feed this new group of seven.

MAY 26, 1944—DAY THIRTY-THREE
NEAR BUTZ, FRANCE
1100 HOURS

After breakfast, Gilbert returned back to the Marcelle homestead. He did not provide specific information, yet he informed the men that he had reached his friends. Seeing that the airmen were bored, Gilbert, along with Goebel, Brinkhurst, and Tucker, went for a walk in the neighboring woods. After ten minutes and without exposing their location, the group neared a cluster of four houses. Gilbert pointed out that the Germans were billeted within these homes and others within the small village. Pausing to take in this information, the three airmen quickly recognized that if they had passed by the Marcelle farmhouse two days earlier without stopping, they would have walked right into a German-occupied town. Stunned by this revelation, the airmen expressed their gratitude once more to the eldest Marcelle child.

Now on a roundabout route back to the farmhouse, Tucker stumbled upon a French helmet partially buried in the underbrush. Retrieving the artifact, he wondered if the owner had been killed or had simply lost it in their haste. Brushing the dirt free, Tucker observed a large dent in the side. Goebel stopped to look and commented that if someone had been wearing it when they received the blow, they would be lucky to be alive.

Later that afternoon, two new visitors arrived at the farmhouse. Gilbert welcomed friends from Charleville-Mézières, a buxom gal named Alyce, and her husband, Emile Milot. Like Gilbert, Emile had also escaped the Germans while being taken to a work camp. Emile shared with the group that he had been taken to Germany in 1940 to work and had escaped twice only to be recaptured. Emile escaped once again the previous December. Unafraid, he stowed away within the engine compartment of a troop train from Berlin to Paris. Emile now worked near the Swiss border and agreed to guide the group through when he returned on the following Tuesday. In preparation, Emile gathered information from the airmen for counterfeit work cards.

That evening after the younger Marcelle children were off to bed, the airmen stayed outside to enjoy the beautiful weather. Feeling pungent, the airmen decided to strip down to their boxers and T-shirts. With hopes that some fresh air would disinfect, they hung their outer garments over Madame Marcelle's clothesline. It had been ten days since their last bath, and it would take more than a couple hours of country air to remove the musky smell. It was Friday evening, and they were feeling filthy.

MAY 27, 1944—DAY THIRTY-FOUR
NEAR BUTZ, FRANCE
1030 HOURS

Goebel and Tucker started off for their morning walk, this time in a different direction. Noticing their route, Gilbert began running after the pair. Catching up, he informed the airmen that they couldn't go in this part of the woods. He went on to explain that he and his fellow résistance members had buried equipment from 1940 and gear dropped at night by the English. To keep it from the Germans, the stash was protected with land mines and booby traps. Understanding the significance of staying clear of this protected cache, the pair headed off on a safer path.

Later that afternoon, most of the group, with the exception of Brinkhurst, went out for a walk with the Marcelle children. One of the middle sons led the group to a wire trap that he had recently set. To the group's surprise, a medium-size wild boar had been snared. Approaching the frightened animal, it squealed and struggled. Assessing the situation, the young trapper tried to stab it, but it would not let him get close. After watching the dance, Gilbert struck the animal in the head with a shovel, killing it with one blow.

Together with the airmen, Gilbert field-dressed the animal. During their return trip back to the homestead, the airmen joined the young children in their search for escargots, a delicacy that Madame Marcelle would roast on the farmhouse cast-iron stove.

When returning to the farmhouse, the group was startled to see the local culture chief on horseback in front of their home. A known German sympathizer, he was unwelcomed by most of the locals. Now paused out of sight at the edge of the woods, the group watched as Madame Marcelle stood with arms crossed in contempt of the rider while he questioned her. After a brief exchange, the chief rode away and the group made their way from the woods to the house. Gilbert inquired to his mother the intent of the chief, but Madame Marcelle would not speak to the matter and motioned him away.

Entering the yard, the airmen realized Brinkhurst was missing. In fact, he had slipped behind the barn when he heard the commotion out front and was hiding in the nearby woods. Such a thorough job he did, the Marcelle children were unable to locate him. Seeing that things were back to normal, Brinkhurst revealed himself. Now together again, the group displayed for Brinkhurst and Madame Marcelle the freshly caught swine and a basket of slimy shelled creatures.

May 28, 1944—Day Thirty-Five
Near Butz, France
1400 Hours

Even with the war on and their homeland under occupation, the Marcelle family still celebrated every Sunday. A French tradition, the entire group of close to thirty enjoyed a massive lunch. Most of the day was filled with food, drink, and friends, who all enjoyed the beautiful spring weather. After their midday celebration, the airmen, including Gilbert and his girlfriend, lay on the lawn, soaking up the afternoon sun.

As promised, Emile and Alyce returned in the late afternoon with phony identity papers for the airmen's upcoming trip. While their stay had been welcomed, the airmen were becoming restless. It was time to move on. Emile's offer to personally escort the seven south to the Swiss border would not work as planned. In exchange, he shared with the group a map indicating the best path forward and offered specific instructions. Beyond that, Emile would return to escort the group back to the train station at Charleville-Mézières. After that, the airmen were on their own. Their plan was set; they would depart on Tuesday.

THE LUCKY SEVEN

The evening prior, the airmen gathered what remaining funds they had from their escape kits and gave a handful of francs to Madame Marcelle. In return, she had risen before everyone else to travel again to Charleville-Mézières in order to obtain the airmen's railroad tickets to Belfort. An industrious woman, she had made the twenty-eight kilometer round trip journey and was back by noon.

The airmen spent their last day close to the farmhouse. In the afternoon, Gilbert's girl brought her sister to visit. The female companionship only made the young men long for home. While the French countryside was beautiful and hospitable, it was time to go.

That evening, the airmen shared their last meal with the Marcelle family. Still unsure how these people were feeding them, the airmen could only express their deepest gratitude. After dinner, the airmen sorted through their remaining belongings, leaving behind all they could, including their overcoats. Before the children went off to bed, the airmen said their goodbyes as the next morning they would depart early.

The French Résistance member above is believed to be Gilbert Marcelle (1945). As seen on his coat, Marcelle is displaying a F.F.L. ribbon signifying his membership in the French Forces of the Interior.

CHAPTER THIRTY-FIVE

Scared Stiff

MAY 30, 1944—DAY THIRTY-SEVEN
NEAR BUTZ, FRANCE
0553 HOURS

AS PLANNED, EMILE ARRIVED a few moments before 0600 hours. The seven airmen were waiting outside the farmhouse as the sun rose over the French countryside. Anxious, the airmen were ready to resume their journey. On foot, the group departed and headed north. It did not take long before the morning dew soaked through their paper-thin shoes.

The normal fourteen-kilometer journey was elongated to nearly twenty in an effort to avoid all population centers. Even spread out, a group of eight men traveling together during daylight was a significant risk. Emile took his time to steer clear of known Germen hotbeds. The four-hour walk was stretched to six when accommodating needed detours and breaks. Unfortunately, it did not take long for the airmen's healed feet to reform blisters, making the walk even more prolonged.

Arriving in Charleville-Mézières with plenty of time to spare, Emile took the group to a known friendly tavern, sympathetic to the cause. The men were treated to a beer and bowl of soup. With still a couple of hours to burn, the group remained in the back and out sight of any customers. The airmen and Emile passed the time by playing cards. With an hour remaining, Emile gathered the group, exited the rear of the tavern, and made their way to the train station. Once near, Emile said his goodbyes and departed from the group.

With directions from Emile, the group migrated to different locations along the station. Safely spread out from one another but still somewhat in sight, their nerves grew tenser as they waited for the train to Nancy. As planned, the seven airmen boarded the 1600-hour train headed south.

Seated separately, the airmen tried their best to look like they belonged. On schedule, the coal-driven locomotive belched as it lurched forward. The airmen could see German rail workers and Wehrmacht officers making their last inspections as they stepped from the platform to their assigned stations. The passenger carriages were surprisingly full of mostly French civilians, but there was a substantial headcount of German soldiers—more than the airmen had even seen accumulated in some time. It was a bit unnerving, to say the least.

Approximately ten minutes into the trip, the door to Goebel's carriage slid open. The ticket inspector, followed by a Wehrmacht officer and an armed German soldier, stepped into his line of vision. Trying not to acknowledge their presence, Goebel continued to stare out the window. Slowly, they progressed down the aisle.

"Billet! Billet!" the inspector demanded.

Row by row, they got closer. Goebel's mouth became dryer as his chest tightened with apprehension. Now adjacent to Goebel's row, the inspector barked the order again. "Billet!"

Goebel reached into his coat pocket and pulled his ticket and identity papers free. He separated his ticket from the papers and handed it to the inspector, who conducted a quick examination, punched it, and returned it to him. At the same time, Goebel could feel the two Germans glaring at him. He folded his ticket into his papers and stuffed it back from where it came. The trio moved down the aisle.

"Billet! Billet!" the inspector called again to the next rows, signifying their progression.

Goebel didn't realize it, but he had been holding his breath the entire time. Suddenly, he exhaled and gasped for air. Astonished by what just occurred, he slowly exhaled, relaxed his breathing, and returned his attention to the vista passing by.

As the train continued south without incident and they passed through Sedan, it was evident that the Allied air offensive had taken its toll on much of the German infrastructure. The allies were effective at targeting Luftwaffe facilities, the German petroleum industry, rail communications, and rail lines supporting the German forces in France. Riding alone on the rail was a significant risk for Goebel and his fellow airmen. Not only did they have to worry about the Germans on the train; his own Allied pilots could target them as they traveled to Nancy.

Arriving at 2000 hours, the four-hour journey seemed to be a success thus far. Disembarking in Nancy, the airmen loitered separately inside and outside the station. Wanting to continue their journey, they were thwarted because the next train to Belfort did not depart until 0730 hours the next morning. After a quick patrol around the small train station, it felt like they had landed in a hotbed of Nazis. Unsure of where to go, the group decided to remain close to the station.

For the next ninety minutes, until the sunset and a German curfew forced them all inside, the seven men each took turns walking a couple of laps around the adjacent town square. Now sequestered in the train station, the men tried to look and act as inconspicuous as possible. Unfortunately, sleep was out of the question as German and Vichy French guards patrolled the station on a regular basis.

Prior to their arrival, a local Frenchman had crossed the Germans and was now on the run and hiding to avoid capture. The Nazis were relentless, making several passes through the station in search of the Frenchman, each time stopping to check everyone's credentials. Unbeknownst to Holton, the fleeing Frenchman was hiding beneath the bench where he was currently seated. In the wee hours of the morning, the Frenchman revealed himself, climbed free, and darted from the station, never to be seen again.

**"5-30 – Charleville Return – Train At 1600 –
Nancy At 2115 – Waiting Room – Cards –
Gendarmes – Nazis – Scared Stiff – Beer"**

CHAPTER THIRTY-SIX

Train to Belfort

MAY 31, 1944—DAY THIRTY-EIGHT
NANCY, FRANCE
0730 HOURS

FOGGY FROM A LACK of sleep, the seven airmen boarded the scheduled train headed to Belfort, France. Happy to be away from the Nancy station, the airmen spread out through a couple of carriages and looked for a quiet spot to rest their eyes. Now slightly more comfortable with the obligatory request for papers, Goebel tried to relax.

During one of the train's regularly scheduled morning stops, Goebel was stirred by a commotion playing out directly in front of him. On the platform outside of his window, he witnessed what looked like two American airmen and a few French civilians being shoved along by several irritated German SS guards. Looking battered, the civilians were obviously under arrest for helping the two airmen. Still dressed in their flight suits, the airmen seemed to be in better condition. Now fully awake, Goebel realized that the two airmen were now prisoners of war. Whereas if he was caught out of uniform, he would most likely be considered a spy and saboteur, only to be executed by his captors. Surely, a fate soon to be realized by theses French Résistance members.

The scene outside was soon in the same compartment as Goebel. Being pushed the entire way with the business end of a rifle, the Nazi guards escorted their prisoners onto the train. The group was now seated in the rows directly in front of Goebel. Too close for comfort, his earlier calm was quickly replaced with high anxiety. Trying to ignore the entire spectacle, Goebel turned his attention back to the window. Thankfully, the guards settled down once the train was in motion. The group sat quietly for the next thirty minutes until it was time to get off at the next stop. Once there, the guards returned to their barbaric behavior and the group debarked the train. Selfishly, Goebel was relieved they were gone.

On their way again, their train chugged through the French countryside for the next five hours without incident. Arriving at 1300 hours, the seven airmen departed at Belfort. A smaller town than Nancy, the depot and the surrounding courtyard looked even more congested with Germans. Now less than sixty kilometers from the German border, Emile warned the airmen that the population would be much more sympathetic to the Nazi cause.

Overall, Belfort was a mess. Badly bombed, there seemed to be a confluence of displaced civilians and Wehrmacht soldiers wading through the open streets. Adjacent to the station was a congested boulevard with shops aligned on the opposing side. With three hours to go before the next scheduled train left for Montbéliard, the group knew they needed to be less visible. After a quick reconnoiter, the airmen broke up into their normal pairings: Brinkhurst and Tucker headed off together to one location; Goebel, Westerlund, and Holton moved in a different direction; and Solomon and Pavelka went about their own way.

Crossing the cobblestone square in front of the train station Goebel, Westerlund, and Holton, quickly found an open tavern. Ordering beers, they were seated at a table near the front window. With a view of the street, the trio had a good vantage point. While enjoying their drinks, a large contingent of Wehrmacht soldiers marched through the square about ten meters in front of the airmen. Looking to be at least three full infantry squads of thirty men, it was quite an impressive scene. These were some of the men whom the allies would face in the coming months.

Shortly after the parade passed, the towns air raid sirens began to whine. Soon, the drone of an aircraft could be heard in the distance. The streets out front became a chaotic scene as soldiers and civilians began scrambling about to seek cover. The three airmen remained seated and did not budge from their location. While sipping their beer, a B-26 Marauder passed over the tavern and train station. The American medium bomber must have already delivered its cargo as it flew overhead without any fanfare. The German antiaircraft guns erupted with no aftereffect.

As agreed, the seven airmen made their way back to the station in time to board the train to Montbéliard at 1600 hours. The quick one-hour ride went off without a hitch, and the group arrived in Montbéliard as scheduled. Emile had provided the group with instructions on how to contact the local French underground once they arrived in town. As directed, the seven made their way through town toward the south and located a local tavern called the Focke Wolfe Works. The group was not inside long before being approached by two unknown Frenchmen. Very few words were exchanged before their new guides escorted them from the tavern.

Once out on the street, they moved swiftly through the small town and headed a couple kilometers to the south until they reached a modest farm. The lead Frenchman entered the farmhouse alone and then reappeared after only a few moments. The airmen were then greeted by Mademoiselle Gabrielle Giesey, who agreed to provide lodging to the airmen for the night. Once she took them in for the evening, their guide departed immediately. The mademoiselle was a young, unmarried woman, living alone in a family home. Her father was a member of the French Résistance who had been missing for some time.

Wasting no time, Mademoiselle Giesey went to work preparing rabbit for the airmen. After dinner and with content bellies, the airmen passed the remaining hours playing cards. Before turning in for the evening, the young matron escorted the airmen to different rooms within the house where the men doubled up on single mattresses on the floor. With less than fifteen kilometers between their location and possible salvation, the seven men would sleep comfortably but with anxious anticipation for the day to come.

**"5-31 – 0730 Train To Belford – Extensive Bombing
All The Way. 1600 To Mount – Billiard. Overnight
In French man's House – More Rabbit"**

CHAPTER THIRTY-SEVEN

Lost in the Woods

June 1, 1944—Day Thirty-Nine
Montbéliard, France
1100 Hours

EXHAUSTED FROM THE LAST two days of travel with little sleep, the airmen did not stir until late morning. Mademoiselle Giesey prepared lunch for her guests before they departed at 1400 hours. Just before 1330 hours, the two French Résistance members returned to escort the airmen away from the farmhouse toward the Swiss border. Prior to departing, Goebel gave his name and home address to the leader of the two requesting him **"to promise to write."** Nodding, the Frenchman accepted Goebel's information but provided none of his own.[29]

With simple instructions to follow closely, remain out of sight, and head in a southeasterly direction, the seven men left the

29 Lieutenant Gassard did write Goebel shortly after the war after VE Day (Victory in Europe Day), in October 1945. Liberation for Montbéliard and return to French control was November 17, 1944.

farmhouse and began the final leg of their walk. Anticipation of freedom amplified their adrenaline as the group walked steadily at a heightened pace for the next two hours. Once securely hidden in the woods, the group stopped a few kilometers from the Swiss border and rested. After providing final direction, the two French Résistance members departed. Made aware that there were many German patrols in the area, the airmen found comfortable spots, then hunkered down together in the brush to wait out the evening. About an hour before sunset at 2030 hours, the group agreed to press forward. Now in the low fifties and raining heavily, it did not take long for the airmen to become soaked through and frigid.

The darkness of the night, compounded with the thick woods and a thunderstorm, caused the airmen to lose their bearings. What should have been an hour walk turned into two hours of confusion. Lost and drenched, the airmen pushed through the woods only to churn in what seemed like large nonconcentric circles. Finally, at 2335 hours, they regained their sense of direction, found the long, narrow clearing they had been desperately searching for, and darted across. Once on the other side, they each climbed through a barbed wire fence, effectively crossing the French border into neutral Switzerland.

Still unsure of their true location, the group continued walking until they came upon a dirt road. As the pouring rain drowned out their footsteps, they followed the muddy road for about a kilometer until they arrived in the town of Fahy, Switzerland. Now a little after midnight, it did not take long for the presence of these seven strangers to alert the authorities. The airmen were quickly greeted by local military police. Blowing whistles, yelling and unhappy with the intruders, members of the Swiss Army aggressively barked directions in both French and German. Brandishing spotlights, rifles, and machine guns, the Swiss approached and surrounded the airmen.

Stopping in their tracks and instinctively putting their hands up, the airmen yelled in reply, "American, American!" Standing in the pouring rain, the airmen stood motionless while their captors searched for weapons. Blinded by the spotlights and the rain running down his face, Goebel stood, shivering. Unsure of what was being said, in a nonthreatening tone Goebel continuously repeated, "American!" Soon, he and the others were shoved from behind toward a parked truck.

Now under arrest, the airmen, followed by their armed guards, boarded the truck and were taken to the Swiss military garrison in Porrentruy, Switzerland. The twelve-kilometer ride took slightly less than thirty minutes. The garrison was an old castle-like structure built of massive stones with a wide portal giving access to the inner courtyard. Ordered off the truck, the airmen were made to line up and face the most senior guard. Still raining, the group remained at attention while shivering in unison.

One by one, they were led into the commander's office where they were interrogated individually. Questioned thoroughly about their intrusion into Swiss territory, each man offered no more than their name, rank, serial number, and MIA date. Once no additional information could be garnered, they were led without further conversation to holding cells. Walking past other cells, they could see that many were already occupied in part by other people. The areas that appeared to be used as stables in the past were now being utilized for detention cells. With no heat, the only creature comfort was a heavy layer of well-used hay covering the cobblestone floor.

Tired and wet, it was now 0300 hours. Under the circumstances, the airmen made themselves as comfortable as possible. Once alone, they questioned amongst themselves the care they were receiving. At least free from the Germans, the group expected more from the Swiss. Damp and cold, their new home for the night was less desirable than what they had become accustomed to over their recent travels. In the dim light of the cell house, they drifted into their thoughts as the steam visibly rose off of each man's clothing.

Feeling ambivalent about their current station, the airmen were grateful for a safe journey and arrival to salvation. Arriving on foot in Switzerland by walking out of German-occupied Western Europe, Goebel unknowingly became a member of the "Blister Club." Well worth the pain, it was not possible without the support and sacrifice of members of the Belgian and French Résistance.

"6-1 – Started Walking At 1400 + Crossed Border At 2335 – Rain + Thunder Storm – Confused In Woods – Soaked – Picked Up By Swiss Police + Taken To Porrentruy"

MAY–OCTOBER 1939
ZURICH, SWITZERLAND

Long before the Swiss National Exhibition in 1939, the spiritual defense of this small neutral nation was growing. A country that has, in effect, been neutral since 1515 with a history of armed neutrality was preparing for a predicted invasion. Nazi Germany had plans to invade its neighbor to the south. Seeing what happened to neutral Belgium in World War I and the German invasion of Austria in March of 1938, Switzerland was preparing for such an occurrence. Within days of Germany's invasion of Poland, Switzerland called up and mobilized 450,000 men in preparation for such an event.

Flanked by serious threats, Hitler's Nazi Germany, and Mussolini's fascist Italy, the Swiss government and the Swiss people fully expected to be invaded. It was not long before Switzerland found itself completely surrounded by the Axis powers and Axis-controlled territory for most of World War II. While not in favor of their neighbor's politics or actions, the Swiss did allow the German war machine to transport goods within enclosed containers from Italy across its territories and the Gotthard railway line.

From 1943, Switzerland stopped American and British aircraft (mainly bombers) from flying over Switzerland during the war. On numerous occasions, Allied aircraft intruded on Swiss airspace; they were mostly damaged Allied bombers returning from raids over Italy and Germany whose crews preferred internment by the Swiss to becoming prisoners of war. By May 1945, there were 115,000 refugees, interned military personnel, and escaped prisoners of war in Swiss camps. Altogether, it added up to some 400,000 refugees, mostly Jews fleeing German-occupied territory and emigrants who had reached or passed through the small alpine country.

PART SIX

Internment

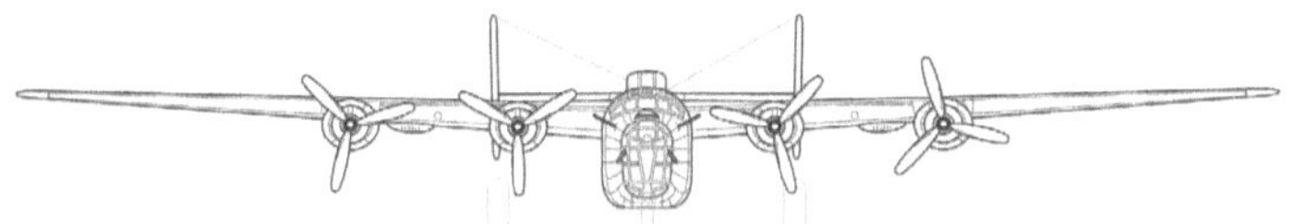

CHAPTER THIRTY-EIGHT

Lots of Indians

June 2, 1944—Day Forty
Porrentruy, Switzerland
0630 Hours

MORNING ARRIVED TOO EARLY. With less than four hours of sleep, the airmen were rousted from their slumber by an unsympathetic guard. Marched into the courtyard for roll call, they were forcefully awakened to the fact that they were in some sort of a Swiss prison. Unsure what to expect, the airmen could only hope that they would not be returned to the border—or worse, handed over to the Germans.

Soon after roll call, the airmen were moved to the decontamination station where they all undressed and took hot showers. After several weeks, this was a much-needed event, especially after the numbing cold they experienced the previous evening. While showering, their clothes were deloused by being dry-baked in a rotating hopper.

The sight of Swiss-enlisted men standing guard at the shower door, ensuring all who entered washed properly, was a stark reminder that they were in prison. A further reminder was provided as they were leaving the shower area. Each man was sprayed with some kind of disinfectant that made them do a two-step as they grabbed their testicles. After dressing, each man was given haircuts that were just short of being shaved. Once properly cleaned, the airmen were allowed to eat: potato soup, rye bread, and black coffee.

Looking around at the other prisoners, Goebel couldn't help but notice the abundance of **"Indians."** In addition to Allied servicemen, the Porrentruy garrison, a reception camp was full of civilian refugees made up of almost twenty different nationalities. One surprise came in the form of a Swiss guard named Wilfred Janssen, who had a unique accent for being a Swiss person. Knowing that he was dealing with Americans, Janssen would speak English to his prisoners. Hearing the young blond guard speak in their native tongue, Goebel and the others became very curious. Inquiring, the airmen discovered that Janssen had lived in East Orange, New Jersey, which was the same town that Tucker hailed from. Janssen had returned home a few years earlier to support the motherland. Because he spoke fluent English, he was assigned to the American and British prisoners.

Later that day, the seven airmen received their first visitor, an International Red Cross representative. Or at least that's who they thought they were meeting with. In reality, this was a British intelligence officer who was there to interrogate them. The Brit fulfilled many roles as there was no American Legation representative available to conduct the interrogations on behalf of the U.S. military. In addition to the line of questioning that they received the previous evening, the airmen were asked about any information they could bring to mind of tactical importance, such as radar installations and troop forces observed along the way.

Now disinfected, the airmen were moved to a cleaner cell, one with new hay. Still no heat, but at least there were lights. The town of Porrentruy remained lit after dark. For the first time since being shot down, Goebel experienced the lights being on without fear of exposure from an Allied bombing raid.

"6-2 – Disinfected – Indians – Straw – Wilfred"

June 3, 1944—Day Forty-One
Porrentruy, Switzerland
0630 Hours

The morning started with the same unfriendly wake up and roll call. In lieu of decontamination, the airmen were treated to a similar tasteless breakfast and some free time to play cards and interact with the other Indians.

At 1230 hours, the Lucky Seven, along with other interned servicemen, boarded an electric train leaving Porrentruy, and headed east to the town of Olten. The three-and-half-hour ride twisted through the Swiss Alps, offering a scenic view of the countryside. Upon their arrival at 1600 hours, the internees were offloaded and marched to the local military police where they were interrogated for a third time—this time by the Swiss.

Once interrogations were complete, the entire group was marched almost eight kilometers up a long hill to a remote camp located in Bad Lostorf. The men marched through the village of Lostorf, witnessing a well-maintained community and many small hamlets overlooking the local vista. As they passed by, the airmen were greeted by friendly locals who offered them chocolate. Goebel and the others noted that this part of Switzerland was noticeably cleaner and untouched by war.

Arriving to their new internment hotel, the airmen were greeted by the Swiss Commandant in charge of the camp. He informed the airmen of the camp rules and the fact that they would be quarantined at this location for at least twenty days. The internees were under orders not to leave the hotel grounds. Under curfew, enlisted men were to be in their rooms by 2200 hours, and officers had until 2300 hours. Guards checked the rooms at curfew and then stationed themselves in the halls to prevent night prowling. There were penalties for infractions of regulations, which included staged durations of confinement to one's room. More severe punishment would lead to internment in a less-agreeable prison camp.

Lastly, the airmen were escorted to their rooms. The five American officers were assigned a room together: Tucker, Holton, Goebel, Solomon, and Pavelka. The room was outfitted with five box mattresses. Finally, they each got their own bed—free of hay. Once settled, the men were able to take a bath and were offered a better meal than they had previously received.

"6-3 – Quarantine Camp at "Bad Lostore" West Of Olten"[30]

30 June 3, 1944, was the last day that Goebel journaled his experience in this shorthand format.

JUNE 4–5, 1944—DAYS FORTY-TWO & FORTY-THREE
BAD LOSTORF, SWITZERLAND
0800 HOURS

Less of a prison and a little more friendly, the airmen were given some latitude in their movement. Over the next couple of days, they were able to trade up for better clothing, such as shoes that fit, and take in the fresh air, read, play cards and monopoly. Most importantly, they were finally able to write letters home. While this provided some solace for the sender, correspondence was held up by the Swiss authorities, and official word of Goebel's safe arrival to Switzerland did not make it to Brooklyn, New York, for another twelve days.

JUNE 6, 1944—DAY FORTY-FOUR
BAD LOSTORF, SWITZERLAND
0700 HOURS

After breakfast, Goebel and the other newly arrived airmen were gathered up and marched back down to Olten where they were interrogated for a fourth time by the Swiss Military. Ultimately, the Swiss were trying to confirm Goebel's story and his status within their country. Like Goebel, all U.S. military personnel who escaped, evaded, and entered Switzerland on foot earned the status of "evadee." Over time, evaders were not kept in camps and eventually were granted privileges, including the ability to leave their assigned housing during non-curfew hours.

Less fortunate internees, on the other hand, were military personnel who landed their crippled aircraft in Switzerland and were in uniform. These airmen were usually restricted to a specific area and kept under guard. In some cases, internees were treated almost identically to POWs under laws of war, except that by definition, an internee is held in a neutral state. While things seemed to be progressing against the Axis powers, the Swiss remained vigilant in their handling of Allied servicemen. Establishing the correct status for Goebel and his fellow airmen was imperative.

Later that afternoon, upon returning to Bad Lostorf, Goebel was informed that the long-awaited invasion of the European continent by Allied forces took place earlier that morning. There was an air of enthusiasm amongst the airmen. The news meant that they were closer to being repatriated. An impromptu celebration with beer was in order.

JUNE 4, 1944
ROME, ITALY
AFTERNOON

After nine months of brutal and hard-fought battle, the Allied forces consisting of the U.S. Fifth Army and the British Eighth Army liberated the Italian capital city. The capture of Rome was incredibly important to the Allies. It was hoped that the battle for the Italian capital might draw German troops away from France and the impending European invasion. Rome was the first capital to be liberated from the Nazi German occupation. The Allied campaign in mainland Italy pushed the Germans and the National Republican Army north toward Switzerland and Southern France.

JUNE 6, 1944
NORMANDY, FRANCE
0030 HOURS

The D-Day operation brought together the land, air, and sea forces of the Allied armies in the largest invasion force in human history. Code named Operation Overlord, the Allies delivered five naval assault divisions to the beaches of Normandy, France. The beaches were given the code names of Utah, Omaha, Gold, Juno, and Sword.

The D-Day invasion force included nearly 7,000 ships and landing craft and close to 3,000 aircraft and gliders. In addition to the over 195,000 naval personnel from eight Allied countries that manned the landing vessels, a combined force of almost 157,000 Allied troops and airmen from England, Canada, and the United States fought on D-Day. Casualties from the three countries during the landing numbered more than 10,000.

The following is a copy of the questionnaire form completed by Goebel as part of his Swiss interrogation on June 1, 1944, while being imprisoned in Porrentruy, Switzerland.

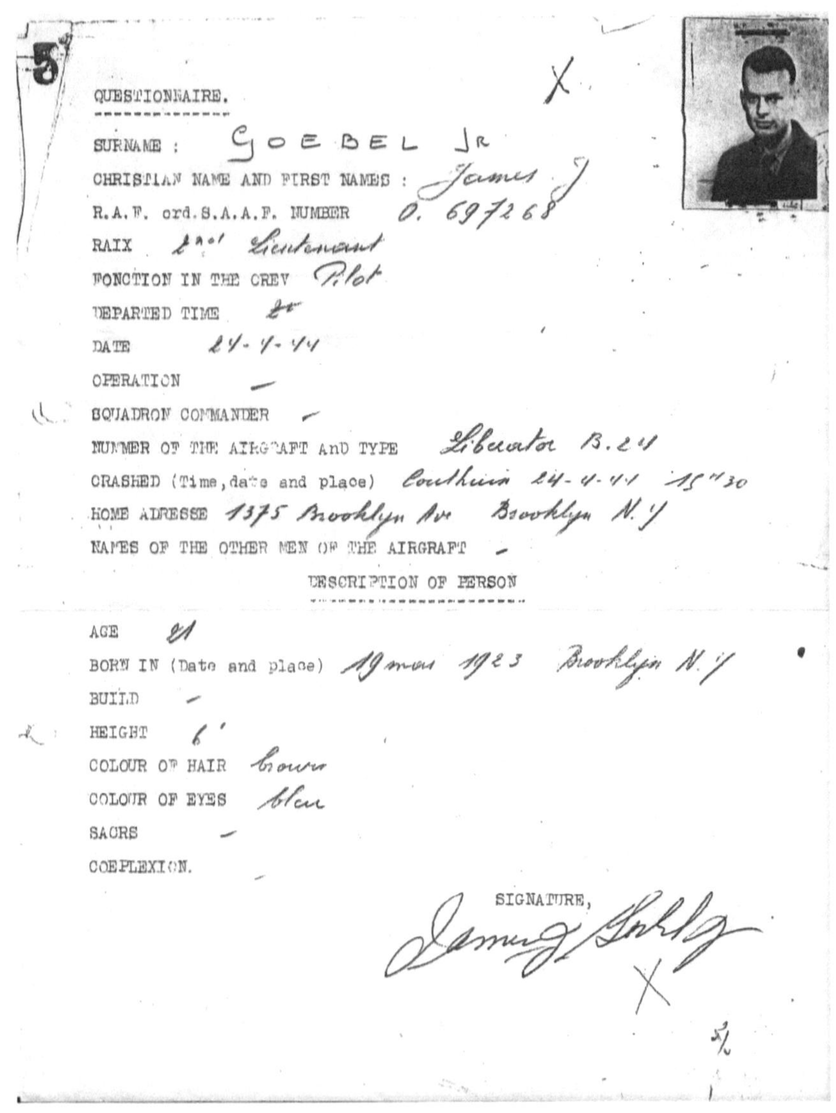

CHAPTER THIRTY-NINE

Quarantine Period

June 7–22, 1944—Days Forty-Five to Sixty
Bad Lostorf, Switzerland
Hotel Internment Camp

THE PREVIOUS NIGHT'S FULL moon was hazed over with clouds and rain. The excitement of possible freedom soon waned by the fact that they would remain in Switzerland until the Allied armies reached the Swiss border. Over the next seventeen days, Goebel and his fellow airmen would be forced to wait out their Swiss dictated quarantine period. Furthermore, under orders, American internees were instructed by U.S. Military Attaché in Switzerland not to attempt to escape from Switzerland.

As each day progressed, Goebel and his fellow airmen received added privileges. Soon, representatives from the American consulate would visit, bringing with them desperately needed clothes and some much-needed back pay. The American Legation paid out in small amounts, and it was heavily controlled. Each airmen received a small portion paid in the form of 100 Swiss francs ($20 U.S.).

For an internment camp, life at Bad Lostorf was not that unbearable. The camp still had watchful guards, Swiss military, rules to follow, curfews, and room inspections. However, there were also plenty of activities to pass the time and defray the compounding boredom. In addition to reading and rest, the airmen were able to go on hikes and play sports, cards, and board games. Every so often the Swiss guards would allow the airmen to listen to the radio and hear news from home where they learned of Allied advances against the Axis forces.

As their quarantine progressed, the airmen were permitted to be on the streets but had to be in their appointed lodging by dusk. Breaking these rules might cause the airmen to be moved to a confinement camp. Eventually, they were allowed to eat in the local restaurants and buy goods of fruits, vegetables, jams, cakes, and other treats at the local shops—the niceties that were absent for many months. Unfortunately, during much of this period it rained a great deal. **"Almost as bad as Ireland, chilly and rainy,"** commented Tucker to Goebel one rainy afternoon. The foul weather limited their ability to walk into town.

Gambling was another primary time-filler and vice that many participated in, from blackjack to poker. When francs were low, the men used cigarettes. The Swiss cigarettes fetched more value in the pot than the French ones, as French cigarettes were terrible. When cigarette rations ran low, men improvised with personal belongings.

There was also plenty of drinking. On more than one occasion, servicemen would be locked in their rooms for three days at a time for being too rowdy, breaking curfew, or being too loaded. The Swiss had little sense of humor when it came to repeated bad behavior. Longing for home, bored, and restless, it was no surprise that conflict resulted from young men while drinking.

The daily arrival of some refugees only added to their irritation. While at Bad Lostorf, Goebel and his fellow airmen often saw well-dressed Italian Army officers in suits arrive with suitcases in tow. These were men who had left their homeland instead of revolting against their own government or fighting the Germans. These Axis deserters had crossed the Swiss border, unwilling to make a personal sacrifice by attempting to correct the wrongs that were inflicted on their own countrymen. Instead, they fled with only self-preservation in mind and were provided the same comforts and freedoms as the Allied servicemen being interned.

SATURDAY, JUNE 17, 1944
BROOKLYN, NEW YORK
1400 HOURS

One day prior to Father's Day, the mail dropped through the front door slot onto the floor. Within the pile was a letter with the return address of The Adjutant General's Office of the War Department. Seeing the off-white envelope, Mrs. Goebel paused in apprehension before reaching to pick up the letter addressed to Mr. and Mrs. James J. Goebel. With trembling hands, she tore open the envelope and removed the contents. Her immediate thought was, *This has to be the worst news.*

Shaking while unfolding the two-page letter dated June 15, 1944, she began to read:

> **"Dear Mr. and Mrs. Goebel:**
> **A report has been received that the above captioned**
> **individual is safe in Switzerland."**

Getting no farther than the first sentence, only to reread it repeatedly, Francis released a yelp of joy and thanked God for the news regarding her son's well-being. This was the first news that the Goebel family received in thirty days since the May 8 MIA telegram. Receiving this letter ended a mother's anguish and heartache, which she had been carrying for the past month.

SUNDAY, JUNE 18, 1944
BROOKLYN, NEW YORK
1000 HOURS

After morning Mass, Francis wasted no time in responding to her son. Following the directions outlined within the Adjutant General's letter, she drafted a letter that she later sent via V-mail. This version would not arrive to Goebel for some time, yet a shorter message did make it through to him while at Bad Lostorf. On June 19, 1944, Goebel received the following radiogram "via Radiosuisse" delivered by the American military attaché:"

> **"received news of your safety letters follow family all
> well all our love mother = mrs james goebel +"**

Copy of the V-MAIL[31] sent by James's mother on June 18, 1944.

31 V-mail, short for Victory Mail, was a hybrid mail process used by the United States during World War II as the primary and secure method to correspond with soldiers stationed abroad. To reduce the cost of transferring an original letter through the military postal system, a V-mail letter would be censored, copied to film, and printed back to paper upon arrival at its destination.

CHAPTER FORTY

Fresh Duds

June 23, 1944—Day Sixty-One
Bad Lostof, Switzerland
0700 Hours

THE AIRMEN COULDN'T ASK for a better day. If the clear skies and sunny weather were indicators, things were truly looking up. As instructed the previous evening, the airmen had packed up their few worldly possessions and were ready to depart their remote Swiss outpost. Lined up, the Swiss guards marched the group from the hotel down the hill to the train station in Olten.

Right on time, the airmen boarded the 0830 train to Bern, Switzerland. A short one-hour ride, the electric train made its way through the Swiss countryside. Arriving, the Swiss guards marched the airmen from the train station to the local police station where each man signed in with the authorities.

While waiting for others to finish their obligations, Goebel and Tucker stood outside soaking up the beauty of the morning sun. As they chatted, a new group of men came into sight. They were being marched toward their general direction. As the group got closer, Goebel pointed out that the uniformed servicemen appeared to be American Flyboys. Also, at the rear of the column, he noted that there were a couple of Luftwaffe pilots. Quietly, Goebel and Tucker watched as the armed Swiss escorts walked past with their newly captured downed airmen. All in uniform, these men were headed to internment camps.

The next stop for Goebel and the others was a visit to the office of the American Legation where they checked in and received additional back pay of 500 Swiss francs ($100 U.S.). From there, they each were designated housing for the evening. The group was assigned rooms at Hotel Bären in downtown Bern. The rooms were equipped with two twin beds, two sinks, and a lovely view of the town.

After a perfect lunch, the group set about and went shopping for new clothes. Goebel, Tucker, and Holton each bought a new sports jacket, pants, shirts, ties, belt, underwear, socks, and brown-and-white shoes. They got the works! Though it cost them each a pretty penny. With their new duds and some spare change left in their pockets, the group decided to hit the town.

Later that evening, the airmen enjoyed a viewing of an American movie, *Till We Meet Again*, staring Merle Oberon and George Brent. While it wasn't their first choice, the 1940 romance film was a hit with the men, if for only ninety minutes it returned them home. After the movie, they enjoyed a few drinks before heading back to the hotel for their 2200-hour curfew.

THE LUCKY SEVEN

The following morning there was no shortage of things to do. First, they needed to get their photos taken. Once developed, they were to return to the American Legation where they each completed many forms for the resident attaché. While there, they each was interrogated again, now for the fifth time.

Once free from all the questioning, Goebel and a few of the guys went out and explored the rest of Bern. They toured the town, stopping in many of its different shops. Goebel eventually returned to the photo studio where he had his headshot taken earlier that morning and bought a 35mm Leica camera.[32]

After a nice dinner at a high-class restaurant, the boys hit one of the local night clubs for some dancing. It seemed strange to be dancing, yet the airmen adapted, and they danced with every woman who was able. They danced with French, Belgium, German, Swiss, and Italian women, many of whom couldn't speak any English, but none of that mattered to the attention-starved young men.

With the drinks going down too easily, the men missed their appointed curfew time. At about 0130 hours, they were picked up by the Swiss police, who had been sent to look for them when they were informed that the boys were not in their rooms at 2200 hours.

---

32 As an American internee, having a camera was strictly prohibited by the Swiss military as it potentially put the neutrality of Switzerland at risk. If discovered, Goebel's possession and use of photography equipment might have come with serious consequences, the worst of which would mean being sent to the Wauwilermoos internment and prisoner of war penal camp.

Like jerks, the intoxicated airmen gave fake names in an effort to avoid any further consequences. They finally arrived back at their rooms at 0200 hours.

June 25, 1944—Day Sixty-Three
Bern, Switzerland
0700 Hours

Goebel and his companions woke early as they were expecting a visit from the authorities. Hearing that the head of the Swiss police wanted to haul them off for their antics, the airmen left the hotel for the morning. After an early breakfast, they rode the funicular cable railway down to the river. Once there, they hung around and watched the locals swim. Goebel and his fellow comrades couldn't help but admire the shapely young Swiss women in their swim attire.

After a few hours, they returned to the hotel for lunch. Before heading back, Goebel made a detour and wired a brief telegram to his parents, which arrived in Brooklyn on June 27, 1944.

**"NLT JAMES GOEBEL
1375 BROOKLYN AVE BROOKLYN NY
WELL HAPPY GOOD TRATMENT EXCELLENT
EVERTHING HOME OKAY IVE EVERYONE
REGARDS ANSWER AMERICAN MILITARY
ATTAHE BERN SWITZERLAND**

**LOVE
JAMES GOEBEL"**

As scheduled, Goebel and his fellow airmen boarded the 1345 train departing from Bern on its route to Montreux, Switzerland, located on the eastern shore of Lac Léman (Lake Geneva). The two-hour train ride was breathtaking as each vista outdid the previous. After arriving, the men took a brief walk from the station to the shoreline. The crescent-shaped lake shared between France and Switzerland was deep blue, clear, and cold.

Unfortunately, at this point in Montreux, Brinkhurst was separated from the rest of the Lucky Seven as the British officers were housed at a different hotel within town. They were still able to mingle during the day and evening until curfew hours dictated that they return to their respective lodging.

From there, they made a short walk to the Glion railway station where Goebel and his companions boarded the small mountain rail car. The inclined railway took the group to the village of Glion, 2,100 feet above the lake and the town of Montreux. Once at the top, the men made their way to their assigned hotel, Hotel de Glion. The small town of Glion had one large hotel that housed about one hundred Americans. The Yanks were the hotel's only guests. Goebel and Holton shared a room facing Lake Geneva with a view of Mont Blanc, a very large mountain across the lake in France. They also had a view of the famous Chateau de Chillon just below on the lakeshore where Lord Byron was, at one time, a prisoner there.

Settled in their room, it was time to meet the gang. The airmen met the other hotel guests, ate a swell dinner, and enjoyed a few drinks. Thankfully, the festivities for the evening were tamer than the previous evening. Dead tired, most called it a night by 2330 hours.

One of Goebel's first photos with his new camera while in Bern.

CHAPTER FORTY-ONE

Hotel de Glion

June 26 to July 3, 1944—Days Sixty-Four to Seventy-One
Glion, Switzerland

OVER THE NEXT WEEK, life in the small town perched on the mountainside was refreshing and relaxing for Goebel and his fellow aviators. Although still grounded, under curfew, and held to very specific house rules, Goebel felt relieved and freer than he had in months. He and the other Americans lodged at Hotel de Glion lived the life of leisure for the coming weeks and months, waiting in eager anticipation of the day when they would be repatriated and flown back to England to rejoin their units.

On Goebel's first full day in Glion, U.S. Army Brigadier General Barnwell R. Legge visited the Americans interned there. A highly decorated general and combat leader, Legge was the acting Military Attaché to Switzerland during the war. Accompanying General Legge was the U.S. Minister to Switzerland, Leland B. Harrison. Unexpected, it was a rare treat for the airmen to welcome and meet the general and ambassador.

Before the war, Montreux was a well-known summer destination town for the affluent people of England and Europe. As a result, most all of the locals spoke very good English. As a vacation town, there were many activities to keep the airmen busy. From swimming, canoeing, and fishing in the lake to riding bicycles and hiking to the many shops, cafés, taverns, and the cinema, there was more than enough to occupy the young men. All together, they were shown great hospitality by the Swiss citizens.

With more than enough free time, Goebel was able to journal some of his exploits during the war and while at Glion. He collected them in "A Wartime Log" published and provided to the airmen by The War Prisoners' Aid of the Y.M.C.A. Goebel was even able to attend Mass only a short distance from the hotel at Chapelle catholique de Glion, which proved to be a much-needed rejuvenation, especially after being hidden in several sanctuaries along the way. On Sunday, July 2, Goebel was able to participate in his first Mass in a true Catholic parish since departing home the previous December.

At this point, the only hazard for these interned airmen was overconsumption, or the risk of missing the last funicular ride before the lift closed, resulting in a rather strenuous and sobering walk up the steep hill to the hotel.

JULY 4, 1944—DAY SEVENTY-TWO
GLION, SWITZERLAND

Day by day, feeling the benefits of a now-pampered life, Goebel became homesick and frustrated with the life of leisure. A short radiogram message received from his father the previous day only made matters worse: **"family pinecliff everybody happy."** Goebel's father informed him that his loved ones were at their family's lakeside cottage on Pinecliff Lake located in West Milford, New Jersey. This news combined with the Glion version of an Independence Day celebration only deepened Goebel's melancholy and caused his pensive mood to worsen.

July 5 to August 15, 1944—Days Seventy-Three to One Hundred Fourteen
Glion, Switzerland

At first, their surroundings seemed like just rewards for the risks they endured from being shot down. However, as time progressed, the idle airmen became restless. The good life during wartime was bittersweet; all the men would have liked to work or expand their education with the time available, knowing that their return to their units and eventually a return to the American workforce would be a challenging and difficult adjustment to make.

With Axis power and progress in regression and the ongoing carnage of war marching on without them, the interned Americans wanted to be back in the game. Similar to many of his fellow comrades, Goebel wanted out of Switzerland.

Just shy of four months since the Kendziora crew was shot down over the skies of Belgium, Goebel received a response to his inquiry made a few days earlier with the Swiss Red Cross. Through the International Red Cross, the Swiss were provided what information that they had, which only hardened Goebel's heart.

"Dear Sir,

In answer to your inquiry dated Aug. 10th 1944, we beg to inform you that we have a

<u>2nd. Lt. Leon CZAPLEWSKI</u>

ASN 0-694342

Prisoner of War at STALAG LUFT III, Germany.

We have unfortunately no record whatever of the other Officers and Non-Commissioned Officers listed in your letter but will gladly make inquires if you can provide us with fuller particulars concerning them.

Believe us

Yours very truly,

Comité International Genéve"

Becoming disenfranchised as time progressed, Goebel developed a form of survivor's guilt. Unable to find out the whereabouts or status of his missing fellow crew members and the knowledge that two Belgium Résistance members gave their lives for his security began to gnaw on his nerves. This sense of uneasiness, coupled with a life of wartime luxury, placed a sour feeling in Goebel's gut.

AUGUST 17 TO SEPTEMBER 12, 1944—DAYS ONE HUNDRED SIXTEEN TO ONE HUNDRED FORTY-TWO
GLION, SWITZERLAND

Three months earlier in Tibenham, Goebel was frustrated, tired of waiting, and wanted to be engaged in the war. Now he was feeling a similar frustration. They could not leave, return to service, or go back home. The spoils and trappings of the Swiss resort town no longer provided relief for the waiting airmen. The adrenaline rush of walking to safety and the retelling of various escape and evasion tales no longer provided comfort or generated the same sense of pride or accomplishment. Only so many stories, jokes, and card games could be replayed.

SEPTEMBER 13, 1944—DAY ONE HUNDRED FORTY-THREE
GLION, SWITZERLAND

Finally, on the morning of Wednesday, September 13, 1944, good news arrived for the airmen interned in Glion. The war had progressed to the point to where the Allied forces were able to begin the process of repatriating their American aviators.

Orders came from the American Legation and Senior U.S. military officials to pack their bags. They would be leaving Glion the following morning. Goebel and the others would take the train from Montreux and travel by rail to Geneva where they would be handed over to Allied forces in the region. From there, they would be transported to London and back to the Eighth Army Air Force headquarters. Beyond that, few details were provided to the airmen as any publicity of their movement could jeopardize any chance of release of other Americans still held in Swiss interment and POW camps.

Receiving the news, the airmen were given a few hours to settle their affairs before being sequestered at the Hotel de Glion. As expected, a celebration erupted, followed by many cheers and drinks, effectively breaking House Rule No. ***"5: There will be no drinking of alcoholics during the day before 6:00 p.m."***

For Goebel and the other members of the Lucky Seven, their five months of escape, evasion, and internment were finally coming to an end. They were going back to London to rejoin their units. Regrettably, Goebel's guilt would not fully subside with this news.

Originally brought together by a sheer stroke of good fortune, the band of fellow evaders, the Lucky Seven would never be united again after this moment in time.

AUGUST 8, 1944
TIBENHAM, ENGLAND

While in Switzerland, Goebel's unit, the 702nd Bombardment Squadron, was cited for distinguished and outstanding performance of duty in combat from May 9, 1944, to July 12, 1944. The squadron attacked fourteen targets in Germany and forty targets in enemy-occupied territories without the loss of a single aircraft or crew. During this period, the 702nd performed 348 sorties and dropped 719 tons of bombs on vital enemy installations. Goebel was not made aware of this citation until well after his repatriation.

AUGUST 25, 1944
PARIS, FRANCE
1530 HOURS

After four years of occupation, Paris was liberated by the French 2nd Armored Division and the U.S. 4th Infantry Division. Light German resistance could not hold back the uprising that began a week earlier on August 19, 1944. By defying a direct order by Adolf Hitler to blow up the landmarks in Paris and burn the city to the ground, the commander of the garrison General Dietrich von Choltitz ultimately surrendered the French capital on August 25, 1944, to the Allies who received Choltitz and his Wehrmacht soldiers as prisoners.

Paris originally fell to Nazi Germany on June 14, 1940, one month after the German Wehrmacht stormed into France. Eight days later, France signed an armistice with the Third Reich, and a puppet French state was set up.

SEPTEMBER 2, 1944
HAINAUT PROVINCE, BELGIUM
0400 HOURS

The liberation of Belgium began on an early Saturday morning. Crossing the Belgian border in multiple locations, the First U.S. Army was on its way to Tournai. The majority of Belgium was liberated in ten days. However, this did not put an end to the German occupation. Two months later, Hitler and the Third Reich surprised the Allies with their last offensive: the Battle of the Bulge.

SEPTEMBER 14, 1944
SOUTHERN FRANCE

Operation Dragoon and the Allies' four-week offensive came to an end, thus liberating Southern France and signaling that the Allied armies had reached the Swiss border, effectively beginning the end of Americans' internment in Switzerland.

The Lucky Seven

The above group photo was believed to be taken near Hotel de Glion in July 1944. From right to left, Goebel, Pavelka, Solomon, and Brinkhurst (top row), and Tucker, Holton, and Westerlund (bottom row).

CHAPTER FORTY-TWO

Repatriation

SEPTEMBER 14 TO 29, 1944
GLION, SWITZERLAND, TO LONDON, ENGLAND

THE EXACT REPATRIATION JOURNEY that Goebel and other American personnel took from their Swiss interment locations back to London and their respective units was not widely documented. Based on other airmen accounts, it appeared that over the course of two weeks, American internees were shuttled by various forms of military transport. It is also unknown if the six Americans of the Lucky Seven—Goebel, Pavelka, Solomon, Tucker, Westerlund, and Holton—traveled together on their return trip back to London.

It is believed that Goebel and his fellow airmen were escorted from Glion to Geneva by Swiss guards. Once there, they were handed off to an American Legation Attaché. Along Goebel's trek back to London, from his journal it appears that he did stay in Annecy, France, at the Nouvel Hotel, located on Rue Vaugelas. Once in Annecy, airmen were reconnected with the Allied forces based in Southern France.

Outlined below is the understood route that Goebel and others traveled from Glion, Switzerland, to London, England.

Leg 1:   Train from Montreux to Geneva, Switzerland (95 km)—2-hour ride

Leg 2:   Military transport truck from Geneva, Switzerland, to Annecy, France (43 km)—1.5-hour ride

Leg 3:   Flight from Annecy, France, to Naples, Italy (539 miles or 867 km)—5-hour flight

Leg 4:   Flight from Naples, Italy, to Casablanca, Morocco (1,302 miles or 2,095 km)—9-hour flight

Leg 5:   Flight from Casablanca, Morocco, to London, England (1,295 miles or 2,084 km)—9-hour flight

Beyond local rail and military ground transport, it is believed that Goebel made most of his journey back to London via a Douglas C-47 Skytrain or other similar DC-3 airliners. Rigged with fixed metal seats, C-47s could transport twenty-eight passengers at a top cruising speed of 155 miles (250 km) per hour and with a range of 1,600 miles (2,600 km).

The 486-mile (782 km) distance between Annecy and London was well within range for the C-47. The elongated Allied repatriation route was the result of two primary factors. Firstly, at this point in the war, within France there was still spotty German resistance, and pockets of the country were still under Nazi control. An unarmed C-47 would be at risk of German fighter planes and antiaircraft guns. Secondly, Allied planes were forbidden from flying over Spain's airspace.

During the war, Spain was nominally neutral. Under General Franco's Nationalist Regime, it was politically aligned with Nazi Germany. While Spain did not actually join the Axis powers, it did collaborate with the Nazis in many areas; therefore eliminating this as a viable flight route.

SEPTEMBER 30 TO OCTOBER 22, 1944
LONDON, ENGLAND

Soon after their arrival in London, Goebel and Tucker were assigned to temporary duty not to exceed thirty days at the 70th Air Force Replacement Depot, AAF Station 594, which was headquarters to the 8th Air Force replacement depot located within the center of the British mainland, only to be returned back to the town of Stone (Jefferson Stone), England, just south of Stoke-on-Trent. A full circle to where Goebel began six months earlier when they arrived as replacements.

Both Goebel and Tucker's immediate assignment was to meet with U.S. Military Attaché representatives at several different intelligence organizations for interrogations, debriefing, and the completion of their personnel records. During these exchanges, the airmen were strictly informed that publication and communication to any unauthorized persons of experiences of escape evasion from enemy-occupied territory, internment in a neutral country, or release from internment not only furnished useful information to the enemy but also jeopardized future escapes, evasions, and releases.

Soon after arriving to AAF Station 594, Goebel exchanged his new duds for an Army-issued uniform. It felt strange after all this time, but it was a welcome change. What wasn't welcome were the unpredictable German V-2 rockets that had been aimed at the island capital.

By early October 1944, the need for heavy bombers in the European Theater was waning. As well, it was U.S. military policy that airmen who had working knowledge of underground networks through their escape and evasion experience would not be allowed back into that theatre of operation for fear that critical information would fall into the enemy's hands. This was a very different policy from German Air Force where a pilot continued to fly until the war was over or death, whichever came first.

On October 7, 1944, General Orders No. 74 issued by the U.S. Strategic Air Forces in Europe, awarding both Goebel and Tucker the Purple Heart for wounds received as a result of enemy action on April 24, 1944.

Upon the completion of their debriefing, Goebel and Tucker received special orders (S.O. No. 296) directing them to proceed to the port of Aerial Debarkation on October 22, 1944. Neither airmen would return to their unit or fly additional combat missions again.

SEPTEMBER 8, 1944
CHISWICK, WEST LONDON

The first German V-2 rockets landed on the British isle, killing three and injuring seventeen. Over the next few months, nearly 1,400 struck London and the surrounding area. The V-2 flying bombs were less accurate than V-1 rockets, but since they travelled at the speed of sound, and no warning noise was presented before impact, it was almost impossible to defend against them. Hitler's V-2 rockets killed thousands of British civilians during the final months of war.

SEPTEMBER 27, 1944
GÖTTINGEN, GERMANY
AFTERNOON

Tragically, in cloud, the navigator of the lead bomber of the 445th Bombardment Group miscalculated, and thirty-five B-24s of the 702d from Tibenham and the other squadrons of the group left the bomber stream of the 2nd Air Division and proceeded to Göttingen some fifty-six kilometers from the primary target in Kassel, Germany.

After their misplaced bomb run, the group was alone in the skies and was attacked from the rear by an estimated 150 Luftwaffe planes, resulting in the most concentrated air battle in history. Twenty-five of the heavy bombers were downed inside of Germany's borders. Three crash-landed, two in France and one in Belgium; two made forced landings at an emergency field in England; and another crashed after it arrived home but was waved off to try again. All tolled, only four B-24s of the original thirty-five returned safely to base at Tibenham.

This was probably the most tragic mission for the 702nd during the war. The 445th suffered the greatest single-day loss by one group on a single mission of the Eighth Air Force, and all within six minutes, resulting in 117 airmen of the 445th being killed in action. One hundred twenty-one were taken prisoner, and only ninety-eight were returned to duty.

The Goebel residence received further correspondence from The Adjutant General's Office of the War Department informing them of James Goebel's status. In a letter dated September 30, 1944, in reply to their inquiry, the Goebels were provided the following update:

> **"Dear Mr. and Mrs. Goebel:**
> **Reference is made to my letter of 15 June informing you that your son, Second Lieutenant James J. Goebel, Jr., 0697268, was safe in Switzerland. A further report has been received that he has returned to his unit for duty."**

Further instructions in the letter from the Adjutant General, Major General J. A. Ulio informed the Goebels that they should not publicize the fact the James was in Switzerland, **"for such publicity is not considered to be in the best interest of the country, and may jeopardize any chance of release of other Americans who may be there."**

A promotional marketing cover for the Hotel de Glion collected by Goebel (above). A casual photo of Goebel in his new duds while in Glion (below).

Above, repatriated airmen are preparing to board the first transit flight back to England. The awaiting C-47 was aptly named the "Impatient Virgin". Goebel on board the C-47 soon after departing from Annecy, France, en route back to London (below).

Heading Home

OCTOBER 25, 1944
LONDON, ENGLAND
EARLY MORNING

GOEBEL AND TUCKER BOARDED a transport plane for a scheduled multi-leg trip home. Their final destination after two days of travel would be the Washington National Airport Army Air Base in Washington, D.C. Upon their arrival, the two crewmen were given separate orders and parted ways. Goebel received special orders (S.O. No. 194) directing him to proceed to the Army Air Force Redistribution Station No. 1, in Atlantic City, New Jersey. He was granted leave and instructed to report to the commanding officer no later than November 18, 1944.

After Goebel's arrival in Washington, D.C., and once relieved of duty, he made an important call. Restricted in his communications and unable to convey his movements, this would be the first opportunity to speak with his family since he departed from New York ten months earlier while on leave the previous December.

Goebel's momentous call home was publicized a few days later in a local Brooklyn newspaper.

> **"A RECENT LONG DISTANCE CALL from Washington, D.C., will probably be the most memorable telephone call in James J. Goebel's life. The message was: "I'll be home for supper." The caller was James Goebel, Jr., who was returning to the States after being declared missing in action following an April raid over Germany.**
>
> **The Goebels had been notified in June that Lieutenant Goebel had made his way to safety and was being returned to his Air Force unit in England, but they had no inkling that he might be coming home until he called from Washington."**

With three weeks leave, Goebel returned home and reunited with his family.

NOVEMBER 9, 1944
BROOKLYN, NEW YORK
AFTERNOON

On a crisp fall afternoon, Goebel received orders redirecting him to the 1078th Army Air Force Base Unit, a convalescent hospital in Richmond, Virginia, where he was to undergo new medical exams to confirm and reestablish his fitness for duty.

Goebel remained in Richmond until December 2, 1944, at which point he was ordered to return to the AAF Redistribution Station No. 1 in Atlantic City, New Jersey. After more than a week, he was given orders (S.O. No. 341) on December 13, 1944, assigning him to the Army Air Forces Flexible Gunnery School at Harlingen Army Airfield in Harlingen, Texas. Goebel was slated to attend the beginnings of a six-week flight instructor training course.

On December 10, 1944, prior to leaving Atlantic City as part of his fitness exam, Goebel was able to log a flight in a Vultee BT-13A Valiant. In the air for little more than four hours, this would be Goebel's first logged flight as a pilot since being shot down more than six months earlier.

DECEMBER 14, 1944, TO JANUARY 9, 1945
HARLINGEN, TEXAS

As directed, Goebel arrived in the border town of Harlingen, roughly 250 miles south of where he attended the San Antonio Aviation Cadet Center almost exactly one year earlier. Another full circle moment, he was now training to be a flight instructor. Goebel began the first leg of his training in Harlingen where he logged additional hours in the BT-13 and one hour in a B-24 as an instructor. On December 22, 1944, Goebel would make his final flight in a B-24.

On January 9, 1945, Goebel received orders (S.O. No. 9) to report to 2526th AAF Base Unit at the Lubbock Army Airfield in Lubbock, Texas.

JANUARY 10 TO FEBRUARY 21, 1945
LUBBOCK, TEXAS

Goebel began his flight instructor training course in early January 1945, continuing through to mid-February. Upon successful completion of this training, he was promoted to the rank of first lieutenant on February 8, 1945.

On February 21, 1945, upon the completion of the six-week training course, Goebel received orders assigning him to Squadron B in the 2123rd AAF Base Unit in Harlingen, Texas, as a flight instructor.

FEBRUARY 22 TO AUGUST 5, 1945
HARLINGEN, TEXAS

Returning back to Harlingen as a flight instructor, Goebel began logging hours as an instructor starting on February 24, 1945, and continued through to July 8, 1945, when he logged his last flight for the Army Air Force. As an instructor, Goebel logged hours in both the Beech AT-11-800 "Kansan" and the North American AT-6D-550 "Texan" Army aircraft.

While at Harlingen, on June 6, 1945, a Pilot Proficiency Board evaluated and passed Goebel with the proficiency instrument flying. The following month on July 7, 1945, he received orders releasing him from assignment and relief from active duty. Goebel was allowed to return home until July 17, 1945, at which point he was to report to the 6th Service Command, Separation Center in Fort Sheridan, Illinois.

On August 5, 1945, First Lt. James J. Goebel Jr., was honorably discharged from the Army of the United States. During his active military service, Goebel was awarded the Europe-Africa-Middle East Medal, the Victory Medal World War II, and the Army Meritorious Unit Citation. Goebel would also receive the Purple Heart for general injuries suffered in parachuting over enemy-occupied territory.

During his time at Harlingen and shortly after the world celebrated the Allied victory over the Axis powers; on Victory in Europe Day (V-E Day) when Germany unconditionally surrendered on May 8, 1945, and then again on Victory over Japan Day (V-J Day) when Japan signed formal surrender documents aboard the *USS Missouri* in Tokyo Bay on September 2, 1945. Relief was felt by all as the Second Great War was finally coming to an end.

SEPTEMBER 24, 1947, TO OCTOBER 21, 1957
AIR FORCE RESERVE SERVICE

By direction of the president of the United States, on September 24, 1947, Goebel was appointed to the Officers' Reserve Corps, Army of the United States. After twenty-five years of military service, on October 21, 1957, Goebel was honorably discharged from the United States Air Force, Air Force Reserve.

First Lieutenant James J. Goebel Jr. while in Harlingen, Texas, prior to discharge, standing in front of a North American T-6 Texan.

Afterword

AFTER THE WAR, JAMES GOEBEL went on to enjoy the spoils and the boom of the Greatest Generation in America. At Pinecliff Lake, Goebel met and fell in love with his future wife, Joan Ann Stewart. They married on September 20, 1952, and thereafter would be together for fifty years until James's passing on September 30, 2002. All together, Joan and James would have seven children: six sons, Stephen, James, Charles, William, Thomas, and Paul; and one daughter, second to the youngest, Jean Marie.

James Goebel would continue a lifetime of love for flight, both privately and professionally. As a career, he spent the balance of 1945 through 1947 "spray" flying and the next four years flying reconnaissance for the U.S. Department of Agriculture. In 1951, James hired on with Eastern Airlines as a copilot and eventually became a first pilot and captain in 1956. James would captain for Eastern until his retirement in 1983.

Upon his passing, effective December 29, 2022, in memory of James J. Goebel, Jr., Goebel Field Airport in Mountain Home, Texas, was established. A fitting tribute to a man who was destined from birth to fly.

Marker at Goebel Field Airport in Mountain Home, Texas.

Never Forgotten

DURING WORLD WAR II, the United States Army Air Force lost 80,000 airmen, more than any other branch of the U.S. Armed Forces. In 1944, the Army Air Force experienced total battle casualty losses of 41,593 personnel and 9,937 first line aircraft in the European Theater of Operations alone. During the month of April that same year, the Air Corps had a combined sum of 1,213 personnel killed in action and 3,096 airmen listed as missing, interned, or captured.

The grave marker on the following page is a sobering reminder that not all souls were as fortunate as James Goebel on that fateful Monday afternoon in April 1944.

The airmen listed were members of the 579th Bombardment Squadron, 392nd Bombardment Group. They took part in the same bombing raid as Goebel. Their aircraft was downed as the result of flak while en route home. All but one member of the crew was killed; the sole survivor became a POW. This was also their first mission.

Photo taken at the Fort McPherson National Cemetery in Maxwell, Nebraska[33]

S/Sgt. Aubrey D. Coble – Engineer
Second Lt. Carl F. Ellinger – Pilot
Second Lt. Ross H. Hall – Bombardier
Second Lt. Neil H. Morton – Copilot

33 In 2004, while on a family vacation to learn more about the North Platte Canteen and to conduct research to determine if James Goebel had passed through North Platte, we visited the Fort McPherson National Cemetery on Memorial Day weekend. Finding the above referenced grave marker was completely fortuitous and very humbling.

Acknowledgments

April 24, 2023
Conifer, Colorado
0700 Hours

THE EVENTS THAT UNFOLDED to create *The Lucky Seven* began more than eighty years ago. However, the inspiration behind this book started for me in November of 1999 during a four-hour road trip from the rolling hills west of San Antonio to Conroe, Texas. With James Goebel in the passenger seat, I was driving him back home after Thanksgiving weekend with the Goebel family. After some small talk and a brief search of the FM dial, I started asking James questions about his wartime experience. For some reason, James chose that Sunday drive to share with me details of events that he did not openly discuss with his seven children. Knowing that most WWII veterans did not speak about their experiences during the war, I felt obligated to share his story. Little did I know this unplanned conversation would be the catalyst of a more than two-decades-long journey.

Unfortunately, James passed away in September of 2002 before I could dig deeper into his personal accounting of his time during the war. Knowing that I had an interest in World War II history, Joan (James's wife) bestowed to me his military and other war-related records, personal correspondence, and photos after James's passing. Within James's documents, I discovered an early version of an autobiography that he had started in the late 1980s called *Now It's Your Turn*. Like many older veterans, James had a desire to record history as he remembered it. In James's memoir we are reminded that it is the responsibility of each generation to seek and secure its place in history. Just as important, it is essential that our forefathers' history and desire for freedom never be forgotten.

It has taken more hours of cross-referencing and researching than I can recount to share this small bit of history; however, I am eternally grateful to James, Joan, and the rest of the Goebel family for entrusting me with James's wartime legacy.

Also, within James's documents were copies of Mr. Robert C. Tucker's personal diaries of the events between April 24 to June 30, 1944. Mr. Tucker was the Kendziora Crew (Crew No.DJ-11) bombardier. He also traveled extensively with James during their time together while evading the Germans. In 1987, when James had aspirations of writing a manuscript about their experiences during the war, Mr. Tucker provided James with copies of his accounts. Though I never had the opportunity to actually meet or speak with Mr. Tucker, I am truly thankful for his posthumous sharing of his perspective and recounting of events.

In September of 2004, during my initial research for James's biography, I was able to contact and conduct a phone interview with Mr. Irl J. Klinginsmith. Mr. Klinginsmith was the assistant engineer and left waist gunner of the Kendziora Crew (Crew No.DJ-11). He was also the only surviving member of the ten-man crew that I was aware of and able to locate. It was a thrill for me to have the opportunity to speak with Irl about his extraordinary experiences.

Mr. Klinginsmith was also kind enough to share with me a copy of his 2001 interview transcript conducted with Thomas H. Miller as part of an oral history program being facilitated by The State Historical Society of Missouri.

In December 2004, to celebrate the sixty-year anniversary of James's venture following being downed over Belgium, I presented the Goebel family with a crude first draft of James's wartime biography. This unpublished first attempt would be the foundation of this book, yet it lacked a great deal of detail. Which frankly, at the time, hadn't fully been uncovered.

In March 2006, the Goebel family received a letter from Mr. Claudy Winant, an author and amateur historical researcher living in Belgium. Mr. Winant was searching for information on behalf of Mr. Edouard Loyaerts, a former Belgian Résistance chief. I responded to Mr. Winant on the family's behalf, which led to a multi-year exchange of information. Claudy's research, intimate knowledge on this subject, and personal relationships with Roger Jamblin and Edouard Loyaerts proved invaluable. With Claudy's assistance, I hope I was able to produce a document that truly celebrates the efforts of those résistance members who risked their lives to aid Allied airmen. I would like to thank Claudy for sharing his historical research and relevant photos. I especially want to thank Claudy for his review and feedback of the 2004 manuscript.

In October 2006, the Goebel family received a letter from Mr. Jack W. Holton, the last known living member of The Lucky Seven. In his first correspondence, Mr. Holton openly recognized his station, and to his credit he unknowingly provided me with the title of this book. He was in the process of writing his own memoirs for his family and was seeking information when he contacted the Goebel family. It was an honor to help Mr. Holton in his effort to retrace events from that period. I enjoyed the opportunity to share in a piece of his history, and for that I am truly grateful.

In June 2014, my wife and I went on a trip to Europe, which included time in parts of France and Belgium. While in Belgium, we traveled through the countryside, stopping in the towns of Couthuin, Héron, and Huy. We timed our trip so that we could attend Mass on Sunday, June 15 (Father's Day) in Liège at La Cathédrale Saint Paul where James had been hidden for over thirteen days during May 1944. This was a very moving experience, and I was grateful for the opportunity to share it with James's only daughter and my wife, Jean Marie (Goebel) Holden.

In August 2019, Jean and I had the opportunity to participate in a twenty-minute flight on the world's only remaining Consolidated B-24J Liberator still flying. For me, it was literally the crescendo event of this two-decade journey and the motivator for me to finish what I had started many years earlier. Thank you to the Collings Foundation for preserving living aviation history and facilitating this memorable experience.

With the exception of a few, the majority of images within this book are from James's personal archives or were shared property of other veterans and or résistance members. I would like to give a special thanks to Mr. Michael S. Simpson the 445th Bomb Group Unit Historian for the approval to use pictures from his website: http://www.445bg.org/.

In the process of pulling together certain facts about James's military history, the following agencies (the National Personnel Records Center in St. Louis, Missouri, and the National Archives and Records Administration in College Park, Maryland) were contacted in writing, requesting military records. Unfortunately, due to a fire in 1973 that destroyed many military personal records, neither agency was able to provide the requested documents.

Last, but most importantly, I would like to acknowledge the Goebel family, especially my wife, Jean, for her continued support and love throughout this journey. I would also like to thank Jean's eldest brother, Stephen J. Goebel, for reviewing a late-stage draft of this book. As Stephen rightly pointed out, he and his six siblings were also the "Lucky Seven." It is truly my honor to bring their father's story to life. Thank-you!

B-24 Liberator Bomber

History

ON DECEMBER 29, 1939, the first of these four-engine aircraft called the Liberator took to the air from Lindbergh Field less than nine months after the prototype began to take shape. Consolidated Aircraft of San Diego, California ultimately produced the winning design (Model 32).

The Consolidated B-24 Liberator was employed in operations in every combat theater during World War II. Because of its great range, it was particularly suited for long over-water missions in the European and Pacific Theaters.

More Liberators (multi-engine heavy bombers) were built than any other American military aircraft in history. More than 18,500 unites were produced by the end of the war in 1945, with 8,685 manufactured by the Ford Motor Company at the Willow Run Bomber Plant. The B-24J Liberator was the variation produced in the largest quantity with a total of 6,678 being constructed.

Statistics

Engine:	4 x Pratt & Whitney R-1830-65 Twin Wasp, 1,200 HP each
Max. Speed:	290 mph
Max. Range:	2,200 miles
Empty Weight:	37,000 pounds
Loaded Weight:	56,000 pounds
Wingspan:	110 feet
Length:	67 feet, 2 inches
Height:	18 feet
Service Ceiling:	28,000 feet
Fuel Capacity:	3,614 gallons
Crew Size:	10 crewmen
Cost:	$304,391
Armament:	2 x .50 caliber machine guns in the nose, top, ball, tail turrets, and 2 x .50 caliber waist machine guns. A total of 5,200 rounds of ammunition were carried. Bomb load = 8,000 pounds.

Source - The National Archives and Record Administration (NARA) and the World War II Database

445th Bomb Group

8th Army Air Force Insignia

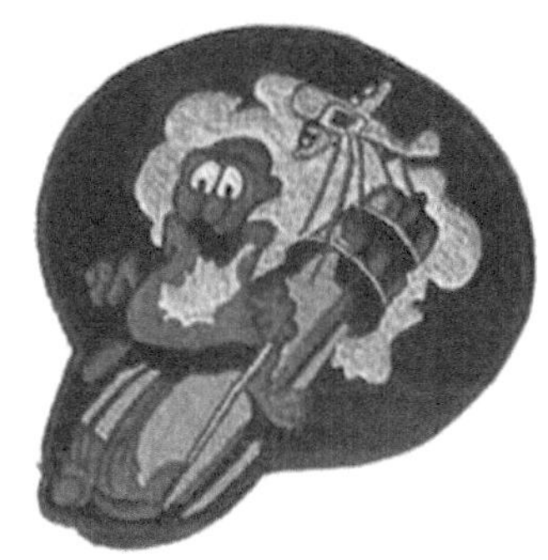

702nd Bomb Squadron Insignia

Assigned 8th AAF
November 1943

Wing/Command Assignment
2BD, 2CBW
January 8, 1944

Motto
The Bison Wing

Squadrons of the 445th BG

700th Bombardment Squadron: Heavy 1943–1945
701st Bombardment Squadron: Heavy 1943–1945
702nd Bombardment Squadron: Heavy 1943–1945
703rd Bombardment Squadron: Heavy 1943–1945

Stations
AAF No. 124 – Tibenham, Norfolk, England
November 4, 1943, to May 28, 1945

Campaigns
Air Offensive, Europe, Normandy, Northern France, Central
Europe, Ardennes-Alsace

Major Awards
Distinguished Unit Citation on February 24, 1944, Gotha

Aircraft
B-24 Liberator

Commander
Col. Robert H. Terrill
April 1, 1943, to July 24, 1944

First Mission: December 13, 1943 / **Last Mission:** April 25, 1945

Total Missions: 282 / **Total Sorties:** 7,145

Total Bomb Tonnage: 16,732 tons

Aircraft MIA: 108

Air Forces Escape & Evasion Society (AFEES)

"The loss of every Allied plane shot down over Europe was a tragedy—every member of a crew that was found and saved and sent back to us brought joy to all his comrades. To everyone who joined in this great work and to each of his family and to all who shared, in those days, his risks and dangers I send assurances of my deep and lasting gratitude."

—Dwight D. Eisenhower[34]

"The History of AFEES dates back to 1964
Before 1961, a Frenchman by the name of Leslie Atkinson, a Reserve Captain in the French Air Force, a member of the executive committee

34 Part of a Letter of Tribute from Eisenhower and a quote used at the bottom of official AFEES letterhead.

of the Army Resistance Organization, and a Helper for Allied airmen, was inspired by the brilliant work accomplished by the British Royal Air Forces Escaping Society. It became his mission to create an association that would bring together American aviators who had escaped from enemy-occupied territory and their European Helpers."[35]

To be eligible for membership in AFEES, a person had to have been a U.S. Army Air Force veteran who had been forced down behind enemy lines, who avoided captivity, or escaped from captivity to return to Allied control.

After the war, James Goebel became a Member, Director, and a Chapter President of AFEES. From reunions, trips overseas, and many years of correspondence, James actively honored those who aided in his escape and evasion from Nazi-occupied Europe.

Below is the AFEES emblem, originally designed and submitted by Harry Minor, an AFEES member who walked over the Pyrenees Mountains into Spain in 1943. The emblem was first made available in 1966 to 1967, and it was worn on a group trip to Europe in 1969.

35 AFEES history as defined by the official website.

The "Winged Boot" in the center of the emblem symbolized *"that all members walked back from their last mission—Fly out—walk back. We felt that no matter how a member came out of enemy territory-whether he walked across the mountains or came out by boat-the winged boot was appropriate for all."*[36] The Latin phrase at the bottom of the emblem, **PRO LIBERTATE AMBULAVIMUS** translates to **FOR LIBERTY WE WALKED.**

Finally, for those who are interested in this subject matter, the AFEES website https://airforceescape.org/ provides a great source of information.

---

36 AFEES History as defined by the official website.

Fellow Evadee Airmen

BETWEEN 1940 TO 1945 a total of three hundred twenty-three Allied evaders were chronicled[37] to have walked in Switzerland from German occupied territory. In 1944 alone, one hundred twenty-four Allied airmen entered Switzerland on foot. Goebel and his six fellow evaders were very fortunate to make this journey.

Like Goebel, the following list of airmen were shot down, considered MIA, and ultimately escaped to Switzerland. These are the airmen that Goebel bonded with while at the Hotel de Glion in Glion, Switzerland. The names are listed in the identical order in which they signed Goebel's Wartime Log. Each airman provided the following information.

Rank, Name, Serial Number
Hometown
Command, Unit, or Squadron
Type of Aircraft and "Call Sign/Nickname"
Position on Aircraft
MIA Date

37 (Anthoine, 1997)

+   *Signifies fellow airmen that were on Goebel's crew.*

**   *Signifies airmen who accompanied Goebel and escaped to Switzerland with help from the Belgium and French Résistance.*

S/Sgt. Joseph Garbish,
35583145
Hammond, Indiana
728BS, 452BG
B-17, "Why Worry II"
Ball Turret
MIA Date: May 26, 1944

S/Sgt. Joseph D. Coss,
1507047
Wellsburg, West Virginia
334BS, 95BG
B-17-E, "Winsome Winn"
Ball Gunner
MIA Date: May 29, 1943

S/Sgt. Howard W. Lawson,
"Cotton", 39456982
Goldendale, Washington
527BS, 379BG
B-17-G, "Duffy's Tavern"
Right Waist Gunner
MIA Date: January 29, 1944

Sgt. Roe S. Woodis,
14041959
Allsboro, Alabama
748BS, 457BG
B-17-G, "Sweater Out"
Ball Turret
MIA Date: May 27, 1944

Sgt. Charles H. Westerlund,
31275855 +, **
Waterbury, Connecticut
702BS, 445BG
B-24-J, "Ruthless Ruth"
Radio Operator
MIA Date: April 24, 1944

T/Sgt. Alexander S. Swider,
33087688
Weirton, West Virginia
594BS, 385BG
B-17-F, "Maxie"
Engineer
MIA Date: February 4, 1944

S/Sgt. Berne L. Johnston,
38124028
Bellview, New Mexico
366BS, 305BG
B-17, "Bessies Bastard"
Left Waist Gunner
MIA Date: February 20, 1944

1st Lt. Joseph Pavelka,
0738019 **
Cleveland, Ohio
702BS, 445BG
B-24-H
Pilot
MIA Date: April 12, 1944

2nd Lt. Walter E. Wiggins,
0692409
Gilroy, California
728BS, 452BG
B-17-G, "Lonesome Polecat"
Bombardier
MIA Date: October 14, 1943

Sgt. John M. Altgelt,
18067576
San Antonio, Texas
15th Air Force
B-17-F, "Chief Wahoo"
Left Waist Gunner
MIA Date: April 30, 1944

2nd Lt. Donald O. Smith,
0813075
Watertown, Massachusetts
384BG
B-17-G
Co-pilot
MIA Date: April 13, 1944

S/Sgt. Lester G. Lillie,
32583420
Gowanda, New York
389BG
B-24, "Naughty Norma"
Tail Gunner
MIA Date: July 17, 1944

Sgt. Milton Katz,
12140624
Brooklyn, New York
369BS, 306BG
B-17
Right Waist Gunner
MIA Date: July 16, 1944

Sgt. Robert A. Price,
11117055
Wellesley Hills,
Massachusetts
369BS, 306BG
B-17-G
Radio - Gunner
MIA Date: April 16, 1944

Sgt. Robert G. Goddard,
11057856
Westboro, Massachusetts
15th Air Force
B-17-F
Ball Gunner
MIA Date: April 30, 1944

S/Sgt. William J. Wilson,
384764898
Stillwater, Oklahoma
389BG
B-24-J, "Naughty Nora"
Engineer
MIA Date: July 17, 1944

2nd Lt. Donald C. Toye,
0691319
Lake Grove, Oregon
703BS, 445BG
B-24, "Nine Yanks and a Jerk"
Co-pilot
MIA Date: April 13, 1944

1st Lt. Philip Solomon,
0682743 **
West Caldwell, New Jersey
702BS, 445BG
B-24-H
Navigator
MIA Date: April 12, 1944

2nd Lt. Judson F. Doyle,
0746646
White Hall, Illinois
381BG
B-17-G
Bombardier
MIA Date: February 9, 1944

2nd Lt. Anthony L. Kosinski,
0811926
Chicago, Illinois
82FS, 78FG
P-47
Pilot
MIA Date: May 10, 1944

2nd Lt. Robert C. Tucker,
0682743 +,**
East Orange, New Jersey
702BS, 445BG
B-24-J, "Ruthless Ruth"
Navigator
MIA Date: April 24, 1944

2nd Lt. Jack W. Holton,
0755948 **
Winston-Salem, North
Carolina
430FS, 474FG
P-38
Pilot
MIA Date: May 7, 1944

S/Sgt. Anthony Ornatek,
36608379
North Chicago, Illinois
385BG
B-17-F, "Raunchy Wolf"
Left Waist Gunner
MIA Date: December 30, 1943

S/Sgt. John J. Chuck,
17151559
Brighton, Iowa
452BG
B-17
Left Waist Gunner
MIA Date: May 27, 1944

1st Lt. Selwyn M. Hunt,
HD5778
Hawke's Bay, New Zealand
Unit: Unknown
Beaufighter
Pilot
MIA Date: Unknown

1st/Sgt. Donald Brinkhurst,
647699 **
Bath Somersey, England
Unit: 101 Squadron
Lancaster
Mid/Upper Gunner
MIA Date: March 30/31,
1944

About the Author

Norman W. Holden is the son-in-law of the late James J. Goebel Jr. and is the author of *Do Better*. Norm is an executive leader in the construction industry. He resides in Conifer, Colorado, with his wife, Jean.

Dear Reader,

If you enjoyed my book and wish to read more of my stories, you can help me in three ways: please leave a review on Amazon, or the online store you purchased from, spread the word to family and friends and on social media, and visit my website at **https://normanholdenbooks.com/** by scanning the QR code below. Once there, please join my mailing list and learn about future releases and other news related to my books.

I appreciate your support,

Norman W. Holden

References

AFEES. (1992). *Air Forces Escape & Evasion Society* . Paducah, KY: Turner Publishing Company.

Ambrose, S. E. (2001). *The Wild Blue: The Men and Boys Who Flew the B-24's Over Germany 1944-45.* New York, NY: Simon & Schuster Paperbacks.

Anthoine, R. (1997). *Aviateurs Pietons vers la Suisse, 1940-1945.* Switzerland: Secavia.

Bodson, H. (2005). *Downed Allied Airmen and Evasion of Capture: The Role of Local Resistance Networks in World War II.* Jefferson, NC: McFarland & Company, Inc. .

Bowman, M. (1989). *B-24 Liberator 1939-45.* Wellingsborough, Northamptonshire, England: Patrick Stephens Limited.

Buell, H. (2002). *World War II Album.* New York, NY: Black Dog & Leventhal Publishers, Inc.

Class 43-J. (1943). *The Eagles.* Eagle Pass, TX: United States Army Air Force.

Files, Y. d. (1991). *The Quest for Freedom: Belgium Resistance in World War II.* Santa Barbara, California: Fithian Press.

Freeman, R. A. (1990). *The Mighty Eighth War Diary* . Osoeola, WI: Motorbooks International.

Gardiner, J. (1992). *"OVERPAID, OVERSEXED, AND OVER HERE": The American GI in World War II Britian.* New York, NY: Canopy Books.

Greene, B. (2002). *Once Upon a Town: The Miracle of the North Platte Canteen.* New York, NY: HaperCollins Publishers Inc.

Lavender, E., & Sheffe, N. (1992). *The Evaders: True Stories of Downed Canadian Airmen and Their Helpers in World War II.* Whitby, Ontario, Canada: McGraw-Hill Ryerson Limited.

Miller, T. H. (2001). *An Interview with Irl J. Klinginsmith as part of an Oral History Program.* Columbia, Missouri : The State Historical Society of Missouri .

Müller, J. (1973). *Liège a la Plume.* Bruxelles, Belgium: Editions Libro-Sciences Sprl.

Readers Digest. (1969). *Illustrated Story of World War II.* Pleasantville, New York: The Readers Digest Association, Inc.

Reda, L. (1988). *AAF: The Offical World War II Guide to the Army Air Forces.* New York, NY: Bonaza Books.

The Editors of Time-Life Books. (1989). *WWII Time-Life Books History of the Second World War.* New York, New York: Prenttice Hall Press.

Websites

The following list includes but is not limited to all websites used for research and corroboration of the accounts surrounding true events detailed within this book.

www.445bg.org/mission-56.html

www.445th-bomb-group.com

www.446bg.com

www.8thafhs.org

www.91stbombgroup.com/91st_tales/38_us_internees switzerland_ww2.pdf

www.94thbombgroup.com

www.accident-report.com

www.af.mil

www.afhra.maxwell.af.mil

www.aircrewremembered.com/adamson-william-ian.html

www.airforceescape.org

www.airforceescape.org/newsletters/index-to-newsletters/ index-to-helpers/

www.alphaeagle.com

www.altus.af.mil

www.americanairmuseum.com

www.archives.gov/research/holocaust/finding-aid/civilian/rg-84- switzerland.html

THE LUCKY SEVEN

www.armyairforces.com
www.aviation-history.com
www.b24.mach3ww.com
www.b-24.net
www.b24bestweb.com
www.cannon.af.mil
www.dfcsociety-nw.org
www.dhr.dos.state.fl.us
www.diggerhistory.info
www.globalsecurity.org
www.heritageleague.org
www.higher.flyer.co.uk
www.history-switzerland.geschichte-schweiz.ch/switzerland-
    second-world-war-ii.html
www.holidays-info.com/belgium/moon/calendar/1944/
www.home.att.net
www.ifrance.com
www.liberationroute.com/stories/181/liberation-of-belgium
www.libraryautomation.com
www.merkki.com
www.mighty8thaf.preller.us
www.military.com
www.nationalmuseum.af.mil
www.nationalww2museum.org/
www.npcanteen.tripod.com
www.npr.org
www.rafinfo.org.uk
www.sanelson.com
www.southernoregonwarbirds.org
www.stable.demon.co.uk
www.swissinternees.tripod.com

www.theddaystory.com/discover/d-day-timeline/

www.tsha.utexas.edu

www.umsystem.edu

www.usaaf.com

www.usaaf.net

www.usafsa.org

www.usmedals.com

www.wikipedia.org

www.ww2db.com

www.wwii-netherlands-escape-lines.com/other-escape-lines/
    mnb-belgian-national-movementmouvement-national-belge/